GREEN POND

GREEN

BY EVAN

NEW YORK

POND

BRANDON

THE VANGUARD PRESS

For Alfred and Marcia Ann

*To my wife and Miss Jensie Underwood
I owe a debt of gratitude for their
generous hours of reading, and to
Mrs. Seon Manley for her enthusiastic
interest and foresight, and to
Mr. Julian Muller, who has sweated
out the editing.*

The fool hath said in his heart,
There is no God. Corrupt are
they, and have done abominable
iniquity: there is none that
doeth good.

God looked down from heaven
upon the children of men,
to see if there were any
that did understand, that did
seek God.

—Psalm 53

Book one

Book one

1

The years ground slow and fine. The earth gave birth to the moon and a voice cried in the darkness upon the molting rocks—and there was no place that doves could bring peace. And the rains came and the sun-hot poured and the red land was made in Carolina.

And Gawd, Mama Amazon's and Victor Thornwell's Gawd, hunted about His earth for a salty people to put upon the red rocky land and there were only the rock-gutted Scotch-Irish to put there, only the Scotch-Irish with enough guts, enough strength, and enough red pepper in their tempers to wring a living from the stubborn red earth. Gawd meant from the beginning that man tend a garden, that every man have a living from the fruity land. The fat tumblebug people He put in soft manure piles, where a living could be got slovenly; but the Scotch-Irish He set down in the hard land, the red sobbing land. He knew what He was about and nodded His sage old head, saying:

"Put em down in you Book, Gabriel. Put em down right. I put plenty red peppers in they tempers so they can blow off and enough guts in they bodies so they backs won't hurt too much. Em's my ole Scotch-Irishmens."

Unto the earth in moonlit Carolina a town was born, Green Pond was born. A dorpish place with greens and airs and furbelows. Hicks came in from the sticks, lighting their lamps that all might see. The town's scrawny railroad and many winding red dirt roads became its trailing placenta.

Thus must Green Pond have begun, mused Doctor Victor Thornwell, plopping along the twilight street to North Bethel Church. His great disused hands swung at his sides as some useless appendages, for no longer were they for hire, for delving and probing, for performing a wonderful proficiency. Fifty years of surgery, fifty years of serving suffering humanity was not too much; but now he was tired, and the little wheel within him wasn't ticking just right.

He was but a deserted and forsaken doctor, touchy and bullheaded, living on borrowed time, hanging on the tree like the last unreachable red apple in the tiptop, waiting for the chilly frost of winter to send him plunging plummetlike to the ground. Splashed thus in red, he would go unhesitatingly. He was a leftover.

His name was not inscribed upon any great marble or upon any golden cup. Nor were there any alabaster Etruscan urns on great pedestals burning in spiral smoke his deeds to his god; neither during his life had his name been engraved upon any silver epergnes, recording his goodness. No place was it so written down that every man might point with finger. These hands of his, now disused and not for hire, no longer alive with intense curiosity or filled with their sensitive probing, questioning, searching, had done their work neither for glory nor for gods to appease. He was marked for oblivion.

This generation, these young'uns, cared not to stop and listen to his slow, methodical talk, his recounting old tales of the years that had been, years of his youth, years when his waters, too, were young and gay and splashing and filled with bubbles and danced over the shoals of time. No—they had to prattle and tattle of their day and time, which was the day and time they thought.

Victor found ole Uncle Simon sitting upon the rock wall that surrounded the four acres that was North Bethel Presbyterian Church's stomping ground—the holy of holies—and smoothing his hand over the evenly clipped grass that came to the edge of the wall. He was so far above the street that his boatlike feet dangled almost up to Vic's head.

"Well, Uncle Simon, I see you have everything in apple-pie order and the meeting going full tilt ahead," said Vic, indicating the Vesper Service within the church.

"Ya'sir, Doc Vic. Everythin's right down to right. That's what the good Lawd's wantin to see goin on down here." He shook his woolly old head and grew positive, "I'm aimin to keep it goin iffen the good Lawd bees willin. Nothin's better'n good preachin onless it's good prayer meetin an singin."

Vic looked up to the wide rock steps that led up to the church-ground and the vast number of steps that led from the ground to the lofty height of the arched church door. It resembled Jacob's ladder reaching into the sky—a stairway running right straight into heaven. Its loftiness was unyielding, unbending. In cold austere dignity it stood.

Uncle Simon politely broke the solitude, "Declare, Doc Vic, you's the spittin image of you pa, Ole Doc. Ah Lawd, there was a case, a heavy case in he's time."

Vic thought a moment, then spoke with a tired voice, "Pop was wise beyond his time, rock-gutted and tough as you make em. The old folks say he was so small when he was born that he'd fit into a quart cup."

Then Vic's eyes turned again to the church and its steps. He knew he needed but to climb those lofty, sublime steps, acknowledge his sins, shake hands with the elders—the few who perchance were present—and the pastor, be sprinkled, provided he hadn't been, and he'd become a living member of the visible church. So rarely did one ever seek the great invisible church, he mused, that it was considered freakish or spiritous and not quite fitting and proper.

Ole North Bethel's steeple reached far up toward the moon and the stars as though it would live forever, holding the royal crown of the Prince of the Universe majestically. For earthly hope and security, Vic needed but look to its utmost pinnacle and there were all his terrestrial tribulations dissolving into the infinite blue, where all human failures passed from finite to infinite. This church a mighty fortress, a solid bulwark, a never-failing helper, fighting like a mighty army—he was amazed at the fights, but North Bethel's members loved Jesus—against its eternal foes: Satan and Beelzebub. When these members got through fighting these creatures, they were as loving as gods and goddesses moving in a supersphere. Green Pond's aristocracies—the noble Scotch-Irish, who cared not for fantasies, rituals, dogmas, but were devout with the Scriptures, qualifications unequaled or unexcelled.

The song the congregation was singing told of going empty-handed. Vic looked at his disused hands and they were empty. There was absolutely nothing in his hands—but wrinkles. He had with him nothing except a mortal body that would end up as a wisp or vapor, some very bad odors, and, perhaps, a spoonful of dust.

"Uncle Simon," said Vic, "you had a white daddy and a black mammy, so they've told me; are your hands full and will you ascend into heaven?"

"The good Lawd will turn all these here stones into souls that surrounds this here Nof Bethel Church, an surer an that He saves my soul. There's a powerful mount of stones about this church. Peers to Me it'd be mo easy fo He to let me into heaven an to turn all these here stones into souls. That's the way I cleans up the church: sweeps the dirt up under the edge of the carpet ontil one of em powerful deacons catches me at em an then I gets em out at one time," he chuckled with churchly dignity.

Victor turned from Uncle Simon and began climbing the royal, lofty steps toward the church, demurely as a guest bid to a wedding, pensively as to a funeral.

The bulletin board, now fluorescently lighted, announced:

THE NORTH BETHEL PRESBYTERIAN CHURCH

Rev. Jacob Emmanuel Thornwell, D.D., Minister

Sunday School 10:00 A.M.

Sunday Morning Worship 11:00 A.M.

Vesper Service 7:00 P.M.

WELCOME

Once in the churchyard Vic could hear the choir better, singing as if they were a pack of coon dogs on a chase, the big ones far in the lead baying the loudest, the little ones yelping in the rear, and the old organist—a suspended piece of animation—with feet stomping, fingers twittering, blurring, playing B natural and the choir singing B flat.

Vic stopped. There was Pop's window. He kicked the paved walk and moved on between the church and the manse. Under the mammoth oaks whose gnarled limbs lapped and shingled, catching darkness, soft and black, he followed the walk that led to the massive iron gate behind which the sleeping dead were resting for ages yet to come.

The choir was now chanting, "In Christ there is no East or West, in Him no North or South; but one great fellowship of love throughout the whole wide earth. Join hands then, brothers of the faith, what e'er your race may be——"

The iron gate squeaked shut. Here under the aged mossy limbs of ancient mimosa trees, whose teary, fenny-fingered leaves gathering darkness had put to sleep in their gray grave robes, Vic stood silent, listening to the little crickets with the melancholy of September in their song. The mossed slabs of stone rose from the ground as spirits; the dead, buried so close they resembled a pile of sleeping puppies, lay with feet toward the east awaiting the great resurrection. The fragrance of honeysuckle, as a nymph bathed in perfumed dew, crept in puddled waves across the ground in the rising dampness of the dying day.

The epitaphs on the stones in this section were so weather-beaten as to be almost illegible. Yet through a hundred and fifty years of wind and rain, snow and sleet, they had held up, as puny fizzling candles, the goodness of the dead. Goodness of virgins and of knights, of fathers and of mothers, held before the eyes of the world lest it forget and construe all to evil, so easily remembered.

The stones in this section pitched lugubrious, nondescript shadows. As Victor approached the mausoleum his maundering softened as a hungry babe with a teat in its mouth. He knelt before the mausoleum to smell the roses the florist had placed there early that morning—the red now black in this darkness. Was his and Mama Amazon's Gawd manifested only in the light? Surely He was of this brown darkness, soft, mellow, soothing. Yet these roses were without color. He must be present if the roses were to be red or yellow or pink or copper. No one had ever seen the color; it appeared so only when Gawd was there. He, the great giver of the light. All art was made of shadows and light; all life was made of shadows and light. It took the great light to make the shadows—and the great light came from beyond, beyond the blue somewhere. *And why?* His question unanswered, Vic put his nose among the roses and drew deeply of their fragrance. This was surely Gawd. His tears dropped as warm rain on the green leaves and the roses.

Upon the great somber bronze door of the mausoleum was engraved:

THORNWELL
DR. THOMAS THADDEUS
1820——1918
"To live in hearts we leave behind
is not to die"

"Pop, Pop," Vic whispered in the dark, his sensitive fingers touching the mausoleum, searching as he would the contracting muscles over an inflamed appendix or a stony gall bladder. "Listen, Pop, I don't feel good. I feel whipped. It's quiet here and I want to stay. I'm tired, Pop; I want to lie down and sleep with you."

There was a fright inside him, like and unlike any that he had ever known. Maybe it came from being tired—too tired, too old; maybe it came from that eternal question, eternally not knowing the only real, important answers.

"Eighty years ago I wondered about the same kind of things, Pop. Even when I was on your lap and everybody thought I wasn't quite all there in the top story."

He leaned his head against the coolness of the mausoleum. Completely gone was his love for the feel of the knife in his supple, defty fingers—that love that had been there almost since he could remember, that love he seemed to have been born with. He gave a long sigh.

"For over fifty years I have gone down into the bowels of men and women—into the upper and lower abdomens, the back, the chest; into the vagina, the anus, the throat. And in all these places I have beheld the intricate, complicated designs Gawd fashioned there, and I have marveled because man is greatly and wonderfully made. Yet in death all are equal."

A lonely wind rustled, scraping through branches, murmuring through leaves. The traffic on the streets sped up and slowed down; horns blew, brakes shrieked, tires sang, suddenly halting, scraping the pavement.

But here was quiet and rest. Vic was still. Surely Pop and Gawd were here. He counted out a prayer on his left hand's fingers as though fingering a violin—as he'd done many years, many times, before hurdling an unheard-of bit of surgery. The prayer quieted and rested him. And he fancied that Gabriel smiled, adding a few notations to the Book of Life, and that Pop was there beside him, whispering as in the long, long bygone; and that Pop showed him the blackened-with-age stones strung across North Bethel's cemetery. So very many stones saying: BORN IN IRELAND—BORN IN SCOTLAND—BORN IN IRELAND. The long way these hot-tempered people had traveled, then lived and died here on the red land of the watershed between the two muddy rivers. They had died stanchly, in the belief of the stardust.

Vic traveled back through time pensively, sopping tats of gravy, filching tidbits, breaking off and pinching away bits of time, munching slowly, nibbling affectionately—gradually creating the delicious feeling of getting drunk. He got up, sat down on the top step of the mausoleum, leaned his tired head back against it, and let the fragrance of the roses, the sugariness of the honeysuckle, the incense of the mimosas and boxwood drift over him. He closed his eyes lightly and his breath came with ease. In this magic hour he did not struggle, for there was nothing in life to struggle for now. He was hidden here from the complicated intrigues of life and the sprawling struggle all about him—the city with its tinseled vagabonds, and those who ritually and reverently embalmed their minds, and those who purged both soul and purse for social prestige.

Vic knew that Jake, his brother, had finished the evening service and had left the church long ago; by now he and Myra had gone to bed. Vic shook his head in doubt. He was an outcast— a recusant as far as the church was concerned; even Jake, his own brother, believed him so. But not Myra. Poor creature! She had been untimely caught in the divine web of righteousness and devoured, her soul and mind torn from her body by the righteous.

Laughingly Myra had spoken the unheard-of once to him, saying that being an honest whore would have been better than what she had gone through.

And he thought of Jezebel, whose recrudescent discontent was running up its thorny blossom. Well, good for her. Her name was still extant within the church books, for she had been a very properly accredited member dealing in brotherly love all her life, and no one had dared openly question her authority or call her to account. People took her contemptuous remarks as slaves their lashings, for she had no elders or betters to call her down. All her life she had been a frenzied obsessor and she had decked herself out in borrowed goodness, entering into hand-to-hand combat in the church for the much-repairing of Jesus.

Vic thought of Mama Amazon, and his heart was overwhelmed with joy and his eyes drafted their tears as his soul was flooded with the tender memory of her. She had raised him as a boy needed to be raised. She had browbeat him, she had made him drop his pants, and she had dusted his behind with her hand. She had scolded him and made him walk the chalk line, and he had loved her as he had never loved anyone else. She was earthy and wise as the eternal hills of the red land; she was sarcastic and filled ofttimes with contemptuous remarks. She was good at clowning, lightheartedly mocking the stuck-ups and scoffing disgustedly at the sloven and lazy. At times she could grow fulsome at it, but to Vic she was as stable as the sun. Storm clouds and laughter were part of her, and she gave them to him and was as dependable to him as the rising and the setting sun.

In his childhood Mama Amazon was law and love and home— it had never occurred to him that she might have a black skin. If he hated anything, it was not having a black skin just like hers.

Her blackness never bowed her in cringing sorrow, but only connoted a better spiritual growth that was genuine and absolutely trusting without one hoot of make-believe. Her living was abundantly arrayed about her and there were no ticklish flurries or flustrations. She had no special incentive to do good, for everything she did was good. In her time she had had contempt for her elders and when she was old she expected the youngsters to have contempt for her.

Now he phrased questions with his lips to ask her, only to realize she was gone forever. For now he was certain she was sousing herself in the Presbyterian stardust as an old hen sifting in the red dirt here on the red land.

Vic looked at the moon, noting that the first thin sheet of the hurricane clouds were sweeping merrily along. He thought of the weather forecast that had come over the radio at noontime: the storm warnings were up all along the coast and the hurricane wind and rain would sweep inland to Green Pond sometime in the night. He already felt the increasing dampness in the wind, making him feel cozily drowsy. There was foreboding in the air. He closed his eyes again, leaned back against the mausoleum, listening to the street traffic which was beginning to let up. It must be getting late. Perhaps midnight. The dampness was getting heavier; and now and then he felt a drop of the approaching hurricane rain.

He was old and tired; and he thought and thought some more. Nearly eighty-five years ago—beyond a golden jubilee, beyond a diamond jubilee, beyond, beyond—stretching into his childhood, and Mama Amazon's pictures of it, and her devils and her Gawd. In the beginning there was Gawd, his and Mama Amazon's Gawd—for he had accepted hers readily, because she had always said it was good to have a real Gawd, a Gawd with some right-much skin on He's bones. It was good to have one to live by, but much better to have one to die by.

His thoughts drifted back, and he recalled how vividly Mama Amazon had told it.

2

Vic saw the amorphous substance, frothy, all veily mist as it was
sometimes over the rivers. There was no beginning and no end
to it. It was without form. It swirled and boiled turbulently, and
there was the great powerful Gawd whose wrath was unmerciful,
whose love was limitless, whose magnificent beard was incompar-
able, whose kindly face was so filled with comprehension and
understanding that there was no need to ask questions. Gawd
trod through the air, His great big feet chunking up and down on
the frothy substance as though He were treadling upon a bi-
cycle. He reached out His hands and He spoke and there were
the creation, the firmament, and the saints—wet, cold, naked—
huddling right up close to Gawd as biddies will do when fresh-
hatched and wet, huddling up to the body of the mother hen for
warmth and protection.

That had been a long, long time ago, just too long to think
about; but then one day, not too powerful long ago, just right
after the Civil War, Gawd and Gabriel came down to the red
land of the watershed here between the two red rivers. It was raining like cats-and-dogs-fighting when They landed in an old worn-
out broom-sedge field. It was the dead of a February night. The
thunder and lightning played rough games across the sky.

GABRIEL: Ho'cum You's got sich thunder an lightnin playin
round, Lawd? You knows that purty nigh scares the daylights
outta me. I don't so much mind em sharp lightnin cracks, fo
they's over quick, but that big boomin thunder is enough to terrorize even the very ole Satan.

GAWD: I'm aimin to terrorize ole Satan. I haves right much
business here on earth an I don't want ole Satan meddlin in it.
That rounder's scart of stormy weather—any kind of water. He's
hidin fro em bolts of lightnin. Iffen not, he'd be right over there
by this broom-sedge field, peepin fro behint one of em big pine

trees tryin to find out what I's up to. I know em fro way back befo buck was a calf.

GABRIEL: Shorely hopes You ain't gonna do too much down here on Earth. I didn't bring em Books down. Good thing. Fo in this weather, they'd get pure ruint. You'd might-night have to start creation all over agin.

GAWD: Shorely don't wanna do that; this ole Earth is been worryation, stubborn an rebellious—an still is. I feels just lack in my head sometimes I'd never birthed em.

GABRIEL: Fo true, but Earth ain't never been contrary as *man*. Earth knowed all along man allowed to be rebellious. That's ho'-cum she didn't want You makin em in the first place. You know how rambunctious Earth got an how she cut up the first time You sent me to get a big handful of dirt to make ole Adam outta. Earth was as mad as a hornet an pouted fo the longest time.

GAWD: Earth got over em, ain't she? Now she'd rather pleasure sheself at birth as doin anythin else. She's fruitful over she whole face. She fount out it'd do no good to rebel again Me. —— Us quit talkin an argufyin an get down to makin Miz Jezebel. Us soon gotta get home so us can keep things runnin smooth.

GABRIEL: Have mercy, Gawd! This where You gonna make she? Right out here in this ole broom-sedge field? An it rainin so you can't see you hand befo you face? I's gettin the awfulest wet-tin, water all in my face an runnin down my legs. Shore glad us spends most of us time in Heaven. I ain't lost nothin on Earth.

GAWD: Aw-pshaw, Gabriel, shut you mouth. You ain't the high power, nohow.

GABRIEL: I knows that, Gawd. But You's shore picked some rough night to birth Miz Jezebel. She must gonna be some powerful vast personage in this ole world.

GAWD: I spect Miz Jezebel's gonna be purty earthy and fleshy —most of em is—so us needs plenty water to work this red mud mo better. Iffen she earthy, she gotta have em fine curves and good-lookin as all get-out. Wit this mud workin mo better, us can naturally get better hair on em. I wants she hair red and wit heaps of yaller an bronze mixed up in em. Let's mix this mud good.

GABRIEL: What color eyes she gonna have?

GAWD: Reckon yaller? Ya, specks of light green on she edges. Folks'll remember em once they look into em.

GABRIEL: She gonna be a saint?

GAWD: Tolt you earthy first. Then see what she do.

GABRIEL: Her Scotch-Irish, enty?

GAWD: You knows blamed well she is. Else why birth em on the red land? What kind of land they come fro is what kind of peoples they is. You can't bring blacks here to this red land and expect em to always be black and you can't bring whites here and expect em to always stay white—not when I created this land fo a red man. You see what I means, Gabrieline?

GABRIEL: I reckon I do; an iffen I don't it don't make no differ. But what I am a-wantin to know is where's the red pepper to put in she temper wit? Us come off wit'out em.

GAWD: Hon, don't you get flustrated over nothin. Run yander to the Leakin Skillet an get a string of red pepper.

GABRIEL: Where'll I find em? Is You shore won't nobody mind? I can't be stealin.

GAWD: You's a case, a heavy case, Gabrieline! That string of red pepper's been hangin beside that knothole behint the door in the Leakin Skillet since befo the Civil War. Folks uster peep through that knothole to see iffen any Yankee soldiers was comin lootin. Hurry up! Us can't make no Scotch-Irishmen wit'out plenty red pepper fo a temper.

The rain slashed down, and Gabriel returned as a streak of lighting ripped across the sky and snapped its fiery tail in a shattering crack of thunder.

GABRIEL: I fount plenty of pepper, but iffen You puts all this in she temper, she'll be one gal. This pepper's ole an mean fro way back yonder.

GAWD: Gimme the pepper. Let's wind up this lil job an get home. I disremembers how long I did set the elements to rage and carry on.

GABRIEL: Fo' true, You picked some lonesome spot to birth the po gal. ——Gawd, is em tats of mud good enough for she breasts?

GAWD: Hold em out mo better. No! Never do! Put sumpin in em so they'll stand out firm an straight. Preachers ain't gonna want to look at no ole flat-breasted haglack creature. Make em so preachers'll say, *umph*. And have some zest fo doin.

GABRIEL: I'll try.—How long's you plannin fo this terrific storm to last? Too hot fo February. Wonder what mens says about this thunder an lightnin?

GAWD: I set the heaviest part of the storm fo the time us'd be down here. It'll let up soon as we gets back. Though I wants the weather to stay damp an squally fo several weeks so Miz Jezebel'll season out mo better.

GABRIEL: It's a lonesome rundown country fo she to season out in.

GAWD: Aw-pshaw. Good country! Been run over lately wit the Civil War, the carpetbaggers, an scalawags. It's fixin to get back on its feet, an when it do, you watch em. Em ole Scotch-Irish can scratch a livin outta this rocky red land. I had no other people to put here right now. I wants all My Earth loved an cared fo. Two wars ain't hurt em ole Scotch-Irish. Em British once burnt my praise-house, Nof Bethel, but the folks fought em off an built Nof Bethel right back up. Ole Sherman came wit he's fire an burnt em out, but em ole Scotch-Irish was just lack ole brier rabbit when he was throwed into the brier patch.

GABRIEL: Us bout ready to diswing off to Heaven?

GAWD: Ya. I think Miz Jezebel's gonna be all right. She haves plenty-fitten curves. Good-lookin as all get-out there on the ground wit that rain water tricklin bout she. —Let's diswing home.

Although the thunder and the lightning had rolled away, the

boiling, angry clouds had not. The atmosphere was turgid with water. It coated and dripped from the trees and dead vegetation. The dripping water was the only sound. It was approaching dawn, a dawn of gloomy gray. The roosters, which were roosted in the fig bushes behind the kitchens over the countryside, were beginning to crow to warn ole Satan and his hellhounds it was time for them to get to the nethermost regions, and they gave their commands with an emphatic metallic sound.

SATAN: Call the hellhounds offen whatever they's runnin. Must be a polecat they's struck out after.

BEELZEBUB: Call em yourself. I'm hoarse fro hollerin after em ole smelly dogs all night long. Us comes on de-big-de-possum hunt an it comes up sich a big thunder an lightnin storm that all us can do is huddle up under a big tree to keep from gettin drownt. Much less gettin the awfulest wettin. I jest naturally don't lack no waters. I tolt you let's not go possum huntin tonight. Gettin too late fo possum huntin. The hellhounds runs polecats all night. Em was bout the fiercest cracks of thunder I ever heardt. You oughtta seen me jumpin fro under that big ole oak tree when that bolt hit it—peelin some of he's bark off to the ground. That's the ole oak tree ole Miz Joanna Thornwell uster climb to get em grapes to make the racy wine fo the holy communion to Nof Bethel Church, enty? Don't ketch me lookin up fo no mo grinnin possum in em in sich rambunctious weather.

SATAN: Wonder who Gawd's mad at? The way He throwed em thunderbolts. Wintertime, too! You reckon He done losed He's mind? He'll confuse lil mens toreckly—not at they ain't already confused. An you—gettin right contrary an rebellious. Won't call em dogs. Here, Queen, *here!* Here, Ring, *here!* Com'on. I can't be out here callin all day, not wit em feather-tailed roosters a-crowin up a storm. Here, Blue-speck, *here!* Beelzebub, you quit you titterin an laughin at me.

BEELZEBUB: You'se that drunk now you's gonna be hard put to get to the nethermost regions befo daylight. Where'd you get that jug of corn likker? That jug's got a red corncob fo a stopper.

SATAN: I took an stolt this lil jug of corn likker fro ole man McCobb. Guess I gotta have sumpin to quench my thirst, I's ever disdainful of water. McCobb makes the best likker in these parts. This corn these Scotch-Irish grows on this red land makes a potent corn likker. It'll knock a bellowin bull fo a loop of Preachin Sundays.

BEELZEBUB: You ought not be stealin Cabelus McCobb's good corn likker.

SATAN: He steals fro the gov'mint. An I don't see as it's so bad fo me to steal fro he. Em gov'mint is got to have they tax, an me, I's got to have my lil drink.

BEELZEBUB: I swear this's some tall broom grass we's wadin through. High as my head. Ole red dirt grows em; em an the pine trees.

SATAN: You oughta quit swearin! You's gettin pure bad. Take you down a notch some of these days. You'll never be able to work on em high elders in Nof Bethel. You's got to toady an truckle to get em. They's pure scart of honest swearin.

BEELZEBUB: Ha, ha! You's done fell down. And on what a funny pile of red mud? Ain't it curious-lookin?

SATAN: Fo true! Shorely is curious, enty? Shaped lack peoples, too.

BEELZEBUB: Ho'cum you's wettin on em, Satan; throwin you leg up in the air lack a dog?

SATAN: Reckon I's gotta wet out some of this here likker I's tanked up wit. An I don't see nare bush right handy fo me to wet on.

3

The hurricane wind whipped the mausoleum furiously, driving its misty spray before it. Victor drew himself up closer to its protecting wall. He daubed his fists into his old, tired, sleepy eyes and rearranged his sitting position, turning his head sideways, against the mausoleum, scrouging closely to ward off the misty spray. He dozed. He sleepily recalled Uncle Prince Blue and wondered how in the devil the old fellow had ever slept sitting on a log. Ole Uncle Prince Blue's gals—Aunt Violet, Aunt Rose, Aunt Lily—kept threading through his mind as a needle pulls the thread through the cloth. There they were in the broom-sedge field as he had remembered them in his youth and as he knew they must have been before he was born, back when the scars of the war had just barely closed in the ravaged soil, back when his father, Dr. Thomas Thaddeus Thornwell, the only doctor on the red land of the watershed between the rivers, rode Star across the wind-swept hills, the tired earth, and the lean fields.

2

In the sea of waving broom sedge, three well spent, withered black wenches patted the red mud into hard sticky cakes. Their rags stuck to their skinny bodies—it was a lean time of year and these creatures were hungry. That February dawning they looked to be unholy witches who had stepped down from the watery clouds that bounced furiously turbulent from hilltop to hilltop, too water-drugged for safety. Their soft voices were akin to the mushy thunder playing in the dripping clouds, and their piercing eyes akin to the lightning that lit up pages of the western sky. The air about them was fretfully damp, a ghoulish world whose tones of modulating grays pined for sunshine.

"Gawd!" shrieked Violet, jumping up with a handful of sticky red mud. "Yander come Ole Doc. Musta took Miz Cora Mathis all night long to have she child."

"Rose, you's goin over there to wash fo Miz Cora Mathis. I ain't about to stick my hands on em nasty sheets," Violet giggled. "An help me Gawd, you's gonna get us some snuff wit that quarter—iffen you gets any money fo washin. I'm tired eatin this red dirt."

"Uh-um," Rose yawned, showing the red earth ground into her teeth, "let's get a quarter fro Ole Doc. An then us won't have to wash. Us can go right on to the Leakin Skillet soon as she opens up. My guts is growlin to pure beat the band fo good store snuff."

"Been tellin you bout eatin so much red dirt, gal. Gonna rot the linin out of you belly."

"Huh. Don't eat no mo'an you. Gotta have sumpin to stick in this ole belly of mine. It's a lean time of year. After crops gets started, taters swellin up in the ground, I'll live on the fat of Gawd's earth. He own it anyway an not the white folks. They's just here fo a little bit."

"Be quiet. Ole Doc'll hear youse."

They crouched, pantherlike, grinning, making mudcakes that they would dry in the sun and then munch upon when they were hard and brittle.

Ole Doc rode up. "Howdy, howdy."

"Mornin, Doc," they greeted, snurly-nosed and with haggly-toothed grins.

"It's so, Doc," giggled Violet. "Just a few mo risin's an settin's of the evenin sun an life is done."

"Gawd, Doc, give me a quarter to get some snuff wit," Rose began, looking at Ole Doc through half-closed eyes. "Prince Blue, he's that triflin an no-account, he's gonna let we's starve. Ain't worked none all winter. Allus dabblin in the conjure business."

"I don't have a quarter. Have to take in peas and molasses. Nobody's got money these days."

"That's what you allus says," cried Violet, who was beside him, rubbing his shiny pants. "No wonder you ain't got no quarters —allus givin em to fine white ladies." Then she cunningly looked him in his eyes, "Miz Cora Mathis done birthed she chile, enty?

"Cora Mathis had her baby over a week ago," Ole Doc stated almost too sharply for Violet's primitive ears.

"She did?" Violet asked in acid surprise. "Us thought that was where you'd been—birthin Miz Cora Mathis. Ho'cum you's out so early an headin right fo the stillhouse? Day's hardly clean yet."

Ole Doc's voice was dead tired, "Oh, I been birthin all right, but not Cora Mathis. You let that slip up on you. What's the matter with you? —Nancy Boylet is dead. You all hurry on to the house and tell ole Blue to go tell what few of her folks are left about it. I imagine they'll want him to make her coffin."

"Miz Nancy Boylet dead?" they chortled in wonder and surprise. They cut their eyes cunningly at one another, then to the ground speculatively.

"How's she chile?" Violet more suggested than asked.

"Child? Who said anything about a child? I said Nancy was dead," said Ole Doc with righteous astonishment.

"Yes, sir," said Violet with a big hoot of laughter. "I heardt you the first time."

"You be sure to tell ole Blue." He rode away, leaving them standing patting the red mud, looking slyly at each other.

"Yes," Lily began, once Ole Doc was out of hearing, "Miz Nancy done birthed a chile." She looked solemn and far-off yonder. "Wonder is Ole Doc the chile's daddy?"

"What I'm wonderin is where's the chile at?" Violet asked significantly.

"Ole Doc sure have pleasured he'sself wit the ladies. Men's scarce since so many of em been killed off in the war."

"Yes, he's got enough stray chillun to half fill a church. Got twins one time: ole Miz Grady had twins."

"Aw. He's too ole fo that."

"Don't look lack it. Why, that lil ole yaller nigger that lays round in Catawba is one of hisn."

"Oh, well. It don't make no difference. He's better an most the whites. He's got breedin. Ain't lack some of this buckra that tries to stay in the field wit you—showin you this an that."

"No, so help me Gawd, I jes naturally wouldn't work fo one of em poor-rumped buckras. I'd scratch out he's stones," said Lily threateningly.

"Let's hurry on an tell ole Blue like he say do. Iffen that triflin nigger'll get busy an make em up a good fine coffin, us won't suffer fo snuff."

"I wants him to go round to Miz Nancy's kitchen an get some meat skins. I know Miz Nancy never got round to eatin up her skins, iffen she's even et all her meat."

2

There went Ole Doc riding away from a labor case that had harassed him all night long, riding upon old Star, whose bridle reins dangled on her neck, whose flanks kept the saddlebags flopping, and who jogged along the stony trail so certain as to appear humanly intelligent, her feet clipping the stones klink-t-klink. Ole Doc folded his hands upon the pommel of the saddle, riding slightly stooped and as loosely as an old untied shoe. His solid rump muscles filled the saddle manly; his big abdomen protruded into the traditional Santa Claus belly; his pants were buttoned with scrutinizing care. He pulled his silk hat, black and shapeless, farther down over his eyes to keep the wind from blowing it to the muddy ground. This, indeed, was a strong February squall. It might last for days. It was too hot for the time of year. The wind swept across barren fields, veiled with black cotton stalks, holding myriads of black burs, each a supplication to the tired wet earth and to Jesus.

He rubbed a fist into each tired eye, trying to rub out the sleep, shaking his head, yawning. It was getting harder on him to keep these all-night vigils. Women always wriggled around so that they would have their children at night. He'd much prefer they select some other time. But so went a man's life here on the red land of the watershed. It was all written out in the stardust of what a man's life would be. Life was but a whirlwind and a short one in a dusty field. Man spouted up—from where? He spouted down—to where?

Nancy, he thought, was getting too old to have a baby. Any woman who waited until she was thirty was taking her life in her hands. Since the war, nature had been cruel to the womenfolks; too many of the men had been killed in the war, so there were not enough men to go around. He knew there would always be trouble when there were not enough men. There was nothing for the women to do. So Nancy had become bored stiff with life and borrowed herself a man, throwing reckoning to the wind. She, at least, had died happy. It had been much easier on her than him. A bloody mutilation always got him in the dumps— he'd have the blues for days over what happened last night.

He shuddered, thinking about last night: Nancy dying. Spider webs and soot were incapable of stopping that blood after that mutilation—nor forceps nor hot irons. It was to be. It was in the stardust, across the whole way of the heavens. Women were the flowers of a nation—God put them here to bloom and to fruit— and man, the bee with a stinger, was to fertilize the seed. So the stars had written long—no man knew how long—ago.

He had covered up for Nancy the best he could. It had been quiet and still there at three o'clock in the morning as he dug the tiny, weesome grave under the fragrantly scented boxwoods and lowered the shoe box, substituted for a coffin, into the wet earth, throwing the tired earth back on the little shoe box. How the roosters in the fig bushes behind the kitchens about the country- side had cried in accusing voices—even so that he had to stop often to listen. Not one single star in heaven peeped through the thick rain clouds to accuse him for his blunderings, although the wind made up for it, howling and hissing as a courtroom crowded with angered spectators.

Now, as soon as ole Blue let the people know, the neighbors would be coming in, prying, peeping, talking in knowing nods and muscular twitchings of the face more than in words. There wouldn't be a copper's worth of nothing hid from them. Still, he had covered purty good, considering everything, but they would make the tale to suit themselves. They'd send her straight to hell. They'd do that if they knew the truth, so what difference did it make? Ole Doc shook his head.

3

The smoke from Green Pond's innumerable stillhouses ascended heavenward as a burnt offering and a thanksgiving of praise to the pure soured corn mash it was stewing. The many crystal-clear creeks of the hilly red land afforded very much cool water to chill the worm that condenses the steam from the boiling mash into fiery dreams—and a great deal of wetting in the bushes.

Ole Doc saw and smelled the wood smoke drifting down along the creek from the stillhouse. It drifted along the winding, flint-rocked road leading beside the creek where the water jumped and splashed over the rocks on its way to the river. Everything was sopping-full of water. The leaves cushioned the road in wringing dampness and Star walked noiselessly. At the stillhouse Ole Doc dismounted, left Star standing by a stunted dogwood, and went into the log-built stillhouse.

Inside it was damply warm and fetid-smelling. Blazing fires ripsnorted at the copper stills, licking them in so many spots as greedy lovers. Ole Doc twitched his nose, sniffing.

"Howdy, Doc, howdy," said Cabelus McCobb, stirring in a large wooden vat of stinking, fermenting mash. "You're out a bit early, ain't you? Of course, it might be later than I think," Cabelus ended, sizing Ole Doc and his situation up quickly with his eager-rodent, shrewd blue eyes. His mustache, twisted pencil-sharp, moved with his lips. He scratched his long chin whiskers. McCobb was thinking desperately and greedily fast. Here was a customer. Early in the morning to boot. Dogbite iffen things weren't picking up. Ole Doc had lost a case somewhere last night.

He wouldn't be here buying likker this early. He had to have likker to drown out his sorrow when he lost a case; that was indubitable. Here was a customer who meant a whole dollar's profit. One of those stinking elders in North Bethel Church, yet a stomp-down good feller. Folks might get indignant because he threw a drunk, but they lacked discretion to openly church him because he was indispensable to the welfare of the countryside. There were always typhoid, tuberculosis and malaria, chills. But as long as he bought and paid cash for his likker, why question more? He was one of the very few who could plank down cash for his likker.

"Been out all night, but I'm aiming to head in with the owls now," Ole Doc replied. "How's that new federal gauger and you getting along these days?—the one the Government sent down from Salem?" Mischief increased in his soft brown eyes.

"He wanted to run things like the Federal Government wanted them run, but we showed him it'd be much easier, more profitable to him to leave the gauge unlocked after he'd checked the little bit the Government allows tax-exempt. Very little," Cabelus twisted the ends of his mustache with serious authority, "can be made on good whisky at a dollar and a quarter a gallon, and if you've got to give the Federal Government ninety cents of that in tax and twenty-five cents for a bushel of corn, there'd be only a measly dime left."

Ole Doc laughed. "Cabelus, you're a skinflint; but if you don't look out for yourself, no one else will."

"Yes, I do have to make a living and lay something up for a rainy day. Money's scarce. Times are hard since the war, and just between me and you, it don't look like they'll ever be any better —not with the Republicans running Washington right and left. Who are you going to vote for this fall?" Cabelus asked.

"Straight Democratic—regardless of who runs on it. A change will do good. We'd never had all this reconstruction hocus-pocus if Lincoln had lived."

"Ole Abe Lincoln was a Republican."

"I don't care," said Ole Doc, shaking his head emphatically, "Lincoln was the only friend the South had. And if the hotheads in the South had listened to him we wouldn't have had this infernal war; a war never does anybody any good—'cept maybe the insidious carpetbaggers and scalawags."

Cabelus shook his head over his treasured possessions and the annoyance in his quick, staccato voice was apparent. "With the Federal Government and the infernal churches stirring up one row after another, sales are not so good as they used to be. Besides, I have to swap too much whisky for corn. About all these free-issue niggers can get, and they have to steal it out of somebody's corncrib."

"Who got up that new law they are trying to push down in Clover?" Ole Doc asked. "I been hearing purty much about it lately."

"Which one?" asked Cabelus. "The one about the crow flying the three miles from the stillhouse to the church?"

"Yes," Ole Doc agreed, "and that'll include barrooms or any place where whiskies are sold. I've an idea that D. D. Inchurch is pushing that. Know how righteous he is."

"That's exactly how I've got it figured out, because several of those old stiff-necked elders from North Bethel came out here and measured. You can't go three miles from here in any direction unless you run into a church. I shore don't want to give up these good rock shoals and move farther back into the hills, but it looks mighty heap like that is what I'm going to have to do. Or maybe since the churches are attacking whiskymaking with such vim, you'll not be wanting to lease me these shoals for another five years?"

"We'll see about that. No need to take a pill until you're sick; then it might not be so hard to get down. Inchurch is going to do all he can to eliminate whiskymaking. He toads and truckles in Clover until he gets what he wants. Still and all, he's been about as good a representative to Legislature as we could have sent down to Clover. He wouldn't be human if he didn't have several faults —we're all too earthy—and perhaps that is the way God meant it to be. You probably have a nice nest egg laid away and won't suffer too much."

"I've tried to be thrifty and saving. I have a little I'd like to invest. Reckon there'd be any chance in me getting a share in those mills you all have planned? You know," he propped one foot upon a sack of corn, leaned over on his bent knee, becoming chummy, "I believe there is going to be a future in that. The country has got to do something or we starve to death. It looks like cotton could be manufactured here as well as anywhere."

"Dogged, McCobb, that's my idea. I think we have something there. I'm going to see can't I do something about it for you. We need a little more money right now. A country is like an army of worms: where the grass is tenderest, the worms have the fattest bellies."

4

Ole Doc jogged along the lonely path. He crowned a bleak naked hill, sitting his horse erect, etched against the dripping clouds. Scotch-Irish, he'd let the whole world know. His grandpa and grandma were the best stomp-down Scotch-Irish that ever crossed the Atlantic. Presbyterian, too. That meant something. They had come from Scotland and tarried awhile in Ireland.

The Lord helped them that helped themselves, Grandpa and Grandma preached. It was written. Up there in the stars. Here in the godly hills and hollows of the red land of the watershed they had finally settled, making themselves at home as if they were a swarm of bees in June before an abandoned hollow tree.

Ole Doc sat there on Star staring dreamily across his red rolling acres. His long stiltlike legs were not over a foot from the ground. His black coat was shiny. After all, he didn't get a new coat every day and Ma had always pointed out to him to take care of what he had—the Lord just naturally gave to those who had. His collar and cuffs, with great gold links, were boardlike with starch. He had foolishly, since leaving the stillhouse, fastened a sprig of mistletoe into his coat lapel. He now replaced his high silk hat and started Star down another hill at whose foot was the old homestead of his Grandpa Andrew Thornwell.

At Grandpa's old house, Ole Doc dismounted slowly, gruntingly, leaving Star standing before the door on the lower level. The house was built primitively and conveniently, as many of the thrifty early settlers did build. The lower floor was of native rocks and sunk over halfway into the side of the hill; the upper floor was of logs and its door opened out a story higher on the top level of the hill. It was near water. It not only showed crude artistry, but thrift and very much animal-like conveniences. Ole Doc fumbled in his pocket for a key. He would stop off here and take a sup from his jug before going on to Catawba. He was in no condition to go on more calls today. If he went home to Catawba, there'd be folks pounding on his door, for there was much sickness and affliction laying his people low in this unseasonable weather. Right now he was very glad that he had never allowed any of his tenants to live in Grandpa Andrew's house, because it was a retreating place for him, situated as it was on the very backside of Catawba's rolling red acres. A body needed solitude and communion with his Maker when things went out of hand as they had done last night.

He built a fire in the fireplace. Fire felt good, he thought, as he warmed himself before the crackling blaze; even though it was unseasonably warm, the air was damp and chilly. He went over to a corner cupboard Grandpa had built so big and heavy out of solid walnut that nobody had ever tried to move it. The household goods were here just as his grandparents had left them. He selected a low blue bowl, with a windmill painted on it, and a pewter spoon, carried them to the round marble-topped table with the fancy carved legs, picked up his jug, and gurgled the bowl level-full of the golden racy likker. He sat down facing the fire, hunkered over the bowl.

He dipped the pewter spoon gingerly into the bowl of whisky, bringing a scant spoonful to his mouth, letting the burning, golden liquid rest cozily upon his tongue, to turn and to flow slowly about his mouth. He swallowed it quietly, feeling its racy taste, swallowing the extra amount of saliva the whisky caused to secrete in his mouth. He felt the tangy warmth in his empty stomach. He reached for the second and the third spoonfuls very gracefully and filled with rhythm. This was the way to soften the horror of last night. This was the way to bring Nancy Boylet into relationship with her Maker and what her Maker had written in the stardust about her. He wondered where Nancy was and he questioned the days of a man's life upon the earth.

"What are you doing here?" asked John Mathis, sticking his head in the open door.

"What are you doing yourself?" Ole Doc responded, the spoon poised in the air halfway to his mouth. "Been out looking your traps? What's that you got there? Come in, dry off by the fire. It's rough outside—raw."

"This is an otter," said John, holding the dead animal aloft by its tail. "It's rare to catch an otter. They're just about played out in these parts. Water's too high in all the creeks and rivers to catch anything. Queer quirk that on a night when I ain't supposed to catch a thing a-tall, I up with an otter. When I send it to that furhouse I ain't so certain they're gonna believe me. But there it is."

"That's the first one I've ever seen," said Ole Doc, looking steadily at the otter. "Have a seat, John. I'm sure glad to see you. I'm kinda down in the dumps—not sad or lonely, but you know, veiled in transparent happiness, the kind that screws you into the shadows and you have that feeling of being and not being." *I'm sure glad old John came along,* Doc thought. *Some folks say he is the barbarous, po'buckra trapper, but I don't know about that. John has always been a mighty good friend to me. Friendship ought to come from the inside. John has had a hard time. The four years of war were downright misery and then he did five years in a Federal prison and that just about sucked the life out of him as though it had been a gaudy harlot. His weak and puny heart has always been without too much courage, but what more can you expect from living with Cora Mathis who has coerced him to obedience as the master his slave?*

"Yes," said John Mathis, taking the proffered chair, "who you fouled yourself up with now? Being a doctor, you are forever cavorting from one shamey gullet to another." *I always feel so delighted to get in Ole Doc's presence, John mused. There is a lingering puberty about him that others do not have at his age. He has an infallible instinct that silts through him as though he were an animal of the woods. Husbandry has always seemingly prevailed over him. Nothing has ever gone to his head and he's never given a whoop for decorum.*

"How's the little girl?" Ole Doc asked, continuing to sup rapturously, looking docilely at John. "Name her yet? Let's see, she's just about a week old." *She pushed into the world like beans cracking the hard crusty red ground. Why is it that everything is so eager to get into the world that it will push and strain so outlandish? But they must get here and grow up and soon begin to rejoice their sexual organs in praise to the great hereafter as they move about with their prattle.*

"Yes, she's a week old today, and right off she has about as much gumption as a fresh-hatched chicken. Cora has named her Jessica, but from the start she's called her Jezebel. I don't go in much for that. Let Cora do as she likes. It ain't likely she would do nothing like I wanted nohow." *That'll be her excuse for not helping me chop the cotton this spring. How she allows for me to make a living with another dry year probably coming up like last year?* "Doc, you'd better be careful how much of that stuff you're sopping up there. You're a long ways from Catawba; you might not get there. Remember last winter when you got lost in that snowstorm—got off your hoss? Couldn't get back on? Know how you held on to that old stock pine, circling it and hollering at the top of your voice for help? You'd froze to death that night if you hadn't had sense enough to keep circling that pine until I heard you." John saw Ole Doc's eyes entranced with some decanting illusion and he was at a loss for words, so he blurted: "Never did tell me, who died on you?"

"It was Nancy Boylet. Childbirth. Too bad—though I hope she died happy. War has killed off too many men," Ole Doc said, shaking his head.

"Seems every dad-blasted one of them has had a kid. Them two oldest gals had theirs without a doctor and they was either born dead or they killed them, one or t'uther. I found one when I was looking my traps. Wonder how come they'd do a thing like that?"

"Scared of the church. They ain't the first ones to trek down the blossomy path of dalliance. Boys and gals have been dallying with one another ever since creation began and got along fairly well without being churched." *It is good to have John here. He is like my very kinfolks. I can say just what I please.*

"You mildly surprise me at saying that, although I have known you to say many special things of wisdom betwixt just you and me. And another thing that has had me overpuzzled for years: how is it that the high elders never church you for supping? And you an elder. You surely must work a medical conjure on them."

"John, you've been trapping and you surely know how hard it is to catch undomesticated animals who have learned to live by their wits? That's me."

"You've always been notorious and flagrant in defying the authorities, but what behooves me is why are they always catching me in trifling things and hauling me before that worldly shrewd and heavenbound Session and churching me? Why, it is getting so I'm afraid to take a chaw of tobacco without first looking it up in Holy Writ. They've churched me that much, I come out right piouslike, drenched, and feel no longer human. I bet iffen Cora Mathis knowed about it, you'd be churched."

"What Cora Mathis don't know don't hurt her. She's not half as good as she lets on. I knew her long before you married her. Though she's about as good as the Inchurches."

"I want nothing that the infernal Inchurches has anything to do with. I got my fill of them when I was foreman there before the war."

"Never cross an Inchurch," said Ole Doc. "He'll get even with you one way or another. They've allus had the grabs and takes and lookouts for themselves. They've ruled that North Bethel Church ever since I can recollect. The whole generation of them have been conniving vipers, concreted and concerted. The only reason I get along with them in that Session is that I toad to a degree and in a certain way. If you are a sharp toader you can get along. I doubt many of them believe they are upholding the word of God. It is mostly their egoism they are subjected to."

"Whatever it is that they are subjected to, I wish they'd continue to be subjected to it and not vamoose me before the Session, churching me in such brotherly love. I feel flabbergasted and like a humbug and would rather be chasing a polecat any day. Who do you think the Democrats are going to put on their ticket for this fall?"

"It wouldn't surprise me if they don't use Charles O'Connor for president and John Quincy Adams for vice-president. I been keeping up fairly well, and it kinda looks like to me that is the way things are shaping up."

"Reckon they'll get it?"

"Don't stand a coon's chance. I can get fooled like the devil. The unheard-of can happen. But the South has got to get better on its feet before it can have too much of a say-so in national affairs. We've been walking around here in borrowed feathers lately."

"Do you still hear from the two Copperheads you turned loose during the war?"

"Why, them rascals have been invaluable in helping us get things lined up for the mills on the river. They're sharp. Now that just goes to show you," said Ole Doc, swallowing the spoonful of whisky, then pointing his spoon at John, continuing philosophically, "that it don't pay to do what the high-ups would have you do. That night I was ordered to shoot them or have it done if there was a charge from the Federal side—I simply didn't have the heart to do it. Told them so point blank. I turned them loose and they said they'd never forget it. Why, Jefferson Harvey and Lewis Ford are two of the best stomp-down friends I've got. Naomi and I went to Philadelphia on our honeymoon to see them especially."

"How is Naomi? You sure pick them young. How old is she?"

"Dogged if I know how old Naomi is. You can't tell about women—some get ripe earlier than others and some don't ever get ripe."

"When was it you told me she was expecting? June? That's a little early, ain't it? You all were just married this past Halloween. You gonna keep on messing around and get churched yet. Though it's about time you have some yard chillun."

"After all, John, it was ketched in my trap. What can the churchly Session do about that?"

5

Late scowling evening wrapped itself about the desolate weather-beaten cabin. The eerie wind of a turbulent cloudy sunset rattled its rotten vertical boards. The one-roomed cabin stood at the edge of the tall soughing pines whose roots flourished in the red land. The wooden window banged with each gust of the harassing wind. The door was propped open with a stick and a crown-nest fire smudged in the rock fireplace.

Uncle Prince Blue knew that he must hurry. Miz Nancy Boy-let had been lying on the cooling board all day long. He had been late getting the black cloth, getting the proper measurements of her body so that her coffin would fit and she would rest.

Prince Blue, decrepit and senile, slick and bald, squatted barefooted in the cabin yard. He nailed black cloth on a long pine box.

He was too old to be a sharecropper, yet Ole Doc let him and the cabin stay here side by side and fall to pieces. The brand of his tribe was burned on the cheek of Prince Blue, a native-born prince of Africa. Such a windy and charming dasher had he been in his younger days that, once free from slavery, he had never had to work only from show-off ways. Ladies were to be had merely by his being there when needed, and his stray chillun were scattered so thickly about the countryside that he had never thought it necessary to have any yard chillun lest there should always be so much confusion about who was who. Life was too short to live in utter confusion.

In his later years Lily, Rose, and Violet had moved in with him or they had all moved in together. It was in such olden times one could not remember. No one was certain where they had come from. No one was certain who they were. They were without age. Like so many Negroes they had been seventeen for ages and then they were suddenly seventy-five since most anyone could remember. They could remember when the stars fell. They could remember when ole Satan had caught up with them in their slacken ways of sin and plunged them living into a smoking pit. They could remember when love conjures worked. So old-timy were they that for them time stood still. Tomorrow was today and today was yesterday.

But Prince Blue was beyond time or time was beyond him, and making a coffin or sleeping in his fireplace he wore many pairs of pants, threadbare, tattered bits of rags that had been patched so many times the original garments could not be told from the patches. The inseams of the pants were ripped from cuffs to strads, giving the appearance of a dress with numerous, dangling petticoats. One puny string across his shoulder served as a suspender. His many shirts and underwear were as void of one piece as his pants.

Lily, Rose, and Violet, like skinny witches, sat on the doorstep singing about Lazarus. Each time the chant was repeated, the number of days Lazarus had been dead was increased by one day until they reached the number ten.

"Lawd have mercy, Rose, Violet," shrilled Lily as a rooster's metallic crowing, "you know Lazarus he ain't been dead ten days!"

"Shore, fo true," chimed Rose.

"You know," shouted Violet, "iffen he'd done been dead fo ten days he'd stunk so bad the buzzards wouldn't et him."

Rose doubled up with short laughter. Lily and Violet saw the fun and they joined with Rose in violent spasms of laughter. And all the time that Prince Blue rapped upon the coffin, his ole gals sat in the doorway, laughing hysterically about Lazarus.

February's wind had switched to the north and was blowing cold. The clouds were ruffling as a broody hen disturbed. The stirring wind that moved them was biting cold. They foreboded snow.

Uncle Prince Blue dropped the hammer from his numb fingers to the top of the finished coffin and walked over to the edge of the bald yard to wet. He stood for a long time fumbling with his many pairs of pants, but he could find nothing to wet with. Lily, Rose, and Violet came to his rescue, down on their knees before him, their swarthy fingers browsing with the tattered pants, parting them carefully, holding each bit of rag out of the way and finally Rose found it.

"Here it is," she cried, "and that cold wind shore done drawed it up."

"Gawd, youse, look comin yander," cried Lily, pointing down the path.

They scrambled to their feet and Rose said, "Declare iffen it ain't Ole Doc."

"Comin fro the stillhouse." There were grinning and knowing looks among them. "Yes, look at that jug swung onto he's saddle. Look how ole Star is walkin."

Prince Blue looked sharply. "He ain't that far gone yet. Ole Star is just getting prepared in case Ole Doc is had too much."

"My guts is pure growlin fo some store snuff," said Lily, pressing her skinny belly, "and I'm gonna ask Ole Doc fo a quarter so I can get me some snuff. Us can still go to the Leakin Skillet fo black dark."

"How you feelin?" they asked when Ole Doc rode into the yard.

"Sorta tolerable, I reckon," Ole Doc replied, leaning on the pommel of the saddle.

"Looks like you'd feel good wit that big jug you got swingin there on you saddle. Gonna make up some medicine wit em, uh?" asked Lily.

"Confound you, Lily. Looks like you're getting mighty old to see so much."

"Ain't half as much as I'm aimin to be seein and ain't half as much as I'm aimin to be tellin bout the countryside." She puckered her withered mouth, looking far-off and all-wise, then turning abruptly upon Ole Doc, she blurted, "Gawd, Doc, give me a quarter fo some snuff. My guts is pure growlin to beat the band." She held out her hand for the much-expected twenty-five cents.

"Confound you, Lily, why don't you lazy dad-blasted folks get out and raise you a patch of tobacco, instead of always hounding me?"

"Us free an ain't got nobody to make us. Now, Doc, you know

I is purty nigh scared to death of em big green worms on tobacco. What iffen one was to sting me?"

"I declare iffen you works wit tobacco, you gets so pure downright sick at you belly that you can't enjoy dippin," said Rose, throwing additional force to Lily.

"Doc, you knows twenty-five cents ain't very much money to a big fine man like you, but you know that much worth of talkin about you and Miz Nancy Boylet would stir up a countryside of stink—though plenty of stink is what everybody wants," Lily added sharply.

He threw her the much-desired quarter. "I hope that snuff rots your dad-blasted red tongue right out of your mouth." He chuckled good-naturedly as he rode away.

6

Passing North Bethel Church on his way home to Catawba, Ole Doc stopped Star in the muddy road, looking dreamily across the cemetery. His memory was sharpened to a screaming point. He saw the two-storied white-frame church standing silently upon the knoll and the cemetery lying to the east and to the back of the church. Out there he knew his grandparents, his father and mother too, were sleeping soundly in the Presbyterian faith. His Grandpa Andrew had given that land for the church and cemetery and so willed it that it could never be used for anything else. Grandpa had been one of the important carpenters in building North Bethel and as clever as anyone with frow and ax. How he had contrived time from his carriage factory beside the river, his flour and corn mill, Ole Doc did not know; but he had been a doer in his time. No work was too hard or tedious. He had a temper like a streak of lightning, for he was rock-gutted Scotch-Irish and God had planted him here on the watershed where the digging was tough.

Doc passed on through the south hills of Catawba's rolling red acres and he came upon a hallowed knoll that was crowned with an ancient oak whose spread was a comforting oasis. At a distance he stopped, admiring the beauty of the aged tree, gnarled and twisted, struck often with lightning; its huge roots were often above the ground, then they would prong back into the salty earth. Here was the oak that his mother, Joanna, had climbed for years to get the grapes from the vine to make the racy wine for the holy communion in North Bethel Church. She had climbed it until she was in her nineties.

Ole Doc kicked Star in her ribs and headed toward Catawba, which loomed up in the distance with its huge weighty wings spread out like a prehistoric bird's wings. Massive, domineering Catawba. Stern like its builder, Andrew Thornwell of the long bygone. Firm and tough like the men who had built it. Cut and hewn from the woods: panels and framing of tulip, pine, walnut, cedar; mantels and great winding circular stairs. The slaves' laughter had echoed through the red hills when the clay was dug from the red earth between Catawba and the river to make the bricks, when the roaring fires were kept going night and day baking the thousands of bricks that went into the building of Catawba. Catawba retained her unyielding sturdiness as the forest's virgin pine she was hewn from, as the stern, rock-ribbed red earth she was molded from.

Approaching Catawba, Ole Doc saw the great front door and he felt sadder than ever, for no longer was his mother, Joanna, there to greet him, to go into a gauzy glow about medicine. She had been the making of him. Ole Doc had been born of an aristocratic mother, proud and a leader, no cheap slattern, no buckra. She had gentle breeding, distinct line, and grace.

As a hickory-shirted shaver, Ma had taught him early how to root for himself, how to bounce out of bed at four o'clock in the morning, how to snitch the fat pine kindling from the wood box, how to rake the mound of ashes from the glowing coals that had been bedded down the night before to keep the fire going, how to lay the fat pine on the coals, and then how to get on his knees and blow up the fire. The slaves would not wait upon him hand and foot—he wasn't growing up around her to be a ne'er-do-well —and she always hammered the good Presbyterian belief that the Lord helps them who help themselves.

He was the lovebug of Ma's eyes; that love grew as a sacred plant. And basically it found its roots in their love for the same thing: administering to suffering humanity. Ma had been the best of midwives, and his earliest recollections of riding her horse behind the saddle was the hurrying. He had ridden behind the sidesaddle and held on to Ma as she hurried up and down the river ketchen chillun at a dollar apiece. She carried her sharp ax to put under the beds to cut the birthpains, and spider webs always checked an ebbing flow of life's blood.

And after medical school, dignified old Catawba grudgingly made room for a medicine room and young Thad had started out in the long bygone. The old folks wagged their behinds scornfully and shook their heads with disdain at first: *He's a sure-enough wild upstart!* But then he went among them. He carefully measured the calomel, May apple, and rhubarb on the point of his knife blade and he dosed them and he physicked them until their bodies were so groggy there was no room left for pain. If a bone needed to be straightened, over his knee it was snapped and cracked to the tune of trickling urine. His torture rack for pulling disjointed bones back into their sockets was a real witch's contraption. So soon he became their sunshine and their rain and their mind-balm. To the old folks, who had so recently looked upon him with scorn, he became Messiah.

The people of Green Pond County marveled, talked daily about young Thad's learning, talked and talked until he was turned into Ole Doc. He was a great magnetic power, better versed in the Bible—the thing that counted—than in medicine, for, after all, the Green Ponders knew full well they were bound to die regardless of who doctored them and it definitely paid to look out for one's immortal soul.

Ole Doc had such a photographic mind that he knew exactly how many verses there were in the King James Version of the Bible, how many chapters, how many Books, and he never tired of quoting the ceaseless passages that he knew. It was a wonder among the people, an amazing thing, how one head could hold so much. He baffled the children with hard catechism questions. If a question of dispute arose or a situation seemed to go out of hand, Ole Doc righteously quoted the Bible and set the issue at peace. And then the controverser would sneak to his home and look up the passage only to exclaim: *Ah, he's right or he'd never said it!* If the physical body seemed to cry in alarm for more medical attention than Ole Doc was capable of giving and the patient tried to spur him into activity, as patients are so wont to do, he would calm the patient's fears with his comforting facts from the undisputable Bible.

7

Low fire glowing in the kitchen of Catawba threw a yellowish light through the open doorway into the murky darkness. Hefty Mama Amazon bent over a black pot nested in red-hot coals on the hearth, steam rising in her face as she dipped up hot chitt'lins bare-fingered, placing them in pans. From the ashes she scraped out smoking-hot sweet potatoes, laying them alongside the chitt'lins. She heaped collard greens treetop tall around the chitt'lins, laid on slabs of corn bread, and over all poured rich greasy pot likker. She crossed the kitchen heavily, placing the heaping pans of victuals on the kitchen table.

"This is the real rations," she said, addressing the three at the table. "This will grease you belly plenty fitten and give you ribs mo power. Honest nigger eatins."

Only dipped his fingers into the victuals, licking them, laughing as if he were a goat. "When I gets through gluttin this night, that lil ole star will be about gone down in the west."

Mama Amazon laughed, "You eat that much and you'll have the cholera morbus again. You know how it was before: you squattin out in the woods that night holdin two pine torches and hollerin wit the gripes." They both laughed. Yellow Sam and Dessa, who had been eating very slowly, stopped.

"Dessa, you and Yellow Sam better be eatin. I ain't gonna stay up all night wit you," complained Mama Amazon, going to the kitchen door, looking toward the front of bulky Catawba. "I reckon Ole Doc's about gone," she said, closing the door.

"You'd better peep about him before you goes to bed," Only said.

"He was suppin wit a spoon an it'll take him a long time to get enough likker in him to pass out, iffen he ever do. I've knowed him to wrap he's legs round a table leg an set suppin fo three days an nights an never get drunk. Set there suppin as though he had a great weight on he's shoulders. Miz Nee-oom-mee ain't so well. She went to bed this evenin fore Ole Doc come in an when I carried up her some supper she wouldn't eat a mouthful. Wonder when she's gonna have that baby? Tryin to keep it covered up, but she needn't. Ain't cuttin up the to-do she did last September when she first rived here," said Mama Amazon.

She snickered to herself when she thought of the first night Miz Nee-oom-mee had come to Catawba. Ole Doc and Naomi had sat up late in the parlor talking. Mama Amazon had been afraid the kerosene lamps would run out of oil, because she had had no warning of coming company and had not prepared and trimmed them lately. Right after Ole Doc had told her that Miss Naomi Mure would be their guest for several days, she had gone up the stairs to the finest company bedroom on the second floor and fixed it up, turning down the covers, checking the heavy canopy, placing the chamber in the room, and then sitting down waiting for her. Women were an abomination. Picayunish and finicky and forever dabbling in the wash basin. When Naomi finally made an attempt at going to bed, Mama Amazon had trudged up the stairs behind her with a heavy bowl of smoking water, as if she were carrying an incense bowl up to some idol. But Naomi had been in no hurry to ascend the impressive stairs. She had been more interested in charming Ole Doc, who with his hog-trough appetite and popeyed frustration had stood at the foot of the stairs looking up. Mama Amazon had stood painfully holding the steaming water and watched the tomfoolery going on in front of her, watched Naomi cavort on the stairs, twitching her hips, crooking her lips into sundry Pandora-box smiles, talking to him softly.

"Who died on Ole Doc this time?" Only asked, breaking into Mama Amazon's thoughts.

"Erah," she responded dazedly, "it was that Miz Nancy Boylet over there in that big two-storied log house on Coon Skin Ridge. She was the last one of em three sisters. Never did none of em marry. Men was too scarce after the war. Ole Doc shore took pleasure wit em," she tittered.

"Who ain't Ole Doc had pleasure wit? I guess they'll bury her tomorrow. Know Uncle Blue mos done she coffin?"

"Bury her over to North Bethel. You know they haves a iron fence about they buryin lot. Makes em kinda stylishlike, but they needn't have been so vast proud, fo white ladies' heads have to lie low as mine."

"Wonder what they's gonna do wit the baby? She never lived to tie hern up in one of em big aprons an throw it in the creek, like she sisters."

"I wonder who they thought they was foolin? Wonder what ole Cap'n David Boylet would say iffen he'd come home from the war an found out about his daughters? They didn't send no wagon way up to Richmond to get he's body an bring it back here lack the Inchurches done their sons. Wonder why the Inchurches done that? Course, Lawd, they's that vast rich an right, they's apt to do anythin. They hauled every one of em back here and buried em out to Pecan Lane in they private buryin ground behind they Big House. I bet em ole nigger servants see just about anythin out there at night. Especially ole Hump, the carriage driver."

8

Ole Doc supped his likker gingerly with a spoon. The jug sat uncorked on the table, nearly empty. The huge grandfather clock struck twelve with a whang. He supped, raising his arm slowly to his mouth, then leaning his head suddenly forward, striking his teeth with the spoon. His saddlebags lay sprawled in the dying glow of fire on the hearth.

He thought of Nancy and of her two sisters. He thought of Captain David.

Life was like a spider's web.

His head fell on the top of the table. Birth and death were funny. They were stupid, useless, unwanted—beloved and grieved—this ending and beginning—and God help the middle. No. Birth was not funny. Death was not stupid. Stupid to die? One died when one couldn't help oneself. Funny to be born? One was born when one couldn't help oneself. Each was as meaningless as the other. Hell. If that didn't give him the creeps. If folks had seen what he saw. Ridiculous. He checked himself. Good doctors knew what they were doing. His secret, he'd keep it.

9

"Miz Big Amazon," said Yellow Sam softly, barely above a whisper, "I'm sleepy. I want to go to bed."

"Me too," said Dessa.

"Gawd, Dessa, you know the way up the stairs; go on up to Miz Nee-oom-mee's room. You can pull that lil trundle bed out from under hern, but iffen she's sleep, you be careful an don't wake she. I don't want to have to stay up wit her all night long. Iffen she asks about Ole Doc, you let on you don't know where he is. You hear me? I'll be here tonight. I'll make a pallet here on the floor so I can be near Budda to let he suck. Yellow Sam, you knows the way up the back stairs to you room. Go on an don let nothin ketch you. You get up in the mornin wit'out me havin to call you twice. Listen youse, youse say you prayers befo you jump into bed. Get down on you knees, too!"

Dessa took a candle from the shelf, lit it at the fireplace, and made her way through the spooky house to the front stairs. She felt weary. Folks expected too much of a lil skinny nigger gal. She didn't like to be Miz Nee-oom-mee's lil black nigger maid, even if Ole Doc did want his young wife to have extra good care.

The Big House almost frightened her out of her skin. The candle cast lugubrious shadows on the wall that flung themselves helter-skelter into the many big mirrors. The grand Chippendale staircase was awesome. The shiny, beckoning stairs tickled her bare feet, sending goose pimples up her skinny legs smack-dab to her rump. She rolled her eyes and unwillingly dragged her feet up the stairs.

The cold stale air in the south wing hall of the second floor shot pure fright through and through her. Any moment she expected one of the heavy doors to fly open and ole Satan, with his horns and forked tail and box of grease, to jump out, grab her, grease his lips, and swallow her whole. She could feel her body going down his throat and her two long skinny feet dangling out of his mouth with no room for them to go down. Lawdy, have mercy, she felt as if something were sucking the breath right out of her body.

Up here in these big rooms were many solid, giantlike beds with double feather ticks on them. Elegant marble-topped dressers with funny heads carved on them. Big water pitchers she could hardly lift, and huge basins where great ladies forever dabbled in water. Nigger's job was to keep em full of water, too.

There was one room with the wallpaper of gay ladies and carriages and traveling by boats. Its furniture had come from France. Once upon a time it belonged to a king. Tonight, Dessa was sure, the old king'd get her, for other nights she'd barely escaped by the skin of her feet.

The designs on the furniture, for Dessa, were hants and spooks of the most diabolic character. She could see them all sticking out their flame-tipped tongues on the big spooky beds. Fo true, white folks were a strange lot. Imps came down in the gloomy-looking fireplaces and laughed in rasping voices at her; the rugs scratched her feet. She just liked good dirt under her feet and sweet-smelling niggers all about her.

She shorely hoped Miz Nee-oom-mee didn't drop that baby outta her belly tonight; cold as it was getting—raining too. But Lawdy, nobody could tell what a woman'd do for she was a sometime thing just like the moon—when the old moon got right she'd drap that chile.

"Yellow Sammy's gonna be big enough to do right smart plowin this spring," said Only, watching the retreating figure. "Might nigh too small this past year."

"It's too bad about his mammy dyin an leavin em. Course it most probably is fo the best—man plans, Gawd unplans. Ole Doc never hesitated one bit about bringing him on here to the Big House when she died. I reckon he belong here, fo Ole Doc's he's daddy shore as the world. Little as Yellow Sam is, you can see he got a whole heap of ways like Ole Doc."

"Don't talk so loud. Listen. Ain't that somebody at the door?" asked Only. His voice raised, his eyes shone catlike in the shadowy light. "Who that?"

"Hit's me," came a thin piping voice.

"Hit's me, who? You better tell me who you is," Only came back commandingly.

"Hit's me, the Uncle Prince Blue," came through in a long, low whine.

"All right," Only raised his voice most manly, "come in. The door is open."

"I don't feel too well fro goin to an fro on the earth an fro walkin up and down the earth," wagged Uncle Blue, entering the kitchen dripping wet. "How is youse?"

"You had better have a lil bite to eat wit us," said Mama Amazon, making ready to dish up food for him.

"I drives the funeral wagon tomorrow to carry Miz Nancy to she grave," he said, and he was sorry to tell them that he could not tarry long, because he must hurry on to the all-night prayer meeting to be held in Weepin Mary and that he was to lead in the prayers. He was going to try to direct the people tonight to eschew evil in the sight of the Lord. He told them of the fine coffin he had made for Miz Nancy Boylet and that he had fitted it on himself, but he was so long that from his knees down he would not go into the coffin.

When he had finished eating and greased himself good with pot likker, he thanked them as politely as a Sunday-school teacher, he bowed like a politician and said good-by like a tomcat, and he backed out of the kitchen doorway into the cold hungry jaws of darkness and the teeth of rain nailed him.

Uncle Prince Blue, son of an African king. Manacled across the ocean and out there in the ocean, in the dark, handed over by the buckras to a dry-rumped white man who came paddling out from land in a rowboat. Handed over for a few pieces of silver, just like the good, good Jesus. He tried to get that ole dry-rumped white man to understand he was a prince, son of a king. He tried to show the claw marks on his cheek. He cried out in agony. But the more he cried out, the more the whip came across his back, the more salt rubbed into his welting, bleeding back. That ole dry-rumped white man taught him what it meant to be a prince, son of an African king.

He faced into the darkness that was filled with howling dogs and screeching owls. He plodded along, the mud squeezed through his toes. His trousers flopped, his egg-shaped head, hatless and boldly erect, defying the rain.

10

Unmindful of winter's rains and ice that had scathed and scratched the red hills, summer came with its leafy green. In Mama Amazon's world the sun-hot poured until at dinnertime the earth, scorched and burned, the very ground cried out in amazing grief with the unbearable heat. Vegetation wilted limply, corn rolled up its leaves protectingly from the searing heat, cotton basked as though at some expensive resort.

BEELZEBUB cried out: Swigger, us needs some of that good Presbyterian water to cool us feets.

SATAN: Quit you grumblin.

BEELZEBUB: You allus teached grumblin an complainin.

SATAN: Ain't wantin no water; I's disdainful of water.

BEELZEBUB: What's it you's wantin?

SATAN: Wantin you to do sumpin wit em high elders in em churches. Fust thing you knows they's gonna discommandment all sin. Wit'out sin, us bad off as can be.

BEELZEBUB: Can't help it that Gawd stirs up so many big thunderstorms in the good ole summertime, drivin em peoples into the praise-houses, scart to death of the lightnin.

But in the utmost sanctuary of Heaven, GAWD cried out: I'm Alpha an Omega—who is, who was—*the great I am!* You hear Me, Gabriel?

GABRIEL: Hears You, my Gawd, yes.

GAWD: I'm aimin to do some birthin on My ole Earth. What's so rare as a day in June? Which one of My ole poets said that,

Gabriel? It's only the poets that understand My creation. Too practical an too earthy are never in accord wit Me. That's where friction starts in. Now let's get this June night ready fo some birthin: silver-threaded moonlight, gardenias, bloomin honeysuckle splashed all over creation, its odor driftin through the hot syrupy night. An dew drippin all over the blackberry thickets, big luscious berries hangin there. That's what I wants My chillun to come through as they enters that ole world of Mine.

3

"I declare to Gawd, you's got more dandruff on you coat," grumbled Mama Amazon, brushing mightily with a large turkey-feather duster. She'd not have her gentleman-doctor sallying forth dallying and untidy. "An loose hairs!" She focused her scrutinizing vision on Ole Doc's head. "Squat down an let me take a good look in your head. You's that vast tall. I want to be sure a fat rooster an hen ain't started a family up there. I ain't got time to be de-fume-gatin you lack when you come out of the war."

He squatted there in the back yard, "I don't reckon they'd eat me up before I could get to you and you'd start making war on them," he said jovially.

"Wouldn't be bad iffen I didn't have so much fruit to dry this summer," she hooted. "Ain't got all the geese picked yet; know they's wantin em feathers off, hot as it is."

"Get some of the field hands to help you pick them geese. They should be through chopping cotton by now," he instructed her as he straddled old Star and rode from under the oaks' cool shade into the brass-bell-like glare of the June sun.

From her watchtower high up in Catawba, Naomi Mure Thornwell, Ole Doc's young wife, watched them in the yard, watched Ole Doc until he had ridden out of sight, then left her window and crawled back into her great four-poster bed.

She would like to draw the curtains and be hidden forever, but she had a premonition that today would be the day. She felt too heavy and tired to get out of bed again and take a step, for her feet felt as lead sinkers on a fishing line. To make her time worse, this prickly-jagging June heat nettled her and she reeked with sweat so unbearably that she no longer felt like the nattiest dresser on the watershed. She bulged out too much in front to even consider her wasp waist, her traditional dressing and lively fixing-up and being gay.

When her mother lived, Naomi had never known the beginning of a day but that she was screwed and laced, tightly and snugly, into her corset. She had practiced hour upon hour walking through the house with a stack of books upon her head until she walked gracefully. Benevolence, grace, moderation, and sedateness were drilled and practiced until they became as artful as the fluttering of her flimsy hands. She balanced herself sitting upon a stool and for hours pivoted her legs around and around inside the hoops of her skirt, never touching the hoops. A hole was cut through her bonnet and some of her hair pulled through and tied so that she would not carelessly pull off her bonnet in the burning sun, turning her milk-white skin red. She must always remember she was definitely white, a great lady—and great ladies did not have coarse reddish skin. She learned to use her fan most briskly and with great care, lest she disturb her curls and look like a crude, uncouth person.

Naomi crawled from her big four-poster bed sneakingly, listening as a woodlike creature. There was no one on the second floor of Catawba. Dessa was in the kitchen by now helping

Mama Amazon with the work—making blackberry jelly and jam today. Lately she was in no mood to have Dessa around more than was absolutely necessary, and not even The Doctor, although he was overanxious about her welfare at this time. She wanted to be alone. She gave one of her little ironic titters of laughter.

A sharp pain stabbed her abdomen. She gasped with a frown, wiped her neck where the prickly heat burned unmercifully. When the pain was gone, she sighed as though her breath were the hot dry breezes rustling the many tree leaves about Catawba.

At fifteen years of age she was the mistress of Catawba, the wife of the erudite Doctor Thornwell. She was going to have a baby. Or something. She was uncertain. Nobody had been certain of anything since the war.

In the low country, where her father had had a magnificent house, land, and gobs of Negro slaves for the house and fields before old Sherman came with his fire, she had sat upon The Doctor's lap when she was only four years old. He was a gallant handsome man and he played with her curls and said she was pretty. He told her he would come back to marry her when she was old enough, but her many fat aunts and uncles had tittered, saying that was what all doctors said. And he didn't come back, but old Sherman did come along with his devilish fire and smoked them from their house as though they were wild rabbits in a hollow tree. Times were hard and they had lived in any place that didn't leak too much. So she had come here on the watershed, all alone, searching out a school to teach, being incredibly positive of what she wanted.

The war had not affected The Doctor too much, for she found him not only gay, but with a line, especially with pretty girls. However he did not have to turn on too much of his persuasiveness with her, because she had been impressed with what he owned and especially this wonderful Catawba.

Naomi looked down at the handsome carpet on the floor and thought how quickly she had fallen in love with this house when she first came here last September. How she had searched things out to find out how much The Doctor was worth. She had prowled Catawba stealthily and felinelike instead of scouring the countryside hunting up some subscription pupils at two dollars each for a four-month term. She searched the bedrooms on the second floor, missing nothing, looking into the beds, turning the bedcovers down, examining the quality of the materials, scrutinizing the furniture, taking her thumbnail and scratching up tats of the varnish to make sure of its genuineness, comparing it with the periods she was acquainted with. She turned the nap of the carpet backwards, looking into its depths, valuing its worth. She compared the colorings of the marbles from the dark brownish to the drifts of palest cream.

On the third floor the furniture was more homelike, with trundle beds, spool beds, plain walnut tables, Windsor chairs. The floors were without covering, but the wide satiny boards were polished slick, so slick that she could see herself reflected in them. The walls were plain pine paneling without the elaborate wallpaper that the second and first floors possessed.

Nowhere in the low country had she encountered such lasting riches as these sprawled here before her. No such house as Catawba, with its three stories, its expansive wings, its turrets at every corner, its magnificent Grecian columns of the half-circled piazza reaching up the three stories, holding the roof with its elaborately carved facing, and the balcony, carved even more elaborately than the facing of the piazza.

Oh, she had been happy then! While The Doctor was out on calls, she had cornered that lovesome Mama Amazon in the kitchen, lifting the lids of her pans and skillets, tasting of their contents, dancing about the kitchen, whirling her many-gored skirt and ruffled petticoats to find out whether a sufficient amount of money and land went with this handsome Catawba.

Naomi's golden laughter had sailed straight up to the rafters when she thought of the possibility of being mistress of this house. Even though The Doctor was old she was sure she could wheedle him into it, because sometimes even old wood made a hot fire, although it burned out rather quickly. That would fix old Sherman—she'd show him. Her life had run into dark days—big clouds were between her and the sun—but if she ran fast enough she could outrun the dark shadows. However, if she were to outdistance the overshadowing clouds, her bundlesome petticoats and pantalets must come off, but no one took them off. Well—maybe, at night. Then she would make the best of the night!

Now she peeped down the hallway of the second floor, listening. Catawba was so still she thought she heard the mice gnawing in its walls. There was no one in sight down the hall, and nowhere did she hear voices. She had no time to be bothered with mice when the muscles in her abdomen cried out that they wished to be delivered of their knotty burden. She must move. She eased, tiptoeing down the hall until she came to the stairway that led to the little-used third floor.

Once on the third-floor hallway, she stood panting, gasping for breath. She felt faint. She leaned against the wall to steady herself. She felt blind, the hallway turned black. She lowered herself to a sitting position on the floor and doubled her head over on her knees until the light returned. Then she tried to stand again.

She must get to the room while she was still able, before the pains became any sharper, before they came too close together. Which side of the hall was the room on? It was at the back end. Once she was behind the door and it was bolted, no one could get to her. There was only one tiny window. She had often wondered why on earth such a peculiar room had been put into the house, but now she was glad of it. She crept along slowly, afraid someone would see her, afraid the very mice in the walls would point out her hiding place, cry out to the world her shame and disgrace. A sharp cramping pain brought sweat to her face. She stopped, clenched and unclenched her hands. Her mouth drew sickeningly white.

Once in the room she surveyed it animal-like, sniffing. It was bare of furniture, the window without even curtain or shade. She wasn't interested in that now. She pushed the door shut and pulled, struggling frantically, until the three iron bars were drawn across it securely.

Nothing could come through that door. She was safe from The Doctor. He could not get to her like a pawing stallion. She didn't want him about her now, to see her in this condition. Wait until this thing inside her subsided. This terrible knot! She wanted him to remember her as she had been before this happened, when he had nosed at her stout little breasts and told her there were no two like them in the whole wide world. Like that. He had been fifty-some years of age, she couldn't remember—but he had surely stirred up a rambunctious fire. And she had thought he was an old man! But she had done what many women had failed to do: she had actually married The Doctor. She was proud of her Doctor, for after all he had been the very best of catches, although he had been a mean old ram and hurt her and the sting of his horn had fouled her up. She had Catawba and her vast red-rolling acres. In glee, her letters to the low country, after she had finally married The Doctor, had reeked and gleamed with its earthly richness. Somehow old Sherman had missed Catawba and Naomi never tired of psalming to her uncles and aunts in the low country of her riches.

She sank down upon the floor in sheer exhaustion, slumping, throwing her hands over to one side of her body. Worn to a frazzle, uncouth and unladylike. She didn't care—right now she didn't care! She had Catawba securely, although this knot she toted was a high price to pay for it.

Her pains grew sharper, closer together. She sweated, for the pains gave her no time to fan herself. If this was only over quickly. Her face was darkly disturbed. She hoped Father was rocking quietly and restfully downstairs on Catawba's veranda— at least she had found a snug home for him in his old age. Sherman couldn't forever smoke them out as though they were rabbits in a hollow tree. The thought made her mad; her eyes blazed and she pounded the floor with her fist.

She pressed her hands hard against the floor of Catawba. Each satiny plank silently shared her anxiety. She would very much prefer the glossy planks right now to the suave Doctor. She'd watch him after this, now that she had Catawba and security.

Her pains grew much sharper. Agonized cries came up out of her, but she bit them off with clenched teeth. She was on the threshold of a most tremendous adventure and she had no idea of how long it would last. She pounded the floor with her sweaty, clenched fist. No, God, *no!* What was this that grew so bulky here in her belly? This big knot that disfigured her pretty, pretty, shapely body?

Was this the way God multiplied the earth? Why multiply the earth? Sherman would burn them out! Was it worth-while to replenish the earth? This knot. This pain. Hell, *it hurt!*

The head of the fetus pressed against the outlet of the pelvic bone. She groaned. There was no stopping it, no putting life down. Behind was a great creative power.

She fell upon her back, clenching her fist, pounding upon the floor. Sweat poured from her. She kicked her feet high into the air above her abdomen. The abdominal muscles were working full tilt. Had not Mama Amazon said it was nothing more than passing a big watermelon? Maybe it was nothing more than a watermelon—a prize winner. She screamed. The room turned black.

2

Mama Amazon never forgot that hot June evening she heard that screaming coming from the top of Catawba. She was right in the middle of pouring the smoking-hot blackberry jelly into the tumblers. The screaming jerked her up so that the jelly-making was forgotten.

"You better see about Miz Nee-oom-mee, Dessa," Mama Amazon shouted up to the second floor.

Flighty Dessa met Mama Amazon on the stairs and stammered awkwardly, "I can't find she nowhere. I looked in all the big rooms. I called. She won't answer."

"You ain't half looked! You'd better find she. Ole Doc'll be here toreckly."

"I—I—" Dessa stammered. "I—know—where."

"Gal, know what? You's actin right crazy lack. I can't understand a thing you say," Mama Amazon grumbled.

"She's locked sheself in the lil room on the third floor. I—think I heard a baby cryin in there—"

"What? What's that you say?" To the second floor now, Mama Amazon gained speed and ripsnorted up to the third floor so fast that Dessa ran to keep in sight of her.

Mama Amazon pounded furiously on the door, "Miz Nee-oom-mee, you let me in there this instant! You hear me?" But the only response she got was the puny cry of an infant. "Lawd, have mercy." She rattled the door knob vigorously. "Miz Nee-oom-mee. Do, Lawd, do do sumpin. She's got every one of em bars across the door." She pounded and kicked the door. "Dessa, get some lamps lit. Hurry! Don't be draggin you feets!"

She wore herself out pounding on the door. At last she fled down the stairs and out into the yard with Dessa at her heels. They wrung their hands and cried.

The great yellow moon peeped over the horizon, grinned at

them through many tree branches, shone down on the climbing honeysuckle, and spangled over the side of the house. Exotic odors of gardenias and honeysuckle filled the humid night air. The ever-singing crickets and frogs sent melody up from the red river.

"I ain't never looked at the full moon through so many limbs but what it brings bad luck. I might a-knowed it. That moon changed to full this mornin an wombs opens then," Mama Amazon cried.

When Ole Doc rode into the yard Mama Amazon wept. "Gawd be praised. It's time you's gettin here, fo us is in awful trouble. I believes Miz Nee-oom-mee is losed she mind. She's up on the top floor. Fastened in that little room and won't answer—an she done had a baby, *too!*"

Ole Doc's violent effort to smash open the third-floor door was to no avail. "*Get a ladder!* If we can get up to the window, we can break the glass and go in."

"But, Duk-tuh, us ain't got no ladder what'll reach up em three stories," she said.

"Get the short ladders. If we can get to the roof of that porch, we can use shorter ladders from there up."

Mama Amazon could find only two ladders; each easily reached the roof of the porch. But the window was still two floors away.

"Get some ropes. We can lash these two ladders together. That'll put us up there."

The moon rocked higher into the heavens, shone down on the red climbing roses, the white blooming gardenias.

Once the ladders were fastened together, they looked almost too flimsy to escalade, but Ole Doc decided Dessa was light, and provided they held the ladders she could climb up to the window.

Scared beyond knowing what she was doing, crying and sobbing, Dessa began the climb, feeling the rungs carefully with her hands, looking back as if she were going to some dreadful place never to return. She reached the window after what Ole Doc thought was hours, yet he had known it would never do to rush that little gal, for she would not climb a-tall.

"Raise the window, Dessa," Mama Amazon called up to her. The window was raised. "Step inside now and open the door. Us goin through a window here on the second floor and come up."

Dessa met them in the hallway, "Youse come quick. Miz Nee-oom-mee, she has *two* babies!"

3

"Dessa, put some mo wood on the fire. Us gotta keep this kitchen good an hot iffen us gonna raise these two mites," said Mama Amazon, fumbling in a box of cotton on the kitchen table, lifting out one of the babies. "Miz Nee-oom-mee done outdone sheself havin two. Ain't he lil? I bet this one won't weigh over a pound. I know he won't weigh two pounds. Warm me some of that lard over there. I wants to grease em, make em shed off they skin so they'll start right off growin." She looked at the babies sharply.

"Dessa, look here, this is a lil caul-headed one!"

"What's a caul-head?"

"Lawd, chile, a caul-headed chile haves second sight. You can't hide a thing from em. They'll see an hear an know things that will never bother a ordinary person."

"Will that thing go away?"

"Sure. The veil will break an the caul will disappear an he'll look just lack anybody else, but inside he won't be lack nobody else. He'll be able to call things outta the air and talk to em. He'll be able to see things in the night lack me and you can't see. Ole Doc ought to be proud to have a caul-headed son. Ole Doc ought to be proud just to have some yard chillun."

She greased her hands with lard, picked up a squirming red mite, greasing him until he sparkled.

"Dessa, go hunt up some shoe boxes and put some cotton in em. We'll have to keep em wrapped up in cloth until us can get some clothes made. That gal ought to be shamed of sheself havin these lil fellers an not even a bellyband made fo em."

Dessa returned with the shoe boxes and cotton.

"Put some grease on you hands and kinda grease that cotton a wee bit, Dessa, then warm it an bring it here. I done got this lil hairy one all greased an ready fo he's box—he's that lil you couldn't hold he on you lap. Fix the other box. When you finishes that, get a lil strip of fat meat, just a wee strip fo he to suck on. You hold that fat meat an let he suck on it while I greases this other un. I'm gonna tend to this lil caul-headed feller myself." And she began to hum and to sing to him right early about the good, good Gawd in heaven above and the mean old Satan right down under the red ground there.

4

Two weeks later, at noon, Mama Amazon trudged up the spacious front stairs to the second floor with Miz Nee-oom-mee's dinner. It was almost a waste of time carrying that crazy gal all these good rations. Mama Amazon had worked her fingers to the bone preparing knickknacks, fancy doodads, to try to whet Miz Nee-oom-mee's finicky appetite, but wait and see— she'd bet anything on a stack of Bibles from here to North Bethel Church that gal wouldn't eat two spoonfuls. Ole Doc tried to pretend that she was sick and in a few more days would be all right, but those days were slipping into weeks and she had noted no particular change; if anything, she seemed much crazier than at first.

Mama Amazon thought bad times were surely upon Catawba, that Gawd had reached down and smitten Catawba with some evil plague. The days were trying, but the nights were worse than the days. Evil seemed to threaten the whole red land. Gawd was bowing them down in sorrow, more sorrow than they could stand. He would come reaping through the fields, withering the grasses, parching up, drying up the earth with sorrow.

She entered Naomi's room with the tempting array of delicacies. Naomi paid the food no mind, but only stared out the window wild-eyed. Her savage eyes roved about with such profound premonition that chill-bumps covered Mama Amazon. "I feels jest lack a hant's done run over my grave," she thought.

"Miz Nee-oom-mee, here is you some dinner. I fixed all em lil things you used to lack when you had a to-do. Come on now an eat," she pleaded in a soft guttural. What was the matter with the crazy gal? This was as bad as offering food to a wooden idol.

"Mama Amazon," Naomi began in a far-off voice, her eyes staring, "I've just come back from heaven. You know, I died last night. I jumped out of my coffin, sitting on the horses there in North Bethel right before Reverend Irvin. You know what I told him? I told him he need not have Cora Mathis slobbering with that wheezing organ over me. Then I hid and they couldn't find me to bury me in the ground. I don't want those white worms eating me. I bet that would hurt like hell. Why don't they go down to the grocery store and catch the groceryman and bury him? He must like worms. Everything he has in that store is wormy—the beans, the raisins."

"Here, Miz Nee-oom-mee, come on an taste this." Mama Amazon pulled up a chair beside the bed, getting ready to feed the patient. She held out a spoonful of food.

Naomi knocked the spoon, sending it flying across the room. "You are trying to poison me. You want me out of the road so you can get in the bed with The Doctor," she screamed, pointing her finger at Mama Amazon. "Well, you are not. I'm going to call Sherman. He'll smoke you out." She rose from the bed.

"Miz Nee-oom-mee, you get back in bed! You know Ole Doc don' allow you up."

Mama Amazon coaxed her back into bed where Naomi looked up at her, remorsefully crying. Then she tiptoed from the room, shaking her head, "Never is I seen the likes of she!"

5

From casual afternoon visitors to Catawba, the ninnies in the village heard of Mrs. Thornwell's peculiar and questionable illness. Being ever hungry for news, they added infinite versions to the original. The visiting committee of North Bethel, who gave out the original version, had added to the story, because even though they'd been right in the house and tried hard, they'd been unable to get any farther than the front parlor where Ole Doc headed them off sternly, though kindly and politely, on their first curiosity call, which they'd pleaded in pure Christian love. Mama Amazon craftily stopped them the second time on the veranda because it was warm and she had pretended Miz Nee-oom-mee to be taking an afternoon nap, although Dessa was at her wits' end and scared very near out of her skin trying to keep the wild, screaming Miz Nee-oom-mee fastened in her room until the servants of the Lord departed. Some of the ninnies were certain they'd seen a white-robed figure of a woman prowling in the moonlight on the many roofs and gables of Catawba and were quite satisfied that something out of the ordinary was going on at the Thornwell place.

6

But after a few weeks of such troubles, Mama Amazon fitted them as snug about her as though they were her old runover shoes. For diversity there were always the twins, rocking in the old wooden cradle before the kitchen fireplace where the skillets and pots bubbled and doodled with cooking food and the big kettle on the crane hook stayed full of steaming water. The eighteenth-century cradle was one that great Grandpa Andrew had made and used before he fled beyond the shining sun to the land of the Presbyterian stardust. There were weird tales told of the countless numbers of babies that had been rocked in it. Once a mother, who sat in Catawba's kitchen doorway rocking her child in the cradle, saw a token: a furly-winged angel appeared in the treetops below Catawba with a white coffin and pointed silently to the child in the cradle and that night the angel came for the child.

Mama Amazon picked the twins up out of the little low wooden cradle and, with a baby in each arm, sat down upon a high-backed straight chair. She took out her milk-dripping breasts and the babies sought them hungrily. She rocked on the loose-jointed chair with much knocking, cozily pampering herself with sweet melody.

She laughed at the babies, "I declare they's rootin like a couple pigs in a new ground." She looked over at her own little black fellow who was beginning to sit alone. "Budda, you's mo' an glad to share you milk wit these lil white boys, enty? Yes, Budda, you know you is. You don't wanna be selfish an greedy, fo that would make you black on you insides. It's bad enough to be black on you outside in this world. Iffen you stays pure an white inside, someday you black skin gonna rot away, then you'll fly away wit the white-winged angels in heaven. You hear me, Budda? I wants you to remember, fo I don't want you growin into black trash. White trash is bad enough."

She fondly mothered the babies with gentle endearments and rocked, bip-bopping on her chair worse than that wood-burning steam-engine train. It had thrown ashes left and right and carried Miz Nee-oom-mee from the low country to this red land last September. And look what she had here in her arms from that trip. Ah, Gawd moved as He saw fitten and His wonders

He did make known, or maybe it was just because Miz Nee-oom-mee was around Ole Doc. Mama Amazon knew it was good he had some yard chillun now.

"Dessa," she continued while rocking, "you'd better be movin on wit some dinner fo Ole Doc. Cause wit three babies to suck, it's gonna take up a good bit of my time. Ole Doc had about four calls to make this mornin and I think he was aimin to meet the southbound train. He's kinda lookin fo em gentlemens fro the Nof, though I hopes he don't come bouncin in here wit em the way everything is runnin behint the times in Catawba."

She stopped rocking and groaned. How work was getting behind here at Catawba. It'd not be that way if Miz Joanna was living. Why, the wool from the sheep hadn't yet been washed and sent to the weavers for the blankets.

"And Gawd, Dessa, you'll have to fix some dinner fo that nurse-thing Ole Doc done brung up here from Charleston to look after Miz Nee-oom-mee. I wonder what the peoples down on the Square thought about she when she stepped offen that train? I bet they eyes popped right outta they heads. But I'm shore glad he's got sumpin to look out fo that rambunctious lady. I's gettin bout half scared of she. A person in her shape might do anything. They shore scrapped to get that butcher knife away fro she yesterday. Where in the world did she get it? It was a kitchen butcher knife."

"Lawd," Dessa said in a frightened tone, "I don't know'am. I shore ain't wantin to be shet up in the room wit she no mo lack the evenin em fine ladies fro the church was here."

Mama Amazon laughed uproariously, "Dessa, you thought you time had about come?"

"Tellin me! That woman had me so I didn't know which end was which."

"These lil ole sweet babies shore ain't payin she no mind. They's layin up here suckin like the doctor says these big black teats is good fo em." She rubbed their heads with her soft warm hands. "I hopes one of em is goin to be a powerful preacher-boy. Wonder which un? This lil dark hairy one or this light caul-headed one that haves second sight? I feels it in my bones that they's gonna be sumpin important." She rocked and sang to them about the big, long-horned, forked-tailed Satan who would get them if they were not good.

7

Upon the first Preachin Sunday after the twins were four weeks old, Ole Doc took them to church to be baptized. He didn't care to take them alone, but with Naomi in such a profound savage condition, she couldn't be expected to go. These kids he could not deny, because they had been ketched in his trap. It was his duty and privilege as a Christian to dedicate his children to God in baptism. He wanted the baptism administered in the church in the presence of the entire congregation, where he would take the covenant that he would teach the boys to read the word of God, to instruct them in the principles of the Presbyterian religion as it was found in the Holy Scriptures of the Old and the New Testament, to have them learn by memory and to recite the Longer and Shorter Catechisms of the Westminster Assembly, and above all to bring up the boys in the nurture and admonition of the Lord. For all mankind was born and was by nature sinful, guilty, and needed the cleansing power of the blood of the Lord Jesus Christ.

Holding the twins upon her lap, Mama Amazon sat in the back seat of the surrey with Dessa, who was taking care of that little necessary extra change. She hoped the twins didn't act up on the wrong end right while the good preacher was laying that strong Presbyterian water on the other end. Yellow Sam drove, and sitting beside him was Ole Doc, spruced up more than a Philadelphia lawyer.

Mama Amazon tittered to herself when she looked at Ole

Doc. He'd spent over an hour in the large wooden washtub out in the smokehouse yesterday, washing all over with strong lye soap and sand. After he'd dried off and got into his long drawers, she'd trimmed his toenails and fingernails and clipped the large hairs from his ears and nose. She'd stood back and surveyed him critically. "You's beginnin to look lack a pure white gentleman's gentleman." And feeling herself a real occasion of this baptism, she'd but scant sleep last night and nothing to eat, because where there was toothsome preaching to be attended, she wasn't in need of these everyday accessories.

She glanced down at her own voluminous pink dress, and when she thought that Ole Doc was responsible for this gorgeous sweeper of thirteen yards of taffeta and lace her eyes grew moist. She had on a great bustle of ribbons and infinitesimal stitches and tucks, high-topped, buttoned shoes, and a flopping cascade bonnet just filled with flowers. She shook her head and muttered to herself, "Lawd, I's just ugly enough to be good-lookin, built lack a Persian mare, an once I plunges into that church with my thighs encased in this pink taffeta, people's eyes gonna pop."

The white-laced dresses and frilly caps the twins wore had been rummaged from some forgotten trunk of an older generation of Thornwells. They were yellow when she dug them out, but she had put in hours washing the fragile things, had rinsed them through three bluing waters, starched and ironed them painstakingly, and it was now doubtful whether anyone could tell that they were over a hundred years old. Moreover, it naturally brought good luck to be baptized in the presence of the Lord in something so old and fine that it could not be told whether it was real or imaginary. The twins were rocked in the ancient cradle, and now to be baptized in the old, old dresses was very befitting and becoming to Catawba. She would have it no other way. Man didn't live by a meat skin—life had to have more.

Comity bore her light-footed up the church steps, because a baptizing with good Presbyterian water was more important than just a plain Preachin Sunday.

The congregation stood agog as Mama Amazon waddled, with a baby cradled in each arm, down the center aisle with Ole Doc and Dessa following. The more saintly female members stopped her often to look questioningly at the twins, their minds filled with downright earthy questions. They had counted on their fingers—what were fingers for?—from November until June. Sucking their teeth, shrugging their shoulders. One of the twins had something wrong with its head. Casually feeling the babies' heads was one way of finding out. They didn't look very much alike; reckon they were twins? Didn't look too much like the Thornwells! Of course, one could never be too certain about little babies. They changed. How in the world had Naomi Mure ever managed to marry Ole Doc? It was more than anyone else had ever been able to do. And she had done it so quickly! All those Mures were poor as church mice, and lazy. Doubtful they'd eat corn if a body'd shell it for them. No one had ever suspected Naomi of going to have a child. Perhaps the Session should look into the matter for church, but Ole Doc was a member of the Session. What an awkward situation! Right in the church!

When the singing was over and Cora Mathis had pumped the reed organ until its very tongue hung out and prayers had properly ended with all the standing elders plopping down upon the benches, the Reverend Edward Irvin asked that the infants be presented for baptism.

Ole Doc, a baby held in each arm, stepped from the second seat to the front of the church to stand before the communion table.

"Do you," began the preacher, "acknowledge your little boys' need of the cleansing blood of the Lord Jesus Christ, and the renewing grace of the Holy Spirit? Answer yes or no audibly."

"Yes, I do." Ole Doc's voice echoed through the still church.

"Do you claim God's covenant promises in their behalf and do you look in faith to the Lord Jesus Christ for their salvation, as you do for your own?"

"Yes, I do." His voice was clear, bell-like.

"Do you now unreservedly dedicate these boys to God, and promise, in humble reliance upon divine grace, that you will endeavor to set before them a godly example, that you will pray with them and for them, that you will teach them the doctrines of our Holy Presbyterian Religion, and that you will strive, by all the means of God's appointment, to bring them up in the nurture and admonition of the Lord Jesus Christ?"

"I do."

"Will the congregation please rise?" asked the Reverend Edward Irvin. He prayed.

Taking up a bowl of water from the communion table, the Reverend Edward Irvin dipped his hand into the water, laying it upon the baby's head that was in Ole Doc's left arm. "Jacob Emmanuel Thornwell, I baptize thee in the name of the Father and of the Son and of the Holy Ghost. Amen."

Dipping his hand into the bowl of water again, he laid it upon the head of the baby that was in Ole Doc's right arm. "Victor Erich Thornwell, I baptize thee in the name of the Father and of the Son and of the Holy Ghost. Amen."

The Reverend Edward Irvin spoke to the congregation: "Let us pray."

8

Mama Amazon trudged into the kitchen with Jake and Vic. "Here, Dessa, hold one of these babies until I gets these fancy lacy dresses off em. It done my soul pure good to see em baptized up right and correct. I felt purty near like cryin. Everybody was so quiet an listenin to the Reverend. He shorely got em baptized up good and they didn't cry."

"There was a heap of peoples there," said Dessa, watching Mama Amazon change the clothes.

"Bout the biggest crowd I's seen there fo it not to be a big meetin goin on. Wasn't so many niggers there though. You know, they's gettin so now after the war they'd rather go to they own church. Now me, I'm goin to the white folks' church long as I lives. I know they'll find some kinder corner to stick me into. That ole nigger preacher over to Weepin Mary don't know nothin bout no Holy Scriptures."

"Cryin John ain't much mo better."

"Here, Dessa," handing her the lacy dress and cap, "fold this lil dress an petticoat an cap up. Tomorrow you get Yellow Sam to help you an youse get some cedar shavins fro out the black-smithy an us pack the lil clothes away in shavins. That'll keep em good. The boys might want to look at em sometime after they's growed up to see what they was baptized in. Besides, a body ought to naturally keep anything that purty. Child, these things was made when peoples had time an patience. Look at em fine stitches. Em lil dresses is over three feets long, an I bet a good foot an half of the tail is got seventy-five yards of pure Irish lace worked in em an em lacy yokes, an look at the needle-work on the collars an sleeves."

She looked at Budda on his pallet, "Boy, how'd you look in one of em things?" She laughed. "Still black!"

9

When the distinguished and noteworthy gentlemen doctors came to observe Naomi, Mama Amazon met them on the front veranda because Ole Doc had told her to be on the lookout for them.

They were dressed in knee-length coats and Mama Amazon thought they ought to burn up in this hot August weather. They wore high-topped buttoned shoes, the mark of the elegantly dressed, extremely high collars, wide cuffs, and high silk hats.

Mama Amazon showed them up the grandiose Chippendale staircase and there the nurse met them, taking them down the south wing hallway to Naomi's room.

"Why, you damned old whoremaster. I've a good mind to cut your damn throat with this damn butcher knife I've got under my pillow here," Naomi screamed at Ole Doc, thrashing savagely in her bed.

"But Naomi, darling, you must—"

"Don't you come no nearer me, you son of a bitch. You want to drown me in blood!"

She jumped suddenly from the bed, landed on the floor, crumpling into a limp heap. Ole Doc reached down and tenderly picked her up, placing her upon the bed. She heaved a wounded sigh. She lay limp and languid upon the bed with only an occasional jerk of an involuntary muscle in arm or leg, an involuntary twitch of a facial muscle. He pulled the covers around her gently.

The visiting doctors stood side by side in the middle of the room, their mouths drawn firmly. They looked, noting and observing in their most profound professional manner. Cold and austere, they calculated, weighed, and measured.

The physiology of the nervous sytem was a muddled jumble in its natural state, but when it became a perverted nervous function—they scratched their heads simultaneously—it was a case of morbid . . . what? The fouled uterus perhaps was pressing upon the nervous system, causing this perverted condition. Foul accumulations in the *primae viae* could cause irritation in the face or even in the heel. This was an internal morbid condition. The remedy for this, they did believe, was correction through the mode of surgery—though poisoning of the blood often followed surgery, leading to inflammation, especially of the liver, and then to death!

Noting full well what the doctors were insinuating, Ole Doc

grew effusively sentimental trying to efface this horror before him. He admonished his mind to turn back to another time. How he and Naomi had sat before the fire in the upper parlor when she had first arrived here from the low country. How they had sat on either side of the fireplace in the Victorian Mr. and Mrs. chairs of Honduras mahogany; until that night he had never realized how full life could be with someone sitting in that Mrs. chair. It was different. This longing that had filled him was something different from any he had ever accosted. There had been about her a tenderness and warmth that made him feel boyish and want to protect her above all. She had been young and vivacious and beautiful. Catawba would never be complete without her. Catawba took on a different meaning with her gay laughter ringing through its halls. And she had become an insatiable need.

He turned to the doctors, bull-like, jaws set. "You're doing none of your experimental whacking on her!"

They stood aghast. "Doctor Thornwell," one of them spoke, "we would not think of such a thing. The point we do want to bring to your attention is that we do not think Mrs. Thornwell will ever be well without the help of surgery. Now, in Philadelphia they are doing some mighty fine work in surgery. The patient is completely relaxed under the influence of this new ether and, of course, the surgeon can work better without too much advice from the patient. The relatives are enough to contend with."

During the heated discussion, Naomi, having regained her strength, propped herself upon her elbows, turning her savage stare upon them.

They looked, including Ole Doc, to make sure there was nothing between them and the door, then toward Naomi, and then in subdued sick-room whispers talked.

"You all," Naomi began, "better go on back to hell where you belong. I'm sure there is a pen of doctors down there. Or are you some of Satan's henchmen? Come nearer," she beckoned to them, "and let me examine your numb watery skulls. Praise be unto my Jehovah, I do believe upon my soul you are doctors. What do you doctors doctor in hell?"

10

Naomi Mure Thornwell, lying white and still as death upon the cot, was lifted up into the baggage car of the waiting train. The nurse went right in with her, talking to her to keep her quiet.

Now the moment approached for Dessa to climb into the baggage car. Her heart pounded chokingly right up into her throat, and she could hardly stand up in Miz Nee-oom-mee's high-heeled, high-topped buttoned shoes that pinched and burned her feet as if she were walking on fire. She knew she was going a far piece into some strange land. Her eyes filled with tears. Lawd, dear sweet Jesus, she was fidgety and jumpy on her insides. She'd never see Miz Mama Amazon again. Or June or July, Gee or Budda, or the little sweet white babies. The big black engine that belched fire and ashes was carrying her away.

Ole Doc was way back there somewhere in one of the strange coaches. She felt the train jerking and lurching, staggering her about over its floor. The cars bumped with a terrific noise, then she could feel the train wheels turning slowly, oh, so very slowly and easily. She was going. Going to a strange place called Philadelphia. In Philadelphia, Mama Amazon had said, a big doctor with a great long knife was going to cut hell right outta Miz Nee-oom-mee. Lawd have mercy! She rolled her terror-stricken eyes toward the lifeless white form on the cot and the white starchy nurse sitting beside it. She must stay and help to hold Miz Nee-oom-mee down, for she might at any moment jump clear slap out of the train. Oh, why had they made her go? She was pure scared to death, a little black nigger gal that was at her wits' end. The train was shaking as if it were a sieve sifting meal in Mama Amazon's hands in the big kitchen.

The clicking wheels sang going, going.

11

Mama Amazon guarded the cradle in August's sultry heat with eyes ever alerted lest some evil eye should smote it.

Satan and Beelzebub pronged their feet up and down the dusty roads, tempting the worshipers in the dusky evening on their way to August meetings, trying to get them to go to the stillhouse or to the barroom.

BEELZEBUB: I see that ol Miz Big Amazon done prided sheself on havin em two yard chillun of Ole Doc's baptized up.

SATAN: I's ever disdainful of that strong Presbyterian water. I fears in the end that water's gonna drown out us fire.

BEELZEBUB: Why don't you do sumpin to she?

SATAN: You ever vexes me—do sumpin to that rambunctious lady? Wouldn't want her holt of me. You remembers how she whooped that big railroad engineer cause she thought he allowed to ruin she virginity. It was one day the train had stopped there while its five flatcars was loaded with em barrels of corn likker.

BEELZEBUB: Ha! She blistered he's butt a bright red wit her bare hands.

Gawd sat in Heaven fanning the hot August breeze from about his ears and watching prayer meetings winking on and off on Earth.

GABRIEL: Hot enough fo all you peoples to get baptized up this August.

GAWD: I's aimin that my peoples don't souse emselves in mo sin an what I can wash em out of.

4

"Come chile, the sun's way up yander," said Mama Amazon as she leaned over the big four-poster bed smoothing Victor's golden hair tenderly. She aroused him from the spirit world gently, lest he should leave the sleepland too suddenly, come to this workaday world with such a jolt that he would be cross and irritable the livelong day. She couldn't worry with a fretting, disgruntled boy; Catawba buzzed with too much trouble as it was.

Victor's brown eyes opened, filled with interest, his lashes so long that his eyes looked as if they were two fern-edged pools. "Mama Amazon, is it time to get up?" He grabbed her fat black hands—the most beautiful hands in his world—and pulled himself into a sitting position. "Come on, Jake!" He kicked his brother with his foot. "Time to get up."

Outside, the pear trees showered down their white petals and a chipmunk scolded. There was so much living to do. Vic didn't like to get caught napping in bed—not this late in the day, when there was such an incessant swelter of living to be done on the outside. All the doodles to tease under the boxwoods, water to pour in the chipmunks' den, the hens to watch up in the barn loft laying fresh, smoking-hot eggs. He'd set and jug with his finger to keep the eggs from coming out, but he never could; they pushed right on out and he wondered why. "Jake, Jake!" he cried.

"Reckon you'll ever get he waked up?" Mama Amazon asked. "Land, that's the sleepiest-headed boy!"

Vic turned her hands loose, pounced upon Jake, shaking him violently. "Wake up, ole lazy bones. Wake up! Wake up!"

"Damn you! Leave me alone," shouted Jake.

"What's that you say, boy?" Mama Amazon grabbed Jake by the arm. "What sorta cuttin up is this? Fust you's takin holt of you brother's heel an pullin youself into this ole world, an now em powerful bad words." She pulled him from the bed. "I'll learn you how to handle em kinda words. When I gets through wit you mouth, washin it wit soap, you ain't gonna know you ever heard sich a word. You's pure bad this mornin. I pure believes the witches rid you all night long!"

2

Filled with pear petals on buttered bread, enthralled with the joyous morning, Vic wandered aimlessly through the many walkways of Catawba's landscaped terrace. He spoke to the flowers and chattered with the working bees. He squatted and talked happily to a scolding chipmunk, hoping it'd go into its hole so that he could pour water on it. Vic knew he would never forget today—though it was hard to separate last week from yesterday. Wandering toward the front of the house, he heard voices on the veranda.

He peeped, and there was Pop on the veranda lying in the hammock and talking to a black man. Grandpa Mure sat there, too, rocking lazily. They did nothing except talk, Vic thought. Did they never tire? Why were they living? They simply sat there breathing the pure fragrant air. They talked mombo jombo, mombo jombo. It was tiring. But the movements of Pop's mouth were interesting. What an interesting hole it made when opened! Wonder what was way down in there?

"Pop," Vic began, coming close and preparing to scrutinize the inside of the big mouth when it was opened again, "I been talkin to the chipmunks." Pop's mouth fell much farther open than he had anticipated, but Vic quickly put his eyes right to it.

Pop pushed him away angrily. "What in thunderation you doing? Take your fingers out of my mouth! You're as quick as a streak of greased lightning."

"Oh Pop, I wanta see."

"See what, son?"

"I wanta see in you mouth."

"Tarnation. What do you want to look in my mouth for? Here, son, come on, look. Take a good look. Don't you miss a thing."

3

When Vic awoke from his afternoon nap he was wringing wet with sweat. Not a blessed breeze stirred the burning August drought. He felt strange when he was fully awake.

He hurried downstairs, trekking across the back porch to where Mama Amazon was snapping green beans for tomorrow when the pot-bellied iron pot would cook them from before sunup until dinnertime, cook them good and black and oh, so greasy.

"It's too hot to sleep," he yawned.

"Fo true it is warm," Mama Amazon replied lazily. "You run on out in the yard yander where July and June is sweepin the yard wit em big brush brooms," she urged, waiting to be free of Victor so that she could keep her work moving.

But Victor was not so easily shooed away. "Run on now, hon. Mama Amazon is got a vast important job to do and I'm behint the time right now."

Vic felt in a keen spiritual perception that he wanted to be nearer her and he came, leaned against her. "Tell me bout Gawd again. I think He woke me right up from sleep."

She looked at him in surprise. They were the same: she had eternal youth and would never grow old, and he had eternal age and had never been young. That was her caul-headed chile. She stared entranced into his soft-laughing brown eyes where she always saw the strangest light. She always had to rub her hand upon his head to make certain he was all there. He had curious-looking hair. At times it looked as though it had come right up out of the red land that surrounded Catawba and then again, in another light, it looked brown as the fur of the mus-krats in the river. Now, Jake's hair was as black as a crow's feath-ers, straight as a horse's mane, and didn't have that queerness of changing colors on her eyes.

"Tell me about Gawd!" he commanded again, noting she was taking an astonishingly long time to look at him. He didn't see ho'cum, but she always did, nearly dropping her eyelids shut with a smile. She said he was curious-looking. Would he have to tell her he had a splinter in his foot to get her to talk to him? He wanted to hear her sweet voice, her terrific spate of words.

"Gawd!" He was never tired of hearing that same old story. So she began for over the hundredth time to tell him the story of Gawd, but he knew it better than she did, and if she veered one whipstitch from the straight story he'd call it to her mind.

"No, the Garden had four rivers."

"Yes," she agreed. "Four rivers an they was just lack the ones here on the watershed. They had a powerful heap of catfish in em an ole Adam and Eve had to be awful careful catchin em catfish just lack we does here, fo em catfish had the sharpest fins an would jug mean gashes in their hands."

The story at last over, a great deal more of the day had slipped by than she realized. "Run on now, hon, and play. Toreckly we'll talk again." She hated to see him go, for he did something to her; he comforted her. He was not like other white folks—he saw too much, he heard too much.

"Toreckly," Victor murmured to himself as he started out into the yard. It was always toreckly we'll do so-and-so. Toreckly was an important word. She had set the little thing inside of him ticking again smoothly. He had wolfed down her spate of words until he felt bloated and the tendrils of his spirit were fastened to the infinite.

In Catawba's sprawling back yard, scented with fig bushes and the acid smell of the lye dripping from the ash hopper, spangled with cool marbled shade, he grew incredibly mystified with the ominous-looking, unreal cumulus clouds banked up in the great blue above him. He smiled lopsidedly, leaned his head farther back looking up into the clouds for Gawd and Jesus. He gazed intently and it was easy for him to see the Divine Trio there working in the soft fleecy substance which Mama Amazon said was heaven.

That was Mama Amazon's Gawd and Jesus up yonder, and his too, he thought half sadly. He and Mama Amazon were tied up here on earth for a while—he didn't know how long—but one day they would be released like birds from a cage and they would have wings, white wings, Mama Amazon said. Hers would be great and big and flopping like the hats she wore and his would be small.

That would be a wonderful trip. He could hardly wait. Somewhere they were going to get on a train, then somewhere they were going to get on a boat—with their wings and everything. He choked right up from thinking about it.

Why, right this instant he bet that Gawd—not Gabriel, because he was too busy writing in the Book of Life—was busy sweeping the back yard of heaven with a big brush broom and getting it as good an clean as Mama Amazon's big black finger got his ears. Catawba's back yard was always swept when Grandpa Mure's people came up for a visit from the low country. Were Mama Amazon and he not going to be company in the presence of the Lawd? Sure they were. Gawd was a polite-mannered person with more love than he could measure. Surely, surely, Mama Amazon had said, Gawd will want us to stay always, because—just plain because He loves us so much.

Well, he could hardly wait.

4

With jelly atwixt a biscuit to eat, Victor and Jacob hurried from the kitchen to resume their playing on the veranda of Catawba. November's chilly wind reddened their fingers that held the bread.

"I hear the train comin," cried Vic. He lay down supine on the floor. "I'm goin to lie here and let it run through me."

"You can't do that. You're not big like the smokin train."

"I feel it here on the floor comin through me. Lie down. You can feel it runnin through you," Vic insisted.

Grumbling, Mama Amazon followed her two infallible heart-throbs through the house, shutting doors after them, and stood in the doorway listening. Out there were a couple of rowdy little boys that not even Gawd had any idea what to do with. But of all the children she had suckled, these two had been the most fascinating.

Victor spied her. "Mama Amazon, ain't the train gonna blow fo the stop?"

"I don't know, chile. It might. You can't never be certain about nothin but death."

"Death! What's that, Mama Amazon?" Vic was alerted as though she had touched some responsive note in him. His eyes sought an answer from her face. "Is that when you wear the tolerable-big snowy-white wings, and me, I wear the lil snowy-white ones? And we go on the long trip?"

"Yes, hon, that's death. That's when you go on the long trip to satisfy you travelin mind. You goes to heaven only iffen you's been good; and iffen you's been bad, the ole Satan will get you and he will jug you with he's long horns an prong you wit he's red-hot fork—ontil it'll seem lack you might nigh can't get you breath any more."

"Mama Amazon," there was a trickle of terror in his voice, "I don't want ole Satan to get me. When he prongs you wit he's fork, that'll hurt. How'll you know when you die? Who will tell you?"

"There! The train's blowin fo the stop," cried Jake.

"I knowed it was goin to blow fo the stop. Else how could the great lady get off the train?" asked Victor.

Mama Amazon stared at him. "What you mean, chile?"

Vic said happily, "The great lady who is comin here to live fo'ever an fo'ever. You know!"

She shook her head in befuddlement. Vic said that many crazy things, but nothing like this before. He scrambled with Jake upon the banisters. They craned their necks, looking in anxiety toward the railway station. Although the train had stopped, they could see no one get off, since the station was out of view.

"Yonder come Yellow Sam in the surrey, leavin the station," said Mama Amazon. "When did he leave out fro here wit the surrey? Wait a minute." She raised her hand to shade her eyes, scrutinizing. "Yes, they's two in the back seat. Lawd, there's Ole Doc an a lady!"

Jumping down from the banister, Victor danced about on the veranda. "I told you. The great lady's comin."

When the surrey drove up before the veranda, Mama Amazon's mouth dropped open in astonishment, her mind incapable of believing. It was Miz Nee-oom-mee!

Ole Doc helped his wife from the surrey and called Jacob and Victor to come speak to their mother. Liking to always show off, Jacob was speaking in his most confidential voice and very, very polite.

"Tell her you're glad she has come home," said Ole Doc.

"*Mama?*" bluntly blurted Vic, holding Naomi's hand, turning his face off as she stooped to kiss him, looking anxiously at Mama Amazon. "How can you be Mama?" He looked at her with lethargic eyes, yet intensely questioning. "You are not black. Mama Amazon is black. She is Mama." He pointed to Mama Amazon.

From the strange look, passing swiftly on Ole Doc's face, Mama Amazon felt like comforting him. Ah, Catawba, she thought, looking upward, you harbor too many strange things. That Frenchman who helped Mr. Andy to build you and then hanged himself in the north turret!

It had been over seven years since Naomi had been taken away. In Catawba it was never talked of. The ninnies on the Square whispered about it, but no one was ever so impolite as to boldly ask Ole Doc a pointed question. Here Naomi was back, looking no more like the wisp of a chattering gal she used to be than Gabriel like old Satan. She was still curved as gracefully as bananas; although her bosom and hips were outlandishly large, her waist was still waspish. She seemed quieter, stranger. Hard to tell what Gawd aimed to do with Catawba. Was this some new weird revival of which Mama Amazon knew nothing? Naomi's eyes looked good, though that wild sparkle had shrunk within the pupil.

That Victor with the variegated mind! He was unpredictable. He must be endowed with more than a sixth sense. What was the light that he always talked of? If Ole Doc heard too much of that kind of outright lying, Victor was going to get thrashed within an inch of his life.

Mama Amazon felt like sitting down crying. She felt as if she would like to fly away to some canebrake, hiding.

"Mama Amazon," said Victor, taking one of her warm hands in his, "don't be sad. The light will not come when you are sad."

"Sad! Sad! What's you talkin bout? I ain't a bit mo sadder than nothin." She burst into protective laughter, flabbergasted at the boy. How could he tell the way she had felt just then? He stood there too innocent. If he would take those eyes off her for just a moment, until she balanced her mind. "Vic, you run on out an play now. Won't be long till it's dark. Maybe you light'll come to you mo better in the yard."

"Mama Amazon, do you see the light too?"

"Yes, hon, I sees the light." Gawd deliver her. What had she done? She had told a bald-faced lie and Vic knew it, too. But anything to get him away from her for a moment, to let her think, piece things together, to get herself so that she'd not be so bumfuzzled.

5

In the church the singing engulfed Vic's eardrums in such oceanic waves that he felt overpowered. He looked up to the tall mass of men surrounding him. Like pines wedged and jammed together in a forest. Here on the men's side, Pop seemed even taller than ever. The preacher droned like a big bumblebee, but Vic didn't see colorful blooms for him to work on; the preacher was a rather foolish bee to drone and never light on one bright bloom.

Words—words! He heard Gawd and Jesus invoked in sundry tones. Surely Gawd and Jesus would not bother with the uninteresting-looking preacher. The big cup of wine was passed up and down the rows of worshipers and most of them sipped from the cup, as most of them had broken off a pinch of the long stick of bread.

Once in the sunshine at home and with the stiff, starchy Sunday dress-up clothes off, there was something important Vic had to do. The preacher had painted a picture in his mind that he could not readily dismiss. So he climbed up into one of the magnolia trees in Catawba's wandering front yard and when he had reached a place where he could stand on two limbs and lean back against the trunk, he freed his young soul of the burdensome picture of hell and heaven. He mocked the Reverend Edward Irvin. His small voice raved and ranted, shouting as many words of the sermon as he could well remember, although he got hell and Gawd and Satan and damnation and sin and temptation rolling out of his mouth so fast that he said some very bad things, so bad that Mama Nee-oom-mee rushed out of the house and ordered him down.

Victor sat on the veranda longing for the sun to go down and the dismal Sabbath to be over. He held the wicked sin he had committed in his breast, harboring it in his heart. He was confused. Gawd made the magnolia, but it was forbidden fruit for him upon the Sabbath. Why did Gawd not want him to be happy and to climb into that big magnolia and yell and holler all he wanted to?

After the sunset and supper were over, Vic went, slipping secretly into the yard to play with the lovesome hoppy-toads that he knew had already returned with the warm days of April. He wanted them to wet on his toes to see if their wet would make a wart. What was there about a pretty toad to make a wart? He yelled and played with the toads and he grew so excited that his voice carried into the depths of Catawba.

"Victor," came Mama Nee-oom-mee's voice to him sharply through the dark, "what on earth are you doing out there? I told you once this was Sunday, the Lord's day, and you should not be making so much noise. Come right into this house!"

He didn't answer right off. He had a notion to hide. Was this dark still the blessed Sunday, too? Surely Gawd could not see him sinning in all this dark.

"Victor!"

"I'm comin."

"Son, didn't I tell you this was Sunday, the Lord's day?"

"Looks like Gawd would go to bed sometime and let me play just like I want to."

6

With the return of Naomi to Catawba, more and more of her relatives gummed up in the house to gobble up Ole Doc's rich food and to rest their war-weary bones in Miz Joanna's downy feather beds.

Sometimes Ole Doc would get fed up with them and throw a good drunk and run every one of them out into the barn where they'd spend the night calling him rough names. Then he would sober up and be sorry and have Mama Amazon begin cooking up such sumptuously rich meals they would take the bowel complaint and fight among themselves night and day.

"I'm ever rushed," breathed Mama Amazon, short-windedly, "wit a houseful of em low-country yappers rustlin bout here in they threadbare floor-sweepers an tattered lace collars."

Also, now that Naomi was home, company came more often to the house, and Cora Mathis and Jezebel were most often that company.

For Cora shouted at John Mathis, "Don't you be down on the churchfolks. Anything decent, you're against it. I'm going calling right this afternoon to Catawba; I'm getting in with that Naomi Thornwell. With what help she can give, I can hold my place in North Bethel. And I'll have you churched come next Preachin Sunday." And she slammed the door in the face of her salty husband and so, wearing her ruffled apron and her gold-headed combs in her red hair, her trim ankles betook her to Catawba, taking along the prying, saucy Jezebel.

That was how Victor and Jake met Jezebel Mathis. Jezebel, a few months older than Ole Doc's twins, might have been born years before, the way she used her yellow eyes, the way she tilted her head back and looked at people—especially little boys.

Mama Amazon saw them coming over the hill and straightway she prepared teacakes for the afternoon refreshments. "I wonder what's atwixt Ole Doc an Miz Cora? Sumpin, he ever sides wit she."

The minute Cora planked her shapely carcass into a Catawba chair she lit upon the subject of the church. North Bethel, Cora informed Naomi, was organizing its first Ladies' Aid Society next Preachin Sunday. She politicked and solicited Naomi's help in keeping the Inchurch womenfolks from getting too active a part. Why Martha—Mrs. D.D. Inchurch—and her daughters, Elvira, Louise, and Irene, would run that church if somebody didn't put a damper on them. All afternoon Cora rocked on the piazza of Catawba, conniving and plotting until she had Naomi well under control, had Naomi so ground down under her burden of sin that she would agree to anything.

While Cora incessantly preached, Jezebel angled for attention. Victor watched her from the yard. There was something about her he did not like, something—young as she was—that frightened him, awed him, fascinated him. He watched her from a distance and knew that he wanted to keep distance between them, yet she drew him, charmed him.

Then Jezebel spotted the boys and, like a bee to honey, headed for them. Jake stood where he was, curious, but Victor fled from the yard to the back porch where Mama Amazon was stringing beans, and made such a to-do to back himself between her legs that he knocked the large pan of beans out of her lap.

Mama Amazon gave a strained hoot of laughter. "Boy, is you lost you mind, buttin in here lack a billy goat? Run on back out there in the yard an play wit the lil girl. She won't bite you —no mo'an you can stand. Don't be a frady-cat."

The hardheaded and have-my-own-way Jezebel put her small hands upon her saucy hips, bent her body forward, and marched cockily about, twitching herself, quite at home.

Jake came up to her and she kissed him.

Vic went, but his eyes stayed moon-round and he was filled with misgivings when he alighted in the yard. Jezebel to him was like some infuriated animal. He remembered the time he had pinched the cat's tail behind the door and how the cat had unsheathed its claws, making the blood fly out of his head. That girl in the yard already looked like that cat and nobody had as yet pinched her tail. He was uncertain what she'd do once her tail was pinched.

He swaddled his spirit and played gingerly; he was so fascinated at watching Jezebel that he could not engage in reckless play. Before Victor realized what had happened, Jezebel had kissed him full on the mouth and told him stoutly that he tasted better than the other un. Victor liked the kiss no more than he liked Jezebel. He wiped it off with his arm, coming across his mouth many unnecessary times with plodding patience to be sure of getting it off.

Then he headed for his official refuge on the porch and sought security between Mama Amazon's knees, feeling the sweet warmth of her breath on his soft neck as it came from her in ripples of laughter. He was quite certain he would not fare forth into the yard again no matter how much she tried to shoo him.

But Jezebel was enraged. Little boys should not rub off her kisses and more especially they should not run from her. She ignored Jake and walked saucily to the porch. She screwed up her face into authority and upbraided Victor.

"Why d'you run to that big black nigger and hide from me?"

"Mama Amazon ain't no big black nigger. She's Mama," Vic asserted positively.

"She is not your mama!"

He turned in concern to Mama Amazon's all-comforting face. "You are my mama, ain't you?"

"Hon, you's got both a white and black mama. That's what makes you so colorful," said Mama Amazon.

Victor whirled on Jezebel, "I got two mamas. I got two! You just got *one!*"

Jezebel's cat's eyes glistened, but there were no tears there; it was funny, Vic thought later, when he saw her another time, how her eyes could do that without tears. She looked him through and through until he could not stand it and buried his head in Mama Amazon's skirt.

"You can't hide from me," Jezebel shouted. Something about him had caught her fancy already, as it had caught Mama Amazon and Ole Doc. "Do you hear me, lil boy?" She screamed her power and her pain. "You can't hide from me!"

7

The little pot within the big pot did a double-roll boil in Catawba's kitchen, because yonder in God's house, North Bethel, a Preachin Sunday was comin up. With subtle wisdom Mama Amazon worked, for as the Egyptians once considered the dung bettle, Old Scarabaeus, sacred, so did she consider the sin-splitting preacher.

She ironed Ole Doc's white shirt board stiff. She shook the hot iron at Vic and Jake who hung about watching: "You Pa's one mo righteous high elder in Nof Bethel, doin a vast work fo the Lawd; an he can't be goin in there in no halfway ironed shirt." She shook her head, laughing. Ole Doc had been a gaffer in his time. "Now iffen you Grandma, Miz Joanna was livin, you'd see some high steppin come this here Preachin Sunday.

Fo goin up an down the river ketchen chillun an goin to church was two things she mo' an believed in. That an climbin that big oak yonder in the south pasture an pluckin the grapes fro the vine to make the racy wine fo the holy communion to Nof Bethel."

Yellow Sam filled the wood box with wood.

"Sammy," said Mama Amazon, "you get right to the barn an to work on the horses an surrey. See can't you have everythin slick an shiny lack ol' Hump'll have em fo the Inchurches. Plait em horses' tails good an tight tonight, fo I don't want to go ridin to church tomorrow wit no horse manure bobbin long in front of me."

Ah Lawd! She would sleep but little tonight, fo there was plenty-fitten heavy preachin to attend tomorrow. She had to have new clothes to go to church, and she had, so Mama Amazon was happy. She was a splurgy, excessively extravagant dresser and Ole Doc always humored her with new clothes. She'd not enter Gawd's house unless she was in proper and befitting raiment.

8

Mama Amazon was up way before day was clean that Preachin Sunday. Her work done, she was dressed fitten to kill.

The sun-bright glimmered hotly in the holy Preachin Sunday morning. At nine o'clock the horses pranced between the surrey staves. Yellow Sam and Mama Amazon waited restfully in the front seat and her pink dress was blinding in the dazzling sunshine.

Ole Doc walked toward the surrey, a rough goat transgressing now to the lambkin green pastures where ran the still waters, to church on a Preachin Sunday.

Naomi came stepping gingerly, the famous twins with her,

and Mama Amazon noted she was dressed like all get-out and her eyes were rather shifty.

Vic and Jake stood in the back and held to the front seat. It was only two miles from Catawba to the white frame building that was North Bethel, yet it was traveled in regal ostentatiousness.

Ole Doc, an elder of North Bethel, arrived at church, having read his Bible *andante religioso* and picked his teeth thoroughly with a toothpick quill plucked from his own geese. In the oblong two-storied building he took the second seat from the front and leaned against one of the heavy columns that supported the galleries. He was near the small reed organ, on the men's side of the church.

Jake and Vic, being little boys, not hairy nor their little horns dangerous yet, were permitted when they wished the hallowed privilege of sitting on the women's side of the church.

Miss Elvira Inchurch, one of the organists, marched forward and sat at the organ, which was in the midst of a whole half churchful of men. She was dressed befitting the occasion. She seated herself, her hat, her dress, her petticoats, her pantalets upon the wobbling organ stool and lifted the lid, exposing its grinning teeth. She placed her trim feet on the pedals and pumped a little air to-hoo, to-hoo.

The relatives and friends talked and whispered happily, finding their places. The church was packed to overflowing. The gallery was filled with Negroes. Miss Inchurch began upon the wheezing organ, the first hymn the preacher called.

The voices blazed forth, unharmoniously; the congregation called in song upon Alpha and Omega to take away the love of sinning—to take back the life they owe—in the mansions bright and blessed—just one glimpse of Him in Glory—soon the pearly gates will open—we shall tread the streets of gold.

The Reverend Edward Irvin rose from his chair in the pulpit

to pray and the elders rose, too, standing piously for prayers. He prayed for rain because it was dry, and for cooler weather because it was hot. He prayed for the Spirit to enter each member of the congregation including the colored brethren in the balconies. He prayed for the widows and the orphans. He prayed for those who would be there and he prayed for those who tried to get there. He prayed that the will of the Heavenly Father be done. He told the all-seeing, all-knowing God all of his troubles, trials, and tribulations. His petitions were endless.

The prayer ended. The elders sat down with a kerplunk into their seats. The high light of the day began—the two-hour sermon.

The elders slept piously; small boys went to sleep and snored, babies wet their honored mothers and were soundly cussed under breath; the heavy deacons were rallied that they might take up the collection.

Horses tied to tall pine trees neighed and made a great deal of dung which the sparrows loved. Mules tied to tall pine trees bit upon the pine trees as though they were corn.

The sermon at last came to an end.

It was dinnertime.

9

Mama Amazon was late entering the church, for she wished the colored brethren to become frog-eyed as she and her clothes plunged down the aisle. She was late leaving the church at dinnertime for she was smart-mannered and knew her place. She could not stand a no-mannered nigger, so how could she expect the white folks to? She had to bustle to the long pine table and spread out the hampers and hampers of food she had brought from Catawba. She prided herself that her cooking outshone anything on the table, for the great ladies were already grabbing for her choice things. After pies and cakes were properly cut, hams sliced, buttermilk poured, and everything made ready, Vic, holding on tightly to Naomi, spied Mama Amazon. He set up such a clamor, making a wry face and kicking about it, that Naomi let him go to her.

The very high elders stuffed their abdomens at the long pine board table under the tall pine trees, stuffed with the elaborately prepared food, and then moved languidly and slightly goggled into the Session House, a squat hut of one room containing the red-dirt-caked, grave-digging implements, to sit in judgment upon those who had been summoned to appear before the Session to answer to the charges of crimes committed against the laws of the church and the prescribed Presbyterian Book of Church Order.

The Session was composed of the Reverend Edward Irvin, pastor; Doctor T. T. Thornwell; Mr. D. D. Inchurch, banker, landowner, possessing great worldly goods along with a super-spiritual manifestation; Captain Isaac Watt, a miller; Joe E. Shams, the cotton ginner; fat, jocose Luke Husk; Ray Lands, who ran the Leakin Skillet; and Archibald Ives, clerk of the Session, who recorded down here in the dreaded book before it was sent to Gabriel for publication.

Juliann: for bearing an illegitimate child. Caught by the nigger wench, Violet. Now humbly seeking the mercies of the gentlemen of the Session. She cringes sufficiently. She is allowed to leave the Session House, henceforward to have her children in the prescribed manner set down in the Presbyterian Book of Church Order.

Joseph Paragon: for losing his nasty temper and swearing at the corn likker he has been drinking. It is doubtful that he knows regret or will avoid such error in the future. Indefinitely suspended from all church privileges. The clerk of the Session will strike the sinner's name from Gabriel's list after it has been read to the congregation on the next Preachin Sunday.

Miss Cathy Astor: for dancing a wicked couplet with her sister in the parlor room of her father's house. The number of petticoats and proper pantaloons worn by the sisters is immaterial. The fact that they had not thought it so great a sin is most material. The sinner is deeply and wonderingly concerned. She begs Gabriel's henchmen that they have mercy upon her and not take the church privileges from her. She wishes to be a teacher; she must have her church. Forgiven in Christian and brotherly love.

Further sinners were examined, split asunder from the church forever or tendered holy mercy, depending upon power and position of family, need for true punishment or only mild embarrassment, past record and character of the sinner, and future promise, gravity of the sin, and degree of cringing before the elders.

The archangel's missionaries filed out of the Session House carrying the dreaded book of recordings.

Knowing looks were directed toward the Session House and great ladies in sweeping, frilly-ruffled clothes smiled coyly behind fans. Whispers danced from shade-tree group to shade-tree group, picked up velocity across wide expanses of dazzling sunshine, dropping into a tittering bunch in a surrey. An elder came to the front door of the church and rang a little hand bell, summoning the members inside the church for another two hours.

The afternoon preaching offered an unusual diversion. Something was wrong at the organ. Miss Elvira Inchurch, who played for the morning service, refused to give up the organ for the afternoon to Miss Cora Mathis. Cora Mathis knew her rights. There was a cat fight two yards in front of the elders. Flowered hats stomped, lace mitts ripped; torn waists with camisoles showing right in church. The elders hesitated to take a hand. The congregation arose and looked. Cora Mathis spat on Elvira Inchurch. The Inchurches had always ruled North Bethel, but it looked like Cora Mathis was about to take a hand. That was going to mean trouble. Cora had too much pepper in her temper; she was pure stomp-down Scotch-Irish even if she was poor. At last some of the men moved in, two to Miss Elvira and two to Miss Cora. The afternoon service continued, with a third party, a mere substitute, at the organ.

Mama Amazon commented to Yellow Sam, up in the high balcony: "Em gals pure craves to play the organ for the Lawd."

Yellow Sam drove slowly homeward from church. Ole Doc and Naomi were wilted and weary. Jake was fretting and irritable.

"It seems that here on the watershed I have the strangest things to learn," Naomi said. "I sometimes wish I had not become entangled with that church. It is like a web."

"The church, my dear, is the seat of any country's welfare. To lose sight of that is to lose sight of everything. You must remember that. That's what we came to this country for. It is built upon that and nothing more," Ole Doc replied.

Victor pulled on Mama Amazon's arm and she stooped to hear him.

"Gawd is soughing in the tall pines, Mama Amazon," his soft voice murmured. "Listen, don't you hear Him? And the pine trees are clapping their hands and shouting with joy."

10

Not a poet's spring came, but a raw spring, like a newborn baby; with chapping winds, sudden wintry blasts trailing and holding to winter tight. Time would snip the umbilical cord. Victor drank the spring and everything that happened in it. And there were some things he remembered beyond others, the spring before he started to school. He did not know what was important and what was not, to Ole Doc or the others, because to him each thing was important in itself and he remembered whatever impressed him, no matter why.

He remembered Pop raving and ranting for days about the scrap in the bank with old Mr. Inchurch. Pop told Mama Amazon all about it and Vic sat under the table and paid close attention. Old Mr. Inchurch didn't want to build a large mill in Green Pond, but Ole Doc and some other people did.

Ole Doc had pleaded, "I tell you, Inchurch, I've an old, run-over field out yonder north of the house that's so gully-washed it won't sprout cowpeas. A large mill there will provide work. That young Charles Coatworthy'd be a good one to run it. He's up-an-comin and what he don't know about needle stitch is not to be known in a cotton mill. This country will go to ruin rapidly with its young men all leaving out for better places. Sheep stay where the grass is greenest, earthworms where the ground is rich and moist. McCobb'll take a good many shares in it, he's got quite a bit of money in a bank in Rahab. Saved from distilling."

Inchurch exploded. "No! I've got the money around here and that's the whipping hand, Thornwell. I'm an honest, God-fearing, church-attending Christian, and I'll have nothing whatever to do with that tripe Charles Coatworthy. He's lived openly with that old Sara down there on the river and they've had about eight illegitimate children. I've got no use for McCobb. He won't quit making whisky and when I tried to get that old log schoolhouse incorporated in the last Legislature, why, he made a perfect fool out of me right before the whole legislative body. And if you insist on leasing those shoals of yours to Mc-Cobb to distill on again, I'm going to have you churched even if you are the only doctor hereabouts."

Ole Doc drank for three weeks because of that. "You can't do a thing with that skinflint Inchurch," he kept saying in the kitchen to Mama Amazon.

"And mind you, Amazon, when I suggested we get Northern help, he jumped all over me. But when he sniveled around and held on to good Federal money during the war, the North was all right. He's allus accusing me of being a rebel. I never wanted that war. I'm going to write Jefferson Harvey and Lewis Ford to see about help. But I bet two to one if I get it and get some additional local capital, ole Inchurch will be the first to jump in and hog everything, like he did the mills on the river when things got to running smoothly and looked safe. I'm tired of being Inchurch's cat's-paw. Oh, well, let a snake bite itself enough times and it'll kill itself."

Ole Doc did write to his Northern friends, because a letter came to him from Philadelphia and he couldn't stop smiling about it; and pretty soon the new mill was started.

That was the spring Vic began going on wild doctoring trips with Pop, the trips that began to open up a wonderful new world. Pop narrated, slowly and methodically, how he used to ride behind Granny Joanna, who was in the sidesaddle, up and down the rivers, ketchin chillun at a dollar apiece. Granny Joanna was the best midwife the watershed ever had. Pop took to a love for healing people from her and now he was proud to have Vic go with him.

Vic met Mr. Saddlebury on one of Pop's doctorings. Mr. Saddlebury was a no-nation member, because he had had a white mama and a black daddy, but now he wouldn't have anything to do with the niggers, and the white folks in Green Pond wouldn't have anything to do with him. Mr. Saddlebury was a sad, kind man; and Vic thought often about him that spring. He was the sort of man who oughtn't ever to have to be a no-nation member.

Later in the spring there was a day when Mama Amazon rushed here and there to get things ready for a big dinner for a lot of preachers and high elders.

"Ho'cum they's all comin here, Mama Amazon?"

"Hon, it's the Presbytery meetin to Nof Bethel. That's gonna be some real times when all em preachers and high elders gets together and starts palaverin—iffen some of em don't go to outright lyin."

Vic shivered a little. One preacher and North Bethel's own elders were enough; but none of them ought to come within the grounds of home, of Catawba.

"Now, Vic, you and Sammy draw me some water fo my butter an cream an then you can help Sammy run me down seven of the best dominecker roosters you can find for the servants of the Lawd. Don't you get none of em what's got bands on they legs, Sammy! Ole Doc's done picked em out fo he's seed roosters—hard to tell what kinda cuttin up a preacher'd do iffen he went to eatin up a body's seed roosters."

11

BEELZEBUB: Don't blame Gawd fo takin the twenty-pound hammer an knockin you outta Heaven. It's too good fo you.

SATAN: Looky here, Beelze, I's the boss-dog of the low regions. What I says goes. I haves heaps thinkin to do. These Scotch-Irish here is hard to get holt to; gotta set down an study em out.

BEELZEBUB: Glad it's summertime an I don't have to wear fine shoes; lack this cool sand runnin twixt my toes.

SATAN: You know blame well you don't have no shoes. That fire'd burn em off. Still—it's good to feel vast proud lack you's got em on, it's just same as havin em on. That's a good way to feel toward em churchfolks. Every time they starts choppin on you wit a hoe, you make lack it ain't hurtin an it won't.

BEELZEBUB: Hee, that's the reason you horns is so sharp an polished: all the years you's been buttin em Presbyterians.

SATAN: Have to butt em; they's stiff-necked. How far us fro Miz Jezebel's house?

BEELZEBUB: Red-headed gal wit em big yaller eyes of

John Mathis? What's brewin in you head, ole man Satan? You head's fo mo' an holdin em horns. Better leave she be! She's gonna cling to that Victor Thornwell an Gawd's done claimed he fo He's own. Jezebel'll cling to Vic so stoutly she'll get across em rotten boards in the end.

SATAN: I can try, can't I?

Victor stands at his window dreaming, living in a purely fantasy world, a creation planted there by Mama Amazon. And dawn is near, the mockingbirds' singing thins the darkness. Ole Satan tiptoes away, afraid of a Preachin Sunday, afraid of too much Gawd around; but he sneaks in Nof Bethel, sneaks in the Session House, butting as many Presbyterians into some sin as he possibly can. For, without sin, he would die.

GABRIEL: Shorely churchin plenty folks in that Session House this Preachin Sunday. I's puttin down some mighty rough things about em.

GAWD: Is they cited any mo stiff-necked ones fo contumacy?

GABRIEL: Had a pile of em up fo defiance of church authority, but most of em broke down an craved the mercy of the Session an got freed.

GAWD: Too much carousin an goins-on down there. My sinful chillun's gotta cut up a wicked to-do. They nature to lean toward the sinful. Miz Cora Mathis didn't church ole John this month, enty?

GABRIEL: No, but she will. I ever said you got too much red pepper in both she and she daughter's temper.

GAWD: Oh, well, don't think my chillun'll get too rough wit one another.

5

"Yonder comes Jezebel, Jake. Hurry up or we'll be late," Victor yelled. His first day he certainly didn't want to be late. He couldn't eat. The thought of school was too wonderful. It made a nervous jerking in his insides. For two whole months he would go to Miss Lizzie Newcome's subscription school; Pop said it would cost two dollars.

Jezebel had been combed and braided so tightly she was cock-eyed. She had been shoved into her long white union suit. Over this went the drawers body, and up came the white drawers buttoned to the drawers body, and pulled up over these were bright airy bloomers. Then a series of petticoats, ruffled, lacy, tucked, and over them a dress, buttoned up its back, making Jezebel into a flouncing butterball. Her long black stockings were fastened securely under the bloomers; other than the moonlike, saucy face and inquisitive hands, no skin was publicly displayed.

So Jezebel arrived in the Thornwell yard with Cora's voice

still ringing in her ears: "Stop by for the twins! I didn't get into Catawba. See what you can do. You've got two to select from." And Jezebel wouldn't have dreamed of not stopping. Boys meant Vic, who watched her with interest but wouldn't let her touch him.

Jezebel, being decidedly clucky, naturally took a spreading-winged motherly interest in the boys. She wanted to walk spunkily in the middle, mindfully holding each one of them with a hand.

Jacob liked the feel of her hot hand, but Victor disliked it. He turned her hand loose and walked boldly down the street by himself.

Jezebel held Jacob's icy hand that frosty morning all the way to Miss Lizzie Newcome's school, but her eyes drank in strangling gulps of the positively brave Victor who walked shyly to himself. Jezebel grunted in her middle as though the ingredients of the Reverend Edward Irvin's inferno were working there. She certainly disapproved of Victor doing her this way, for when the memory flooded her of how lovable his lips had been in Catawba's back yard, she knew he was her loadstone. Her hands and lips wanted to stick to him as the viscid fluid in daffodils or the white milk from poinsettias. About him was a communicable laughter that she wanted to get inside of, to harbor forever in her heart, but when she approached him there was mocking laughter that shut her completely out of his world and he became more than ever like a mirage to her. The tendrils of her soul might take root somewhere if he would only pay her some mind with his infectious smile.

Mama had said there was something wrong with him when he was born—something about his head; but Jezebel didn't see him that way. To her he was a tat of lovesomeness.

If he were only an ugly boy she could easily dismiss him as though he were a haphazard blackbird; but here he was, the most adorable lopsided creature who had ever entered North

Bethel Church and now Miss Lizzie Newcome's subscription school.

Although she held on tenaciously to Jake, her soul liquefied itself as lard will do over heat for the creature who walked by himself down the street.

Victor could not believe what school was like: it had not been that way in his imagination. The children did nothing but sit all day. There was no use for him to sit there looking at the queer old lady who told lies. Vic was not sure how he knew they were lies, but he could not believe Miss Lizzie Newcome. She didn't look like someone to be believed. Besides, the room was filled with a most noisome odor.

Catawba did not smell that way—it was home, and home was fresh air and sweet-smelling Mama Amazon and her laughter and her doing about. Why couldn't you learn at Catawba—why couldn't you learn outside and learn what you wanted to, what interested you? Oh, he could not be shut up in the lonely schoolhouse!

He did not cry. But that night at home he put away his slate forever. When Pop and Mama Naomi heard him muttering about it, they looked at each other with sharp ridges of surprise daubed on their faces. Why?

"I won't be going back to school," Victor shouted, repeating so often he got excited and stuttered.

They were astoundingly shocked. He was so emphatic—and he had looked forward to it so much. What had happened?

Victor proclaimed, beyond the shadow of a doubt, far beyond their mere questioning, what was wrong with school. He mocked Miss Lizzie Newcome. He grew quite voluble with his lopsided talk. His reasons were clear, but they could not understand them as he did; that was evident. They did not see into his heart or know that there was a fierce disappointment there. They did not, because Pop took him back to school himself the next day.

In spite of Victor's honest horror—to which Pop had always given due consideration before—in spite of his pulling back, his tears, his whimpering, sticking his toes into the ground, the next morning Pop led him back to Miss Lizzie Newcome's school.

And there he learned. Miss Lizzie Newcome thrashed him often with a stick, rared upon her tiptoe she poured it to him so hard and so often and she never poured it around him. Often he was whipped three times a day.

Jake was never whipped. He was good.

2

To err was to erase the slate and to start again.

If winter's school was an error, the spring rains washed the slate the cleanest Victor could remember. With the spring plowing going full tilt in the fallow fields that sprawled rakishly, yet securely and promisingly, over Catawba's wandering red acres, Victor found life chock full of living. Above was the blue up-yonder, the Presbyterian stardust, to watch over him and to guide him.

He and Jake played in the fresh-turned furrows, rolling over in the warm earth, letting its goodness creep into every fiber of their bodies. They barely had time to jump out of the furrow before another plow sang by, cutting the earth asunder, piling it into fragrantly glistening heaps.

"You boys, go bring us a drink of water," said Yellow Sam, halting his team before them, wiping his face with his shirttail.

"I don't have to carry water," impudently asserted Jake.

"I'll see about that," said Yellow Sam, picking up a stick, making for Jake. "You know good an well Ole Doc's done tolt you to do what I tells you. You hurry up or I's gonna wear you out agin wit this stick."

Only, who had stopped his team behind Yellow Sam's team,

snickered, "Makin em lil half brothers of yourn step about, enty?"

When the roastin' ear patch was hoed, Yellow Sam had Jake and Vic as helpers, although he thought them a mite puny to hoe briskly and swiftly, but Ole Doc gave orders to be obeyed without argufying. Yellow Sam showed them how to hold their hoes, how to thin the corn out to a distance so that it'd make two big ears to the stalk, how to dig deep into the ground, getting all the roots out to keep it from sprouting up again. Jake and Vic dug with manly vigor, their small arms flailing the hoes through the hot air, but they swung them awkwardly, as though they would cut their bare feet.

Vic was unmindful of Yellow Sam's big talk and did as he pleased, lingering behind and clipping the corn off barely under the ground. It was too hot to hoe corn and he wished he were under the big boxwoods in front of the house teasing the doodles there, telling them their house was a-fire. His hoe cut an angleworm half in two and he fell upon his knees, grabbing hold of the half worm that bored rapidly into the ground, holding to it gently, making it ease itself out of the ground.

Before he got the worm halfway out of the ground there was Yellow Sam rushing madly down the dusty row, grabbing him up, flailing him with his big yellow hand. Vic didn't know which hurt the worst: Yellow Sam's big yellow hand, Mama Amazon's big ginger-colored one, or Pop's hickories.

In late spring the pigs were castrated.

Uncle Prince Blue, looking like a character right out of the Old Testament, came out of the woods and headed straight to the pigpens behind Catawba where the lanky field hands scuffled and played, waiting on Pop to sharpen his knife on the grindstone. Vic watched him test it for sharpness with his fingers, and it was as sharp as the razor Mama Amazon carried.

The field hands threw the harshly squealing pigs to the ground, holding them there by brute strength. Ole Doc's shining knife slit the skin over the testicles; he probed the incision with his fingers, taking hold of the testicle, pulling it out, easing the knife down the testicle cord, cutting it loose deep within. Ole Uncle Blue, hunkering close to Ole Doc, held out a dented pan to receive the bluish testicles. Lard and turpentine were smeared over the incision to keep the blowflies away, the pig stood on his head for a brief moment, and then dropped back into the pen, running off whimpering, huffing to himself.

Vic squatted beside Pop, thrilled with the ceaseless string of pigs being castrated. He watched Uncle Prince Blue's pan mount heapingly high with the oysterlike testicles. He watched the sure-fire cutting and itched to cut like Pop.

Vic whimpered so piteously to cut that Pop gave him a chance, but he was so slow cutting, recutting, smearing around in the bright blood that it turned dark under his fumblings and Pop had to take the knife away from him and straighten out his mess. Thereafter Pop told him he would have to eat a great deal more mush and milk before he could remove the testicles without killing the pig.

But Victor had felt the knife in his hands and his hands exploring in the hot flesh and his longing to use the knife swelled up within him and he longed to do wonderful things with it. It began that day and it did not cease. That craving, that coveting the knife, the shining bit of steel.

"No, sirree," said Uncle Prince Blue, bowing low to Ole Doc and picking up his heaped-high pan of the bluish testicles. Not this delicacy, he would not let his ole gals have one mouthful of it to eat. For ladies to eat such eatins would make em jerk their hips too swiftly and saucily and he was much too ole to tend to that.

Only teased the boys with his voluminous store of information about ole Satan. Satan today was a long-horned, forked-tailed creature who was slicker than a rattlesnake. But once upon a time he had been a high and mighty angel in heaven, but like a lot of white folks he got too vast proud and teased Gawd too much. One day Gawd was busy in his blacksmithy sharpening plows for the angels to plow with and Gawd could stand ole Satan's devilment no longer; so He whapped him in the head with a twenty-pound hammer—knocking him down to a lake of fire. Then Gawd felt sorry for him being singed in that seven-times-seven hot fire and threw him down a seven-pronged pitchfork to prong his living from that fire and He sent him a bunch of hellhounds to lick and lap his sores and a bunch of aggravating lil devils to assist him with his work of doing evil throughout all this land. Ever since then ole Satan and his gang have been pronging around, pronging up plenty-fitten evil.

The stories never made an impression on Jake, for indifferently he shrugged them off, but for Vic they opened up a mad world—a world that was all right in daylight, but once the dark of night came and objects became indiscernible, things took on incredible shapes and forms and Vic's terror and imagination knew no bounds. Yet it fascinated him—even this terror—fascinated him as much as the gal Jezebel. In bed at night, with his head well under the cover, although it was hot weather and he thought he would smother himself to death, he could feel the huge seven-pronged pitchfork of ole Satan coming through all of Granny Joanna's patchworked quilts and sticking right into his flesh. And he thought of the knife at the pig cutting and he felt the warm sticky-hot blood on his fingers and he knew that would be the way to rid himself of ole Satan, perhaps to free the earth from him. And then the hounds of sleep overtook him and he drifted off from sheer exhaustion.

3

The dews were heavy each chilly dawn. Vic's choking curiosity filled him with a gusty rambler's spirit and he moved through the late autumn fields and by streams his free days, studying greedily with nature.

He wandered aimlessly through the fields where Mama Amazon's children were picking cotton; they stopped to play and to talk.

The children looked scornfully at their half brother Budda, who was with Victor, knowing he didn't have to pick cotton because he was Only's child. July and Gee quarreled about who their daddy was. Gee allowed she was lighter complexioned, not favoring July, and she knew fo true that her daddy couldn't possibly be the same as his.

"Ole Uncle Prince Blue musta daddied you," laughed Gee, cunningly smiling at the cotton burs.

"You know blamed well that ole ugly nigger ain't daddied me." July's angry eyes blazed. "That ugly thing, he's a African. Me, I's Nof Kerlina."

Budda struck out to running toward the woods, with Vic and Jake scrambling after him. Blindly they came out of the big woods right behind Uncle Prince Blue's cabin.

Ole Uncle Prince Blue sat asleep, leaning against his house in the sun. His mouth gapped open, his red tongue hanging out on his white wool covering his face.

Budda picked up a straw and tickled the old man's tongue, jumping backward out of his reach. Uncle Blue knocked nonchalantly at the straw without awakening, thinking it was an aggravating fly come to torment him. Budda repeatedly tickled his tongue until Uncle Blue started and jumped out of his chair.

"Whose lil black boy you? Slippin here ticklin me. I'll tickle you toreckly. You ain't foolin me, I knowed who you bees all along," laughed Uncle Blue harshly, the woolly hairs flying up and down on his face.

He told them that he was a prince, son of a king, from faraway Africa where the good black people lived. Often they ate one another's flesh, but they didn't bother the spirit. He showed them the great holes in his ears and nose where he had worn many bones and rings. He showed them scorched marks on his body that were the marks of a king. He told them how he could make both good and evil conjures. He took from his pocket a small box of grease and told them that by greasing his lips with that grease he could swallow little boys like them whole just like a powerful king snake swallowed other snakes.

"Uncle Blue," said Budda, "Dessa, her's gonna way to school come Monday."

Uncle Blue doubled with short laughter. "Where's that lil nigger gal gonna get learnin?"

"Her goin to Emancipation Proclamation Academy," Budda stated stoutly. Did Uncle Blue not know that Miz Naomi had been teaching Dessa to read and to write? Since Miz Naomi had been saved by the grace of the Lawd Jesus Christ she fully intended spending her time teaching cullud chillun to read and to write. She would miss Dessa's help around the Big House, but Gee would be brought in from the fields and trained to do housework and then she was going to teach him and Gee to read together. Mama Amazon had never gone to school a single day in her life and could do nothing more than tetch the pen and make her mark, and she was overly anxious for her children to be able to read about the pictures as well as to look at them in books and papers.

Uncle Blue said that to mention Emancipation Proclamation Academy recalled such olden times as most people had forgotten. It had been founded for Negro children by a Northern white woman who was a missionary and had come with the scalawags and carpetbaggers to the foreign Southland, although she was afraid she would be eaten alive, to teach the heathen to be kind to one another and to be like Jesus. But the white heathen scoffed at her, so she had founded the academy for nigger children. He thought Miz Purdy Purdue had done some mighty fine big talk when she came. She died soon after the school was started and was buried on the schoolground and a great monument had been raised to her later.

"Emancipation Proclamation Academy be bad for Dessa," Uncle Blue said.

For a cullud person to get book-learnin was bad. One could see what book-learnin had done to the whitefolks. Their minds were no longer than his fingernail. They were as fidgety and nervous as a mule tied over a bumblebee nest and the bumblebees stinging him under his tail. Instead of wise, people became ignorant and sinful from reading books. A man of wise counsel had no need of reading, because Gawd gave man everything he needed on earth, but the instant one of the ignorant ones thought of a book, sin began popping as though the earth were hell and white men became foolish in their minds. Thought they could catch niggers and sell them—and they did!

Time passed swiftly and the sun dropped out of sight before they realized it, so they bade Uncle Prince Blue hurried good-bys and fled toward Catawba.

Darkness overtook them in the big woods and Miz Purdy Purdue laughed at them from behind every large pine tree. They saw the shape of her hipbones in the tall treetops. Her skull grinned among the knotty limbs. They sped faster, panting for breath. Once through the dark woods, they could feel her tearing after them, reaching out with her bony hands, beckoning them to come back, not to leave her alone in the dark woods, because she was oh, so very lonely.

For Vic, Gawd splashed the colors riotously and in all His creation there was an overflowing of abundance. For Vic all things were pure as Gawd had intended in the beginning.

4

And Victor knew, but couldn't explain it, that Gawd was way up yonder somewhere. He was there in the winter's cold and the summer's hot.

The humid sun-hot made the bean vines throw their arms above their heads, shouting with joy for Gawd's creation. The vines were busy making little beans filled with lots of flatus that would eventually bestir and bemoan in the Green Ponders' bellies. Gabriel had to record each queer-sounding note the flatus made in the Green Ponders' bellies.

GAWD: Gabrieline, quit you writin jest a minute an us study lil mens out mo better.

GABRIEL: That lil yaller-eyed Jezebel shorely is twitchin she behint these days; might nigh jerk sheself in two.

GAWD: Ain't I made she right much woman?

GABRIEL: That You's done done, Lawd.

GAWD: You know, I's right proud of Ole Doc: the way he's been helpin that po lil Charles Coatworthy out the last few years. Old Doc is got him head of that big new mill—what they call em?

GABRIEL: 'Big Bertha' is what I put down fo em.

GAWD: Yah, that's em. An Charles Coatworthy is shorely runnin em. Makes em mill hands step round. He's climbin, too. You watch em. Him an ole Sara took a notion to get married up wit they chillun all lookin on wild-eyed as hants. An I's awful proud of em fo marryin up. Of course you can't hardly call they chillun yard chillun, yet stray-ones won't quite suit. But I reckon it don't make too much mind. An I shorely didn't lack to see my chillun get pushed around lack Inchurch was trying to do em. Good fo Ole Doc.

GABRIEL: Oh, you can't do nothin wit em Inchurches. They's gonna have everythin. You know how they sent way up to Richmond right after the Civil War to get the bodies of their boys, haulin em away back here to Green Pond in they wagon, fightin the buzzards off all the way.

GAWD: It's in they nature to hold on to the impossible. You been recordin anythin mo interestin?

GABRIEL: I's been recordin plenty bout em baptizin Miz Willie Carter in the river. They dipped she three different times in the river an each time they'd bring she up, her old man'd holler, "Dip her agin, by crackey, she ain't fitten, dip her agin. She hit me in the head wit a rollin pin, dip her agin."

All during the summer Satan worked hard, pronging up piles of sin for the people to fall into. At times he would get wore out and disgusted and sit down.

BEELZEBUB: Us jest bout gonna lose Charles Coatworthy an Cabelus McCobb.

SATAN: Shut you dirty mouth! All you can think of this evenin is discouragin trouble. Good as McCobb's corn likker was fo my parchin tongue; I's ever disdainful of water!

6

None of it made sense. The big words of the church droned in Vic's mind like a bee: justification, immortality, predestination ran through his mind without any meaning. There were many more: purification, redemption, remembrance, sanctification— the list never seemed to end.

Here in church he wished fervently that Mama Naomi had left him at Catawba. He was pure lonesome in his middle. While sitting with Mama Amazon here in the balcony of North Bethel was delightful, he'd be more delighted to sit with her by Catawba's hearth where she kept pots and skillets doodling with the good things he liked to eat. This was a dreadful tied-up Preachin Sunday and he couldn't get into a swelter of living; surrounded with church he couldn't submerge himself into his own world, so instead of listening to the preacher he picked out the members of the congregation, sizing them up.

Jake was getting on fast and already sitting on the men's side of the church. He had no need to camouflage his emotions, because this preaching was what he liked. He had nothing to do but twirl his thumbs and recite slowly to himself and awe listeners with the many verses of Scripture and prayers he'd learned. He stood in the middle of his most earnest and devout prayer-age.

Cora Mathis played the organ and Elvira Inchurch snickered at her playing behind her fan. "What she's playing could never be put down upon paper," she tittered to Naomi. Naomi wondered, if Cora strained herself, who the elders would get to play the organ.

The church was overcrowded and the air grew unbearably hot. Salvation, justification, predestination—Victor hoped that he could be a vastly great man before he fled to the Presbyterian stardust, although it took such a dreadfully long time to get prepared for living in the stardust that he didn't believe he would ever get there.

His heart quivered with the lonesomeness of pine trees, and he indulged in a whim of using integrity and reasoning with himself. He sat down with himself and pacified himself with thinking of the keenest pleasure he could derive.

He remembered the time when he and Jake stole the Inchurch horse and sulky, while Mama Naomi was on a visit there, and drove away in it. Jake was scared.

"Sumpin might get us," he quaked.

"I ain't afraid of nothin. Gawd'll care fo me."

"How you know He'll take care of you, Vic?"

"I can feel Em."

"I don't feel no Gawd. I'm scared."

Vic did not know how Jake could learn so many verses and prayers and like to go to church so well and not trust Gawd. That was just before the Inchurch sulky got stuck between the trees.

Mama Naomi had screamed with horror when she found out they had been caught stealing. She knew something dreadful would happen to them for this terrible thing. Vic kept his mouth tight shut, looked at her much concerned, and recalled the number of times he had actually seen her snitching foolish things and toting them to a hiding place in Catawba, but no one had ever caught her. And now she screamed so violently that Pop led him and Jake right straight down to the Inchurch bank and they were made to bow real low before ole man Inchurch and to humbly beg his forgiveness. Vic did, but he wasn't a sincere repentant. Jake did too, but he managed eventually to wriggle all the blame upon Vic's shoulders and to sun his righteousness every way possible.

Vic saw Mr. Inchurch across the aisle from the Inchurch women and he shivered because he remembered how Mr. Inchurch's ice-blue eyes had glittered when he and Jake had cringingly bowed for his forgiveness.

He glanced down at Mama Naomi sitting beside Elvira Inchurch and he thought he would keep a watch on her to see just what she cunningly slipped out of Elvira's pocket. She'd take sumpin. She took things every chance she got. He had seen her take things out of the stores and drop them so swiftly into her bosom that no one ever saw her. Once she had slipped a golden angel from the Leg & Leg Department Store, dropping it somewhere into the folds of her dress. He grew round-eyed thinking where the golden angel had gone; but women had so many contraptions fastened onto them it was doubtful where it landed.

The preacher said, "Let us pray." And all the elders stood up piously. Vic noted that Robert Inchurch, a newly elected elder and son of ole man Inchurch, stood up as proudly as the old man. He was a humpback, with a great big head screwed down between his shoulders, and he always wore a long-tailed coat and walked about as a disjointed bantam rooster. He was getting a good bit of age on him. Folks had always whispered about him, wondering would he ever marry to perpetuate the Inchurch progeny. They had said he needn't be picayunish about whom he married, he was going to have to be glad to get whoever would have him. He'd always fascinated Vic because his body, even to his shriveled-up seater, looked so much like a baboon's and his great head so haughtily proud and his long reaching-out-yonder arms.

Sitting with Miss Lizzie Newcome on the women's side of the church, Jezebel could easily look up to Vic in the balcony. And when she saw him, his adorable eyes and kissable lips, she forgot all about preaching and Miss Lizzie Newcome and scratched herself. She wished Vic would deck himself out and not be so admirably dirty—sitting up there in the balcony all alone with that ole nigger woman! But then her thoughts grew so deep and abiding within her that she didn't give the slightest heed to what Vic did. Anything would please her, anything from his lopsided smile to his unfathomed soul would suit her. Without him this so-called life would be an unreasonable experience and she couldn't conceive of such a catastrophe happening to her—no place in her life for such absurdities. She overruled such vicious possibilities. She piled her dreams high as the dainty frosty sherbets served in Catawba's spacious dining room.

Someday she would live in Catawba. She could see herself right now descending those spacious front stairs. She was far more beautiful than Naomi and someday she would marry Victor and move into Catawba, the largest house in all Green Pond County. She would be Mrs. Victor Erich Thornwell. It seemed almost impossible for her to wait.

And Victor saw Jezebel sitting there with Miss Lizzie. That was because Cora was at the organ and she had said that Jezebel was not to sit with John on the men's side. Victor was glad that Jake liked Jezebel; she might always be trying to get even closer to him and tag him even more than she did if Jake wasn't around a lot, too. But in spite of Jake and in spite of trying to keep out of her way, Jezebel made it her job to get intimate with Vic. She was always putting her hot little hands into his clothes and telling him he was sweet.

When people scolded him, he felt weighted down by sin for a while, but soon after that he would perk up and find his own way back to Gawd. He didn't believe in repenting as much as everybody else did. The Lawd, he felt sure, was not holding anything against him, so why should other folks?

2

Firmly rooted in the red earth, Vic was now shooting up like a bean sprout. He was so dreamy-eyed and lazy-lipped that he sent shivers fleeing up Jezebel's backbone. She often wondered did he ever talk, but he wrapped himself about Catawba and listened: North Bethel was being rebuilt.

Once North Bethel had been burned to the ground by the devilish British, but the rock-gutted folks had run the British away, cussed and shoveled the ashes out of the way, and with frow and ax hued themselves another praise-house out of the tall soughing pines, using wooden pegs for nails.

Two bloody wars had been fought here on the watershed, men had bled and lay down and died for what they thought was right. And now they thought nothing of rolling up their sleeves and erecting a praise-house to the glory of God because they thought they were right.

Now since the Civil War, the folks were again brazen enough to stand upon all twos. No longer did they haul the old iron pots, many of them smelted in old Andy Thornwell's foundry, away down to the sea to boil water to get salt. No longer did they have to hide their animals from an approaching army or peep through cracks at approaching soldiers. No longer did they have to dig holes in the ground to bury their greasy hams to keep the Yankees from gobbling them up. Now they could openly fry them on the kitchen hearths.

The congregation of North Bethel prided itself of the fact that when the form of government of the United States of America was chosen, the devout Fathers practically copied the form of government of the Presbyterian Church.

But one thing that the congregation of North Bethel did not mention openly was the fact that it usually had a real honest-to-goodness, holier-than-thou species of she-hen who ruled the church roost by hook or crook. She kept her eyes open, watching that no one got a higher sacred seat than she before she could plunk her churchly seater into it.

Cora Mathis was now finally North Bethel's reigning queen and she ruled regally.

She had openly snatched it from Mrs. Daniel D. Inchurch. And the old sainted patriarchs, sleeping in the churchyard, would gladly tell, if someone would wake them up, who old Mrs. Inchurch had snitched it from.

And Naomi fell prey at last to Cora's conniving. Cora held the whip in the church, striking whomever she wished, and since Naomi's new-found religion had bewildered her even more than she was already bewildered, causing innumerable shortcomings always to be in her road, she found solace and condolence and refuge in the infallible, impeccable arms of Cora. Thus, Naomi became so close to the source of power that she never felt the sting of the whip.

Now that the congregation of North Bethel was continuing to remodel and add a great deal to the church, the members stayed as angry at one another as a nest of bumblebees into which water has been poured. There was backslapping, tongue lashing, sulky faces with soured countenances, blazing angry eyes in the congregational meetings. There was taking sides. There was lining up, ready for the draw. Controversies arose over first one and then another vital matter.

The weather boarding on the outside of the logs, some fifty years old, was argued upon. Not one blessed, sainted splinter of it was to be removed. It could be brick-veneered as readily as the logs. Neither were the handsomely carved balconies to be moved nor the stately, dignified solid round columns that supported the balconies, that had the grapes, leaves, and vines climbing up them, to be moved. People should have a mind tearing into God's house.

If an afternoon thunderstorm boiled up in the west and moved thunderingly toward North Bethel while the bleating lambkins spewed and pawed within over contumacious things, the losing side, casting holier-than-thou eyes out the open windows, wished —even prayed—that the approaching storm might destroy their enemies right here in the portals of North Bethel. They themselves, of course, would escape unmolested, to bear good tidings that Jesus had smote the enemy down.

During the rebellion so many preachers' tail and wing feathers were snatched and strewn helter-skelter that it appeared as the goose-picking time, including the squawking the goose does when its feathers are jerked out. And the Reverend Irvin's feathers were plucked out by great handfuls, he saw a more sinful pasture, and fled from North Bethel to where the Lord called him, even as a naked old rooster.

North Bethel was changed from a rectangular building, hewn smooth of virgin pine logs, to an enormous brick octagon edifice with seats for over a thousand people; great storied windows; a sublime bell tower that reached up and up, several hundred feet straight up into the stardust.

3

Chaos came to Catawba on all fours, challenging its arranged security. Ultrapious Naomi had failed to invite David Kingsley to a party she was giving for her boys.

Ole Doc was called off on a mysterious trip that morning before Mama Amazon had uncovered the coals in the kitchen fireplace to start breakfast.

"Lawdy," she breathed when her sleepy eyes beheld Ole Doc

jumping astride Star and racing toward the Square, "is sumpin done stung him on he's tail? Been makin out lack he's too old to ride a hoss. Don' act lack it." She gave a stouthearted chuckle. "Knowed all along he'd never keep David Kingsley hid."

Riding down Main Street before sunup, Dr. Thornwell thought how the place was growing. In a few more years, if this growth kept on, Main Street'd pass by Catawba. There'd be no need for him to move into town as many of his country yokels were doing. The town moved at a trot, and it'd move faster if he'd sell more land between here and Catawba. But the land between Main Street and North Philadelphia Street he intended keeping. There might come the day when he'd get a hundred dollars per lot.

From Catawba's rolling acres, he had dug them as saplings and planted them—the huge elms which had grown, shading the street, their limbs forming a high cloistral arch on the upper blocks of North Philadelphia Street. Behind them stood the spacious two-storied houses, rich with verandas, columns, porte-cocheres, flowery embellishments; befitting abodes for the aristocracy, for those who climbed society's ladder on the rungs behind the Inchurches.

Before one such aristocratic house, whose intense dignity was startling, Ole Doc stopped, hitched the horse to the handsome hitching post, went through the iron gate, walked stiffly up the boxwood-lined walkway. He knocked with the shiny knocker on the handsomely embossed front door and was received by a young Negro girl who wore a colored dress covered with a white pinafore.

"Right up the stairs there, Doctor Thornwell, an turn to the right."

Knocking, opening the door, entering the smartly furnished bedroom whose feminine odor smacked him full in the face, he said, "Why, Nora, you don't look a-tall sick. Sending for me at this hour, I thought you were real poorly."

The stately young woman, whose beautiful body alerted him, whose line of neck and face revealed charm yet concealed a will of cold flint rock, laughed ironically, "Really, Doctor Thornwell, you've never known me to be sick?"

"Come to think of it, I can't say I have."

"Oh, have you really forgotten when David was born?"

What was she after? His mind groped. What was she conniving for? She had something up her sleeve. "Why, that's been a long time ago, Nora. A long time ago."

"I thought you'd remember without too much prodding," she said curtly.

"I don't get the point," he spoke in bewildered awkwardness.

"I'm sorry about arousing you so early, but I thought you'd be up early because of the ducky birthday party that lovely Naomi is throwing for your bratty sons."

"I don't understand, Nora."

"So you don't understand." Her voice was insolent. "Then I'll be more than glad to explain." She used a descending, boorish tone. "You surely remember David, Doctor? And you'll not deny that he's yours and my child and that he's only six months younger than the famous twins at Catawba."

"No, no. Let's just keep quiet."

"That's just it, I've kept quiet too long. When David was born you urged me to blame it on William Shams, because he was a young single man and you were married—that I did to shield you. Oh, I was a fool to listen to your mealy-mouthed, salivating words, but I had ambition. I thought I could get you." Regret crept into her voice. "I can't change what's been done, but Doctor, you mark my words, I most certainly can steer the boat from here on and you're going to help me.

"David wasn't invited to that party at Catawba for this afternoon. He was the only child left out here on North Philadelphia Street. So, Doctor, you're going to see that he's invited. I can't help it that he looks so much like your Victor. He's just as much yours as Victor is and he's every right in the world to go to that party. To take spite out on an innocent child is too much for me. So you're going right back to Catawba and see that that stinking, churchgoing, hypocritical Naomi invites him."

Jumping up, she crossed the room. "Moreover, I'm not selling my mill shares to you or to anyone else. If you think their value will increase, it'll increase for me as well as anyone else."

"Nora, Nora, calm yourself. You're getting wrought up—"

"Wrought up, my foot. David is my child and I'm fighting for him. Do you understand? Let me tell you, you'd better see from now on that David's put on equal footing with Jake and Vic."

"Nora, Nora—"

"Shut up, don't you be Nora-ing me. When I think of what a fool I was over an old codger like you—" She walked to the mantel, leaned against it. "Well, Doctor, I'm not blaming you for what happened. I'm not that kind of woman. I let you do what you did. I at least wasn't raped, as so many of your Southern belles are—"

"Nora, you shouldn't try to impose your Northern ideas upon the South—"

"Of all the smelly goats there are in this town, you win the prize for being the most stinking. Years ago, when Grandfather and I first came here, you were very much interested in Northern ideas —or was it chiefly the Southern exposure that took your gleaming eye?" She threw out her hands in a helpless gesture. "Doctor, let's not bicker over the good old bygones. I hold nothing against you. I threw all my cards upon the table and lost. I'm not complaining. Now that Grandfather has gone, all his money is invested here and left to me, I've no intentions of selling out and running away. Why should I run? I've done nothing but have a normal healthy child! Everything here that I have someday goes to David and you're going to see that he's treated decently."

Going to the door, opening it wide, she stood aside, holding it. "Now go on home to that sweet Naomi of yours and tell her you were called to see me and that I had the smallpox, because I don't want her running up here with any of her descending visiting."

Old Doc ambled through the doorway.

"Remember, Doctor, what I said about David." She laughed teasingly, "Come back to see me sometime. I've better days. You remember?"

4

This morning, Vic thought, was the love feast of his life. Today was his birthday. What an age!

He climbed until he was higher than tall, domineering Catawba. He saw the town sleeping at the foot of the hill, hating another workday. He looked at the untiring river curving through mist. He beheld Big Bertha whose hot chimney ever smoked. He saw the lonely moon sinking in a mist. All over the watershed of the red land, as far as his eyes could see, he beheld the beauty of the approaching day.

It was cool in the top of the oak with the damply chilled breeze blowing over his naked body. It was doubtful whether anyone could find him here. If he were found, there'd be more tattling talk. He excited people enough as it was. He could twist his head sideways, say nothing, look at folks impudently, and make them fighting mad.

"Vic, you come down outta that tree this instant," squawked Mama Amazon, peering up among the leafy-crowded branches. "I ain't got time to fool wit you. Ho'cum you didn't answer me the many times I's called? Havin me an Gee an Yellow Sam runnin all over creation, hollerin us heads off—an here you sets in the tiptop of the biggest oak in the yard. Did you crawl out you window to get there? Enty know you haves a party fo this afternoon?"

Vic climbed down into her sight.

"Gawd have mercy," she laughed, "you ain't got one rag on.

Is you losed you mind? Out here naked as a woodsy animal. Them low-country yappers see you out here wit'out any clothes on they'll fall in a dead faint. Get in the house an get some clothes on an you can go wit Yellow Sam into Green Pond."

Yellow Sam and Vic hurried toward the center of Green Pond, Sam shuffling his feet in the dry dust, swinging his rump that looked disjointed and too high-placed, singing the blues about the yaller gal and the big red rose. Victor trotted to keep up with Yellow Sam's speedy, swinging gait. Right downtown on North Philadelphia Street he was to leave a written message at Miz Nora Kingsley's house and then go on to the office of the Green Pond *Observer* to leave the write-up of the party that Miz Naomi was very anxious to have come out in this week's newspaper.

Coming before Miz Nora Kingsley's stately residence on North Philadelphia Street, Yellow Sam told Vic to stay at the iron gate until he went up on the veranda to deliver the message. Vic leaned on the gate waiting. While waiting, a boy about his size came around the house and down the walk. When Vic first saw him, his eyes widened in astonishment: that boy resembled him to a startling degree. How come that?

"What's your name?"

"Vic."

"Vic. That's a funny ole name. My name is David Kingsley. I've been afar, staying with my aunt, and just come home last week. Where do you live? This's my house here. I'm going to a party this afternoon, so I heard Mother say. Are you going to the party?"

But before Vic could answer there was Yellow Sam ready to come through the gate and he and Vic went up the street.

"Yellow Sam," asked Vic when they were out of hearing, "Ho'cum that boy looks so much like me?"

"Does you think that boy looks like you? What makes you think so?" Yellow Sam, like most of the Negroes in Green Pond, had an uncanny way of finding out the white folks' secret lives.

"Yes, I do," Vic stated positively. "When he first came around the house, I thought he was me."

Yellow Sam told Vic that he was getting to be a big boy and there were lots of strange things he was going to find out about people.

The reason he and that boy back there at Miz Kingsley's house looked so much alike was because they had the same daddy and that both of them had taken their looks after their daddy. Miz Nora Kingsley had grown David in her belly and Miz Naomi had grown him in her belly. Vic wanted to know all the minute details. The more Yellow Sam told him, the more he questioned.

Suddenly Vic blurted out, "That's nasty." He spat upon the ground, feeling a queasiness in his stomach.

"Oh, you just feels that way about em now," Yellow Sam laughed teasingly. "When you gets mo bigger an you stones swells up some mo, you'll be just lack a lil boar pig runnin loose."

When they left the Green Pond *Observer's* office, Jepson and Ossie Grady stood in the doorway watching them go down the street.

"So," said Jep to Ossie, "that's one of Ole Doc's yard chillun?"

Folks said that Jepson Grady resembled Old Doc too much, had ways like him, and ought to have been a bird dog because he had such a good nose for ferreting things out of the grass, and that his twin sister, Ossie Grady, ought to have been born a little fyste dog, since she was always yelping and scratching fleas.

Jepson, tall like a sapling, lanky like a vine—his news was always like tendrils—never talked if he could listen. In a roughish way he was decidedly handsome, appearing indifferent, yet hearing and seeing plenty, and for proof the citizens had to do nothing more than read the Green Pond *Observer*, which they did, scrutinizing it meticulously, wondering why such and such a thing ever got into the weekly newspaper. Ossie was a clever soul, flouncing and bouncing as grease in too hot a skillet.

And their newspaper was Green Pond's heart, pumping the

life-giving blood down its streets, through its alleys, out its by-ways, over its dusty, bumpy roads twenty-four hours a day. It kept a strong pulse at the wrist, at the temporal, at the heel, beating, hammering—as a hammer on a white-hot plowshare.

5

Sometime that summer Victor found Ole Doc's tucked-away medical books and he opened the books, opening a door into a new world. He couldn't make head or tail of all the words, but the pictures excited him to new interests—a nettling curiosity. He'd have to learn all those big words so that he might know all about the pictures. There was a stern man with the whole side of his face and mouth torn away. What did it say? Cancer of the lip? What was cancer? He looked at the suture needles, the twisted suture. There was the dislocation of the elbow, of the shoulder. There the flesh was laid open on that woman's neck; look at the needles with threads stuck in them! What did it say: T-U-M-O-R? He spelled it out. What did it mean? There was a man with a bloaty bag under his chin larger than his head. It was another tumor!

Biding his time, there was no need to hurry, no use to rush, he had all today and all the night if needed. He lugged all the books to an unused room on the third floor and there he spent his time wandering through them, picking out the things that interested him most.

Going to and from his trysting place, he did a great deal of hiding from the grownups, his own family and a houseful of summer visitors. Catawba swarmed with Mama Naomi's relatives. Some were fat and dragged heavy rattling skirts over the rich carpet, and some were skinny with wasplike waists and cackled like wet hens, their laughter ringing, bell-like, from hallway to hallway. The only times they were quiet were when they had their feet under the dining-room table and then it was never exactly quiet, because they made a great deal of noise crunching on chicken bones and exclaiming over Ole Doc's rich food. When their talkative and laborious feasting came to an end, the piles of chicken bones would be so high in front of their plates that they could hardly see one another to carry on their gibberish chatter.

Pop didn't take so kindly to Mama Naomi's relatives eating up so much of his enriched rations. He declared to himself and to Victor, in one of their secret and secluded moments, that he believed they simply came up here in the summertime to fatten up so that they'd not have to eat much during the winter. Work was a menial and disagreeable task to these proud people who carried deep grudges and hates from one generation to another. Their gibes were sharper than their teeth. The only reason they didn't fall to fighting among themselves here in Catawba was because he kept them so full of heavy food that they could hardly breathe from one meal to another. They were short-winded and doggedly opinionated.

Their great Aunt Tiffy had a gleam in her eyes and had had one ever since the close of the War Between the States. Her fellow had been killed in the battle of Gettysburg and she had become so angry at the Northern army for killing him that she had jumped into a cheese hoop of eggs, which she was saving during the war to make her wedding cakes, and jumped up and down until she had smashed every egg—that, Old Doc thought, was getting the North told in no uncertain terms. She fought the battle of Gettysburg once a year all over her place; she was getting wrinkled and cracked, but she'd be able to fight the battle of Gettysburg for years to come.

Biding his time, there was no need to hurry, no rush, he had all today and all the night if needed. In his trysting place with the big medical books, Vic began slowly and tediously to unravel the fascinating mysteries that were hid in them. He had all the time he wanted, because Budda was away in the fields and Jake had so much elegant talk to do to the relatives that his day was filled.

When Vic could catch Pop off to himself, which was rare since he had so many irons in the fire he hardly knew whether he was coming or going, he'd amaze Ole Doc with some astonishing questions about medicine. Pop would stop for the moment and scratch his head, wondering where the boy was getting so much information, and then good-naturedly chide the boy with some quip that sent him back to the medical books to probe more diligently, scratch himself, and mumble.

6

Autumn came with its disagreeable school and not a speck of hope in sight for the forlorn Vic, who dragged his weary self back to the miserable schoolhouse, there to be shut up, to be buried. To be shut up when a gossamer mist beckoned from every hill, when the laughing rioting colors came tumbling down, froze the sunlight within him. He felt unadmirably tainted in his middle. The swallows had flown from Catawba. The goose-picking time and the fruit-drying time at Catawba had folded up until another summer.

One morning he stopped by the Ives garden, admiring Mrs. Ives's chrysanthemums that were wrapped in icy dew, and there he saw a bird taking a bath atop one of the huge blooms. The bird stretched out full length, ruffled her feathers, turned over and over, getting herself as good and clean as Mama Amazon used to get his ears and neck. He leaned on the fence, looked at the bird so long that he completely forgot about school and for a brief moment Gawd stood there with him and all creation and all eternity stood still.

Vic came down to earth, realizing where he was and where he was supposed to go. But he couldn't face Miss Lizzie Newcome's crabby schoolhouse now nor would he be tied down or hemmed in. He looked about. If he fled fast enough, he could be out of sight and no one would see him. Once he reached the woods, no one'd find him and there for the day he could enjoy himself, because it'd be fresh-smelling and not noisome as the kids in school.

He hid his books in a stump hole, ate a mouthful of lunch from his pail, and stuffed the pail into the hole with the books. He wanted no cumbersome burdens. He elf-danced into the woods, throwing his legs high into the air; each time a foot came up he smacked himself on his belly with it and clapped his hands above his head. Tired of this he turned handwheels, spinning down the woodland trail. At the creek, he pulled off his shoes and long stockings and waded in the water, now blue with the sting of autumn. He caught a crayfish, turning it over and over in his hands, studying it carefully, then gently let it back into the water, watching it use its tail fin as a rudder. He soaked up the woodland beauty until he grew tired, then he curled up in a sunny spot and fell asleep.

It wasn't Miss Lizzie Newcome who used the hickory that night, it was Ole Doc.

And not long after Victor fell heir presumptive to the rosewood piano in Catawba, hyphenizing Jezebel and Catawba almost as easily as he fell heir to so many lickings.

This was brought about by Naomi and Cora trying to out-oh-ah each other or, as Mama Amazon put it, outshine. Naomi, while unmusical and caring nothing for music, wanted, actually she craved, the rosewood piano for Catawba's upper parlor to flaunt Cora Mathis, because of the burdensome church yoke Cora had so cunningly hung about her neck. So she bedeviled Ole Doc until he took her to Rahab and got it.

Now Cora, seeing the piano shining in Catawba, hereby turned almost into a heretic—at least, a good mischievous, churchly sprite. She beshook her brain for ways and means of having some connection with that piano. So she came to Naomi

for the good of the church, saying that Jezebel needed music lessons and a piano for practice in order that God's house shouldn't
suffer for sweet sound when her days were over pumping the
wheezing organ. Cora's house was too small to harbor such a monstrosity as a piano: thus wheedled the overzealous, crafty Cora
poco più animato.

Naomi, punctured flat, gave in so quickly, permitting Jezebel
the use of the upper parlor every afternoon after school, that Cora
scratched her thighs, thinking up some reluctant acceptance. So
she slyly suggested that Naomi's boys should study the piano.

Naomi thought it dreadful that boys play the piano, never
heard of such a thing: their big awkward fingers on those delicate
notes! But Cora insisted, tittered behind her fan, so glad to
salve her conscience.

Once the piano lesson was under way, little mousy Miss Waters
was amazed at Vic. His relaxation at the keyboard was astonishing; it welled from something deep within him, the firm hard
touch in the tips of his fingers brought out the singing quality in
the tones. She showed him how to keep his hands ball-shaped.
He must learn to spread his fingers so that as he grew older he
could reach far beyond an octave. She was so glad that she had a
boy taking music. All the great pianists were men. All the great
composers were men. She counted along for him, "One-lee, two-
lee, three-lee, four-lee." Relax, she cautioned him over and over,
emphasizing the word by nudging his elbow. Make the tones
sing deep within. No, no, he must never *strike* the pianoforte
keyboard. He must *attack.* Singing tones. Watch his fingering carefully. Accuracy was the first point in good pianoforte playing.

Vic ate it up, but to Jake and to Jezebel it was very distasteful.
Jezebel practiced with the boys, as Cora had arranged, and had
plenty of time for other things besides. The rosewood piano was
left to Vic, and Jezebel and Jake dawdled their tune away. This
parlor held a great gold chair that fascinated Jezebel. It had lion
heads on its arms and its back and here she spent the greatest

share of her practice time. It was like a throne, and she felt like a queen sitting in it.

The thing that spoiled her throne was that Vic. Of all the boys she knew, and she was now definitely boy conscious, Vic was the most fascinating. She felt drawn to him as metal to a magnet. If he were here at her feet, her cup would certainly be full. How was she to get him? He paid her not as much mind as he did a brickbat in the back of the fireplace. He kept his back to her, his head bent forward, playing the piano.

Jake was easily obtainable. He could already kiss almost as well as David Kingsley, but so far his kissing had not affected her as David Kingsley's had. She yearned to know how Vic would kiss.

There had been a time she thought he was going to kiss her, so she had her mouth willing and waiting and he had slipped away, fooling her so much that she actually blushed. Someday she'd get him; he couldn't always be so elusive. In the meantime she'd play along with Jake.

To Cora's shocking amazement Miss Waters informed her one day that she couldn't teach Jezebel; the child had the peculiar talent of playing by ear. There was no need in wasting time giving her lessons. Miss Waters was very sorry about the matter, but Jezebel's condition couldn't be helped.

Now that their love for one another knew no bounds, Cora came dashing to Naomi with the news about Jezebel. Cora's face was tear-stained. But Naomi thought it was wonderful to be able to play by ear like Jezebel. God had sent her an unusual gift. God had great plans for Jezebel. Through Jezebel He would probably prosper the work of North Bethel. It was divine, a divine gift!

7

Jezebel had to give up her afternoons in Catawba and there was nothing much left for her to do but sit at home and listen to the disgruntling of Pa and Ma.

Beyond Green Pond, across many red hillets, was the T-square, four-room house of John Mathis. Old John was as soddy as the overbold earth—salty too, if he was rundown at the heels. He reminded everybody, at the oddest times, that the T-square house and the eighteen acres of land upon which it snuggled low to the earth were his.

However, Miz Cora, biting and shrapnel-piercing, pointed out to him daily that it wasn't paid for—in fact, if it were not for her raspy, panic-pulsing work and her ever-haggling him, he'd never keep the interest paid.

"John Mathis, look at this kitchen. If you had as much gumption as a goose, you'd have it ceiled. These old blackened two-by-fours and joists, sticking out with greasy ham bones and side meat hung about on them! There's no place for Jezebel to have company. Why I ever let myself get tied to such a ninny as you, behooves me. When I could have continued teaching and made something of myself."

"Now, Coree, look in yander at the two front rooms: they've got plastered walls and that's where you're supposed to have company. People ain't supposed to have company in their back-houses. Jezebel can have all the company going right in there. You're supposed to have meat in a kitchen, Coree. Meat in a kitchen looks good. Iffen you've plenty of meat an bread you don't need nothin else. Come on, Coree, put your rat-killins on the table. That skillet of side meats's rarin with a smell."

"Oh, you fatuous imp. Here I am, hamstrung to old smelly he-goat you. I'll say, company in the backhouse. John Mathis, you know your smelly eighteen acres of land has never hazarded a backhouse since you've been on it. No wonder I got copper-head-bit that time out there squatting in the tall weeds. You'd been glad had I died. And I'll have you understand that every stitch of furniture in the two plastered front rooms is mine. I taught school and paid for that. You're not going to get it, either. I've a will made, John Mathis. Then see what you sleep on. Lying upon my good feather bed snoozing. No wonder you never want to get up in the morning."

"I was tired after the war and then five years in a durned Yankee prison a-freezin to death and eatin cooked housecat —though they billed it as rabbit—"

"Shut up, John Mathis, I don't want to hear that—General Lee and the Atlanta Constitution is all I hear out of you—morning, noon, night. The Inchurches went through that little old war: look what they have. Why don't you have the gumption to get out and do something like they do? No little war ever got them down in the mouth—the Lord helps them that help themselves."

John swore. "Them Inchurches is crooked—every dad-blamed last one of them. And that Robert now: he's just born crooked —the way he's all scrouched up."

"At least," Cora Mathis snapped, "Robert is an elder in the North Bethel Church now and he ought to have you churched. It's been a good bit since you've been churched and I'm going to turn you up now right early. You just watch me and see."

Jezebel sat at the oilcloth-covered table listening to their pin-pricking impeachments winking on and off as a firefly's light. She was never understandably concerned or made any effort to ferret out their troubles, for she was too interested in dig-ging from each the favors each was most capable of granting. Pa'd turn his pockets wrongside-out and give her his last nickel, though it was seldom nickels were there. He'd brighten her gloom when Ma thrashed her for not getting her lessons, and if she scurried to him fast enough, she could usually hamper the whipping. But aside from these two favors, he was sadly lacking. Ma saw that she had new hair ribbons and got to do as she pleased in the complicated innards of the intricately controlled Presbyterian Church, and she learned the technical know-hows early in life.

Nobody needed to tell Jezebel that she was beautiful, for she was the image of Ma. And Ma was the best-looking woman that walked into North Bethel. Jezebel knew that her blend was as singularly effective as Cora's.

Why Ma ever married Pa she didn't know. He was an incurable old clown who anticked up even when he was churched and did everything all too casual. It did look as if, with the beauty that Ma had clotted about her, she could have done better in picking a husband.

And she thought of Victor, and eternal spring welled up within her and the joyous paradise it spread before her was unimaginable. But it was so seldom he touched her. Oh, the earth possessed only one Victor Thornwell. So true a loadstone he was to her, so singular, that sometimes it did not matter whether he ever touched her or not. And that was remarkable for Jezebel!

8

Now there was an evening, a cold winter evening of wind and clouds and Vic leaned on Catawba's gate and looked up at the clouds in the evening sky and visualized Gawd chastising ole Satan.

GAWD: I'm mighty tirt of you vexin em Presbyterians, Satan. I'm gonna have to bring you down a notch or two, ole boy, else chain you some of these days in the bye an bye.

BEELZEBUB: Tee hee, haw-haw.

SATAN: Quit you laughin, you dung-rollin beetle.

GAWD: I despises uppitiness in chillun, breeded or unbreeded.

GABRIEL: Yah, Satan, ho'cum you's allus carryin along that lil jug of corn likker?

SATAN: Needs to quench my thirst. Sumpin fo my parchin tongue.

GABRIEL: Next thing, you'll be smokin!

SATAN: Smokin! Not hot as that fire is!

BEELZEBUB: Gawd, You know a big weddin's brewin in ole Green Pond?

GAWD: I wish youse'd be less nosey. I ain't made up my mind bout that weddin yet.

7

If the dying of autumn filled Vic with an uncanny devotion to the spiritual, the first white frost of winter set the little unknown wheel within him spinning so rapidly that his nerves tingled as Christmas bells. Joy abounded in every brown blade of grass, in every leaf that gave up the ghost and floated tranquilly to the earth, in all pines and berried hollies reigning royally in winter's splendor, in the gnarled limbs that reached into the blue praying.

He skidded through the frosted fields before daylight when the decanting moon slipped down the western pathway roiled with its night's journey, to check his rabbit boxes by mossed rail fences, along brown hedgerows and in wooded patches, and occasionally he got a rabbit to drop into his ever-ready sack. He wheeled the red land of the watershed for more joy and he was consistently and frankly happy with the commonplace.

After the piano practice on Saturdays, he wandered with intuitive skill, searching hollow trees for owls, squirrels, possums and, if perchance the hole was the home of one, he twisted and screwed the varmint out of its home with a forked stick and carried it back to the pens where he kept his caged animals and birds—his patients; and he ever studied them and was ready at the drop of a hat to administer to their ailments. He stroked their fur or feathers, he studied their anatomy and their habits. It was inborn in him.

He lived in utter terror of Mama Amazon killing and eating some of them. She bedeviled him, "A good fat possum'd be the thing fo Sat'day night's supper. Rabbit sausages make my mouth pure water lack a river. Squirrel brains an dumplins is the best goin."

Vic made a beeline to the cages first thing in the morning and first thing after school, fervently checking them. "There'd better not be one of my patients gone." He guarded them jealously.

Only laughed at him continually. "Boy, that's ho'cum you hair grows so long, so you kin ketch the woodsy things?"

The astonished boy, his face scratched and marked with the claws and beaks of the creatures, answered, "Laugh all you wantta. I like em."

Only dried the laughter from his face soberly; his mind took on a philosophical mood. "You can't go far wrong when you lives wit the creatures of the woods as you does. You'll be all right, hon."

December's bespewed ice and besprinkled frost covered everything in the mornings. The invigorating air made Vic want to draw in two breaths simultaneously. He loved the sharp tang of the frosted red land.

Only and Yellow Sam awoke Vic by four o'clock with their laughing and talking as they built the roaring fires preceding the hog-killing. By the time he had jumped from his bed, slithered into his scanty clothes on the run, called to sleepy-headed Jake, raced down the stairs and out to the fires, the first four hogs were killed, lying with the blood running from their cut throats before the scalding barrels.

When frosty dawn arrived, the fat hogs, scalded and scraped hairless, hung on a hickory pole ready for Yellow Sam to take the butcher knife and gut them.

Snotty-nosed Budda shivered by the fire. He kept his nose wiped with his sleeve, complained of his eyes turning watery red from so much smoke. He had brought along a cane, cut from the creek bank, to blow the pigs' bladders into balloons to dry for Christmas.

Mama Amazon came from the house with her dishpans, pails, and knives and looked the situation over critically.

The defty fingers worked swiftly. Only ran to the fire often to warm his fingers; grumbled that he wished the sun'd come up toreckly. It was going to be the middle of the day before this white frost got away. Mama Amazon declared it was fine weather to kill hogs; the moon was just right so that she could get every drop of grease out of the cracklins. If hogs were killed in the wrong time of the moon, the sausages'd not fry out right, they'd swell up in the pan; perhaps give a body all sorts of pains if eaten. She was gonna store these sausages in corn shucks; and Lawd, the eatins they were gonna have.

Mama Amazon wanted to save all the chitt'lins and the paunches, lights, melts, and feet. White folks were a sinful and wasteful lot. They'd throw the best parts of the hog away. This meat'd warm a body through and through to the bone. What greater happiness could one have on earth than to have a full belly, to feel drowsy, and to sit talking by a warm fire while the rigors of winter's night pawed at the house's boards trying to get in?

Vic loved her and he listened intently and with huge curiosity to Mama Amazon's philosophical talk. It comforted him, it calmed him as no earthly opiate could. Here with her, relishing her untroubled utterances, he had no other desires on earth. If anything went wrong between heaven and hell, she knew how to fix it. Long ago, if the day was cloudy and the sun didn't shine and he cried to her that the sun'd never rise, she consoled him, "Hon, that sun's been up. It's cloudy up there and you can't see em. The day you don't see that sun come up, that'll be the Judgment Day and you had better be ready an waitin, fo you Lawd'll be comin fo to carry you home."

2

Vic soaked the cold from his fingers in hot water until well-limbered, then he crept into the upper parlor and silently slid upon the piano bench. It wasn't his time to practice, but since it was Christmas Eve, the time of peace on earth and good will toward everything, his playing wouldn't be considered too objectionable. What was the piano for, if not to be played? Jake didn't practice enough to know his lesson when that time rolled around. No one cared for the piano but him and he was usually denied it—and that piano was a part of him. He'd stay at its keyboard all day if he were not driven from it.

Vic picked out a motif he'd heard Yellow Sam singing the other night on his way to prayers at Cryin John and worked it over, varying it from one key to another. It sounded as Christmas music.

When Vic first started playing, Pop looked at Naomi and they both looked at him, but neither said anything and turned back to their reading. Now Pop came toward the piano. "Son, what's that you're playing?"

"I don't know," Vic replied. "Sumpin I like."

"I thought you had to know what you played before you could play it."

"I know, but it don't have a name. How can I tell what it is iffen it don't have a name? You can't see the things inside my head. You ain't that good a doctor."

"No, I can't see the things inside your head, but that tune is familiar. I've heard it all my life. Anyone that's heard it would never forget it. It's something I remember hearing the Negroes sing when I was a boy. I remember hearing them sing it at night when they'd be going somewhere. Hear that same song you're playing here on the piano. It ought to have a name."

Vic looked at Pop. Who'd ever thought that Pop had heard a tune when he was a boy and could still remember it? "Yes, sir; it should have a name but I'd not know what to call it. I heard Yellow Sam singing it the other night on his way to Cryin John for the prayers. I don't think there're words good enough to name it. It has too much loneliness in it." Vic dropped his head. What was he doing talking this way to Pop? Pop'd not understand.

For a moment Ole Doc fought tears in his eyes, thinking it'd never do to let the boy see tears in his eyes. So that boy sitting there on the piano bench was his son. Sure a very part of his being. He'd not die when he died, but he'd live on in the heart of Vic who was sensitive enough to reach out into something mysterious for that fragile tune and remake it here on the rosewood piano. The thousands of times he'd heard it, how it lingered in his mind. He conjured up his mama, Joanna; her dying voice flooded him, "Tad, boy, don't you forget me. Listen to me, son—you listen. I'm going, but I'll live on in your heart and I'll not die. I'll never, never die!" Had she?

While Pop meditated, Vic slipped out of the upper parlor. Ole Doc suddenly realized he was alone by the piano. How'd the boy slipped so sprightly away without his seeing him go? It was uncanny. But the boy had always been uncanny and when he was gone there was an emptiness, a vacancy in the room that was terrorizing to Ole Doc. He had felt, the few moments that he stood there by the piano talking to Vic, that he lived in some ethereal world that was peopled with absolute goodness. The light coming from the fire, falling on Naomi with her eternal reading of the Holy Scriptures, intensified it.

Ole Doc moved across the room, his hands in his pockets, stood before the fire, pulled his pants tight across his buttocks, warming that part of his anatomy.

"Did you hear Victor at the piano?" he asked Naomi, gazing profoundly at the solitariness of the piano keys.

She raised her head slowly from the great Bible, looked in a daze at him. "Who could miss it? Victor slips in here and bangs too much at that piano as it is. I believe I'm going to have to lock it to keep him off. I'm sure he'll ruin the finish on it and I'd not have that happen for the world."

"But you should have listened and took in his playing just now. It'd have made everything in your Holy Scriptures look sick."

"Doctor! You say the most ghastly things. I'd be ashamed to even have such a thought, much less to utter it."

"Naomi, I doubt seriously whether you get the full meaning and great depth and beauty out of your Bible reading—though I know you diligently strive to. We simply don't have the ability to grasp it. I know I don't."

She drew herself up with goatly dignity and spoke in a severe voice, "Doctor, I knew you were an old man when I married you, but I had no idea you were a crazy one."

"Unruffle your feathers, my dear." A twinkle impishly played at the corners of his eyes. "You fly to conclusions too soon. Jump at the ending without knowing anything about the beginning or the middle. At the best, you and I and all the lot of us are mere one- and two-talent people. We're not the thing— the five-talent, that's rare—that people remember. We're like common days, not the hottest or the coldest which is so easily remembered, but common days hooked one onto the other with nothing outstanding about us. There're millions like us. It has always been that way since creation began. But if you'd heard Victor play that wistful tune just now, you might have some inkling of what I'm talking about. He has grasped something that's of an infinite world. I don't know a thing about music. I'm sixty years old; I've lived long enough to know and fully appreciate that man doesn't live by bread alone."

"Well, are you through?" Naomi sighed faintly. "Or have you run out of wind and waiting for another breeze? I'm sorry I ever let the boys start to studying piano. Jake would drop it tomorrow, but Vic torments the daylights out of me practicing —why in the world Cora ever suggested such a thing—" She stopped abruptly, looked at her hands and Bible lying in her lap. "Do you know one thing?"

"What could it be that I don't know?"

"I'm quite innocently beginning to catch on to Cora Mathis. Forbid that I should ever stoop to gossip about her, but—well, Cora's real reason for wanting Jezebel to study music in the first place was simply to throw her into more contact with Jake and Vic. I've caught on to her. She's using her church wisely!"

Ole Doc dropped into the chair by the corner of the hearth, stretched his legs out to the fire, letting the heat soak into his feet. He studied the cheery fire while his mind raced back over the years. So now Cora was wanting to get Jezebel into Catawba? He counted the number of them there had been in his day. There must be something about the house that attracted women as molasses did flies. What was its secret sweetness?

"What's made you so quiet?" Naomi asked.

"I was thinking of the tune Vic played. I remember hearing it sixty years ago; and tonight was the first time I ever heard it played on an instrument."

"My goodness! I can't see what's in Victor's silly playing that'd make you mope like this."

Ole Doc dreamed again. "Let's see . . . Vic's fourteen? Time he's getting gals on his mind."

"Don't you put that into his head," Naomi demurred. "He'll get that way soon enough. Why, Jake was trying to shave himself this evening, with your razor, too. You ought to have heard those colored girls teasing him."

"They have to grow up. There's no standing still. One must move on. That's in the plan, in God's plan."

Naomi sniffed. The Doctor was a good one to talk about God's plans, when he'd only just spoken so scornfully of the very Bible itself as he had.

3

March was steadfast, seemingly trustworthy; the days were warmly bright with drying winds. The nights were lazily warm. Folks rushed with their gardens, the ground was plenty warm to sprout the tiny seeds. The plows turned the red earth from sunup to sundown. The fragrant aroma of newly broadcast manure floated over the county in the humid night air.

From Catawba's kitchen door, Mama Amazon watched Yellow Sam drive Ole Doc and Naomi to the Inchurch funeral. "Fo true," she said to Vic, whose gangly legs were wrapped about a tree in the yard, "that's goin to be some powerful funeral."

"Let's go watch em go into the church," Vic urged, knowing she was itching all over to go.

"You's fixin fo Ole Doc to bust you wide open. Know you mama done tolt you to stay here an behave. Been ramblin all mornin because of no school on account of respect fo Mr. Inchurch. Where's you been?"

"Pecan Lane, where they're goin to put ole man Inchurch."

"Better say Mr. Inchurch; respect the dead!"

"I never liked that ole man."

"Ought to respect he, because he was a vastness in that North Bethel Church."

"Yah," Vic scoffed. "I saw him once, leerin ugly, beatin a frightened fyste out of church—beat it wit a broomstick—and the lil dog was only scared of the thunderstorm. I think Inchurch had a wormy soul."

"Hon, you's a case, a heavy case."

"Let's hurry so we won't miss nothin. Hide in the honeysuckle thicket across from the church."

"Iffen I goes an Ole Doc ketches you—Been over a month since you got a good thrashin. It's just back here in February Ole Doc caught you an thrashed you fo birthin that cow. But Lawdy, you arms went pure up in that cow to you elbows an you turned that calf's feet first so he could get into this ole world. Saved the cow and calf, too; but Lawdy, Ole Doc pure tore you up."

But Mama Amazon's heart was always with Vic's and they went.

Mr. Inchurch, while angrily foreclosing a mortgage on Cyrus Hill's rundown, gully-washed farm, suddenly had grasped both hands over his chest. He'd ceased to think and to talk of the notes due, of the mortgages to foreclose, of the money he loved. Deep within him there was a pain that he couldn't understand. All his life he'd reached out getting whatever he wanted and now there was this monstrous pain he could do nothing with. It was devouring him in its hungry jaws. He tried to reach back, to grasp, to hold on, but to no avail, for the hungry jaws had him. Surely, surely his God hadn't sent this. The God he knew yonder in North Bethel wouldn't visit this terrorizing pain upon him—not him, an Inchurch.

Now Green Pond was properly draped in sorrow.

Mama Amazon and Vic were snugly hid in the honeysuckle thicket long before Uncle Cy began to toll North Bethel's big bell. They saw the hearse with its glittering sides of glass, its heavy velvet black curtains, and its sparkling brassy knobs sticking flashily upon its four corners pull into sight. The two colored drivers, dressed in somber black with white gloves and tall silk hats, sat up on top of the hearse driving the four black-tasseled horses. Never in her life had Mama Amazon seen that hearse pulled by four horses or polished and shined as it was this day. Lovebird and Lovebird were stepping about. They wouldn't have any trouble collecting for this job. Sometimes Lovebird had trouble with po' folks and niggers. If payment didn't come purty soon, Lovebird'd slip out to the house of the deceased at night and draw a coffin in the sandy walkway and then it'd not be many days until the folks'd rush in with the money.

In a few more hours, D.D. Inchurch would be cemented into that fine brick sarcophagus in Pecan Lane. He might think he was resting securely with the heavy stone slab pulled into place over him, but once Mama Amazon had seen a sarcophagus that the rats had burrowed into, the snakes sliding right behind. So with pecan roots to help the rats out in Pecan Lane, they'd soon make a rhapsody out of his sarcophagus, because Gawd was no more respecter of the important than he was of her—the whites' heads had to lie low as the blacks'.

Life was a circle. It was like the tiny buds puffing out of the naked trees in the springtime and then the trees naked again when the next winter came. Life was a circle. Part of the time was spent in sleeping in the warm and comforting grave and part of the time preparing to go to it. Time would move on. There'd be many warm south March winds blowing softly and kindly over Pecan Lane and the brick sarcophagus of Mr. D.D. Inchurch, because one could do nothing with that which was predetermined.

4

Miz Cora Mathis had hired Uncle Prince Blue to pump wind into the new Moeller pipe organ for the dedicatory services being held in North Bethel and had given him bony Katie Lou to ride.

Wearing a long green overcoat in July, Uncle Blue chortled portentously to the old mule as he clambered astride her bony backbone, knowing she'd cut his buttocks smack-dab half in two.

Victor and Mama Amazon were in Catawba's back yard when Uncle Blue passed by and Mama Amazon spoke with fancy mockery, "Goin to pump wind into the organ, enty, Uncle Blue?"

"Iffen Katie Lou don't break down wit me."

"Katie Lou breakin down or no breakin down, you'd better have plenty-fitten wind in that organ, else Miz Cora'll wind you."

Already Uncle Prince Blue heard the church bells in Green Pond cutting up a to-do. None of them rang as powerful as that new North Bethel bell. The Baptist bell, a block away from the Presbyterian bell, sang out like a fyste, "Shall we gather at the river?" And the big Presbyterian bell boomed like a big bulldog, "No, not one." The Presbyterians, being on very much higher ground than the Baptists, knew full well they had the start on the Baptist in a sight-race to Jesus beyond the shining blue. It took a mighty heap of tramping, tramping to make heaven their home.

Ah, Lawd, he was going to pump wind into an organ to save the sorry white folks' souls. The hellhounds were already after them and it was doubtful whether wind in an organ would keep them away. White folks were a strange, sinful lot. Restless, discontented souls. They tried hard to hide from Gawd's wrath, but Gawd had His eyes upon them, eventually He'd mow them down, and there'd be no use reaching back grabbing.

After hiding Katie Lou in a brambly thicket, as Cora had instructed him, Uncle Blue met Uncle Cy at the church door and the old fellers moseyed down the church aisle.

"You keep wind in that organ fo Miz Cora, you'll pull that long green overcoat off," tittered Uncle Cy.

"They do say she's a vast power at the organ."

"Power! You don't know nothin! Go on an get behint the organ an be ready. I got to get the dust offen these great curved pews fo the white ladies gets it on they bottoms."

"I expect lots of fine white ladies is got dust on they bottoms an can't nobody see em."

With Vic at her heels, Mama Amazon bustled up into North Bethel's new balcony, dying with curiosity to know what the new preacher looked like. The last preacher hadn't stayed long enough for the pot to boil, because he and Miz Cora had had a run-in. Cora had unflinchingly accused him of keeping her off one certain social committee and he'd rebuked her, charging her with thinking too much of her personal gains and not enough of the church. She snatched his tail feathers and he fled. Then Miz Cora had come to Ole Doc, wailing, an array of extravagant tears rolling down her cheeks, and Ole Doc had consoled her in what Mama Amazon thought were too endearing terms. She'd never been able to figure out Ole Doc and Miz Cora—sumpin twixt em.

After sitting down, Mama Amazon said, "Gonna kick off my shoes an rest my foots. Doubts iffen I get em back on wit'out a slipper-spoon. Shorely lacks to rest my foots. Sunday was jest naturally made fo rest an church."

"Yon Miz Elvira Inchurch," said Yellow Sam, slipping beside Mama Amazon. "Married herself a fine No'then husband—Pawtucket, Rhode Island—I hear say."

"Erah—she's Miz Dodge now. Say she feathered she nest. Inchurches is allus had money, holds to it, an marries mo."

Vic let his eyes rove over the congregation slowly and he

spotted Jake sitting with Jezebel two seats from the organ. He saw Jake was holding her hand—her very hot hand—giving it little pumping squeezes. Vic could easily feel Jezebel's hot hand; he knew how her hot hands felt when she ran him into the barn loft and ran her hands into his clothes, making him decidedly boyish. He shuddered. He could feel her warmth creeping into his scalp, creeping down his spine, creeping into his shoes to his very toes. Shaking as with a fever, he sighed so deeply he disturbed Mama Amazon.

"What's wrong, hon?" she whispered.

"I was feelin Jezebel's hot hands."

Mama Amazon rolled her eyes as though she had seen an apparition. "Gawd, boy, what in the world's wrong wit you? You can say some of the craziest things. You fixin to lose you mind lack you ma? Don't you start to actin up here in the very high church of all places!"

"Mama Amazon, be quiet!" He looked at her scornfully. His scorn was a quiet thing. She had put it in him, long before he knew how to use it. He could easily carry a chip on his shoulders, arrogantly daring anyone to knock it off. He could be horsey and look at people as though they weren't there. He accurately remembered everything he heard, his mind photographing cameralike. Nothing abashed or shamed him, chagrin and embarrassment unknown.

Cora Mathis seated herself at the console of the showy Moeller pipe organ, the weirdest contraption yet to reach Green Pond, unless it was a cotton mill or a stillhouse. She spread out her dress of great yardage upon the organ bench, pulled it up very slightly from the foot-manual to show her many ruffled petticoats, but chiefly to display her shapely ankles to the gawking elders who looked mealy-mouthed at her.

She selected befitting stops to let sacred wind through the pipes. She tapped lightly upon the console for Uncle Prince Blue to fill the air chamber with air. *Andante religioso* she placed a hymnal—definitely a hymn book, since the church long ago had fought bitterly over hymns and psalms, the church dividing, the hymnodists, thinking God liked hymns, hymned, the psalmodists, thinking God liked psalms, psalmed—upon the organ opened at the appointed page.

Jake squeezed Jezebel's hot hand and Jezebel raised her yellow eyes heavenward in anticipation of anything that might happen, for she wasn't choosy this blessed day. Mama ruled the church, the preacher too, and Mama was happy today; she could see it on Mama's face as she sat at the organ. Jezebel knew her joy was limitless today, because each time Jake squeezed her hand delight shot from the top of her head to the bottom of her feet.

The choir filed into the choir loft and the Reverend Benjamin Flemming went into the pulpit, opened the large gold Bible while currying his goatee.

Miz Cora gave a stormy, befuddled blast at the console, the Reverend Flemming lifted the congregation with his hands, and they sang the doxology.

Then the Reverend Flemming prayed with extemporaneous aptness in mighty gulps; thereafter the congregation plunked down into the pews with a thud, starting at the front and rolling toward the back of the church as water sloshing in a trough.

Mama Amazon shook her head in doubt when her eyes fell upon the preacher. She was not sure whether he was a genuine reverend. That knee-length coat looked a little too fluty. His collar, while starched stiff enough, ought to have been ironed better. His cuffs were about far enough beyond his coat. His tie seemed proper, but that little goatee puzzled her. But after, he waded good and deep into his sermon and, looking straight at her, he started to popping his fist and speaking in a ringing, staccato voice that boomed through the mouse-still, vaultlike church, telling the congregation that hell was hot and getting hotter. Mama Amazon raised herself upon the edge of the seat, sniffing, "Where's that fire that man's talkin bout?"

Once the singing ended, Uncle Blue slid down into his seat behind the organ and became drowsy. He hoped he had pleased Miz Cora Mathis. Above all he wished to please white ladies. To displease white ladies could be painful for his buttocks. He remembered the times he had been strapped across a barrel. The times he was tied to a tree, his body drenched with molasses so that the flies and ants would aggravate him to death. Keep the nigger in his place, the white folks shouted. Where was the nigger's place? Pump that organ, sweep that floor, plough that cotton, hoe that corn. Get down on your knees, nigger—praying to Jesus.

He felt tired and exhausted. The warmth worked deep into his bones. His drowsiness increased. The last thing he remembered was the droning voice of the preacher, popping his fist on hell.

"Wake up there, nigger!" There was a bold white man standing over him, telling him to pump that organ. Miz Cora Mathis had knocked almost all the skin off her knuckles trying to get him to pump and she was already quite red in the face. The congregation was snickering. The more the congregation snickered the redder Miz Cora's face turned. Uncle Blue spluttered and, half asleep, grabbed the bellows' handle, pumping manfully.

Miz Cora had leaned her smart bosom and gloved arms upon the keyboards, nervously waiting, and when the first rushing wind came through the organ there was such a horrid noise that she nearly jumped from the bench, putting all her weight on the foot manual, causing another loud blast that was more terrifying than the first. The congregation's snickers turned to audible giggles, ricocheting over the vaultlike church and high into the rafters.

After the service each member shook the Reverend Flemming's hand, *andante religioso*, at the front door. The Reverend Flemming's voice boomed at the members in salutation; he squeezed their hands viselike, shaking vigorously. The line moved steadily, evenly, spilling down the church steps, gathering in small knots in the street, gabbing and gossiping.

After the last musty organ note had died away, after the last hand had been squeezed by the Reverend Flemming, Uncle Prince Blue, tired and weary, dragged himself from behind the organ, his long green overcoat buttoned tightly, his shoulders tired and stooped, his battered, wormy hat in his gnarled fingers, and started across the church in front of the chancel rail, sliding his feet over the rich carpet, looking up at the great gold Bible.

"Nigger," came a sharp voice from the organ, "the next time you go to sleep on the job, I'm going to have you flailed with a barrel stave." And there was Miz Cora coming from the organ, dashing rip-roaringly angry across the church toward him, her eyes blazing as two coals of fire.

Mama Amazon, Yellow Sam, and Victor stood up in the balcony, looking at the commotion.

Jake and Jezebel, holding hands, followed Cora.

The Reverend Flemming, whose self-satisfied smile burned across his face, turned, looking toward the front of the church, his whole face filling with consternation.

"Yes, ma'm, Miz Cora Mathis," Uncle Blue said, turning slowly to face her.

"Nigger," she was now right into his face, "I'm going to have you blistered until it comes a month of Preachin Sundays." She squinted her eyes, gritted her teeth.

Uncle Prince Blue looked at her in all humility.

"Yes, ma'm, Miz Cora Mathis."

5

That night Vic lay in bed thinking about Uncle Prince Blue and Cora Mathis. Ole Satan must be at the bottom of it somewhere. That old feller would slide about the church with the grace of the serpent, Mama Amazon said.

BEELZEBUB: Satan, you's had a great outpourin of sumpin on you carcass other than a red-hot Sunday-school lesson.

SATAN: The troubles of Job! I's got a big inflamed carbuncle burnin on my seater.

BEELZEBUB: Settin an waitin fo em Presbyterians to backslide?

SATAN: You jars my head wit you prattle——Listen! What great noise is that I hears whirlin way up in the air?

GABRIEL: Ah, hosanna, The Pink House, Magnolia Grandiflora, whose period of puberty is beginning, put on your cassock and begin psalming to Dixie. Polluted poll tax, the corrupt white primaries whooping up in their own spittle. Race? How old is race? What is a race? Around the royal race you run, you big black bum. Call out Second Samuel, Emperor Ruler of the Ku Klux Klan. Man'll have imperial wizards. Who's to say what's right and what's wrong? Who's to bring the yardstick to measure a reputable people? But I say unto you, you Jesus-jerkers, better quit that burnin em crosses in the night!

GAWD, hurrying up rapidly: Gabriel, is you losed you mind? I's never heard such a noise.

GABRIEL: Oh, I was jest blowin off at the mouth. Jest predictin. You don't mind, Lawd?

GAWD: I reckon not. It's good to blow you noggin. I fixed em Green Ponders so they can blow off.

GABRIEL: That was good.

GAWD: I made all things good an nothin bad.

GABRIEL: Uh, I wish you'd look down yonder at that triflin Jake Thornwell. He ain't no mo choppin cordwood lack Vic than nothin. He'll let Vic chop while he complains in the shade.

GAWD: He ever was tricky.

GABRIEL: Toreckly he'll help to cord it up, then he'll hold out fo half the money. It takes a good chopper to make a dollar a day lack Ole Doc pays. Vic'll make it—the way he can swing that ax. Choppin cordwood fo the lil steam engine that pulls the railroad train. Lil mens is funny. Ever wantin to ride.

GAWD: Jake's gettin outta much work as possible an spendin he's time studyin Miz Jezebel. Vic'll work, but he's got that doggone much devilment in him he's downright unpredictable. I see Jake's longin fo the sun to go down so he can spark Jezebel somewhere. Declare that shorely was a bad fight him and David Kingsley had over her the other night. Ole boys'll get that way, but Jezebel, she ain't studyin em. Jake wasn't about to tell nobody about that black eye David gave him. He put up some other tale about it.

GABRIEL: Lie right outta it an plenty other things beside. I watches em.

GAWD: I can allus depend on Vic fo the truth and sometimes he's truthfulness get he into a passel of trouble. That's the way men is. But I can allus depend on Vic. I didn't create em evil.

GABRIEL: Amen.

8

Two days of riding scrouged up in the surrey was too much for Vic. He sat screwed up on a footstool with Jake in the bottom of the surrey. All he could do was to look out at the hot dusty fields and watch the dancing heat over the wilted cotton and corn. If it rustled the corn blades, Pop'd say that was God out there walking, stirring up a summer shower. Or he could watch Mama Naomi, who had on a new hat arrayed with lumps of flowers and ribbons streaming down the glory-hallelujah road. Her high-necked collar came right up to her ears. Vic continually debated with himself: what sort of crazy thing'd Mama Naomi do next, what would she swipe?

Up in front, Mama Amazon and Yellow Sam had the best seat where they'd plenty of room to stretch out their legs, to lean back comfortably, and to enjoy themselves. As soon as he could, Vic aimed to find some excuse to ride up there with them. But he had to be careful. Pop might lay a hickory to him again; he'd already worn him out two days ago to make him come to Goose Creek Camp Meeting. Pop thought he was winning sumpin with those thrashings, but they ran off Vic's back faster than lightning down a greased drain.

Yellow Sam broke the monstrous, devouring monotony of the dust-sifting surrey wheels and the clop, clopping of the horses' hoofs, "There's sure been some big snakes crossin this road. Look where that bigun went slidin through the dust there. He musta been big as my leg."

"That's a sign of rain," said Mama Amazon. "When big rusty snakes starts searchin out a cooler place, it's bound to be hot an dry."

"All signs fail in wet and dry weather," stated Pop.

"Can't tell bout these snakes up here," Mama Amazon retorted. "These mountain rattlers is got sense purty nigh lack peoples."

"I think snakes are purty. I like to play with em," said Vic.

"Victor," squawked Mama Naomi, "you're the most horrible boy!"

Mama Amazon and Yellow Sam snickered impulsively. Vic stuffed his hands into his pockets and squirmed. There was silence.

Vic thought: *Ole bonehead! What'd she like to snitch now? Another angel? How well I recall the time in the department store she snitched the golden-haired angel. Gosh, reckon two weeks of religion'll do her any good or will she drag away the whole mountains? And why does Pop wanta come to camp meetin anyway? Preachin, preachin. Too dry and hot for a preacher to preach about a burning hell.*

Jake thought: *I'll be glad when we get to Goose Greek Camp Meeting because Jezebel'll be there; she might miss sumpin if not there. I can't keep her from my mind. I wonder how much farther up the road ahead of us the Mathises are? I won't have to contend with David up here; his mama is an outcast and attends no preachings. I'll have Jezebel all to myself.*

Pop thought: *If we don't get there today, we can always get there tomorrow. The world wasn't made in a single day. Crops in this section look good, but need rain. Hope not until camp meeting is over, for the things of God must come first.*

Yellow Sam thought: *White folks are a power to have thunder-lightnin religion in the summertime, big storms drivin em to it. Better to be in the praise-house than under the bed, down in the closet, jukin from em big bolts of bright lightnin.*

Naomi thought: *The Doctor sits so straight for an old man, definitely rounded stomach, his pants so neatly buttoned. Some men leave their pants unbuttoned, but not The Doctor. Today we're fulfilling the Scriptures. These hills are so uplifting. This journey is restoring my soul more this year than ever. The thought of being on our way to camp meeting is so very comforting. This I need, if I am to keep the steady course I've set for myself. No one must have the least suspicion. And if I go to meeting, I've nothing to fear. I can continue to store up and still appear stove up.*

2

The second day of the journey found the Thornwells into the edge of the foothills. The road was more winding than Moses' and Pharaoh's squirming snakes and the increase in altitude was noticeable.

The road was filling, overcrowding with unimaginable vehicles that kept falling into the main road every whipstitch, poking right out of the bushes along the road, magically.

The caterpillar movement of this pilgrimage——

——wagons pulled with field-plowing mules—the passengers sitting erect on straight chairs—women nursed babies who held greedily to the flowing teats in the burning sun——

——dilapidated, antique buggies, their steel rims doing a tooth-edging turn in the gritty road, their occupants so overcrowding, drooling over the edges, mashing the springs down until they were unsqueakable, being pulled by a lone skinny mule who grunted and farted over every bump in the road——

——oxcarts pulled by slow clumsy oxen, whose horns flared out long and piercing sharp, whose yokes seesawed on their necks as burden-grinding as they were primitive, whose extreme slowness was their beauty——

——surreys, greatly varied from the very rich to the very poor, from the old and tested to the new and dashing, from the newly shined and polished to those that looked like claydobbers' houses——

——surreys with a top and surreys without a top, the tops shot off in the War Between the States and never mended——

——buckboards—sulkies—and numberless riders astraddle——

The pilgrimage moved onward up the road into the hills—— men and women that'd rather have Jesus: Santa Claus was fo the chillun. Jesus was for everyone and especially for the Methodists and Baptists and Presbyterians of the red lands of Carolina. For salvation, to the rock of ages, the pilgrimage moved into the hill country. Tramping, tramping, tramping, trying to make heaven their home.

3

At the camping ground, Vic jumped from the surrey, mischievously relieved.

It was the same old campground. The same old ring of hovels around the arbor. The ring was usually three layers deep, but this year it had been increased to four. He made a beeline to theirs to find Only, who had driven up in a wagon a few days earlier with chickens and hams aplenty to give them strength to praise God.

From all the hovels supper preparations were dabbling underfoot; the lazy-blue smoke curved and curled skyward.

Women washed and babies squalled madly. The tettered animals gnawed corn, munched hay, gnawed the bark from the trees.

Throughout all the camp meeting ground there was happiness and expectancy. Talk—garrulous gossip—the talk ran to the spiritual feast the reverends would dish up and serve out that night, the first night of the two-week meeting.

With the first night's service well under way, the insects, the many whose ancestors had gone into the Ark two by two, buzzed about the pine-torch lights, falling down the folks necks, falling into the women's long hair. Vic climbed up into a nearby tree and sat upon an overhanging limb where he might observe the entire goings-on.

Their singing voices snapped and cracked with sheer zealousness. The preacher walked belligerently across the pine-slab platform, ran his fingers continually through his hair, shook his head, drank cool mountain water from a gourd, and whipped ole Satan around the sassafras stump.

The preacher mopped the sweat from his brow with an extremely large handkerchief, hung it over the pulpit to dry, and called out the mourners' hymn. The congregation began to sing. He threw out his net and fished for the wayward sinners. He rammed and jugged among them with his sobbing pleas, but not one small minnow would dart forward into the net of righteousness.

"Get down on your knees and pray!" the overbold preacher cried. "Bow your heads and close your eyes and keep them closed for Jesus' sake! God is working. I can feel the spirit hover nearby!"

Vic watched intensely. Often he noted a slightly raised head, a peeping eye, and the head dropped back as suddenly as it had been raised. They were snitching on the preacher and he didn't know it. Vic wondered if the preacher caught them at it, what he'd do? But they did it too coyly for him to catch them.

4

A patchwork-quilt dawn arrived the next day—a dry, multi-colored sky, weird and foretelling, with thin rickrack clouds. It threw a wonder-hued light over the campground. It was so dry that during the night not one drop of dew had had the energy to form itself upon anything. The dust hung thick in the old-fogyish air, covered everything in a thick layer in which pictures and writing could be done with the forefinger.

The worshipers rose with the sun and Vic, knowing well that he was thoroughly sinning, skipped Mama Amazon's steaming-hot breakfast and hurried into the woods that stretched out so invitingly from the camp in every direction.

When the sun was high into the heavens, he felt hungry and turned toward the brush arbor. Descending a hill toward it, he walked out upon a large, overhanging boulder. His ears caught the distant singing in the brush arbor and he stopped. "They've got that one off key and outta rhythm besides." Then he listened more closely. There was a voice nearby. Fear seized him; a feeling of guilt quilted him. Pop'd get him sure as the devil for cutting that singing this morning. He strained his ears listening. That wasn't an old voice—rasping and cracked. That was a oung voice—and two of them.

"Uh-uh," he thought, "that's Jake and Jezebel. Where are they? Scaring the livin daylights outta me! Boy, for a minute there I could feel Pop's stiff hickory cuttin across my butt. What're em saps doin, anyway? Somebody else ain't likin song service so well this morning. They must be down under this ledge of rock. I'm gonna lie down and lean over the edge and see iffen I can hear what they're saying."

JEZEBEL: No! I never did any such thing. I don't like David that well. He don't mean a thing to me. I don't even like his mama. She was bad and she's Northern—queer, too, folks say. Why, she doesn't even go to church! Guess she don't feel like it after what she's done.

JAKE: I don't care a thing about David Kingsley's mama. She don't have a thing to do with this. Sudiebelle said you'd been kissin David a heap o times. Said she'd seen you.

JEZEBEL: I wouldn't believe a thing she says on a stack of Bibles as high as North Bethel's steeple. Jake, you don't believe her, really?

JAKE: Why'd she tell that iffen it wasn't so? She said she saw you kissin him over two years ago. Is it so?

JEZEBEL: No. It's a lie. I've never kissed him. Why won't you believe me instead of that Sudiebelle Wilson? Or do you like Sudiebelle better than me?

JAKE: I can listen to what Sudiebelle has to say without liking her, can't I? She's told somebody else the same thing.

JEZEBEL: Oh, you do like Sudiebelle. Shame on you for liking a part nigger! Why, she's old man Saddleberry's daughter. Her mama was desperate for a place to live after the war and she stooped to living with old man Saddleberry. And there she had Sudiebelle. Queer as old man Saddleberry was, anybody could tell he was part nigger—everybody knows that, Jake. Shame on you! Why, when the elders churched old Saddleberry's ma for havin him she lied out of it and said a big black bull had frightened her and marked the child and that was how come Saddleberry was so black. I know better. Mama said so. She remembered all about it.

JAKE: That's not so.

JEZEBEL: 'Tis so.

JAKE: David said the same thing. He told Dudley Ives he'd kissed you plenty of times and that you knew how.

JEZEBEL: Shame on you, Jake. He said I know how—what? What do you mean? You say the strangest things. I'm surprised at you.

JAKE: You know a whole heap more than you let on to.

You're tryin to cover up something. He said you knew how to kiss. Don't you try to deny it.

JEZEBEL: Why, I'm not denying a single thing. Really, Jake. Honestly. Do you think I'm trying to deny something? Honestly? I'm not keeping one single thing from you.

JAKE: David told Henry Leg the same thing. They've both told me. You can't deny that. Two against one. They'd not both tell the same thing—the same lie!

JEZEBEL: I think it's a shame for those boys to go around talking about an innocent girl like me. Why, Henry Leg is lots older than me. You can't expect much of David Kingsley, being Northern and all. Jake, this's dreadful. You really don't believe them?

JAKE: Sure I do. I believe every word they said.

JEZEBEL: Why, Jake, that's terrible—taking sides with those bad boys—they're common.

JAKE: Will you face em and tell em that?

JEZEBEL: Tell em what?

JAKE: That they're lyin. They're common. I dare you. You won't do it.

JEZEBEL: Jake, you can put a poor, innocent girl into the most embarrassing positions. That'd be the most terrible thing. I just can't imagine you—"

JAKE: Jezebel, you're hidin something. You can't fool me. You're coverin up. If you weren't, you'd face em.

JEZEBEL: Honey, darling. You've the awfulest thoughts. How could you ever imagine me doing a thing like that?

Vic picked up a large stone and let it roll over the edge of the boulder. It dropped noisily to where they were. He meant to lie down quickly upon the rock, hiding from them, but they came from their trysting place and looked up so quickly that they spotted him before he had time to conceal himself.

"Ha, ha," laughed Jezebel. The stone had not frightened her

in the least. It had helped her to shake Jake off with his too-private queries that were making the road hot for her. Moreover, she was tickled to jollity to see Vic, glad to have something on him.

"You've been hiding out from song service, Victor Thorn-well! I'll tell Doctor Thornwell on you, boy," she giggled, the whip now in her hand. "I bet he won't like that a-tall; him being an elder in the church for lo these many years. They'll church you and fire you from the church, old boy." She was flippant and altogether too spurty, because she had him in such an unfavorable position. She didn't care what sort of devilment he'd been into, she was glad she'd caught him to further her own gains.

"*Like hell they'll church me!*" He was as indignant as a disreputable-looking rooster. She had always fascinated him and he loved her for it, but then the sight of her and her sharp tongue rattling upon him broke something up in him and he was ready for a fight right now with her. No one could stir him up as quickly as she could.

"Victor Thornwell! Such language. I never heard the like in all my life."

"Shut your damn ears and you won't hear it!"

"Vic, are you swearing at me? You're the most uncouth—the rudest boy. What'd the Reverend Benjamin Flemming and the elders say?" She manipulated her purity as one does an umbrella against the shifting rain.

"I don't give a damn what they say. You go take a squint up their behinds. You nosy busybody."

"I've a notion to go tell Doctor Thornwell every word you've said. Insulting me." She wallowed in sheer goodness.

"Do, angel," Vic sneered. "I can tell sumpin, too. I've a purty good idea what you an Jake were doing. Who do you think you're fanning?" He became sleeky moody, pulled himself within his cozy shell; completely independent of his brother or her or anyone else.

"I detest an eavesdropper—up on that rock snooping." And she had thought she had him right where she wanted him. She was furious, so furious that she slapped his face.

He drew back unabashed, "Oh, no; I just found you lying in my path with your sorry lovemaking. Can't you do it no better?" He roared at her with imagination and inexorable right. "What notion induced you to lie in the woods while in that brush arbor yonder, a-top Goose Creek Ridge, your ma's yellin her heart out to save your lousy soul?"

"Victor Thornwell, I thank you to remember that I belong to the North Bethel Church and *my soul* has been saved. And you—you have never acknowledged your sins before the Lord. Jesus will surely deny you and tell you to depart into outer darkness, that He knew you not."

"Well, if you're one of the saved ones, Gawd have mercy upon the unsaved." He astonished Jake. How did Vic know how to be so apt? How did he dare be so impudent?

Jezebel ruffled her feathers and twitched herself.

"Victor Thornwell, I fail to see one single thing wrong with myself."

"Glory hallelujah." He flung his sarcasm fervently at her. "Hallelujah!"

The trio walked in silence through the woods to the brush arbor.

Jake thought: *Her eyes never turned green one single time when he poked fun at her back there! What is there about Vic? She lied to me and thinks nothing of it and I go on loving her the more. Her eyes never once turn green at him.*

Jezebel thought: *How can I make him sit up and take notice of me? I want him. It's useless to try to make him jealous. Oh, well, there's time yet. I'll not be pushed off so easily. I'll get him yet—there's time.*

Vic thought: *If she keeps on, she is going to be the best-look-ing gal in the country, but I wouldn't tell her for the world.*

5

Rumors flew thick and fast all through the camping ground that upon the last Sunday, which was the breaking of the meeting, which was the long-looked-for day, which was the day the Lawd'd do the greatest work, a young Herculean from on high in the steep mountains was coming down to preach. Some said he'd come barefooted, wearing a simple bearskin robe he had skinned from a black bear that he had killed with his two hands. He'd bring along a little honey, for the Lawd said take along a little honey. He could not read or write until he was thirty years old. The Lawd had called him one day as he minded his pa's still on the high mountainside by a cool mountain brook where the worm sweated indiscreetly twenty-four hours a day condensing the pure corn likker.

The Lawd had called to him to get up offen his seater and to go—to go straight yander, with impudent tactlessness, straight as a martin for his gourd, to Goose Creek Camp Meeting. His mind was young, strong, vigorous. It hadn't been oppressed with the lightsome, stupid things people said in books. His mind had had time to grow and to develop. He had been taught by the wild woodsy creatures, by the stinging wind and the pelting rain, by storms and fair weather, by the summer's hot and the winter's cold. But once he opened the great Bible, the Holy Spirit led him into reading, taught him to look for the craftiness and cunningness in evil men's minds. There was no need for sinners to hide behind any sort of leaves, because he could easily move the leaves aside and see them with his fierce animal-like eyes.

"Make room," the cry went out throughout the whole camping land. And the old preachers sat back and took notice, looking up at the young Hercules, looked up at young Typhoon Ai, who saw all their sins.

6

August was deep-set at Catawba again, rich and abiding after the long camp meeting. Victor rambled in the dusty heat and refurbished his soul with showers of happiness.

Coming in late one evening, Vic noticed a decided number of turkeys were droopy and unable to fly into the ancient oak with the rest of the flock that was already high into the tree turking, jumping among the limbs, seeking a perch to their liking, one where they might comfortably hang their long necks straight down as they slept.

Vic ambled among the sick-looking birds, his hands rammed into his pockets, and scrutinized them, diagnosing them as being poisoned. Pop was away and he didn't know what Pop would say about his cutting into the turkeys to satisfy his hunch; yet that was the only way to make certain of his diagnosis, the only way to obliterate all speculation. Any other way would be purely a guess in the dark. Still . . . Pop was funny. He'd thrashed him more than once for such carrying-on.

Vic felt his knife; it'd cut mighty slick. He'd have to have thread, a needle, cloths for sponges. He grew drunk with excitement: that desire to probe, to explore, to mend. For a moment he felt weak. He felt like jelly with two uncertain legs for support. It was the sudden shock of thinking what he'd like to do to the turkeys. *Would he dare?* After the cow-and-calf affair? The temptation was more than he could stand.

The creeping-up darkness filled the air. The barnyard creatures prepared for bed with soft guttural sounds. Yellow light streaked from Catawba's windows and the open kitchen door. The restful earth bedded down for the night. Vic leaned over the turkey Only held on the improvised table and with his defty fingers snatched the feathers from the bird's crop.

"Jake, hold that light so I can see better; I don't want too much bleeding," said Vic. Only tittered and Budda looked on popeyed.

"You ain't got a bit of mercy on that turkey," said Jake, "pullin out his feathers while he's dyin. Why don't you let him die in peace?"

"Who said he was gonna die?" Vic retorted.

"I bet Ole Doc's gonna bust you wide open again when he finds out you done kilt one of he's fine turkeys," solemnly warned Budda, his voice hinting of strange evils that could lurch up from this carrying-on here.

"Budda, I ain't killin Ole Doc's turkey." Or was he? What was there for him to get hold of, to stake trust in?

"Ho'cum you know they's not gonna die?" asked Only. "Death is allus certain."

"I know. That's ho'cum."

His knife slid across the taut skin of the well-packed crop, laying the outer skin open, exposing the inner crop. He noted the muscular movement of it and plunged the knife into it, opening it with one deft whack. He felt the blade cutting across grains of corn and gravel and the opened crop exposed a mass of food waiting to go down to the gizzard to be ground up for nourishment.

He dumped the contents of the crop upon a piece of board and got down close to it, running his knife through it, picking it apart. Suddenly he held up a piece.

"Nightshade—deadly poison. That's what's wrong. Budda, run an tell Mama Amazon to send us some lard," said Vic.

"Here, Budda, you hold this. Let me get the lard. I'm sick as a dog," Jake moped toward the kitchen, trying to vomit.

Vic looked into the incised crop, put his finger into it, exploring. His finger found the opening that went on to the gizzard and down this his finger went, the fingertip reaching inside the hot gizzard, and there he felt the healthy angry gizzard grinding upon his finger as though it were food. This was unearthly sweet music to Vic's inmost being.

Mama Amazon waddled up with the lard; Gee and Dessa trekked behind her. Great concern encompassed their approach.

"What's youse doin?" Mama Amazon asked, and then she saw the cut-open turkey and rolled her eyes violently, "Gawd have mercy, iffen youse done kilt Ole Doc's turkey—*umum!*" Her mouth clamped shut, her lips sucked in an array of evils that could crop up from this going-on here.

"I ain't kilt his ole turkey! It'll feel good by morning," Vic floundered, desperately clutching.

"Cause he dead, he'll feel so good," she swooped in mockery. Yet, she thought, that was her caul-headed chile. Couldn't tell about him. He'd been right with the cow, although he got thrashed within an inch of his life.

"Let's have some lard." He picked up the inner crop, spread the incision with his first and second fingers and with his free hand scooped in lard. "Hand me the needle that's threaded. I'll tie my own knots!" He pushed the needle through the inner crop, drawing the incision together; the flesh between the stitches stood up in little dark beads. This was the important incision to sew, the outer incision would be easier.

Jake did not return, but the others stayed with Vic and good-naturedly chided him, making cutting remarks, but their admiration increased as he worked. Vic finished fourteen of the turkeys and had only one more to do when Ole Doc suddenly appeared upon the scene. Time and Pop had slipped upon Vic.

Vic tried to explain to Pop what he was doing, the reason for doing it; he went into every detail about the case. He tried to talk man to man, doctor to doctor. He thought to bear everything he could think of to defend his actions—but Pop said he was a crazy upstart, young and foolish, having no more idea what he was doing than the man in the moon. He forbade Vic to operate on the other turkey.

The others stood abashed, with smirky smiles and imps of mischief playing on their faces.

"You've killed enough turkeys!" Pop exploded. "Fourteen of them. Let the other alone. We'll have nothing for Thanksgiving and Christmas. Go away from here for five minutes and the things you'll get into are unnamable."

Pop's sting of correction drove Vic to bed whipped. He sobbed into his pillow. He felt as if the poisonous nightshade of the remaining turkey was in his stomach. Nausea spread through him. Pools of saliva gathered under his tongue.

In troubled sleep the turkey haunted him. He felt it dying. He saw the lofty buzzards gliding through the sky for its rotten carcass. The distorted faces of Only and Budda and Mama Amazon leered at him, laughed and snickered, crescendoing to a screaming pitch.

When the sunshine of morning crept and glided into his room, he pulled the covers over his head. Today he had no desire to rise, to stir about; his eagerness to live was gone; his incurable spate of laughter was gone and the joy and sunshine had flown from him. His gloom surpassed all the accumulated miseries he had ever known in its downward plunge.

"What you doin, playin possum?" asked Mama Amazon, sweet-voiced Mama Amazon, yanking the covers from him. Her eyes shone with jetty light, her laughter its same old familiar lovesomeness. "You'd better get on out yonder an carry off that dead turkey before the buzzards comes flyin after em."

"Where's Pop? What'd he say?"

"Gone to town. He wasn't talkin a-tall this mornin; mostly lookin."

"Did he know that turkey died?"

"Ought to, he's out there before day was clean-lookin. Spent enough time to resurrect that dead one."

"What'd he say about the fourteen livin ones?"

"Nothin. Wasn't talkin a-tall; but doin some powerful lookin at em turkeys turkin around."

7

After the operations, their eyes met at the dinner table for the first time. Vic played with his food and glanced at Pop each chance he got when Pop wasn't glancing at him. They played a game of peepeye. But their guarded looks fell out of turn and they found themselves staring into each other's eyes. Pop's crow's-feet wrinkles about his eyes worked up such an inviting smile that Vic spread his wide mouth in a copious grin that was effusively sentimental.

"I wish you two'd wipe those silly grins from your faces," said Mama Naomi, toying with a dainty morsel of food, and her trim feet silently treadled the fly brush, moving it slowly backward and forward over the bent-to heads of her relatives who gobbled up and sloshed down Ole Doc's rich eatin's into their ever-craving bellies. "You've been secretly smiling at each other since the meal began."

"I thought everyone was so engrossed in masticating food that there'd not be time for conversation," he indicated the relatives, "so I hadn't realized a little grinning'd be so very objectionable, *my dear*," said Pop.

"No one said anything about it being objectionable. *It's silly!*" She drew herself up with dignity.

The Mure relatives snickered, gave one another sly winks, but took no time from their hoggish eating.

"I'm sorry if we're silly," said Pop.

"Have it your way. I'd as soon argue with a brick wall as you.

I think without your stubbornness, you'd not quite be there. I'm quite thankful Jacob takes after the Mures and not you. With you and Victor as identically stubborn as a donkey, I'd never be able to stay in the house with the three of you."

"*Three!*" Pop looked at the Mure relatives contentedly munching. "Son," Pop said to Vic, "you want to go with me to see old Dave Latham this evening? You've a hankering."

It was all right with Pop about the turkeys.

8

Vic held the reigns tightly and the lively horse took the bouncing buckboard briskly over the road at a sprightly pace. Pop leaned back in the seat and took life in his quiet strides as though it were mere trivia.

Grasshoppers chirred in the ripening grass. In the distance a sultry dry fly sang his wound-up-to-run-down song. Insects chirruped in fruited fields. Quail called. A buzzard circled in the lofty blue. The hot dry wind blew in their faces.

"Son, we're going to see a man whom I operated upon a long time ago. I think you'll be more than interested since you seem to possess that yearn to mend," Pop said dryly.

"Did he get well?"

"Oh, in a way. I give him a few more years—cancer is usually a slow death."

"Where was it?"

"On his penis. I cut it off right back against his body and it was a big long one."

"How does he pee?"

"That's a likely question for you to ask. He cut a cane from the creek bank, pushed the pith out of it, and uses it; when he isn't using it he carries it in his pocket. He gets along well that way. There's always a way for doing things."

Ole Doc grew reflective, "But regardless of what is advocated or practiced in this day and time, the state of mind has an overwhelming influence on any disease. I firmly believe that since Dave's cancer started to acting up several years ago, his longevity has been due to his pleasant state of mind.

"Son, as you grow older and get behind the scenes and probe into life as you seem hell-bent on doing, you're going to find that a great wise force created this world and started it into motion. Man'll always have a religion. You could destroy all the religions on earth today and tomorrow there'd be a new one spring up."

On the return trip Vic's mind chirred as though it were filled with the multitude of grasshoppers that fed in the fields. Grasshoppers gorged themselves beyond capacity, knowing that their eggs must be laid into the ground to rest the winter long there, and with the coming of spring, the trumpeting of the spring rains, a new generation of grasshoppers'd hatch out, starting a new life, knowing with certainty as they fed that their death awaited in frosty autumn.

"Pop, does Mr. Latham know he's dying?" Vic asked.

"No, I don't think so; if so, his mind is prepared. Death to the old is what love is to the young. God has a way of preparing us in advance for the stages in life that we must pass through. Why do you ask?"

"He looked so pitiful. He's the most dried-up, shriveled-up human being I've ever seen. I could see every bone in his hands and face. I could see the dents in his skull. Why'd you want to fix it so he'd live so long and come to this?"

"A doctor's duty. You've seen him at his worst. He has had better days."

"Then you're not certain whether your operation made him live longer?"

"Couldn't be certain. Nobody could. When you come to the place in the road that it forks and you can take only one of the roads, there's no earthly way of telling how it'd be down the other road. There's no turning around, going home, and starting all over. In your mind you'll always speculate how it'd be down that other road, and you'll always wish more or less that you'd taken that other road—so easy to picture the nice things down it. But, son, let me tell you one thing, when you're older, if you're ever a great doctor—there'll come days when you've diagnosed, performed, prescribed, and then you'll wish you could go down that other road. There'll be days when you stand at the forks and have no idea which way to go, days when you stand at the forks certain the one is right, only to find out later that the other was right.

"It does something to you, son, knowing that no matter how much you know you can't always be sure. Knowing that you—your own mind, all your powers of judgment—have failed. That somebody died because you thought wrong and that there is no turning back."

They clopped along and Pop was in his own thoughts of the forks he'd known in his years and Victor was only beginning to see the differences in the road he had thought was straight and clear and beautiful and easy to see his way down.

Then Ole Doc added, "Each patient is an individual case; no two alike—though their parallels are astonishing. The most difficult thing in ethical medicine is diagnostics. You must learn to not look at a patient as an impersonal hunk of meat. Not to see the patient as Mr. Cancer Lip, Mrs. Diabetes, or Miss Diaper Rash. But to look into the mind; there's more in the mind than most folks dream of. Ma always preached that to me and she was far too wise and strong-minded for her time—and she did nothing more than go up and down these rivers mostly ketching chillun, birthing at a dollar apiece, or she'd trade it out in goose feathers or dried fruit. And she was good at abating a fever, alleviating a painful boil with salty fat meat or soap."

Victor saw all the long way down the lonely road, the millions of ailing people; patients, patients, and there was joy in never having two of them identical.

9

The time was gone when Jezebel's games had too much kissing in them. They weren't games any longer; and where Victor had once run from the yard or scrambled up the barn loft to get away from her, he now simply withdrew into himself and kept a distance. Even in the same room he kept a distance that had nothing to do with space, and Jezebel could not figure out the elusive creature or figure out a way to bridge the distance between them. When they were younger, when they were scrapping kids, he had not been able to hide from her. She had swiftly scrambled up the barn loft after him, easier than a cat, quicker than a squirrel. She rolled her yellow eyes and taught him many little tricks, making him decidedly conscious that he was a boy and she was a girl. To Vic it was alarming, but Jezebel scoffed at him and plunged her hot hands into his clothes.

Now it no longer alarmed him, because he knew how to shut her out and she did not touch him. She waited for him to touch her and there was more joyous excitement in that than in the touch of all the other boys. Jezebel could scoff, but she couldn't scoff half as scornfully as Victor.

10

The churches of Green Pond saw a great cloud of sin winging about over Green Pond and decided to clip it with a big united revival. Typhoon Ai, long-haired, booming-voiced Ai, was looked upon with maximum favor as a revivalist and was called to do a month's preaching in Green Pond. Two thousand years ago John the Baptizer couldn't get into the Temple: so today Typhoon Ai made no effort to get into the temple, but brought along a big tent and pitched it in a bramble honeysuckle thicket and whanged at whatever he thought needed to be whanged at.

The Green Ponders loved Typhoon Ai's whanging. The tramping worshipers to the flapping tent beat the earth into silt and ground Robert Belcher Inchurch's honeysuckle thicket there on Third Street into oblivion. Night after night their songs rent the air, dashing madly to the throne of grace for divine attention.

Night after night Typhoon Ai preached, whanging away at old Satan, reminding the people of their sins.

Night after night there was singing, the moaning and the crying air rushing across the human vocal chords, screwed into agonized frenzies, battered into a sweet concoction, a sweet glorifying sound.

Typhoon Ai preached.

He called upon God to meet him down there in the middle of the tent, at one of the sturdy tent posts, at one of the chunky posts that held the kerosene lanterns, to help him to wrestle old Satan out of Green Pond, for Satan was about to take it over. Typhoon Ai rushed from the pine-slab pulpit, fleeing wildly down the aisle, stirring a bulky cloud of stifling dust. God met him at the tent pole and they wrestled Satan in the powdery dust. Typhoon Ai threw his hands out in wild gestures, he shook his heavy mop of long black hair, and the people saw how wonderful Ai was when God met him down there in the middle of the tent at the tent pole.

He sadly lamented his walk back to the pulpit, bamboozling them all with his shaking of his great shock of hair.

He pounded the platform with his heels, the pulpit with his fists. He whipped old Satan around the mulberry bush and always came out victorious. He called the congregation stinking polecats. He called them pussyfooting, likker-drinking hypocrites, demoniac buzzards, Goliaths of Industry, money-loving Judases, cruel Ahabs of covetousness, disbelieving Nebuchadnezzars, Rahabish whores, and King David whoremongers.

One of those nights, in the semigloom of the yellow-lighted tent, Ole Doc and Naomi sat toward the rear. Ole Doc listened attentively to the preacher, and once as he went to recross his legs to rest them he chanced to glance down between the seats, and there in the gloom he saw Naomi's ungloved hand reach out to the hip pocket of the man sitting on the pine-slab bench in front of her. She carefully eased her fingertips—it was diabolic and unbelievable, he hardly dared trust his own eyes—into the man's pocket and cautiously extracted his pocketbook without the man having an inkling of what was taking place.

Ole Doc watched her sharply, being careful that she didn't catch him. She brought it to her lap, then quickly covered it with her hands. Now she relaxed, looked the congregation over unconcernedly. She slowly worked her hands, opening her handbag and pushing the wallet into it. She smacked her lips and brushed her fingertips softly.

Ole Doc lost track of the sermon. He concentrated upon the little drama that had been enacted before him. He recalled the time communion was served in North Bethel and Naomi had slipped two whole long sticks of communion bread up her sleeve. When the wine was passed, she had drunk over half the cup and said she didn't care for bread. He remembered once she had cunningly filched dried peaches from a man's pocket.

The rest of the evening Ole Doc was profoundly quiet, because his mind was so asphyxiated with Naomi's pilfering trick which she'd manipulated so ennoblingly. To purloin as she had done right before his eyes was enraptured genius. What on earth did she do with the queer assorted articles that she so ardently pilfered? She was as agile and diverting at it as the most goatly magician with all his concerted efforts.

11

Cora Mathis paced her parlor. She was twitteringly nervous. She was doggedly tired waiting. She boiled over with expectations. This waiting got under her skin, vexed her beyond her limits.

"John Mathis," Cora's scissor-clipping voice bounced to the

pine ceiling of the room, "you sit there like a pair of runover shoes. Why don't you do something?"

"What's to do?" John questioned from the cane-bottomed chair he seemed to be screwed to.

"What's to do?" She circled the parlor, grimaced at the unpainted ceiling. "That's it, you never do anything. Ever since I can remember you, you've never done anything but sit on your rusty butt, yet somehow your mouth's always hanging open at mealtime for my food to fall into it."

"Coree, you're havin one of your nervous spells again. Sit down and wait. They'll be along by-and-by."

"When it's the greatest moment of our lives, you sit there in the chimney corner and tell me to be calm! Shut up, John Mathis, anything that's decent, you're against it. Jezebel should have a decent chance at marriage! It was something I didn't get, not with the thing sitting there in the chimney corner that I did get."

"If she gets him, she won't have anything to brag on in a husband. Why, I think Robert Inchurch looks like an overgrown spider. That's the way Robert Inchurch looks. His head's purty near that big, if it had a neck to set on, but there's that big head screwed away down between his shoulders. And them long, reaching-out-yonder arms and legs. And always wearing that long-tailed coat, swishing around—"

"Shut your dirty mouth! At the rate you're going, we'll not have turnips this fall. Perhaps if Jezebel gets a chance to marry the Inchurch fortune we'll have turnips, at least."

"So, it's the Inchurch money you're thinkin of? Well, Coree, that's an old fortune and old fortunes're mean. Man can't fare so well where money accumulates and is held. It becomes like a slimy pool of water without an outlet."

"Aw, shut up. You tire me. I may have to have you churched now right early some Preachin Sunday."

"Just remember, Coree, this's my eighteen acres of land and my house to boot."

"Isn't that something to brag about? You ninny! Oh, I wish they'd come on."

She went to the window. The clock struck on the mantel; she counted the strokes. "Ten o'clock. They should have been here an hour ago. I'm not having this."

"I'd stop it. It'd be the best thing you ever did," John said.

His wife sneered. "What you got up your sleeve? No, keep it to yourself. I don't want to hear it. My mind is set on the course for Jezebel to take. When opportunity knocks at her door, as it has done this blessed night, there isn't any reason for her not to accept it."

Jezebel entered as a whirlwind, suddenly, slamming the door shut, stamping across the pine floor.

"Jezebel!"

"What?"

"You could change your tone of voice, Jezebel, when you're speaking to your mother."

Jezebel flared and spurted, "The next time, don't you be egging that stinking Robert Inchurch into bringing me home from the revival, Ma! Do you hear me? That was a cheap, dirty trick. Why, he even took me to the drugstore! Of all places!" The brightness of her Jezebel-face darkened. "He had me go in with him to have a soda, and everybody in town looking on. The whole crowd from the revival passing right by there—looking in! Oh, the folks in this town'll never sleep tonight, not from gossiping. Ma, Ma, how could you do such a cheap, low-down trick? I'll bet half the boys I know were in that drugstore tonight. How can I ever face them?"

"Jezebel, I thought I'd trained you to be a Christian, and here you're acting like a wild savage. You'd think, the way you're cutting up, that you'd committed a crime. You did nothing but have a soda and ride home with Robert Inchurch in the carriage. And if you ask me, I think he's a wonderful boy—and an elder."

"Nobody asked you. I think he's a stinking mess."

"Jezebel!"

Jezebel stalked from the room.

Bitterness swept her. She stormed back and forth on the bare boards of her cramped-up bedroom and swore to herself in an unholy, unladylike way.

She saw Robert Inchurch's small, deep-set, and too-close-together eyes looking at her, taking her all in greedily and letting her know he wanted to eat her up. She saw the pallor of his whey-white face and the thin lengthy fingers, cold and icy when he touched her. She could feel his creepy hands on her again. Why did he have to paw like that? There was no pleasure in his touch, no pleasure or excitement as there was with the boys she knew, with David or Henry or Jake—or just in the thoughts about Victor Thornwell. Robert Inchurch's touch was an ugly thing that made a knot tighten inside her.

She knew what was exciting Cora: that money and that power in the church. But if she couldn't stand somebody, what matter did the money make? "Let him keep it!" she shouted, and startled herself with her voice. Oh, if it could only be Vic who was so overanxious to bring her home! Then there would be something to look forward to, something to dream of—why couldn't it be Vic?

But people did not flaunt elders of North Bethel, and Jezebel Mathis knew they did not. Jezebel had North Bethel and all the ways of the stardust ground into her, ground in well from her earliest memory. She was between the fire and the frying pan.

She was driven so against the wall, clutching about so desperately, that she did something she had never done before in her life. She spoke right out in the open and right up to the Lord as though He were there in the room.

"Listen, Lord, you listen to me. Listen to Jezebel Mathis! Help me out, Lord, help me. I'm in deep trouble, deeper than you'd think. Do *something*." And then she added in a voice so small as to seem a whisper, "Please."

12

In the cool of the evening Mama Amazon sat easing her feet on Catawba's back steps and talked to Victor about old Typhoon Ai who was stirring up such a rambunctious dust in the revival tent on Third Street.

"Fo true," said Mama Amazon, "I know most Gawd's rared back enjoyin that big noise of heavy preachin."

"I doubt it," said Vic. "Not the noise Typhoon Ai is making."

"Oh, yes," said Mama Amazon. "Why, iffen you had the power you could set right here on these steps and hear Gawd way in heaven somewhere talkin, and way down yonder in the fiery pit you could hear ole Satan, too."

In blue paradise, Gawd stood enjoying that big tent revival Typhoon Ai was whanging at in Green Pond. He shook His gray head, for the singing was good—off key but loud. But as long as His chillun were agreeable, He didn't mind a little noise.

GAWD: Ole Typhoon Ai is doin some powerful good preachin in that revival tent in Green Pond. Noisy and kinda hurts My ears; but I enjoys em. Say, Gabriel, who's lil gal chile is that playin the organ? I can't tell fro here. I just bout needs specks. But I dreads goin to one of em ole eye doctors. When's the last time us let one of em rascals in up here? I's particular who fools wit My eyes. Maybe, iffen I go to the next one that just fresh arrives up here, he'll be so glad to get here he'll take some pains wit Me. I'll wait. No need to rush; took Me six days to get that ole green earth rollin.

GABRIEL: Lemme see, lemme see—G H I J—Jezebel—It's Jezebel Mathis. Yes, it's her rared back playin. You shorely remembers birthin her? Never fo'get that stormy night.

GAWD: Give she plenty credits. She's shorely rared back there pumpin that lil organ. Did that organ come from Sears, Roebuck? I's particular about the contraptions folks uses to praise and to glorify My name wit.

GABRIEL: They ordered off fo that organ to She-cog-o.

GAWD: Em shorely is smart peoples in Green Pond. I'm gonna bless em good and plenty heavy when I finds the time. You remind Me to do it.

In the synagogue of blasphemy, the region of the second death, ole Satan shed crocodile tears of joy with a new stumbling block.

BEELZEBUB: Gonna deplume she, enty Satan?

SATAN: I'm a highly successful imp an when I plants a tiny seed in Miz Cora Mathis' head, it'll sprout sooner or later.

BEELZEBUB: I'm shorely up on my prongin.

SATAN: Ole lawd of dung, you'd better be well up on you prongin, fo there's gonna be a prongin time in the ole town.

The earth slanted away from the sun in autumn, yet it sent its weakened, yellowed beams among the communal foliages about Green Pond, making a pleasant place for the amphibia to sun themselves. The land was kissed nightly with pungent rills of crystal frost and the sweet Green Ponders moved indoors, shut their doors, and built themselves fires, because they now had matches and needed no longer to borrow a coal of fire. The tree leaves painted themselves in brilliant colors and danced gaily to their deaths, but the Green Ponders smelled and predicted dire evil.

Victor Thornwell was at a swelled-up age that fall. Like a dangling vine he walked, early in the frost, down Main Street to school. His temperament had deepened. The things about him that were not all boy were pure fantasy, the folks thought, but Mama Amazon shooed him off as being unpredictable and a disarming phenomenon that ran gaily across the portals of her life. There was about him no contaminated venom, but a highly contagious laughter which came from all over him and molested folks' goings-on. He was incurably honest and possessed an undisciplined curiosity which exasperated folks and caused them to predict a very unholy end for him. Yet there was something amazing about his still boyish grin, his awkward, slow-blunted speech that got under the females' skins and caused them to go romantic.

He stopped and leaned dreamily upon old Mrs. Ives's picket fence while his famished soul drank morning gulps of the stately chrysanthemums. The bouquet was wholly wrapped in high-spirited dew. In remembrance he lived here in the long bygones and nothing had a beginning or an ending.

Jezebel came along and caught him at the fence and leaned, because he was leaning, and told him, jealous of Mrs. Ives, that the old lady was crazy and they were going to take her away any day now. Jezebel would punish old Mrs. Ives by sending her to some far-reaching place of unrighteous madness.

"What're they gonna take her for?" Vic asked. A friend was going, he thought.

"You goose, because of her mind—and, I imagine, these flowers. Always so many flowers! They say she tends them at night to keep the frost off."

"If Mrs. Ives is crazy, the rest of the folks in this town had better get crazy, because she's getting more from life than most of em."

Old Mrs. Ives sat hidden behind her curtains and was in love with Vic, though she had not heard a word he said. She knew he was just like herself and so she was simply and innocently, without regard to age, in love with him.

Victor and Jezebel walked slowly on to school; he carried her books; they were happy and gay and talked.

"Vic, I wish you'd drop that music. There's something queer about a boy playing the piano. Why, every time you play for assembly the kids titter. Why, there's not another boy in all Green Pond that'd be caught dead in the woods playing a piano."

He was sharp. "I don't like that, Jezebel. If you were a boy I'd cuff your ears. If I don't play the piano, what's there for me to do around here? Come down to the drugstore and hang around with the fellers listening to their smutty talk about the female population of Green Pond?" She was endowed with a tendency to incite him to anger. Eventually they'd be inveterate foes.

He scratched his head. "No, I'm not quitting piano. Jezebel, you ought to come over some night and let me play the Moonlight Sonata for you. Boy, Beethoven had a time and a struggle, but he can't be beat with that moonlight."

With the mention of moonlight, there went that unnamable something in his voice that turned Jezebel upside down. "Yes, Vic," and she reached over to take hold of his free hand.

He jerked it away. "You turn my hand loose. That's the way babies get started."

"Victor Thornwell, you're the limit!"

"It's so. Folks start holding hands, then fondling and kissing and feeling, feeling—"

"I don't think I'll have a baby from touching your hand." She repented of her overhasty action. She had been on the brink of warm intimacy with him and now it was gone for today. It took only a breath to blow it away. She belabored her brain as to how she could bring back that warmth again.

She did not know that even when he bickered at her she warmed a spot in his heart that was on the brink of something very big. He was too much of a puzzle to her for her to sense anything that went on inside him. He was so unpredictable that he overwhelmed her often, but she loved him regardless and there'd never be another to take his place. Although—she thought suddenly of Robert Inchurch's attention, persistent and continual for the last year. She didn't want to overestimate her ability or overstep her lines where Ma was concerned. Ma's head was set, Ma could be far more bullheaded than a dozen elders. She could easily handle the elders, but Ma remained the great question. She could lie out of things naturally, but this time Ma was against her.

Either Victor read her mind or saw the Inchurch bank looming up the street. "When you get the bank," he teased suddenly, "you can live like Cleopatra."

"Spider!" she exclaimed.

"Huh, they're no spiders. The Inchurches are a tradition. They can trace their family back to the War of the Roses. You'll be made a queen—was there ever a Queen Jezebel?"

"Don't you plan such big things for me, because the first thing I'd do is have your head chopped off," she retorted light-heartedly, and her laughter was as gay splashing water. She was fair and the rising wind blew sharply upon her and she girlishly dismissed her cares.

"You'd have everything; why'd you want to take spite out on me? I'm only human."

"Oh, I'd just be a woman; so awful mean from living with that humpback. I'd exploit the earth. I'd chew off anybody's ears who got in my way."

"When he comes to see you, does that make you mean? What do you do? Hold hands?"

"He sits in one corner and I sit in another and Ma peeps through the crack in the kitchen door. Oh, it's divine—the three of us!" she laughed.

He wanted to fish out her secret; he smelled something very tainted. "Ho'cum you let him come to see you?"

"Oh!—you don't know my ma! She says I should feel more than honored to have a high elder call upon me. She says it has great weight in church affairs to be on familiar terms with the elders."

Jake saw Jezebel and Vic sneak into the geometry class while Professor Aberdeen drew the geometry patterns on the blackboard and cunningly take their seats. Jake burned with an inhuman jealousy. Jezebel had promised to walk to school with him and here she came sneaking in with Vic.

That day in school Jezebel did not itch, because she had pulled off her long underwear and hid it at the foot of the hill in the honeysuckle thicket before she came out to the main road.

2

That evening from school, Jezebel and Jake walked hand in hand, in their moon-eyed weavily-wilting way, down Main Street. The evaluating folks in the doorways of their sleep-webbed stores watched them and thought them as handsome a pair as Green Pond had to offer.

Alf Logan—founder of a dynasty, years later a string of cotton mills—stood in his hardware store and saw them. "Thar she blows like a bitch in heat and you never know which dog is followin her. Dog-bite-it, Green Pond's comin."

Farther down the street, Henry Leg bounded across the street toward them, jumping the piles of animal dung, grumbling at animals in general for making dung.

"Where're you two birds goin?" Henry asked.

Surprised, they dropped hands and turned their faces to Henry. "Home. Where you reckon folks go after school?"

Henry looked intimately at Jezebel. "What you doing tonight, doll?"

"Studying."

"What kind of lessons? Inchurch Banking System?" He was cocky in smoking out what she was up to with her coy negativeness.

Jezebel blushed. "No."

He turned to Jake and spoke carelessly as if to a child, "Small fry, how about taking yourself off down the street?"

"You make me," Jake growled, and he was already a bulldog.

"Don't you all start nothing over me here in the street," Jezebel chirped, "with people standing in their cobwebby stores looking." For she knew that each doorway contained at least one garrulous gossipmonger, whose eager-listening ears, round eyes, and pursed mouth were ready to sop up choice tidbits which might be displayed in an otherwise dull street.

"Who's starting anything over you?" Henry cut cruelly. "You must be stuck on yourself!" He laughed ironically. "Is ole humpbacked Grandfather Inchurch already gone to your head? Is he coming to see you tonight?"

"Henry Leg! You're the most brazen fellow." For a moment she'd have liked to fly on him as though she were a broody hen and flog him good, but she composed herself quickly. She tossed her head and poured red-hot words at him. "You're cheap dry-goods trash. I wouldn't go in that Leg & Leg Department Store—that dusty cobwebbery—to buy another nickel's worth of ribbon for anything in the world." She turned brusquely, with an air of finality, and walked stiffly down the street. "Come on, Jake, it's getting late." She gave her behind such lightning-like jerks as though she'd paralyze it forever.

Jake fled down the street after her and took hold of her hand. "Aw, Jezebel, I'm sorry."

"You've done nothing." She squeezed his hand. "You are so sweet."

They met David Kingsley coming out of Mrs. Ives' gate with a large bunch of chrysanthemums. His handsome deep-seated smile flashed. "Hi."

"Why wasn't you at school today?" Jezebel flashed at him. Her eyes searched him with avid admiration. There was nothing snobbish or ingratiating about him—his candid face, flowing animal lines, his turbulent hair. Didn't he look like Victor? The similarity struck her more forcefully today than ever. He was as good-looking as Vic, too, yet there was about him a certain loftiness that Vic didn't possess. Something about Vic that drew her and David didn't have it.

"Thought I'd give the teachers time to catch up with me," he laughed. "Needed to help Mother, too."

Jezebel giggled. Everybody in Green Pond knew that David was the smartest boy in school. Some of them said he knew more than Ole Doctor Thornwell who lacked a lot of being anybody's fool and that was one time Ole Doc had bred to a smart woman. Smart as a whip, sharp as a brier, any of them'd say any day about David Kingsley. Then again, they'd never known an illegitimate child that wasn't smart.

David smiled to himself when he noticed the twitching of Jezebel's behind, and how she rubbed her hands up and down her hips so that he could see the print of her hipbones through her clothes. Then he spoke intimately to Jake. "Come over and see me sometime, old boy."

Jezebel noticed David's devouring look and flushed and grabbed Jake's hand again, pulling him away. "David Kingsley had better shut up," she thought. She hurried Jake down the street. The sun was in their laughing faces and laughter came freely from them as the wind over the wind-swept hills.

Their hands were hot between them. They felt each other's blood coursing through them. There had never been a time, an evening, that their hands had been as hot as they were this evening. Even the cool breeze, with its chilly sting, blowing ceaselessly from the west, didn't dampen the hotness of their clinging hands. They had to get somewhere.

At Catawba's gate they hid in the heavy bushes, in the darkly concealing shadows the leaves made. They lingered and their hands didn't want to part, but to hold on forever and forever.

Jake pulled her to his body, kissing her greedily. When his body pressed against her, he was surprised to find she wore such few clothes that he could feel every dent and curve in her hot body. Jezebel pushed her belly up against him, urgently. Her hot-moistened tongue clung to his mouth.

The sun dropped from sight. The chilly dampness rose up from the ground. The stars came out with evaluating winks and frankly scattered the stardust throughout the whole way, predestining all the trafficking that a man would do with a maid.

3

Contentment prevailed upon Catawba's threshold as it nuzzled against the bosom of God's earth and cuddled itself down for the winter as a bear for its sleep. The days were short and filled with smoky gray and the lamps were lighted early in the evening. Pop sat up late and talked of the long, long bygone which seemed so remote and infallible to Vic that he didn't think it could have possibly ever been—but it was so, Pop repeated. He recalled case after case that made Vic's shirttail stand straight out. Vic dreaded to see bedtime come, wondered why he and Pop couldn't sit all night by the hearthstone and talk medicine forever. But Pop told him they could not, that they must sleep some.

Then came the cold night of lullabies played in the conifers about Catawba and fires crackling in the fireplaces. The elder Mathises visited with the elder Thornwells in the great upstairs living room and he and Jezebel in the parlor downstairs.

"Did anyone ever tell you that you were beautiful?" Vic asked, a soft smile played about his lazy lips, his brown eyes dreamy and far off. "You are, and your hair is the most gorgeous, and your eyes—they've allus fascinated me."

Jezebel wriggled among the cushions and carelessly dropped her hand on his knee. She moistened her lips, closed her eyes, and thought that this was as the Garden of Eden.

"You know I want to be a surgeon?" He wanted to talk to her intimately, acquaint her with his spirited desires.

But Jezebel groaned and opened her eyes in sheer disgust.

She was undeniably alarmed at him for bumping her so suddenly off her selected perch, casting her among thorns and thistles. First he'd talked of her beauty, so she'd thought he'd kiss her, because fellows usually didn't have that sort of talk without wanting to kiss, then he'd abruptly changed the subject like that!

"It'd be fascinating." He tried to commune with her.

"But—where'd you get such ideas?" With harmony and prosperity cradling him, she thought in her sheer misery, why did he want to probe and delve into such ungodly things that surely helped no one? Here he wanted to cut on people! Had he lost his mind? It made her hopelessly sad for him to behave like this, when she had so many other things planned. Oh, why was he so elusive? So uncommunicative and something she couldn't touch?

"Pop's been a good doctor all his life and Granny Thornwell was a good midwife."

"So you want to be a doctor? Because your pa and granny were doctors before you?"

"Sure. Be a great surgeon with a big hospital here." His overbold ideas were on a rampage as the red rivers when gorged with too much water.

"A hospital!" She was sharp with amazement.

"A hospital'd be a good thing for Green Pond. Hospitals are going to come here." The room filled with his excitement. His words tumbled out and his thoughts clattered as dishes in an earthquake. His voice, she thought, held all the emotion she wanted for herself. "We've been studying anatomy in Biology and I've delved more into Pop's medical books and magazines. Why, take you here." He placed a hand on each of her pelvic bones, which were not cushioned with fat or clothes and easily felt, and she trembled. "From bone to bone there is right at ten inches. If you thought your appendix was acting up, I'd feel right there and I'd feel the muscles contracting over the inflamed appendix to protect it, or if you had a fibroid tumor, I'd feel right there—I've felt calves in cows. felt em turn over—"

She shivered and jerked from him.

"Victor Thornwell, I'm no cow!" She jumped from the sofa. "You're the limit. Do you think I'm some sort of frozen meat?" Jezebel was crying, her tears coming from a taut sexual anticipation she'd created in herself and from her adoration of him; from a host of ununderstandable things.

"I didn't mean any harm. I'm sorry."

"Sorry!" She spoke sharply. "You're hopeless." He was impossible. Yet his lips, his eyes, his hands, everything about him called her, wanted her to reach out to take him; how that feeling lingered, dug into her, bored down deeply. She was desperate. She was obsessed of the desire of wanting him.

Vic stood in the middle of the room, boyishly awkward. "Golly Moses, girls are funny."

4

Upstairs in the south-wing living room—the big room that cut across the entire end of the hallway, with its enchanting fireplace flanked on both sides by expensively curtained and draped windows, the big room with the homelike, livable furnishings and atmosphere of inviting warmth, the room that always threw welcome across its threshold—the conversation flowed freely, seemingly amicable enough, yet beneath it lurked a scowling darkness.

"My, my, some people have everything," said Cora Mathis, looking the room over, waiting to be asked to be seated, tapping her heel lightly on the rug. *This could've been mine*, she thought. *Why, my whole dinky house is hardly as big as this one room. Why I ever tied myself to that sloven, slipshod John Mathis puzzles me yet. Still, there were so few men left after the war. Better a piece of a man than none a-tall. Better than drying up upon the vine.*

Won't you take the sofa here with me in front of the fire, Cora?"

Naomi asked. "And we'll let the menfolks have the big chairs beside the windows." *Cora Mathis is taking this room in as though she had never been in it before. She can't fool me with all her carrying on in the church. She's more up her sleeve than a plump arm. I don't believe I've ever seen anyone in my whole life look at anything with so much covetousness.*

"Looks like we're in for some rough weather," said Ole Doc. "We need some good cold weather to kill out the insects. Right now, it'd check this rage of colds that's going about. Where there's unsettled weather, it always breeds colds." *Why are they looking so intensely at me? Do they not think I'm a human being? You can never tell about that fellow John. He seems to get more out of life than most. But I bet when the sharp-tongued Cora gets through picking on him—although it's probably her tongue that has made him as he is. Naomi thinks she has me buffaloed. I've learned to watch her. And Cora's getting older. Good bit of gray in that red hair. Still good-looking. I remember her when she looked like Jezebel.*

"Weather ain't so bad long as you've a roof over your head," John began in his turtle-sticking-his-head-out voice. "But when you've got to sleep on a brush pile, like I did in the war, night after night, with the rain turning to ice all over you and the brush and the water running all about, that's bad. Folks are discontented in this day and time." *Why do they look at me? If they'd been through what I have, they'd not stare that way. I gave up the best years of my life to the Cause and it was lost. Nobody cares for an old soldier and his lice once the wars have cooled.*

"Yes," Naomi nodded to John knowingly, "Father said it was simply dreadful. He talked of it ceaselessly until the time of his death. Poor Father. He gave his life for the Cause." *The Doctor has his eyes upon me. I can see the cunningness as he looks at Cora. And he acts just like he was a cat and I was a poor defenseless mouse. I shall show him. He doesn't know I have a storeroom. I'm saving up.*

"Heaven declare His glory," blazed Cora, "that's all I hear morning, noon, and night at home. John sits reading Robert E. Lee." *I wonder what Tad Thornwell's thinking of? I wonder what he'd say if he knew that golden opportunity had at last knocked at my door and that I am taking advantage of it? I played with him and lost. He remembers it. He doesn't forget that easily. This time I'm not losing.*

5

Catawba's mellowed red bricks became most intensely home when across her color wheel was that lovesome black and richly gleaming Mama Amazon to iron out every trouble between heaven and hell and even talk right up to Gabriel. Mama Amazon was going to have more downright fun out of the candy pullin than anyone. Much of life she left to inference and innuendo, for there were always things cropping up that nobody understood and she didn't care to act unbecomingly. She understood the ages from seven to seventy and each in his age was all right. Gawd placed her here to laugh outright and to furnish niggers fo the world and she had shorely been pleasing in He's sight.

In the spacious dining room she had the fire in the big fireplace throwing its flattering light over the rich furnishings with the subtle eye of fancy decorum. The crocks of molasses boiling on the hearth in nests of glowing coals sent their steamy breaths of fragrance up into her face as she worked over them. This candy pullin gave her a good excuse to get to cook by the fire and she did hope Naomi didn't become unset in her mind and suddenly take a cheap notion to want to close up this fireplace and put in some sort of cranky stove. She laughed softly to herself and stirred the crocks often with a long-handled spoon.

Outside, the crunching of ice and snow under the horses' hoofs rang out sharply. When it was nighttime, the moon came up creeling and spreading its wide mouth from tip to tip and dipped out quantities of laughter, and the dark spot in the moon—caused by some ill-natured, unrighteous sinner burning brush on a Preachin Sunday—spoke darkly to all that sprawled thereabout in the imbricated shadows. The air was invigoratingly raw. Fat icicles glistened as shiny silver on all Catawba's eaves.

Jezebel came riding straddle in the saddle with Henry Leg and her laughter was as moonlight and her eyes were filled with stardust. Abigail Bell, a mousy girl, lifted her countenance in horror and actually blushed so vividly that the trees were lighted up as by a flare when she beheld the sparkling Jezebel riding straddle. But the catchy and colorful Jezebel spurned curtly anything that Abigail might be prone to think, for after all Abigail was merely a scrawny female with no gusto and Jezebel dismissed any obfuscate feeling that perchance might smolder in her heart and laughed loosely with the boys in a childishly independent way. Throughout the evening her quick temper, laden with some trite peevishness, flared up and down as a pianist running scales, but she always successfully maneuvered things so that she had a boy at each side of her.

Jezebel frequently had to climb Catawba's spacious staircase for numerous graceless reasons, and one out-of-breath swain escorted her up and two different ones escorted her down. She feigned shyness and was suave and giggly.

When the crocks of molasses had boiled themselves into thick popping syrup, Mama Amazon poured it on marble, worked it into lumps, and then the boys and girls, with well-buttered hands, pulled it—a boy and a girl hold of each piece. They threw the sticky substance back and forth, changing ends recklessly, giving it innumerable twists with each jerky pull. The fondant was pulled until creamy white, then snapped into sheeny sticks. The boys and girls laughed gaily, the boys filched brushing kisses and caressing looks. Mama Amazon sat in the corner of the homely hearth and her reward was steadfast, notwithstanding the fact that she was working later than usual, but where those boys of hers were concerned there was no shy shrinking from work in her.

Vic was fascinated with the decided feminine way of Abigail and he felt substantially enriched tonight when he had the pleasure of being her partner.

Jezebel watched, as a hawk watches when outstripping a field mouse, Abigail and Victor throughout the whole candy pulling. She boiled thicker than the molasses and she popped much louder. Who in the world did Abigail Bell think she was—what sort of worldly girl? Jezebel clicked her heels and twitched her behind most disapprovingly and she was immodestly bold about it—Abigail was spoiling her evening of fun as too sharp spurs often spoil the trip for the horse. Jezebel's partner, David Kingsley, had to remind her frequently that they were pulling candy. David, knowing only too well what was wrong with her, openly upbraided her mischievously, but it did no good. Once he was tempted to bemean her before everyone by calling their attention to it, but that would have been too cruel and to nobody's welfare so he refrained. David Kingsley knew how to get along with people; his mother had taught him to be conscious of it.

Victor played for the crowd and Abigail was entranced with the music—and Jezebel reflected upon what this could mean. She was edgy and mistrusted the way things were turning out. She'd have been as well off to have stayed at home and entertained the spider. A shudder careened over her body and she muttered darkly to herself. It was a good thing that Ma didn't know that Robert Inchurch was coming tonight or she'd never have got to come on this sprint. Her throat constricted with fright and she smiled blandly to herself and tried to comfort herself with the thought that perhaps the weather was too bad and he would not come tonight; but if on the other hand he did come, there'd be the devil to pay. For when Ma's tongue got through whacking on her and her jeering voice rattling in her ears, she didn't know whether she could face such an upbraiding. Everything seemed so unendurable and insecure for Jezebel the way that Victor Thornwell was acting up. Honestly, she believed he was simply manipulating things around to aggravate her. He knew her ardent nature would be no trouble whatever to agitate. The evening was absolutely and wholly wasted. She noted sourly that everybody was clapping with great gusto for Victor to play again and Abigail was leaning over in his face. That was impolite—Abigail was the rudest girl. Jezebel thought she'd suffocate in her own miserableness.

It was late. The candy pulling had ended. Everyone was scurrying around getting ready to leave. Some of the boys were out looking about the horses; most of the girls had gone upstairs after their coats and hats and mittens.

Vic sauntered through the hallway that led from the south parlor, passing behind the staircase to the north parlor, where he purposely maneuvered to bump into Jezebel. He asked her what on earth had got into her tonight, but she had punished herself so unmercifully all evening that right now she wasn't even interested in him, so made as if to brush past him rudely. He threw out his long arms and stopped her.

At first she squirmed as if to get away, but his touch so fired her that she stopped, trying to interpret his motive. This was most flabbergasting, she thought. He was so fascinatingly strange. Was that what drew her to him? What sort of misdo was he up to this time? He'd fooled her so much. She had struggled so desperately for this lately and here it was right before her very eyes and at the most inopportune time—had she misjudged? Would he forever be so unpredictable?

At first she wriggled, trying to free herself without knowing why she made this feeble struggle to escape. But then his arms tightened on her and slid to her waist, pulling her against him. Now he so excited her that she struggled desperately and franctically.

"Who do you think you're fooling?" he breathed into her ear.

She felt his warm sweet breath on her neck, in her face. She melted into his arms.

His face was in hers, he had her off the floor, kissing her with consuming hunger. Their lips clung together for an eternity. They must never, never part, Jezebel thought. This that had come to her from beyond the stardust must never go. This boy, this man-child from the heavens above was hers. Hers!

Then he let go of her slowly, his arms and hands and fingers easing away; and Jezebel and Vic looked at each other with a love light in their eyes. Their hearts pounded as the thunderous hammers of creation. They had no need to ask questions, for all life and the world lay at their feet waiting, like a rose waiting for the rising sun to unfold its petals.

"You're the strangest boy," she said under her frightened and trembling breath. "You get the wildest ideas."

He shook his head at her and smiled shakily. They looked and looked at each other, their cheeks highly colored, their eyes glowing. She was still looking as she moved backward toward the stairs. He was all she had ever wanted in this world. Ever since she could remember, there had never been anything but Victor. She couldn't imagine why she didn't fling her arms around his neck and hold him so that he'd never, never get away again. But then she turned and started up the stairs. These were Catawba's front stairs, and very, very important stairs, and there were a lot of people about. Victor would choose a time like this!

Oh, well, Jezebel thought as she went up the stairs, everything was all right now—forevermore she would be happy. The long waiting was over. She had her love, nothing else mattered.

Victor stood and watched her vanish up the stairs and watched until he saw her coming down. With her by his side, there were great wonders in the world that he could do—hills and mountains he would move.

When Jezebel came down the stairs, waltzing importantly,

there was David Kingsley, suave and tall, topcoat on and hat in hand. "I'm taking you home, Jezebel. The sulky's here if you're ready to go."

Jezebel left with David, and Victor followed them to the door, watching them drive away in the snow, and Victor's heart pounded with such madness that he thought he would never sleep again.

On the way home, Jezebel slapped David's face every time he leaned near her, and he wondered what had brought about this sudden and significant change.

6

Catawba was comfortably bedded down for the winter. The cane had been run through the mill and its juice boiled into thick molasses; the sweet potatoes dug and hilled with cornstalks and dirt; the fruit all dried and sacked away; beans and peppers strung on strings. The garden was full of winter greens, turnips, and carrots. The hogpen was filled with such fat hogs they didn't care to get up to eat, and all the fig bushes and trees filled with roosting chickens and turkeys.

The wind blew icy cold and the old mules backed their butts against the barn wall, standing there wriggling their long ears and prophesying more snow.

And at night Vic and Pop popped popcorn, listened to the fire on the hearth, and they talked of all the things that had been in medicine and the things that they thought would come.

And Vic thought, "Let all my days be like this."

7

GABRIEL: Lawd, sich a big weddin us got on han down in Green Pond.

GAWD: It's good to see Yellow Sam an Gee gettin married up. Sumpin big gonna come outta this.

GABRIEL: What besides a parcel of yard chillun?

GAWD: Sumpin mighty interestin. You know em white mens took it upon emselves to kill off the red mens and took it upon emselves to ketch emselves a parcel of black men and bring em here. Well, that ground down there was made fo just one color of people: red. They can't sin agin Me.

GABRIEL: Yellow Sam tolt Mama Amazon he wants all his chillun to be good yard chillun. Mama Amazon was awful happy. She say Gee better treat Sammy right. He's a good settled boy and he'll be good to her. He's too much like Ole Doc not to be.

GAWD: Gee'll do it. Mama Amazon done brung Gee up right. She never did raise up none of her chillun to be trash. She say if black trash was any worse than white trash they'd be gettin some low.

GABRIEL: It was nice of Ole Doc givin Sammy that land yonder south of town. Got a good house on em, too.

GAWD: Well, long as Yellow Sam and Gee haves the land, they have everythin. But look at po Cyrus Hill down yonder walkin along to the mill. He done been driven fro he land so long ago he's purty nigh fo'got bout em. It displeasures me much to see Cyrus workin in the mill. See how longingly he look to the fields, to his bright red land he was drove from. I created the lovely red land and all things fo the red land. I filled it with worms to plow it, filled it wit growin things. I didn't create the twilight hour fo walkin to no mill. Man done that. I create only goodness.

GABRIEL: I heard Cyrus cryin out against You the other night, Gawd.

GAWD: What was he sayin?

GABRIEL: He say You ought to look down on Green Pond an stop this carryin-on. He say You intended man to tend a garden because man love the earth; that You intended him to plant seeds. He say that man ought to get prepared an ready to lie down in the earth wit he's mother, to sleep the sweet sleep in the earth, an he can't do it in the mill. He say You ought to see man is where You intend he be.

GAWD: That makes Me pure sad, Gabriel. I do My best, but man keeps thinkin up things.

Ole Satan hung around the T-square house of John Mathis, courting the living daylights out of Miz Cora.

BEELZEBUB: Satan, ole boy, it's too cold wit all this snow an ice here on the ground to be hangin round Miz Cora's. This wind an cold done turnt me so ashy, doubtful I ever gets thawed out again.

SATAN: You's the grumblingest man. When us got all this important work here to do!

BEELZEBUB: I don' think jest one ole woman is worth all this freezin.

SATAN: It ain't so much what one ole woman is worth, it's what jest one ole woman will do. Look what I got ole Eve started at.

BEELZEBUB: All right, have you way.

Then came the inevitable time that Cora betook the wagon whip in her hands and inelegantly meddled with the everlasting stardust. She stood over Jezebel and breathed fire and clutched John Mathis' wagon whip in her hand.

Cora emitted her brightest sarcasm upon Jezebel. "Since you're so innocent today, my dear girl, I'll explain. Robert came last night and you were gone. I had to entertain him to keep him from being too disappointed. And I did a thorough good job of it—I told him where you'd gone. He seemed extremely disappointed and hurt."

"I didn't tell him to come. I didn't tell him to come—" Jezebel began her lengthy defense. Her eyes flared.

"Oh, you didn't?" Cora shouted. "I can easily imagine that. But you knew he was coming. Having him drive over here and you running off. I know you and your cunningness. You're dreadful."

For a moment Jezebel's eyes dropped to the floor, but she

brought them up suddenly. "I wish that stinking Robert In-church'd leave me alone. He's hounded me so, I despise him." She shook her copper-colored hair. Her face filled with loathing.

"Jezebel, you may as well cut out your tomfoolery," and Cora changed her tone to absolute authority. "You're going to marry Robert Inchurch."

"I'll not!" Jezebel raised her voice beyond the ceiling.

"You will," Cora declared. Jezebel stamped the bare pine boards with her energetic feet, her eyes hard and unflinching, lips taut. "Oh, you cunning Jezebel." Cora cut the wagon whip threateningly on the floor. "I know what you've been up to. I've suspected it for several years. I could tell every time it happened here lately. You're a dead giveaway—to me, at least. I've been wondering what to do about it and now I've fully decided." She brought her eyes to narrow squinty slits.

"What do you mean?" Jezebel broached slowly, threaded her way.

Cora cut Jezebel across her arm with the whip. It popped loudly in the cold air. She grew caustic. "I'm having it out of you this morning or I'm cutting you so full of watery blisters with this wagon whip you'll not be able to move for a dog's lifetime. Your carrying on with Henry Leg: I know about it and don't you for one second try to deny it to me. I'm not so dumb as you think. What I want to know is: how did he get himself into you? You had on long underwear, drawers, and bloomers."

Cora hurled and charged the defenseless Jezebel, inveighed against her dishonorable ways. And Jezebel cringed. Jezebel, who had never cringed before. But now she felt humiliatingly defeated and hopelessly woebegone.

Cora cut Jezebel with the whip, shouting, "Out with it! How'd it happen?" She knew how to blow the fire manfully once the wood was ignited.

"I took them off."

"Where? Behind the schoolhouse with Henry Leg looking on? Have you no decency?"

"No." She halted, because nothing seemed any longer paramount in her world.

"Where? Answer my question!" Cora was superbly adept at arduous undertakings.

"On the way to school—down there in the big honeysuckle thicket at the foot of the hill."

"Jezebel Mathis, do you mean to say that you stripped stark naked down there in the honeysuckle thicket in broad daylight—in the outdoors?" Cora's uncertain voice was as a sick woman's. "What did you do with your underwear?"

"Hid em in the honeysuckle thicket until I came back."

"So that's how Henry Leg got himself into you? How many times? How many times did he fiddle with you?"

"I don't know—I never kept count."

"So you don't remember? Perhaps if I prod your memory you'll tell me more. When did you start in with David Kingsley? Or did you take them on week about? Or one in the morning and one in the evening?"

Jezebel drew herself into a knot. "Ma, how'd you know about David?" The sluices of her heart opened suddenly, draining all the blood from her body, leaving her bleached, leaving her frightened at last, as she saw where this was leading and where Cora's driving would end it.

"Oh, so it's so?" Indignantly Cora fetched the words from the storeroom of her soul. Now it was a mere matter of time until she got her way.

"Yes." Jezebel felt as though she were being separated from the things of the earth.

"And now it's Jake Thornwell! Am I not right again, Miss Jezebel Mathis?"

"Yes."

"So you're trying to wedge yourself into Catawba?" Cora smacked her lips a little.

"I don't like Jake Thornwell." Jezebel stated it bluntly, quite stiffly.

"Don't like Jake Thornwell? This, indeed, is astounding. Pray, tell me whom you like, other than Jezebel?"

"Vic."

"Another one? Will the line never cease? Tell me, has he tried it too?" Cora was rimmed in subtle irony.

"Oh, but, Ma, no. He's different. Ma, I love Vic." Jezebel spoke in sheer honesty, pled in desperation.

"You might as well forget him. You have a chance to marry Robert Inchurch and that's what you're going to do! The Inchurches have the money and you have a chance at it!"

Jezebel struck wildly at the oncoming landslide. "No!"

"Yes, you are! He's coming again tonight. I soft-pedaled for you last night. I've cut out every underbrush—the way is clear. You're nearly eighteen years old and unmarried. It's time you quit raping all the boys in the county and get married and settle down," Cora said with brutal savagery.

"I won't, I won't, I won't!"

"When I get through with you, you will."

"I'll kill myself!" She would try the unheard-of, the fantastic, anything that offered escape.

Cora laughed mockingly. "Go ahead. I don't have any objections. I'm saying if you should decide to remain alive, you're going to marry Robert Inchurch. A poor girl like you seldom has the golden opportunity that's knocking at your door. Of course, your good looks help some in his wanting you," she inveighed cautiously.

"What does Robert Inchurch care about looks? He's never had a girl in all his life."

"Well, at least one of you'll go to bed a virgin." Cora cut the whip. "Listen, young 'un, I've had a little experience. Thirty years ago I thought I was able to get into Catawba. So Tad Thornwell and I did just what you've been doing, but you see, somewhere along the road I lost. And that old codger went scot-free. All I have out of the affair is security in the church, for Tad Thornwell, being an elder, wouldn't be brazen enough to have me churched. So I've kept him reminded of that all these years and been able to get what I wanted in that church—even to having more than one stubborn, bullheaded preacher glad to get away from it." She came down from on high.

"*Ma! With Ole Doc Thornwell?* Oh, my gosh." This must be held over from some other life, from some other world.

"After all, you do have to be young before you can be old. That's beside the point. The important thing is that you decide to marry Robert Inchurch. You can have Green Pond at your feet. I tell you, opportunities don't come often like this. And you must strike while the iron is hot if you'd bend it."

"I won't, I won't, I won't. Oh, Ma, I can't." It was a bitter, horrified wail.

"You'll be glad to or I'm going to whip you within an inch of your life. I won't have this kind of disgrace pulled down around my ears because, you mark my word, Jezebel Mathis, those boys'll never marry you. They're already laughing up their sleeves. They'd talk right now if they weren't so young and still afraid of the wagon whip at home. Later they'll talk. It'll be on everybody's tongue, every slut in town. But once you're married to an Inchurch, they'll never let that cat out of the bag. You'll be quite safe."

"But Vic—I'd hoped someday—"

"Forget him."

"I can't. I love him."

"That makes no difference. You're a woman. There're lots of things women have to put up with. This has been a man's world, you goose, and don't you ever, ever forget it. But Jesus is setting us women free through the church. The church is helping us women lots and you've got to learn early to beat men at their own games. For if you don't learn to win early and stay on top and never, never give them a chance, they'll get you down under their feet, and once they do they'll trample you to death. . . . Now, Robert is coming tonight—"

"No, no. I can't face him. Not after all this."

"Jezebel, I'm tired arguing with you. He may be like his father and not live long. You'd better grab him while the grabbing is good. Your little affairs'll leak out some of these days, for boys like to brag about any new territory they've explored—it's in their nature. And it'll get into the church and we'll be ruined. You'd better cover up while you've got a chance."

"But, Ma, those long spidery arms; he'll be so hungry for a woman."

"Good, it'll be the easier for you to get your own sins covered up the better. For a while, he'll be blinded with his new-found joy."

"No, Ma, please."

"Jezebel Mathis, I'm tired fooling with you. I've a good mind to let you go. Let the men tramp the life out of you. Let them spill your blood about the roads, let the dogs lick it up. I've a good mind to do just that, because that's exactly what you're asking for. And I don't know but that it'd serve you and John Mathis right." Cora became unusually calm, and spoke quietly. "Robert will be here tonight. Have your answer ready. Where money is concerned, he knows, which is real good; and where women are concerned, he doesn't know, which is even better. Your answer had better be yes."

Cora Mathis walked from the room.

2

The natural, beautiful process of aging by nature takes time. It is not done overnight nor in the batting of an eyelid. The juice from the apples makes the cider and the cider ages into the vinegar, golden vinegar the color of Jezebel's hair. The golden vinegar is on top, the dregs—as Cora—are settled dark and ugly at the bottom of the jug, and there they repose calmly until some outer force strikes the jug, and then roiling begins that clouds the whole contents.

Tonight, a cold dreary December night, Jezebel sat in their parlor before a radiant fire that was so hot she was forced to sit almost in the middle of the room. Jezebel had become, in something over eight hours, almost unrecognizable, except that now she looked almost exactly like Cora. She had aged without time.

Her beauty, while never of a classical quality, was superb and natural. She wore her Sunday-best dress. Her hair, naturally curly, was fixed upon her head in mysterious-looking coils which the firelight toned into many shades of red.

There was no longer any laughter about her mouth. Her hands lay folded in her lap loosely. Her waist was pulled into an eighteen-inch waistline. Her eyes, no longer cunning and mischievous, were filled with bitter hate, although she was being crafty enough to keep that well concealed. So Jezebel sat in the parlor waiting, patiently waiting for the spider to come to sit with her.

There would be no use for Cora to peep through the crack in the kitchen door tonight, keeping her nervous, fidgety vigil. She could stay in the kitchen and roll on the floor with her new-found joy.

"I, Jezebel Mathis, have sinned." She glanced at her hands and for a second the bitter hate was gone from her yellow eyes, and in that second it looked as though tears would come, but with one quick batting of her eyelids she brushed them away, letting the bitter hate return. "The wages of sin would be getting tossed out of North Bethel Church. The wages of sin would be having the high elders look down their noses at me. The wages of sin would be having the women cut me cold. The wages of sin would be having the whole town pick me to pieces."

She listened keenly. There was someone walking across the porch. She heard the loose floor boards rattling. She fixed herself resembling a lifelike oil painting and faced the door.

The knock came on the door.

"Come in." Her voice was so dead that she didn't recognize it as being her own. The door was pushed open and there stood Jake Thornwell, startled surprise on his face when he saw her.

"What in the name of God has happened to you, Jezebel?"

"Nothing," she said in a cold voice filled with subdued fury, "nothing a-tall! Go away. Do you hear me? Go away! Go away." She spoke in such icy tones that shivers ran over Jake's skin. "Go on home. Do you hear?"

Jake went as if he had been caught plotting rowdy mischief. His barometer of fear embalmed his face with lines of fright. One backward look showed him Jezebel recasting her pose, preparing for the spider to come into her.

He jumped upon his horse, riding away into the night. He told himself over and over, with continuous ripples of fright shuffling over him, that what he had seen at the Mathis home was either a ghost or Mrs. Mathis. It was impossible for that to have been Jezebel. He could never be certain in the fire's yellow light, because it threw too many tricky shadows. It surely was Mrs. Mathis. She and Jezebel resembled one another to a startling degree. Jake laughed shakily. It was uncanny going to court the daughter and getting the old woman. Well, there were other nights. He would see her tomorrow at school. Strange, come to think of it, that she was not there today. It was seldom she ever missed a day. There were too many other things she'd miss if she missed school.

3

Robert Inchurch was preparing for his leavetaking, having duly and properly courted Jezebel in the correct style of an Inchurch, having asked for her hand in marriage, and having been accepted to his personal satisfaction and ultimate joy. He had been as methodical and cautious as though reading a mortgage paper in the Inchurch bank. He had lusted for this girl for too long; he had endured her scorn for too long. His pride rose at his victory and he desired her more than ever.

Even when a choleric old spider asked her to marry him, it should be sealed with a swooping kiss, Jezebel thought. After all, she had spent the whole evening anticipating what that kiss would be like and what it would be like to go to bed with a great high elder of the North Bethel Church. But his affair here had been too dull. While Jezebel was an excellent pouter, she had no intention of pouting her whole life away just because she was going to be tied to a spider. She already knew the vague shape of other plans.

So Jezebel helped him into his topcoat, being fussy, feminine, and fluttery with the process, using an astounding amount of soothing brushes with her hands. Cuddle-wuddley she buttoned his coat, letting her head brush against his shoulders, and she knew it was coming before it arrived.

He had his arms about her and his lips sought her mouth. Jezebel thought, "Oh, my gosh, this's gonna be right easy. He's squeezing me like a big bear." She shut her eyes, but curiosity bade her open them to slits. "Gosh, his eyes are tight shut. His breath is gasping. I'll kiss him good, this spider—I'll give him something to remember. Perhaps it'll shock him to death. He might die—"

Robert turned, groped blindly for the doorknob, and was gone the quickest she could ever remember him going. Jezebel stood vastly proud in the center of the room as a great general who has whipped and subdued a rebellious people. She knew she had rocked the Inchurch fortune, shaking it to the very bottom. She tapped her energetic foot on the floor, surveyed the four walls of the dingy, Victorian parlor. There surged in her the desire to conquer new horizons, new territories. She would have no more use for such trite things as jealousy, greed, envy, malice. Why should she need these paltry tools? Didn't she now have the whip in her hand? And she had so easily donned the churchly garb with the Inchurch fortune. Who was there to call her to account? Or what would the charges be?

4

Jepson Grady came to see Ole Doc and stayed to hear Victor play—and to study him.

This old, well-preserved house and this boy went together; they were as much alike as two bolls of cotton, Jepson thought. I wonder who tacked the name of Victor to him? It's as though whoever named him had reached into the air and caught hold of a nothingness and stuck it onto him and it has turned into a name. That high, aquiline nose, sensitive as a squirrel's; those eyes never seem to look at you—first they're as far away as Tibet and as mysterious, then they're back burning, burning a hole through you with their searching. I wonder, could I trust him? I've a notion to try him—he might know something.

Vic felt he'd always known someone like Jepson Grady. There was something about him he couldn't forget. The way he held his pipe. The way he crossed his legs. The way he fished into his pocket for a match to relight his pipe, grumbling that he had forgotten and let it go out. It was something, he didn't know what; did he need to know? There were things that neither words nor pictures could convey; perhaps some could be told in music; perhaps some in surgery. Didn't life have many unexplainable things in it? Why make everything plain?

"Do you know Jezebel Mathis very well?" Jep asked casually, watching the smoke from his pipe.

"I'll say. She took me to school the first day I went. She wanted to hold my hand and I didn't want her to."

Jep laughed. "Why didn't you want her to hold your hand?"

"Too fussy or something—like a hen trying to crowd too many biddies under her—"

"If I tell you something, you'll not tell? It's a very dark secret."

"What is it?"

"You'll not tell?"

"What do you think I am?"

"All right. Did you know Jezebel Mathis was going to be married?"

"No. Who to? Robert Inchurch, bet a dime."

"How did you know? I thought I was telling you something."

"I don't know—it's just a hunch I had." Vic crawfished. "The Inchurches always get whatever they want one way or another—the crabbiest of the cozeners—or that's what Mama Amazon always said—and what she don't know about folks in this neck of the woods is hardly worth knowing. And what she knows, I sooner or later find out. She has filled my head so full of things that happened before I was born and when I was born that I sometimes feel like I'm living two different lives. I look at my hands and I'm not certain whether they're my hands or Pop's hands or my Granny Joanna's hands. It's the same way with my eyes. I can't get away from that feeling of living two lives—that feeling of being through all this once before—like a play—like a rehearsal. The same thing going over and over. Why, right now I feel like I've told you all this a thousand years ago."

"I get you; but don't you accidentally let it slip out about the marriage."

"How'd you know about it?"

"It's all down at the office raring and snorting to be put into the paper—picture, too. Wedding's going to be in June, the exact date hasn't been set yet. It's not coming out until Christmas Eve, so keep your mouth shut. I'm not wanting to tangle with the Inchurches. I know which side of my bread is buttered and I want to be sure I keep the buttered side. Dry bread isn't so good—I've had too much of it. There's lots of things lots of times

I'd like to print, but I remember the buttered side of the bread."
The firelight flickered against Jepson Grady's face, and Victor
thought he saw shadows there that were not made by the fire.

Long into the winter night, after Jep had left, Vic lay looking
at the fire and thinking about Jezebel.

5

When the Green Pond *Observer* came out Christmas Eve, it
caused the severest shock the human body could take and remain
alive.

Jezebel Mathis was to be married to Robert Belcher Inchurch.
Green Ponders gasped.

Jepson Grady smoked his pipe and listened.

Christmas, Santa Claus, and Jesus were forgotten. "Have-you-
heard" was the holiday in Green Pond. Small children, who were
too young to realize, cried for a bright-red Santa Claus. Very
old people, who had had too much bright-red Santa Claus, cried
for Jesus and the church bells. But everyone else talked only of the
news.

Henry Leg turned white when he first heard it. He forgot to
unwrap the dry goods. He forgot to carry the merchandise from
the stock room to the shelves and the counters in Leg & Leg
Department Store. Everything looked identical to him. He
couldn't tell the long underwear from the bloomers. The news
went around and around in his mind.

David Kingsley read it sitting before the fire in his mother's
living room and he was mildly amused. He was learning to smoke
a pipe. Mother thought it'd add so much to the room to have a
man smoking. He laid the paper down, took a deep draw from his
pipe, blew smoke rings, and looked at them. Life was like those
smoke rings: it faded away just as fast.

When he read it, Jake Thornwell knew a kind of fear he'd
never known before. The world was suddenly filled with spider

webs, sticky and tangling. He refrained from talk and stared into space. Tomorrow and tomorrow were the same. They were filled with sticky spider webs. That was the net, the net of righteousness. And the spider web kept tangling around him and every day was the same.

But Victor scurried through a snowstorm that Christmas Eve, scurried through bleakness and desolation, scurried over the wild wind-swept land and carried a heavy basket of Christmas parcels. Uncle Prince Blue was sick and would have no Christmas unless Vic got there. When he saw the basket, Uncle Blue's face lit up and he was filled with dry, brittle laughter. "I been prophesyin fo sumpin lack that. I wishes Christmas would last always." But Vic told him that too many goodies would be bad for his old belly. Then Uncle Blue cackled, "Next time you's comin this way, bring me a passel of good meat skins, some what's got right much meat left on em, and I'll show you can my ole belly grind em up."

6

Men and books are fallible. What is accepted today was not accepted a hundred years ago and will not be accepted a hundred years hence. Green Pond was not certain then, nor is it certain now.

However, Jezebel lolled in the parlor holding the hand that wore Robert Inchurch's impressive diamond. And she knew that it was more than a stone, for stones were small rocks that one threw, most likely at one's enemies. Well, she would see: what else was there for her to do but gaze at this great glitter? She couldn't go into Green Pond shopping. There was no way. The fiancée of an Inchurch didn't ride down Main Street in a dilapidated, steel-tired, mud-spattered buggy pulled by such a beast as Katie Lou. It simply wasn't accepted in Green Pond. Moreover, the Inchurch in-laws were not going to accept her readily. Well, she had this stone; she'd see. This betrothal was a burdensome yoke. This was being old before her time. But she had got herself trapped into it because there wasn't any way out, and if she could bear it a while she would get used to it, perhaps, and it would not be hard to bear. She would make everyone sit up and take notice all their lives, as they were taking notice now. And those Inchurch womenfolks, her in-laws, she was all ready for them. She would chafe and irritate them just as being engaged to Robert Inchurch irritated her.

She had two people watching her—by day and by night. Ma was watching closer than ever now and Robert watched her as a buzzard its offal. Robert's jealousy and desire increased from night to night. He was a busy man these days, he told her, yet it seemed that never a night rolled by without his coming to see her.

Robert was building a grandiose Pink House, a gilded cage for his dove, erecting it on Third Street over the hallowed honeysuckle thicket where Typhoon Ai had expunged ole Satan. On the way to the bank every morning, ole Hump drove Robert past the Pink House in order that he might punch up the workers and see the architect's plans unfold as pink peach petals in April. His long arms and legs and weightless body enabled him to crawl and scan and jump the framing hurriedly. The carpenters stood in awe, watching him as though he were a dreaded spider. And when he'd prostrated the law to the carpenters, Hump drove him on to the bank to see which mortgages and notes were in default.

On Sundays he came to take the Mathises to church, so no longer did they have to go an hour earlier to hide Katie Lou and the mud-splattered buggy in the thicket from the critical eyes of the congregation.

Now they rode in regal splendor; now Jezebel was forced to sit with the Inchurch in-laws in their pew—the most important and expensive pew in the church. Jezebel had known the Inchurch womenfolks all her life, but now they were in-laws—her cat eyes shone and she beat her tail on the seat, and the Inchurch womenfolks could feel it coming right through their seaters.

No pew in church was as expensive as the Inchurch pew. No one in church could help looking and looking at Jezebel—little, red-headed Jezebel Mathis who now sat in the Inchurch pew. Well, that was some comfort, she thought. It would be more. Later. When she was married. She would show them. And there would be more diamonds. And finer furnishings in that Pink House on Third Street than there were even in Catawba.

But no Victor. Victor belonged to Catawba. She wondered what he was doing. She had not seen him in so long—how long had it been? Since she quit school. He'd be studying somewhere —all the Thornwells were bookish. She ought to see him—ought she not? There should be a way if she put her mind to it. If she put her mind to it, she could get around Ma.

Jezebel sat all day looking into the fire and holding the hand that held the diamond. What else was there to do but to sit and to dread her first night with Robert Inchurch?

7

Vic suddenly realized it was June and his last summer at home for a long time. All the earth was still with the stifling heat. There had been no rain since early April and the red land parched dry. Tomorrow and tomorrow continued to slip up over the horizon, dry-eyed, red-eyed, and promised no rain. Wells dried up, small streams trickled at night, pitifully slow, and mysteriously hid their waters during the long hot days.

Vic went over Catawba's parching acres. He had never realized that there was so much beauty as he found now—a small patch of corn in a low place that didn't suffer, the damp coolness about Catawba's ever-copious well where it looked to him as if all the toads in the country were habitating, each toad, cheerfully panting, making its bed in the damp sand.

The earth belonged to Gawd, Vic thought, He'd do with it as

He pleased. Somewhere beyond the shining blue it was written in the stardust, predestined about a man's life here on the red land between the two red rivers. He accepted in serene discipline and becalmed his upbraiding fears, for there was nothing to fear.

Mama Amazon said, "Discouragin tryin to raise a crop this year; but it might be a good year after all. Pays to hope. Hope's good to live by, an still better to die by."

For no apparent reason typhoid jumped up and started on a wild rampage. Ole Doc very near pooped out trying to stay on the go day and night.

The days grew incredibly hot and it was hard for Vic and Mama Amazon to stay lighthearted, especially with such scurrying about in Catawba.

Great Aunt Tiffy lay with sedulous death, decked out in borrowed feathers as though she had an inborn incentive to go somewhere. During her lifetime her chronic colitis had turned her into a ravishing eater who wolfed down all comestibles that she could lay hands to, thereby weakening her bowels to such pin-pointed bleeding that when typhoid fever jumped astraddle her skinny frame the fever bugs had no trouble boring millions of holes in her flimsy guts.

"Ah Lawd, her an ole Sherman can strike matches together now," said Mama Amazon to Vic, and she rolled her eyes to the front part of Catawba where the Mure relatives fetched gallons of tears to their eyes, kissed and swooned most elegantly, and never missed a meal during the whole to-do of getting Great Aunt Tiffy off on her farewell journey.

Pop shuffled in from calls, tired and irritated. Somebody had to make enough money to buy her a coffin. He couldn't recall how many of them he'd buried, the numbers he'd fed and clothed, often handing them folding money as a gift, for the vast proud Mures would take it no other way.

Vic dropped on the back steps with Mama Amazon and they

talked of Miz Joanna who was a stomp-down good midwife and
healer and who attacked the deadliest and most insidious diseases
with downright superintuition. Some were born with the telltale
signs of healing in their fingers.

They listened to the fowls go to roost, smelled the soap-spiced
odor the fig bushes emitted, caught the drift of bees and overripe
peaches coming from Pop's new orchard, which he'd budded
and grafted himself. Vic had learned and could use the knife, the
wax, and the string to bud and to graft as well as Pop.

After the funeral, Mama Amazon said it was plenty hot for
Ole Doc to take his yearly wash-all-over. So Vic got him sitting
flat down in a large wooden tub out in the smokehouse and
scrubbed him with lye soap and sand.

"Got plenty dirt on your back," said Vic.

"That's dead skin; rub it off," said Ole Doc, vindictive toward
this washing all over.

"Ole folks shed their skins like snakes?"

"No. And you hurry up. It's not good for me to stay in this
water too long. You'll loosen up the pores of my skin too much
and no telling what I might catch. If the Lord had meant for
me to stay in the water, He'd have gave me a skin like a frog."

The nights grew so hot that sleep was impossible and Mama
Amazon got up quarreling. "Name of Gawd, June and July, you
hear me? I want you to take that heifer to the bull right this
mornin fo breakfast. She bawled all night long fo the bull. Ain't
youse got sense enough to know that that heifer want to go to the
bull just lack fine ladies?"

8

Through moonlight, great white magnolia blooms, the hot
heavily scented night, The Green Ponders had come to North
Bethel for the wedding. Coveys of twittering women filled the

church, their taffeta petticoats rustling; gleeful men and round-eyed boys and girls. The organ played and the candles marched in saintly parade.

There were hushed murmurs, "Isn't she beautiful? Who'd ever thought to see John Mathis in that riggin? I'd like to get a closer look at that dress; Cora Mathis made it, but she's clever with the needle. Looks like that dress cost a fortune. That veil came from Rahab; it was used by Great-great-grandmother Inchurch at her wedding a hundred years ago. How did they keep it so long? Did you ever know the Inchurches to turn anything aloose once their claws were hold of it?"

Jezebel thought, *It's a long way down this aisle. It's the longest church aisle in Green Pond. I shall abide my time. There's no hurry. There's only a spider waiting for me at the altar. I have seen spiders many times before. I once saw a spider spill its eggs and scramble madly to protect them, but my foot was down too quickly upon the spider for it to escape. It's good these stupid ninnies do not know my plans. That's Victor Thornwell yonder at the altar I'm going to meet; he's not there yet, but he'll be there. Ah, Jezebel Mathis, you have sinned. The wages of sin are death. You shall surely die. When I am Jezebel Inchurch I shall be reborn. I shall be free of sin and sorrow. My sins shall be washed away, blotted into oblivion.*

Through the humidity, the flattering candlelight, and the high-toned atmosphere came the Reverend Benjamin Flemming's voice reading, "Entreat me not to leave thee, or to return from following after thee: for whither thou goest, I will go; and where thou lodgest, I will lodge: thy people shall be my people, and thy God my God: where thou diest, will I die, and there will I be buried: the Lord do so to me, and more also, if aught but death part thee and me."

In the balcony Vic watched and listened and thought, *There'll never be another like Jezebel.*

9

Throughout the rest of that summer Jacob wandered aimlessly and nearsightedly. His heart was filled with squalid, noisy turbulences that would not give up, lie down to die. The palmy days of Jezebel were gone from his life forever. His was a frozen world, a world without hope. To whatever hilltop he climbed and looked down he saw Jezebel. He felt the warmth of her breast, the softness of her belly, and from these nostalgias he could not run. He blubbered effusively sentimental sadnesses, obsessed with the longing of her.

Victor laughed at him, begged him to accompany him on field trips now that the fields were filled with specimens that they could collect to draw. But Jake shook his head. His brother was one of earth's craziest creatures to want to spend his time in studies through the fields. School was out, the books were closed. Why probe into old sores? Yet Jacob continued to tear the scab on his wound and to start afresh the bleeding.

From the moonlight, from the soughing of the summer wind in leafy trees, the song of birds, he drew memories to feed his distressed mind. He never, that summer, walked down Third Street past the Pink House, but his mind was there through his wakeful hours and in his dreams.

Mama Amazon looked him over and spat on the ground, made a cross with her toe in the dust of the yard, and asked the Lawd right out there in the open to keep the evil plait-eye off Catawba. Looking up to Catawba she shook her head, for she knew Catawba had had many evil days and had withstood them.

At last the looked-for rains came falling gently all night upon the parched sad earth. The roots of the trees and plants of the fields, awakening from their morphic drought, pushed out new white roots, plunging them further into the sopping wet earth, drinking greedily. The crops were saved in the nick of time. The grasses turned green and stood up soldier-erect, sparkling in the sun as though they were bedecked in gleaming medals. And the people of Green Pond felt a renewed interest in life, and went about their work with gladness.

But nothing revived Jacob; he continued wilted as though the dusty drought was still over the face of the land. Man's life was as a rock plunged into the pond: it made a puny kerplunk, sending the water up in a little squirt, then rolled away in vanishing circles. Strange times were here, and he knew nowhere to turn. He groped desperately. If he sank into the depth of hell, God would hound him there, for God knew. There were no words on his tongue that he might utter to Him in self-defense. If he took into the hills, to hide in the leafy boughs, God was there soughing in the leaves. The more he searched out a hiding place, the hotter he burned for Jezebel, the more he wished to press her against himself to relieve his longing, to feel her lips pressing greedily against him. Nor in the darkness of night could he hide, for God knew his lying down and his standing up and his walking about.

When the annual revival was held in North Bethel Church in August, Jake went to the services morning and night, going alone, going close to the front of the church to listen attentively, seemingly in a trance, to the preacher. Then toward the end of the revival he thought the Lord called him to preach, so at one of the morning services he went forward, when the invitation was given, and gave his heart to the Lord.

His application was filed with the Presbytery. And the Committee on Ministerial Education inquired diligently and searchingly into Jacob's character, his spiritual, mental, and physical qualifications; and he was found ample and not wanting. So he became a candidate for the ministry under the jurisdiction of the Presbytery and went away for the four long years of college and the three years of work in the theological seminary that were required.

10

Sweet Cora lay lightly upon her bed. Her sunken eyes were far brighter than earthly fires, cheeks as a red sunset, her breath thick and heavy in its passage, and her body dry as new-mown hay. The body was too tired to struggle with the foul typhoid and she could not hear the neighbors say she should have strained her drinking water.

Her yoke, indeed, was as light as a feather in a breeze, for in this perilous typhoid time her soul felt immortality, and death and life were so united that it was impossible to tell where one began and the other left off.

The folks took turnabouts sitting with her to mind the flies away that buzzed continuously through the day and hummed at night on the ceiling as they stuck their rumps high into the air and washed their hind legs, rubbing them briskly together, then washing their front legs more stylishly and ladylike than a cat. The oil in the kerosene lamp ran low, Cora's oil of life ran low, and the flies buzzed and it was clammy hot. And the neighbor who sat fanning sweet Cora dozed in her chair.

Cora hovered between life and death—suspended by a flickering thread that could be so easily snipped. The darkly browned fuzz on her tongue grew mossier and thicker with the symphonic movement of the typhoid, the air came out of her coarse and hollow and rushed across her parched and burning lips, her body smelled and its fetid stench soused the room. Her bowels rotted and rotted and rotted. The cool water from some rock spring that she forever mumbled and motioned for to cool her parching tongue was forever denied her. Her mind was a wearying fugitive from the demon-infested fever bugs that burned and bored into her.

It was troubled times in Green Pond. Trouble smote the red land of the watershed. No one knew what the stardust predestined: no one knew what was written of a man before his time upon the red land nor what was predestined for him after he left the red land. Time was trouble.

11

Vic stood in the back yard of Catawba bidding Mama Amazon good-by. When he glanced up at the swallows' empty nests about the eaves and realized they'd gone for another season, his heart quivered with such dogged loneliness that he felt suffocated. Profound bewilderment choked his thoughts of leaving, but it was the only way to get what he wanted.

"You's gettin mo better-lookin every day. Just knowed right off when you was lil you was gonna be sumpin powerful important. But nothing lack this," said Mama Amazon. "The good Gawd put me here to furnish plenty black chillun fo this ole world and I's been pleasin in He's sight, but it looks lack I's had heaps o other things to do besides." She looked up at him misty-eyed.

Vic felt the quaver in her voice surge through and through him and he bit his lower lip to choke back the too intimate feeling that was rising there so sharply.

"We can't always stay together. There has to be a parting along the way." He looked at the ground and made a mark with his toe, then straight at her. "Which one of us, Jake or me, was born first, Mama Amazon?" Funny how it seemed important at this odd moment.

"Lawd, hon," she clapped her hands loudly, "nobody on this earth knows fo sure. Gawd in heaven only can answer that question rightly."

"Then you really don't know?"

"That's mystery. I can only guess."

The train seemed not only to be pulling him away from her and Green Pond, but to be pulling the very heart out of him. What was there about it that held such a spot so deep down in his heart—its dung-tramped streets, its dusty stores, its howdy-do folks, its old-fogyish airs, its sun-hot? There he passed Big Bertha and he knew that inside was Charles Coatworthy tongue-clipping the hands and ole Granny Swaps who'd swear and never miss tieing a knot. He saw Betty Mae Hill leave the Leakin Skillet with a piece of fatback. He passed through Pecan Lane and he saw Inchurch's sarcophagus awaiting in empty time. The train was gaining speed and he recalled the times that he and Jake used to cut cordwood for the train at a dollar a cord. Jake'd lie in the shade and not work and in the end beat him out of the money. Life was a ludicrous blunder, burlesque trivia.

Now the engineer was blowing the whistle and its sound floated back across Green Pond to the Pink House where Jezebel and Robert sat at their evening meal while a great covey of white-coated servants hung about. She looked up at great old Catawba on its hill and her face grew masked with shadowy sadness. Robert noted this and was greatly perturbed because she had ways of tricking him and bringing on strange spells as bedtime approached. When the train's whistle pierced her ears, she stuck her fingers into them, jumped from the table, and fled to her room, locking the door behind her.

12

In the Low Regions, Satan was stompingly angry because things were not moving along as smoothly as they should.

SATAN: Start all over there, Azazel. You's supposed to lead the marchers. It's that hot tonight all I'm gettin done is wipin sweat.

BEELZEBUB: You needn't be whammin an shakin that pitchfork at me so rambunctiously. I's got the presence of mind. Good mind.

SATAN: You Drunkards, keep youselves together. Don't you be tryin to slip in there an mix up wit the two-faced Hypocrites. I can't stand a parcel o laxness.

BEELZEBUB: Com'on, Sinners, don't have me cuttin you across you rump wit this wagon whip. Here you's got to learn to whirl fast in this burnin furnace. Don't have me allus throwin shovelfuls o brimstone on you parched an burnin heads. March up there in line, you pesky Backsliders an Gossipers. Us don't have to put up wit no such hypocritish ways.

SATAN: Quit you laughin, Beelzebub, an make em Liars an Thieves keep marchin. Ole lawd of dung, you big ole beetle, you blister-bottomed creature, ho'cum you's got to hang around so slovent-like an laugh?

BEELZEBUB: Ole Satan's gettin too rambunctious an I wonders ho'cum?

SATAN: Sinners, Earth knowed all along youse allowed to rebel against Gawd before youse was ever created out of the red dirt an Earth didn't want youse created. But no, Gawd done like He pleased an here youse is down here to worry an vex me to death. The fire is not quenched an it burns an burns fo'ever an fo'ever an fo'ever.

Cora Mathis no longer fretted over any earthly thing. She nodded to death. The fuzz on her tongue was dark brown and her breathing was rasping.

In Heaven, Gawd sat under an old apple tree, watching ole Gabriel grinding apples through the mill, making up some of the sweetest sweet apple cider.

GAWD: How's My chillun gettin long down in Green Pond?

GABRIEL: They thinks they's cunnin and You won't know no better; and You knowed they'd do that anyway.

GAWD: I ain't worryin My head about em. Lil mens ain't gonna wriggle emselves into no mo troubles than they can wriggle emselves outta.

GABRIEL: I know that. An mo'an at, they'll tell You right now, iffen You'll just listen to em pray, what's what. They's got only one thing, an that's the give-mes.

GAWD: I created em, an I'm enjoyin em.

Book two

Book two

11

For fifteen years the red sun rose, sailed gallantly across the blued upyonder, and saw that Green Pond's golden vinegar was unroiled; but its dreggy mother lay dark and ugly at the bottom of the grave. Jezebel, the gorgeous wench, led Banker Robert at a gouty trot and righteously set the pace of Green Pond's society. Each night the moon came up careening through the blue, star-dusted sky and looked over the sky's edge at Green Pond and laughed.

The train was running south from Washington, clipping through the moonlit fields. In a Pullman, Doctor Victor Thornwell, surgeon, lay propped upon his elbows, his muscular, lithe body over on its belly. He stuck his heels up against the upper berth and looked out the window at the moon-washed landscape.

Going back to Catawba, Vic thought. When he'd wanted to give up and come home, when the going was hardest, Pop had written, "You keep right on. I want you to have a chance I never had. The next fifty years will see a great revolution in medicine. No use starting without finishing. The world was not made in a single day. You're only a young whippersnapper and you have to learn from the ground up. There's no rush; take your time. What am I for, if not to help you?"

And now Vic felt as soused in the Hippocratic oath as though he were Hippocrates himself.

Then, as sleep came gradually creeping upon him as the cold of a winter's night seems to steal up from the ground, Vic's mind drifted to the doctors who had taught him. *Young man, have a care there. You've got to learn to feel.* And his hand was steered down into the gaping incision. *Feel the scar of this healed ulcer. That right ovary has a little cyst growing on it.* His hand was led deeper into the dark, foreboding pathological structures. *That appendix is bound down with adhesions. This left kidney is filled with stones.* And then the case of a child and the tense appendix that is twice its normal thickness. *Gotta be careful with this kind of appendix.* And the voice went on, *No book can give you the touch; some folks are born with it, some few learn it. You've gotta learn it from watching, then doing. Tie that blood vessel there. There's art in knot-tying.* Then the ghoulish voice another time, *There's the gall bladder sticking up there. Filled with stones. Take it out. It's unfair to the patient to just drain it and let it fill again with stones. Let the old feller grow something besides rocks. It takes fine sewing in here with a liver.* And Vic knew that was what he wanted. Knew that was what he had been born for. *Old-fashioned granny knots are a good stand-by. Tie em three times, because a poorly tied knot may break, once the clamp is removed, and there'd be a serious hemorrhage. You only learn surgery by doing. Practice.*

That was the highroad to surgery, to new and thrilling adventures. Then Vic was fast asleep, lying on his belly as unconcernedly as though he were one of the numerous bodies in the dissecting rooms in the medical school. Oh smelly cadaver, what would you cabbage now in sweet death? Your pilfering life is at an end; yet you lie here, oh treasured cadaver, to haunt me!

2

This girl, Missy, and that boy, Clay, walked down North Phil-adelphia Street in Green Pond this bright June morning, the two eldest children of Yellow Sam and Gee. They had large baskets of soiled clothes atop their heads, balanced evenly and unheld by hands. The baskets of smelly clothes kept in time with the rhythmic swing of their lithe, supple bodies. Missy and Clay were carefree, barefooted, and rich in earthly contentment. Missy at fifteen was a girl whose reeking beauty startled. She was much lighter in color than Clay who, at fourteen, took his light ginger color from Gee. They flashed each other bright smiles and jested and gesticulated in conversation.

"Ho'cum, Missy, you don't wanta go work fo Bigma to Catawba?" Clay asked, quickening his step, hoisting his rump in quick staccato jerks. The young'un, bound to be different, had taken to calling Mama Amazon simply Bigma.

"You jars my head, Clay, wit you blabberin." She twitched her rump saucily, continued to speak in scorn. "Bigma's gettin too ole. Fo true, they say she'll work the socks offen you. Mo'an at, Catawba ain't so fine a place as the big Pink House and now I's all done promised up to Mis Jezebel. She seemed mo'an glad to have me when I tolt her yellow Sam Thornwell was my pa. She was pleased all over sheself."

"You'll be sorry, Missy. Bigma ain't gonna like that—no nare bit."

"I ain't studyin what Bigma likes. I'm tired carryin these clothes every day fo Ma to wash. Ma say I can go into service, iffen she get my pay."

"You won't get to go to the public school no mo."

"*Huh*, who wants to go to that ole nigger schoolhouse an have that Miz Dessa contraption twist you ears?" Missy asked flatly and unbecomingly. "Ma says she have the big head because she graduated offen Emancipation Proclamation an that gives her an excuse to twist nigger chillun's ears off."

"Fo true, Miz Dessa can twist you ears iffen you don't know you lesson; but that better an what Bigma do. She say drap you pants, kneel over, an get that skin tight fore she starts in."

"That's the way wit these ole niggers," Missy tittered ironically, "acts lack it was still slavery time."

Clay tried to evoke the evil plait-eye. "Bet that'll be ten times mo better an what you gets done to you in that big Pink House!"

"When I gets in that vast Pink House, I'll be Nof; this down South is just nigger. That big Pink House has spigots and runnin water an a telephone an I won't have to work so hard."

"Gal, where you get em big ideas? Catawba has spigots, electricity lights, an a bathtub—as well's a telephone," added Clay, taking up for the place Bigma worked because he felt that the place Bigma worked was bound to be close to heaven, for Bigma dealt in no sin concoctions. Then Clay stooped suddenly, picked a Coca-Cola cap from the street, and talked on, "Wish I could get aholt of a whole nickel so I could buy myself one of these fine new drinks folks's talkin bout these days."

"Stead of wantin, you'd better be shore you's still got that money tied up in that rag fo this wash, else Ma'll do you."

"There's 37 blowin," said Clay. "Listen. It's blowin fo the stop. I'm gonna see who's vast important enough to make that train stop here." He scurried across Main Street and on to the station, forcing Missy to gather up more speed than her great ladylike attitude bade her do, but she kept right behind.

Alf Logan stood in his hardware store's doorway. "There goes them Thornwell niggers. Now, that gal's some looker. Purty as a picture. Hardly tell she's a nigger. I'd not mind a little pleasure of that some night."

Arriving at the station just as the train did, Missy and Clay stood gawking at the long line of cars as they began to halt. There was scrambling and scurrying at the baggage-car door as several large trunks were pushed out and, from the end car, a lone passenger emerged. Missy beheld the passenger and was awe-struck.

"Gawd, Clay, look yonder. Is you ever seen such a fine-lookin white gentleman in you life? He's bound to be from a long ways off. Don't nobody here in Green Pond look like that. Not that fine-lookin. Why, he'd near put you eyes out iffen you looked at him too long. Fo true, enty some good-lookin?"

3

Victor Thornwell was back in Green Pond wanting to feel impersonal, wanting to be as a stranger when he beheld electric lights and running water in Catawba, when he saw the gray in Jepson Grady's hair, when he saw how suave and dapper Attorney David Kingsley was. But he couldn't be when lovesome Mama Amazon's soft voice struck his ears.

"Hon, you's been gone a long time and Gawd changes things every day to suit He's notion, an disregards man's give-mes."

"You weren't happy when Mama Naomi put in the range and you had to quit cooking on the hearth in the kitchen," Vic reminded her, and laughed when he saw her old fury at the range return to her shiny face. "Aw, Mama Amazon, it's so good to be here with you."

Her eyes filled with tears, her voice grew croaky. "The years is creeped by, but Gawd's seen fitten to send you home." She'd always expected big things of him, but somehow nothing like this: him handsome and speaking like Jesus Himself. She couldn't get it through her head that once those manly lips had gnawed and suckled at her big black teaties. But she'd cast forth her milk willingly and now it'd returned to her seven times seven. Gawd, indeed, had an infinite love beyond all understanding. He'd shorely meant for her to do more than furnish niggers fo this ole world.

Now she had Jake's boy, Tommy, a big husky boy looking just like the Thornwells. Ole Doc and Naomi had brought Tommy home to her from Virginia when Jake's wife died, and he was the fourth generation of Thornwells in Catawba under Mama Amazon's loving care. "He's a rounder. Growin up fast," she lisped.

Ole Doc lacked a lot of being old even if he was getting up in years. To Vic he was as he had always been. He doted on Tommy and beamed on Vic and hung in a kind of worship over Vic's huge array of instruments from the medical centers of Europe. He talked of the changes about Green Pond's countryside, but was amazed at the new things that Vic told him were cropping up in the medical world.

Naomi was still Naomi—ceaselessly delicate, too feminine, and craftily springing about with high-strung nerves that were well controlled; ceaselessly infuriated by The Doctor and by her strange son, with his deep mocking laughter and his outlandish indifference to decorum. She had one grave consolation: Jacob, the pixy of her soul, lived a normal life and preached and walked in the accepted ways of her God. Whenever she could escape Catawba, fleeing to Virginia to visit him and devour the wonderful sermons he preached, she was strangely comforted. So singularly comforted that she could easily snitch a small toy Santa Claus and hide him between her overlarge breasts. Jacob looked fondly upon her and caressed her with his smiles as he did his congregation.

4

Only and Budda dragged in late from the fields and Mama Amazon dished up their supper and they sat talking of the strange happenings of the day.

"Vic still play that pianna lack he uster?" Only asked.

"Only, you ought to heardt he play today when he got here," Mama Amazon replied. "Played a piece fo Tommy that was bout horses goin through the clouds—sumpin bout a opera. You could hear em horses foots comin right up outta that pianna an tearin through the air."

"Good Gawd, you know there ain't no horses what can get away up in the air."

"Only! Don't you dispute my word! Vic said it was so an I heardt em wit my own ears. An Vic allus could see strange things."

"Fo true, he musta been in some strange part of the world fo horses to be flyin through the air. It must be some misunderstandin somewhere. I ain't never heardt Uncle Prince Blue tell a tale that big. An you got to get around to outdo Uncle Blue wit a big tale."

"Now, Only, iffen you don't believe me, you go in yonder an look at em big trunkfuls of curious shears, knives, and things an see won't you just about believe anythin. —Let me tell you, sumpin else happened."

"What?"

"Miz Jezebel was yappin on the telephone late this evenin, wantin Vic to come see her. What I want to know—how'd she know he was here so soon? Well, I didn't tell him, fo that cat will be in that cream jar soon enough."

5

Long after Mama Naomi and Tommy had gone to bed, Ole Doc and Vic sat in the lower parlor talking.

"We've got a new doctor here in Green Pond," said Ole Doc, "but I don't believe he's had too much training. And folks will naturally distrust a new doctor."

"Who is he?" Vic asked. "What does he do?"

"That last question is absurd," said Ole Doc. "You comb some of the kinks out of your thinking, son. You've too many ideas up there that won't work in Green Pond. You'll scare all the frogs and they'll jump back into the water. Once they're wet they're twice as hard to hold. His name is Roy Daniels, if there's anything to a name, and he's a general practitioner—takes a clumsy stitch now and again."

"So Green Pond doesn't have a hospital yet?"

"Hospital for Green Pond? Who'd go to it? I wanted you to be a good doctor, but you seem to be beset with wildness."

"Pop, between you and me, there's one certain thing: I either have a hospital here in Green Pond or I shall leave and go to where there is one."

"I see rambling over half the world for the last fifteen years has not taken one grain of stubbornness out of you. You're going to have your way or else!"

Victor jumped up from his chair and shook his finger in Pop's face. "I see absolutely no need of me devoting so many years of my life to the study of medicine and then come home to sit down and rot. All the books I've waded through, the painstaking, diligent work I've done in smelly dissecting rooms working on cadavers! Making notes, the studies I've made, the greasy drawings I've filled notebooks with. The laborious hours spent serving in hospitals, grueling hours spent watching operations, the frightening, maddening process of learning to deal with a living carcass!"

"Young man, sit down!" Pop raised his voice.

"Like thunder I'll sit down. Oh no, Pop, I'm not starting to rot this early. I'm too young for that."

There was a piercing knock on Catawba's door.

"Who in the devil's that at this time of night?" Vic asked.

"This is a doctor's house—that means that anyone can knock upon that door any one of the twenty-four hours that best suits him and not the doctor," Pop spoke, dryly sarcastic. Then, commandingly, "Go to the door, you nitwit, and see who it is. Surely, surely you can be hospitable without being in a hospital."

For a moment Vic thought that he'd have to pick up a kerosene lamp to see the way; then it dawned upon him that the house now had electric lights. He hurried into the main living room, switching on the lights as he went. Arriving at the front door, he snatched it open and stood glaring at the man.

"Is Doctor Thornwell in?" the voice asked.

"I'm one Doctor Thornwell," Vic replied.

"I want to see the old one."

"Oh, all right, come on in. He's sitting back in yonder," said Vic, indicating the direction for the man to take. Vic closed the door, feeling abashed. "So it's the old doctors they trust," he grumbled to himself. "Why, that man looked at me as though he thought I were a piece of offal filled with maggots. Well, then he's the blowfly." Curiosity cleared Vic's roiled temper, so he hurried on into the lower parlor to see what was up. Pop was a positive believer in shaking hands, and now he was standing, shaking hands, greeting the caller.

"Well, well, Doctor Daniels, what on earth brings you out at this hour? Won't you have a seat? You look all petered out."

Doctor Daniels? Vic thought. *Wonder how long he's been around here? Well, it's about time the watershed had more than one doctor. But this one is the most nervous, fidgety doctor I've ever laid eyes on. Obviously that fellow's in some hell of trouble.*

"Doctor Thornwell, I've a patient over in Green Pond that belongs to your church and I want you to come over there right now and pray with him," abruptly blurted Doctor Daniels, being barely seated.

"That, indeed, is a strange request. What's the trouble? Drunk? Been in a fight?"

Vic went over to the piano, sat down, toyed with the keys.

"No, no, nothing good as being drunk. Childbirth."

Vic's ears perked up. Pop asked, "Childbirth? Thought you said it was a man you wanted me to pray with."

"Sure it's a man. Andy Thorpe. His wife's trying to have a baby and she can't. I can't save her and the child, too, and he won't make up his mind which he wants me to save. We can't be dallying much longer; she's in none too good shape."

Vic's ears were more alerted.

"If he'd let me mutilate the child, I'd soon have things under hand, but he says that'd be a sin to destroy that innocent life. Then if I suggest saving the child and letting the mother go, he says maybe she's not prepared yet to die and meet her God. So I thought if I came and took you over there, you might get him to see one way or the other."

"Who did Andy Thorpe marry? Wasn't it one of the teachers here in the academy?"

"Maybe. I know she's too old to have a baby."

"Andy Thorpe, Andy Thorpe," Pop took his head between his hands, thinking. "Now I have it. Andy Thorpe married a Miss Pope that taught here."

"Miss Pope!" exclaimed Vic. "Miss Pope? You don't mean," he said, looking at Doctor Daniels, "you're going to stand there and let Miss Pope die? Golly Moses, Miss Pope was my art teacher and she was a stomp-down good'un. She's the teacher, Pop, that sent me home from school because I drew the ugly picture of the ragged rooster running the dominecker hen." Vic smiled in recollection. "Bet she knows what it is now for roosters to run hens!" Then he grew as serious as a mountain. "Doctor Daniels, how about a Caesarean section?"

Doctor Daniels was sardonic. "Nice. Who'd do it?"

"I will."

"Okay. The joy's yours. But it's going to be a wild gamble if either of them'll let you do it. You've no time to lose. She's been in labor a long time."

"Is there anyone there to help?" Vic snapped impatiently.
"The would-be father."

"I'll have to have some help. Pop, can you go? You can hand me
the instruments. I'll go get Mama Amazon. There'll have to be
someone to care for the child. She'll be good at that.

"Doctor Daniels, you take Pop on with you while I run for
Mama Amazon. Get the patient to sleep if possible. Set up for it
in the kitchen, boil plenty of water, have the kitchen hot and
damp. That light there'll be bad, but I'll put up with it."

Vic took out a pad and pencil, writing and talking. "Pop, I'm
making a list here of the stuff I want you to take. What you don't
have you'll find in my trunks. Better take two or three cans of
ether; get Number 2 catgut for that uterus and Number 1 catgut for the peritoneum and we'll use silkworm gut for the skin;
two scalpels, twelve artery clamps, eight long pendicle clamps."
He checked rapidly over the list, "There're twenty things to get,
Pop. Don't overlook any. Oh yes, Doctor Daniels, sterilize six
sheets, about eighteen towels, and a dozen handkerchiefs."

Vic climbed Catawba's back stairs and knocked on Mama
Amazon's door and listened to her grumble, "What in Jesus'
name you want, boy? Ho'cum you ain't in bed gettin some good
rest?"

"Ho'cum you ain't in bed gettin good rest you'self?" he asked
when she had flung the door open.

"Gettin ole, got lots to think bout," she laughed. "What's
happened? None of you hedgin, now. I know you tricks."

"Want you to go with me to do an operation."

"*Operation!* Is you lost you mind? In the middle of the night?
Gawd, boy, I thought you was case enough that time you rammed
you arms up to you elbows in that cow's behint an turned that
calf straight to face this ole world—an here you's gettin mo
worser!" She cooled her frown and looked backward into the
room. "Only, you and Budda hear what this boy's talkin? Opera-

tion on real peoples in the dead of the night! Ain't changed a bit. Still that same lil boy." She turned slowly and gazed up at Vic. "What you wants me to do?"

"Ketch the chillun lack Granny Joanna uster."

"Oh my Gawd! Thought it was a operation! You's a case."

"Cut em out."

"This I's got to see." She grabbed up her old shoes, split for her corns and runover by her excessive weight. "I'm ready. I can travel mo better barefeeted."

6

At three o'clock in the morning, the sweetish smell of ether reeked over the steamy atmosphere of the Thorpe kitchen. Mrs. Andy Thorpe was anesthetized, sweating profusely; her breathing came easily and regularly, ticking with the assurance of the grandfather clocks in Catawba. Her swollen abdomen, ripe for delivery, was exposed.

Nervous Doctor Daniels stood at her head, holding the ether can, letting drop by drop fall on the sponge over her nose. The ether can vibrated, wavering as a bird balancing itself upon a wire in his hands, and he sweated as in a sudden gusty shower because of his taut nerves and not from the overheated kitchen.

The silent, would-be father cringed sickeningly in a corner. He didn't know whether his heart was in his body or his mouth; he didn't know from which end he wished to vomit, his illness was of such incredibleness. Such nausea arose in him as to make his saliva overflow his mouth. His stomach felt desperately hollow.

Mama Amazon stood sure-footed, although so awe-struck she could scarcely breathe, and what air she was successful enough to ensnare was wheezed in and out of her lungs with such vim as to be heard all over the kitchen. She rolled her eyes as though this were the Judgment Day and she was fixing to behold the graves opened with the sounding trumpet. She knew the world was a curious place, but with this before her eyes, it was getting much more curious.

Pop stood, hands gloved, opposite to Vic, ready to hand him the instruments.

Vic took the scalpel in his hands, leaned slightly over the drum-like abdomen. His feet were rooted as sturdy as two oak trees, and from his waist up he was as relaxed and loosely waving as bunting in the wind. He laid the abdomen wide open with a long midline incision, clamping, tying off.

Oh, dear sweet Jesus, Mama Amazon thought, *is You ever seen fingers fly an move so fast? But that's what he allus wanted to do, Gawd. Yes, sir. That's my caul-headed baby boy, born wit a veil over his head. Gawd, I just knowed all along You knowed what You was a-doin wit these here Thornwells, fo I knowed I didn't.*

Vic nicked the peritoneum. There was very little bleeding, Pop marveled. He cut rapidly into the upper portion of the uterus, grasped the infant by his heels, bringing him forth, then, clamping the cord in two places, he cut the cord in two between the clamps, tied it, and handed the boy directly to Mama Amazon, who began to grumble and to complain and to smack the infant.

"You breathe in some good air now and don't you be all day about em, so help me Jesus. You's mo' an anxious to get here an started to livin. Come on now, haste-maste. Don't let me have to remind you agin."

Pop was stammeringly abashed. He twiddled the instruments in his hands abstractedly. And his old brain was fired to such intense thinking that he heard or saw nothing about him. He conjured up case after case, identically like this, that had engulfed his whole medical career—cases where he was but a mere stumbling, awkward, gawking boy, all hands and feet. The question of embryotomy—to be used or not to be used on a viable child—always stared him in the face, nakedly, accusingly. It was as the voice in the night crying out its accusations. His answers had always been mutilation. Cranioclasis, crushing the head of the fetus, removing the cerebral matter, smashing the bones together to reduce the size of the head, and then removing the entire fetus; or the cases of hacking the body of the child half in two or severing the tiny head of the fetus. There was Nancy, so very long ago, before Victor was born. The long night of struggle, with not a soul to turn to for help. No family to consult, the decision had rested painfully upon his inadequate shoulders. The mutilation. The blood. Nancy's terror-stricken screams. Then he'd buried the tiny shoe box under the heavily scented boxwood, buried his own ignorant blunderings. He remembered the long hours of working with Fanny and the comforting decision of her husband, Will, who said to save Fanny, because she might not be ready to face her God, and to destroy the child, for Jesus comforted the earth in His love for little children.

Pop through his fixed, staring eyes saw Vic motioning for another instrument, saw Vic, this lad, across the kitchen table from him, and realized that this night Vic had well-nigh wrought a miracle. He, that boy over there, his son, was working here as though this were mere spittle and clay. From Granny Joanna through him to Vic—it was inborn, a deep-seated antipathy for disease. And Ole Doc knew he'd never die, but live on in Vic, that son of his with a natural dislike for ill-bred demons who devoured the human body.

Vic heard the lusty squall of the delivered infant and he shook his head, coming away from the misty fog that he had been secluded in. "Doctor Daniels, you may stop that ether, for it'll be only a matter of minutes." He muttered, working rapidly, "It takes fine sewing with a uterus as well as a liver."

No one paid any attention to the father, Andy, who had slumped in the corner in a faint. Mama Amazon thrust all her love and devotion upon the whimpering baby as she greased it with lard and gave it, to Vic's horror, a generous strip of fat meat to suck.

Working swiftly, unmindful of his surroundings, Vic removed

the placenta and afterbirth. His movements were definite, rapid, his brain in the tips of his sensitive fingers. Now the uterus was carefully sewed up, then the peritoneal toilet done, the peritoneum stitched; out he came, working quickly in sections and layers until this woman's abdomen was put back together again; now the fascia was sutured and then the incision of the skin whipped together, leaving only the thin sewed line as a permanent memorial.

There were tears in Pop's old eyes. Tears of thanksgiving and praise to God, because of the many children that he had begat from the Lord in his long and fertile years there was none to equal this boy of his beyond the kitchen table. Could Granny Joanna, he thought, have lived to see this, her cup would surely have been lipment full. Man's life is as chaff before flooding waters, as crab-grass seed before the wind, as weed seeds in horse manure. There is no putting life down, nor putting it asunder, for it will rise up from the very bowels of the earth as this had come from this woman's belly. And it was all in the stardust—if only one could read it.

7

Mama Amazon, Vic, and Ole Doc scrouged into the buggy and rode back to Catawba in the grayest of dawn—tired, ashy, and fully gratified. Mama Amazon straightway shook up the breakfast.

Ole Doc stood in the yard watching the mist over the river, looked through the gray foggy dawn sharply with his shrewd, steady-gazing eyes. Within his brain thoughts were whirling, churning more turbulently than the red waters of the river when it was gorged with too abundant rainfall and burst from its banks tearing through the lowlands on a rampage, uprooting trees, sending houses and barns asunder. He could not drive the scene of the night from his mind. Myriad times he had felt just like this after an all-night vigil: bitter against himself. Now he reflected upon this and he lamented. He compared his failures with Vic's success. Nowhere in his analysis of himself did he cushion his conscience with a muttering of lies and excuses. He looked cold and calculating right down into the bottom of the well of naked truth and he felt freer than he'd ever been. Freeheartedness and good will shook him as though he had a chill. The trivia that had corroded his life swam before his eyes and he murmured softly and pityingly, "When you've lived into the eighties, it's so easy to see a new heaven and a new earth which was so hidden from you in your youth; but at eighty you can only advise those that are younger, and the young don't want advice. Is it something that God planted within man so that he ultimately will destroy himself? Is it not written? Have there not been many civilizations that reached a certain stage of progress and intelligence only to destroy themselves? Leaving but a few clay tablets, but a few bones, but a few implements, but a few scrolls for the next civilization to paw after, to delve for, to test the cunning of men's minds? So man continues to befool himself—"

8

Victor was no schemer and he was beset with the desire for a hospital and, once obtained, how he would beguile the sick and mangy inside, for he knew the Green Ponders were of wile and subtlety when it came to getting out of a cutting-doctor's way. He might have to resort to some sort of schemey affair yet.

Mama Amazon cackled gleefully, "Hon, you's gettin right now. Tole em into you trap wit some sort of good bait. You can ketch most nigh any sort that way," she ended, looking at him and Tommy sitting there in the buggy ready to go on some calls.

Vic smiled and looked down at her. He knew and she knew how the Green Ponders were talking, how he'd shocked them with what he had done to Helen Thorpe. The town was a-buzz with their talk of it. It rang in his ears night and day.

——They say he gutted Helen Thorpe that night just like you'd gut a hog. Why, he ain't got a bit more feelin fer a body than iffen they was a sack of guano——

——It'd of been better to let her die as to be a-whackin and a-hackin that way on her——

——Iffen I get sick, I shore ain't a-wantin em sendin fer him. It's no tellin what that fool'd do to a body's livin gizzards——

——Helen Thorpe'll never have another kid. It'll be years before she can get up and go about now as it is——

——They say Andy can't get any of the wimminfolks to come in there and wait for her, fer they're all scart to death she'll bust open——

——It's downright heathenish cuttin on a human bein thataway: a human bein with a soul!——

——Ole Doc's been a good doctor and didn't go in fer all this cuttin. Where'd this boy of hisn get em quare ideas? I'll bet Ole Doc could outbeat him doctorin——

——Ole Miz Joanna never lost a case and she never went in fer this cuttin and whackin——

——By God, he ain't a-cuttin on me with none of em sharpened-up European things. Iffen he's a-fixin to pick up where Ole Doc leaves off, I'm findin me another practitioneer. Ole Doc's pills has been good enough fer me fer years and I ain't in favor of no changin——

——Don't much mo' an get the scalawags an carpetbaggers an Republicans run outta the country an have a little peace over the land an here comes an upstart wantin to cut on a body——

Vic frowned, pursed his lips slowly. "When I'm called to lancinate a simple boil, Mama Amazon," he complained, "the parents have to run their children down before they get to the tall weeds." Then he laughed at her looking up at him in the buggy, ran his fingers through Tommy's hair. "All right, old man, let's go hunting." He picked up the reins and drove out of Catawba's yard.

The lucent sun fell upon Vic and Tommy on their grazing calls, in town and country; birds reeled in drunken reverie; in the country the plowmen exhorted one another of the dangers of crab grass eating up their crops. In town the shady spots felt good and there was always someone who'd prop a friendly foot upon buggy hub and loose a wagging tongue.

"Uncle Vic, why won't you go see Mrs. Robert Inchurch? She's the purtiest woman in town," asked Tommy.

"What in the devil are you doing studying about the women?" Vic retorted.

"I can look, can't I? And you ain't answered my question yet."

"Huh, don't know the answer!"

Passing Uncle Prince Blue's old house, they found him drowsing in the good sun-hot, which he had never spurned. His old gals, he told Victor, were all dead long ago—so long ago that the spoons, medicine bottles, cups, and saucers placed on their graves had withered into nothingness. And now he was alone with merely his dreams of faraway Africa to keep him company.

His old mind rambled on. He was waiting now. Any day he looked forward to going home. He'd laid his burden down long ago and spent all his time watching and waiting, ever ready, because that was one train he didn't want to miss. He had missed so much as far as worldly things went, if they mattered. His ticket was ready, he was waiting to hear the whistle and to climb upon that sweet train.

Bewildering perplexities screwed his voice into a wild outcry when he heard that Vic had been across the waters to a strange and faraway land. He wanted to know right quickly how Vic had escaped so soon and was not held in slavery time, because that was what the mad waters were for: to carry one so far from home that one could never, never swim back, to carry one to a place where the people made a detestable slave of one. Was it the cold time or the hot time of the year, that Vic had so successfully escaped?

On the way to Granny Joanna Thornwell's old homeplace, Tommy was greatly disturbed about what Uncle Prince Blue had said, and Vic patiently pieced the tale together. The noontime sun-hot burned the buggy top and scorched along the dusty way and Vic communed with Granny Joanna, visualized the ups and downs she had contended with in her day. They stopped at her old homeplace to talk to John Mathis, who had finally lost his precious eighteen acres of land when the golden mortgage of forty years standing at the Inchurch bank had turned to brass.

John Mathis shaded his nearsighted eyes with his hand and gazed intensely at the approaching strangers, then, upon recognition, he said, "This that you see about me is all the place I have, by-crackety. There ain't a soul lived in this house since way before the war, so I moved in and kinda fixed it up and been living here now for a number of years. Ole Doc's about the last person left in these parts that'd give a body a roof from the elements; but this's your Grandma Thornwell's house and I've about got it rigged up like she had it when I first come to these parts."

Now John is free as the squirrels of the wood, Vic mused, *and here under this great walnut tree that Granny grafted the nuts fall abundantly in autumn. Here he lives upon the fat of the land; here is his contentment.*

John said to Vic, "I told Cora not long fore she died that I would never have peace of mind once I vamoosed to that there banking institution of the Inchurches and signed my life away for a paltry hundred dollars of the bank's boodle. I would as lief had a she-bear slapping me any day as that dudelike grafter sending me duns every whipstitch for interest on that boodle. I stay flabbergasted trying to pay the interest. For years I foment cunning plans to keep it paid and now mind you, never getting a bit of the principal paid—interest'll eat you up. That whooping spider thumps me more and more and I gulp and gasp; but he thumps the more. For years I fight right along to save my divine, human rights; but then I realize that old roach is going to swipe me out to the right and to the left. I am tired psalming to that old sham—there's a limit to the number of times you can lick one single behind in a lifetime. So one day, with the interest far in arear, I walk into that cahooting institution; I walk in there as scrumptious and with as much gumption as though I had et a bellyful of billy goat and I tell him to get up offen his sorry behind and come and take this place of mine.

"No, I never see Jezebel any more. I hear she's too busy running the town to bother with the likes of me. Well, she allus was a lot like Cora in that. The church, too. No, it won't make any matter iffen I never see her again. She's got one road to travel and I have another. With all the prattling and careening she does in that town, she'll certainly keep everybody flabbergasted. When she gets through prying with the humbugs, she'll petrify the very Lord. Me? I'd rather duck out here on what time I have left as to cahoot with them so-so voices.

"So tell Ole Doc I'm tarryin here the rest of my life, for I don't wish to cavort with the spider generation. Tell him I'm here where God hovers. Tell him that here I wish to make my peace, because should I die now and go straight to hell, there'd be the crafty Cora standing with a big shovelful of red-hot coals to throw on my head right off."

9

"Name of Jesus," growled Mama Amazon late one evening, "I wants you to haste-maste, Vic, an go on an see that Miz Jezebel contraption. She's wore me frazzle-assed callin fo you on the telephone. She's called four and five times a day ever since you's been home—an you ain't gone yet!"

Victor thought of a shaky kiss and a shaky smile by the front stairs of Catawba, long ago, and of the great Pink House that belonged to Mrs. Robert Inchurch, and smiled because he knew Jezebel and what she would be like. But he did not know any more what he thought of Jezebel—and he was afraid to find out.

"Why must I go, Mama Amazon?" he asked humorously.

"She says she haves right much pain. An I'm beginnin to bout believe she."

Someday soon he'd go. He thought he knew what she wanted; but now, after the years, would she still be that way? He thought of how it might have been had there not been Robert Inchurch. That was a puzzle. That was something he'd never understood, something he could never find in any book. Women were—unpredictable, funny. After she'd tried so hard, finally waked him up, she'd suddenly run off down another road. Was he to follow? But now so much had come between—like the rivers that carried the red land into another part of the watershed; and she would not be going his way.

His way was for mankind and its illness, the way of suffering and healing. Surgery. Even at the old table in the kitchen he could feel the slender delicate instruments in his hands. His hands, always carrying a life of their own, beating out prayers or sonatas on the piano, curved now about shining steel and cutting and repairing, working with defty movement. Blood and action—rapid action. He lived and breathed surgery; even his thinking was in its terms. One could only speak a language when one could think in it; he could think in surgery.

He would come back to Pop and they would talk: talk medicine. He talked of it, of operations he had seen and done. Surgeons he had known. And Pop listened to Vic as the dry parched earth for the approaching summer shower.

And Ole Doc said, "There's no means to discern the inner man, just what goes on in his insides. Perhaps it's best that one man can't look into the inside of another, for there he might see things that are best left unseen."

10

Summer nights in Green Pond are short and filled with the out-cries of millions of low-flying insects that, Vic knows, buzz about ole Satan's face when he and Beelzebub go pronging about its ways, swagging with sin.

SATAN: Don't you try pushin me into that water agin, Beel-zebub. You think I'm Baptist? Baptist always wantin a coat of water to outstrip my fire. Get down and roll emselves in it lack hogs. My fire gonna win in the end.

BEELZEBUB: Quit bein so disgruntled.

SATAN: Shut you mouth. Us got to get on over to the Pink House an see can't us hatch out a snazzy idea in Miz Jezebel's head. You know that Victor Thornwell's home?

BEELZEBUB: That church wench ain't one bit happy wit that Robert Inchurch. Reckon us could get she to do sumpin to he—sumpin to get he outta the road?

SATAN: I doubt that—be sinful.

In Heaven Gawd sat out in the yard under a pink-topped mimosa tree fanning with a limb of the tree of life and listening to Tommy Thornwell's prayers come up through the hot summer night.

GAWD: I declare my Miz Big Amazon surely believes in strong an proper prayers. Listen at her, Gabriel: "Tommy, drap down beside that bed an say you prayers. I don't care iffen you is a big boy. What'd you papa say bout you wantin to jump into bed an en say you prayers? Him a big fine preacher out cuttin the lard outta ole Satan every Sunday. Mo better fo that floor to hurt you knees an ole Satan to ketch you soul an carry em to that fire what's seven times seven hotter an it ought ta be."

GABRIEL: Yes, sir, Gawd, declare that's some fine prayin. Never heardt mo better.

12

Jezebel's tempestuously urgent ringing of Catawba's telephone, untiring night and day, had finally brought Doctor Victor Thornwell to call upon her. As he tied the horse to the handsome iron hitching post in the street before the Pink House, he cast sidelong glances at the bulky edifice and smiled. This call would surely test the Hippocratic oath, but his professional manner arrayed itself about him as though it were old clothes accustomed to every elbow and every knee. Vic marched boldly, clicking his heels soldierly upon the tiled walkway, and rapped impatiently and brazenly upon the gracious door with the great gold knocker.

Hump opened the door of the Pink House and invited Vic in with his most polite bow and crocodile grin. His coat was as stiff and white as the pinion feathers of a white dove; his pants and shoes shone as freshly oiled skin. He asked Vic to wait a moment and he'd call Missy, Miz Jezebel's pusnal maid, and she in turn'd lead him into Miz Jezebel's presence. He went off up the grandiose marbled stairway, slightly stooped with his hands on his knees, and mumbled about the strangeness of the times and what in the name of Gawd'd white folks think of next? Nothing better could be expected of this sinful day and age, and he and his grumblings vanished as thunder after a summer shower.

Vic waited and looked about the immense living room. He knew that these handsome pieces of furniture were the most costly that money could buy. There was no sham here from the floor to the ceiling—the rugs, the pictures, the mirrors, the tapestries, the entire array of furniture reeked of rich living.

Missy stood immaculately dressed before him. Every line of her was graceful and dignified. So this was the girl that Mama Amazon had bewailed as so unbecoming and accursed to Catawba, Vic thought. She walked tactfully proud. Here were no dragging, shuffling feet, nor larkspur heels; here was becoming dignity, graceful bearing. Her personality overshadowed everything in the house. Her hair was not in strings; it was freshly oiled and gleaming, combed down her neck to its nape and there turned up, resembling the wigs the Egyptians had worn thousands of years ago. Come to think of it, she resembled an Egyptian, especially about the eyes and nose; her skin was smooth as a ripe plum and its color a smoky-pink sunset.

"Doctor Thornwell, this way, sir," said Missy, turning to the stairs and beginning to climb. Vic followed. So young Doctor Thornwell was led up to the highest pinnacle of the Pink House to behold Jezebel, the devil's beauty, the ruler of any hen roost she might by chance find herself within.

Vic knew that Robert Inchurch was a contented and prosperous man in these days, waxing richer yearly. He greedily received Jezebel's scrimpy kiss every morning and hurried on to the bank, knowing that all was well in the Inchurch household, knowing there were many golden mortgages to keep in tune, knowing there were many loose people needing to be noosed with one.

It was rumored among the ninnies that Robert's passion for Jezebel was unwavering, more ardent than ever. He'd spared no money in educating her after marriage by private lessons in the arts, and several times he'd accompanied her on trips to Europe. He'd placed costly gifts at her feet and arrayed her in the world's finest clothes. Her good deeds not only wearied North Bethel members, but in Synod increased their tempo with jingling money, and in General Assembly she rolled forth her vast richness. Robert had purchased her a summer home in the cool mountains of Babel, the holy of holies, where she cahooted with the mighty church fathers of the South and fought the Northern Presbyterian Church worse than an old soldier.

Vic was led through many winding, splendid hallways in the Pink House; past doors that showed many rooms resplendently decorated and furnished; past bathrooms where the water sluiced and gurgled and babbled equal to the fountains in the Persian yard; past uppish servants who looked down their noses at him as though he were once again a small boy with chicken manure between his toes; and then he was led into the room where Jezebel lay upon a couch surrounded with many polished mirrors. When she saw them approaching she threw a large towel over her pelvis, leaving the rest of her massaged and creamed body exposed to his view.

"Miz Jezebel, you want to put on you clothes now?" asked Missy, who had been grooming Jezebel when she had had to stop and go fetch the young Doctor Thornwell.

"No, Missy, you can come back and finish as soon as Doctor Thornwell has examined me. You may go now. Close the door behind you." She slowly turned her yellow eyes on Vic. The lips of her lucent mouth parted in a triumphant smile of sheer gladness.

Victor stood stock-still, astonished. This was beyond belief.

This was engendering a fettering of his nerves, screwing them as a corkscrew goes through the cork of the cork oak, producing a violent nausea in his stomach worse than any he'd ever had in the dissecting rooms in medical school. The Jezebel he remembered was a mere playful kitten; this before him was a full-grown tigress, a mature woman, whose coyness and cunningness knew no limit. Indeed she was the devil's beauty. Every curve of her lithe body showed the slick, smooth beauty of the deceitful serpent.

"Doctor Thornwell, you still stand and gawk like an awkward boy. Will you never grow up?" She was definitely poking fun at him. She stretched her arms high above her head to show him the firm youngness of her breasts.

He looked straight at them and thought how he would handle this. "Mrs. Inchurch, what seems to be your trouble today?" He spoke professionally, keeping his voice as dry and matter-of-fact as possible.

"Really, Vic, do you and I have to be so formal here in the privacy of my room? You surely remember that my name is Jezebel?" She saucily stuck a leg into the air, twisting the foot at the ankle, admiring herself and giving him another chance to note that she possessed this unquestionable pair of trim legs.

Vic spoke positively. "I'm a doctor. I come to administer to the sick body, to cut out the corrupt portions that offend, not to lust with nor after the rich and righteous. If you've nothing wrong, why have you sent for me?" A frenzy of indignation boiled in him.

"Oh, Vic, why do you have to be this way? You're as cold and calculating as a tombstone. I have all sorts of pains," she touched her abdomen and her breasts with her well-manicured fingertips, "here and there." Her voice grew mellow with seductiveness and at the same time wind-swept with lighthearted desperation.

Vic stood silently and stanchly in the middle of the room,

surveying her, feeling the incredibleness of the situation. She'd
jade the saints in heaven. He was urged to grab her, turn her
over, and lay his strong hand to her bottom as Mama Amazon
used to do him. But no, he couldn't do that to the richest and
most beautiful woman in town—and the leading Christian in
North Bethel Church. Why, he'd be hanged or tarred and feathered before nightfall. Men's deeds could be stopped, their
tongues easily silenced. He wanted a hospital more than anything on earth, he wanted to be a good doctor, but somehow—
this, this, *this!*

"Just think, Vic, of the things that Robert and I could do
for a poor boy like you," she said. Vic noted in her voice the
drawled coo of the amorous dove. He was filled with a mixture of
emotions. So she wanted once again to run her hand into his
clothes with her erotic fondling?

"Who said I was poor?" he cut irritably, his lips drawn in
thought, his eyes wandered away from her.

"Why, Victor Thornwell, everyone knows that without being
told. Just because Old Doctor Thornwell has raked and scraped
together a great deal is no saying that you have anything. Everyone knows that you're a mere upstart pill-peddler. And cutting
on Mrs. Andy Thorpe! Do you know how this town's talking?
They're about ready to run you out right now," she hurled at
him vehemently.

"Gawd heap damnation on your rotting carcass, Jezebel Inchurch! What if I had no place to lay my head but with the
possums in hollow trees? After all, the possums are sincere when
they play possum." His blood cruised to his head so violently and
suddenly he felt drunk.

"Victor Thornwell, I thank you not to be swearing in my
house and calling me vile names. It's not nice. It's against the
rules of the Book of Church Order. Robert and I," she em-
phasized the latter, "can easily have you churched. You know
Robert is the elder who has the say-so now." She pawed him

gently as the cat paws the mouse before eating it. She was rapt with alertness.

"Dammit, how in the hell can you have me churched when I don't belong to the church?" he hurled at her.

"Victor, you mean to tell me that at thirty years of age you have not yet joined the church? Don't you realize sometime you must die?" There was lofty superiority, descending scorn in her voice.

"I'd much prefer to walk alone with the possums as to become entangled with you scribes and pharisees of *that* church." He found himself becoming calm and he spoke sadly, "Jesus said, 'Beware of the scribes, who love to go in long clothing and love salutations in the marketplaces and the chief seats in the synagogues and the uppermost rooms at feasts, who devour widows' houses and for a pretense make long prayers.'" He turned abruptly, making straightway to leave, but he heard Jezebel's tearful voice.

"Oh, Vic, how can you be so mean and cruel? I thought you were a doctor and would comfort me here on my bed! But you quote me, 'Jesus says'—which is old and can't apply to me—and start to leave me. Vic, Vic, Vic!" She sat bolt upright in bed, scornfully drew her knees under her chin, lamenting as though her well-groomed coiffure were smeared with black sooty ashes.

Vic turned and looked at the defected form in the bed. Undeniable pity for her flooded him. He walked over to the side of the bed and stood looking down at her.

"Don't leave me, Vic," she managed through her tears. "I've waited so long for this. You're the only thing in the whole wide world I've ever really wanted or will ever want. I have everything else, but I want you, only you." She looked at him and he knew it was true and remarkable. "Please." She pleaded with a voice that was filled with such melancholia as autumnal winds. She was now quiet and empty of energy.

He stood lonely and far away in his heart, far away as the

sound of night wind, and yet he was by the side of Jezebel's bed, gazing down at her, at her tender, pinkish skin as gleaming as the cheek of an apricot, his nostrils flooded with her scent, faintly fragrant of mountain arbutus blooming under snow. He beheld her seductive charm. She was made for what she was fondly offering. There was honest hunger for him in the flecked eyes with the long waxed lashes; yet deep within those eyes of hers he saw a foreboding darkness. For a moment she aroused in him such emotions as he did not know he possessed.

She saw him weakening and her heart leaped. If this could be for now—right early and no putting off until tomorrow! She wanted to grasp this yearning moment. She wanted him more than anything on earth. She wanted to live and breathe and be wholly consumed as never before in her life. He could do it and he alone. The years she'd waited and planned for this! Her famished soul reached out to him. She reached out her hands to him, murmuring, calling him her little rooster, her little bull, her little he-goat.

He placed his hand on her naked shoulder and her hotness momentarily shocked him. Then he was clean of emotion, halted by something he could not fathom. The medical touch crept into his fingers. "Jezebel," he said, "you'll have to put this out of your mind. It won't work. It'd sooner or later get us both into trouble. Why aren't you satisfied with Robert? You have everything but a child, and I'd suggest that."

"I detest him! It wasn't ever my idea of marrying him!"

"Then why in the world did you marry him, Jezebel?"

"The only person that knows is dead." Her voice was hollow, her eyes closed so tightly that the upper and lower lashes seemed as one. "No one else shall ever find out. I'm quite capable of keeping a secret. I know a great deal more than you think, but the thing that puzzles me," her unreasoning eyes looked up straight into his, "is your stinking goodness."

She spoke with venom in her voice. "Nothing in this day and

age is achieved with goodness! Only simpletons know no better. You've always been so good! When you want a thing, as you did me just now, why don't you reach out and take it? That's the only way you can get anywhere. Good, good, good! That's all you've ever been and I hate you!"

"Jezebel, Jezebel, listen—"

"You're a stinking, dirty coward. We'd be as safe as the first great lovers in the Garden of Eden. Yet you'll not make one move toward our happiness. It's always your stinking goodness.

"I know whereof I speak. I've not lived with the Inchurches for years for nothing. Not that Robert and those in-law sisters of mine! They reach out right quickly and snatch up anything they want. Pa said that had always been their policy, for he'd known the older generations of Inchurches. He quarreled over me marrying Robert—said he'd rather see me in my grave!"

"Jezebel, do you know where your pa is? Do you know he was driven from his farm?"

"No. Moreover, I care less to find out. He'd be better off dead. He's another that got what he asked for with his eternal kindness."

Victor's heart closed over the warmth he had felt for her. "Jezebel, it's only the old who find beauty in living. The young are too filled with the breeding lust to live. If you think for one instant that a hen merely laid an egg for you to eat, or that beans grew upon the vine for food, or that grain waved and fruited in the field that you might have bread, or that little bulls bred cows in the green and cool pasture that you might have milk, you're crazy, Jezebel, Jezebel Inchurch!"

He excited her as nothing else ever had. Wildly she caught his hand and held it against her breasts and they were warmer than ever. "There's no one else to take your place! For years I've comforted the spider's ugly bed and thought of you. I've made his bed warm; there've been mornings that he—oh, the fortunate spider!—that he's been so weak he was forced to crawl from the bed because of my zealous loving. And he hobbled to the bank and his golden mortgages!" She laughed recklessly. "But what the spider doesn't know about us won't hurt him. With his little bank and his little mills he can heap our coffers lipment full. What's nearest your heart, Vic? I can grant you anything you'd wish. My darling, anything. I'll give you anything—if I am not enough!"

Victor said, "A person who's chosen to sleep with the possums would have very little need for anything your money could buy. You think you can buy anything—even me and what I don't want to sell. No, Jezebel, look elsewhere, or better still, get a eunuch, for he'd be much fatter than I and not nearly so dangerous. I'm healthy and I might disfigure your body! Yes, I'd prescribe several good fat eunuchs; you could alternate them from day to day and wear them out more evenly!" He was astounded at his own venom.

"So, Mrs. Robert Belcher Inchurch," be bowed stiffly, his voice filled with mockery, "I'm sure you'll find my prescription, properly used, will bring profound relief."

He turned and walked rapidly toward the door, his heels clicking on the satiny floor. He snatched the door open so hastily that the eavesdropping servants had barely time to jump out of his way.

Jezebel bounced from her bed as a tigress after prey. She snatched up a heavy jar of cream and hurled it after him. She hurled, paying no attention to what she hurled—mirrors, combs, brushes, boxes—as fast as she could throw. And when her useless fury had exhausted her, she slammed the door and threw herself onto her bed—her empty, empty bed—and screamed and wept into the pillow until at last her thoughts corroded into a stupor.

Her servants gathered themselves together in her kitchen and ate slowly and talked softly.

2

Once Vic had fled into the street from her, he hurriedly un-hitched the horse, jumped into the buggy, and drove toward Main Street so swiftly that his medical bags nearly lurched off.

She wasn't going to like his running away. She'd hatch something else in that fertile mind of hers. And she'd be after him, although with what cunning, what tool, he knew not.

Was he being foolish running away from her, considering what she had to offer? She would gladly give him that hospital that he so desperately craved; that he had to have if he continued in surgery. He had no intentions of spending the rest of his life driving about in the country, contending with these formidable adversaries, dueling with these antagonists, struggling with adversity, operating under haphazard conditions. He visioned his hospital; he could feel himself strutting down its halls, entering its rooms, its wards; he could smell it—its ether, its disinfectant destroying bacteria, its chloroform. That hospital, what a dream-to-come-true! He'd do anything for it, pay any price. Or would he?

He calmed himself and drove slowly toward Main Street and he changed his mind by carefully observing as he went. The silt of dust kicked up by the horses and mules and vehicles softly oozed through the breeze and filmed the shrubbery and porches along the street. Women and girls on the sidewalks carried umbrellas to shield themselves from the burning sun and held their dresses up out of the dust and dung. Some stopped to wave at him and to stare; many of them blushed because he was a doctor, but then they liked to cut coyish eyes at him. Many stopped and turned around, following him down the street with their eyes.

Across the street he saw his shadow, David Kingsley, going from his office to dinner. Vic noted that he was still the smart, fancy dresser he had been in his youth. David threw up his cane at Vic, both their smiles flashing. So he'd turned out to be

Green Pond's top lawyer and Vic wondered, was he not the Inchurches' lawyer? Dave never lost a case. It was said that if he took a notion, he could outargue ole Satan and convince him that he was wrong. It was said among the Green Ponders that he was as sly and smart, tricky smart, as a crow, and the Green Ponders, never tired of their trivial gossip, were prone to compare David Kingsley with Ole Doc in their hand-to-ear whisperings.

Vic disappeared down the street, leaving a whirl of dust for the Green Ponders to blow violently out of their nostrils and to start in with their small talk about him. The two blocks of Main Street, this hot summer day, harbored a sprinkling of groups whose sole ray of joy in life was talk.

Suddenly near the end of the street, Vic jerked powerfully upon the lines to keep the horse from running over the staggering, wildly disheveled man who ran into the street and fell to the dust in front of him. Vic pulled the horse to the side of the street, jumped out of the buggy, and ran to the man, turning him face up. It was fat, jocose Archibald Ives, owner of the sawmill and clerk of the Session of North Bethel, who did all the recording down here in the dreaded book before it was sent to Gabriel for publication. Vic saw that his belly was badly mutilated, the cuts crisscrossing like so many intersections.

An out-of-breath man, who had been following Ives, ran up to Vic and explained that at the sawmill Ives had lost his temper with one of his workers and grabbed the Negro by the back of his collar and furiously kicked his butt; but the unfunked Negro reached back with a long-bladed knife during the kicking and ripped Ives's belly to shreds.

Vic quickly took in the situation. "Lay him on those boxes over there in the shade—I'll see what I can do." They carefully picked up the groaning, bleeding Ives and placed him in the shade.

"Run to my buggy and bring me my satchels," Vic said.

The commotion gradually had attracted the furzy Green Ponders who ceased their talk and congregated, circled tightly about Vic and the victim, who by this time was being anesthetized.

Vic knew he was very probably attacking the impossible. He ripped off Ives's pants, exposing the hairy, blood-sotted gashes oozing blood and feces. He hoped the bladder wasn't punctured. His only hope of saving Ives was speed. Clean him out thoroughly and sew him up; cauterize his surgeon's instruments the best he could in an open fire; and hope to high heaven that he could work faster than the ever-infesting microbes could incubate.

He worked swiftly, his fingers doing fly-by-night curves and twists. He mopped up the blood, caught up what squirters he could see, cleaned out the dirt, scooped out the feces. The bladder wasn't punctured, he found out as his fingers worked deeper into the hot bowels. This was now a real gamble. He hoped above all else that the Negro's knife had been razor sharp.

The ever-curious ring of Green Ponders pushed in closer, and their clamorous, tart-tongued talk set up a louder ringing than the church bells. Vic thought he would suffocate, they pushed in so close and talked so loud.

——It's Unchristian to be a-cuttin on a body like that. Dog-bite-it, iffen I'd let that young rascal do me thataway——

——It's the Lord's will. His will will be done. Ives's time was up. You can't do nothing with God——

——The Lord has His eyes upon Ives. An eye for an eye, a tooth for a tooth——

——I ain't never knowed a rapscallion to meddle with the Lord's works as he's a-doin there——

——No good'll come to him——

——It's an outrageous sin. The Lord oughtta strike him down——

——You see him? He's a-burnin em knives until they're red
hot——

——Ole Satan's allus got to have red-hot things——

Victor saw Ives hauled away in a one-horse wagon, snoring
peacefully upon a pile of straw, but he stood there lonely and
far away until the crowd had dispersed like fog before the morning sun. Then, alone, he gathered up his instruments, put out
his fire, climbed into his buggy, and hurried on down the now
dispeopled street, although the air from their overheated tongues
came from their cobwebbed stores and followed him. Within
Vic was a mad ecstasy that not even the microbes could touch.

Vic rode on. He felt free as a bird in the wind. There welled
into him an uninvited joy. He sighed. The wind of the watershed blew softly and he could smell the water and the red land.
His pent-up emotions cooled.

Casually indifferent, he wandered into gloomy North Bethel
Church. He stopped, letting the meditative quiet cushion his
spiritual iniquity, letting it cloak him in infinite richness. Here
the insatiable need of the little wheel within him was filled. He
looked up to the sublime height of the hand-wrought, intricate
design of the octagonal ceiling and noted the new electrical
chandelier, like a thousand butterflies. He moved down the aisle
and he came to Pop's pew. He stopped and looked at the cushions and wondered did he and Mama Naomi sit on them or lean
back against them. As a child, when he had complained of the
hardness of the church pews, hoping that would make a gate-
way for him to get to stay at home, Pop had told him that if his
mind were on the things of God in God's house he wouldn't
mind the hard pews. He chuckled.

At the organ he marveled, for it was a magnificent organ,
given by the Inchurches, whose names were graven on it on a
handsome bronze plaque.

He switched on the organ and played in a meditative, elegiac mood, and there was no shy shrinking or diffident feeling

in him. Here for today he found a sweeter rest than he had
known since coming back to Catawba.

He played until the street lights were on. The belated clopping of horse hoofs, hurrying in for the night, sounded in his ear.
There was the feeling of contented bedding down. In Victor
there was no feeling of an outcry to outstrip the wind, to stretch
taller than a tree, but only the old longing to wrap his arms
about the bosom of the earth.

3

Worn to a frazzle, Mama Amazon dragged herself to the kitchen
and sat down on a chair at the end of the table to wait. For tonight the Holy Spirit had her low in her mind. She fully intended sitting here waiting until Vic came. What in the name of
Gawd was keeping him away so long? He'd been gone since
early this morning. He'd be rambling out here in the kitchen
hunting a bite to eat and that was the time she'd planned to
ask him. She'd been wanting to ask him ever since he came
home, but her shyness of approaching him with that kind of subject had kept her from it; although she'd raised him and he was
as simplehearted as a dove, she still felt ticklish.

She propped her elbows upon the table, formed a cup out of
her hands for her chin, and sat listening to the mockingbirds
singing in the honeylike moonlight that crept among the leafy
boughs. It was a lonely night; she'd never remembered a night
that the birds sang this lonely.

She waited to waylay Vic. Surely it'd not be much longer before he came. These summer nights were short and she needed
all the shut-eye she could get, but worse than needing shut-eye
was her plain flat need of seeing Vic in private. She'd counted
for thirty full moons and the thing continued to grow in her
belly. That was too long. That door ought to have opened with
the tenth full moon, opened wide, letting that which grew inside

her escape, for that was according to the plans Gawd had written in the stars. How much bigger would she get? This thing swelled and grew on now for thirty full moons. There had been a flood of hope in her with each full moon, only to be disappointed as the full moon waned.

Anybody that knew as much as Victor did would know the answer right off. To think that she had come to this! When she'd held him in her arms, when she'd suckled him, when she'd spent days fixing his baptismal clothes, nursing him in the surrey to the church!

Then she heard him coming across the porch toward the kitchen, hungry as ever.

"What're you doing here, Mama Amazon?" Vic questioned, the bright light of the kitchen making him wrinkle his face into a frown and squinch up his eyes. "You're surely through with your work? Pop ought to get someone else to help you. No use working day and night. Moreover," there was a devilish grin on his face, "I wanta bite to eat. My ole belly won't let me sleep when it's empty and gnawing."

"That's what I'd figured out. I's got everythin ready. Even kept it warm just lack ole times. Is you never gonna outgrow you tricks?" She chuckled low. She brought his supper from the stove and placed it on the table. "Eat fore it gets cold. I bet you ain't had a bite to eat since you left the house."

"No, been too busy." He picked up a forkful of food. "Wandering around." And he told her about sewing in Mr. Ives's cutout guts.

Mama Amazon listened until he'd finished. She waited, watching him a minute. Then she said, "Hon, I's done run thirty full moons and I ain't had no chile yet, an I's gettin mo bigger an mo bigger every day I lives."

"What're you talking about? You don't mean to stand there and tell me that you're trying to have a baby at your age?"

"Miz Sarah, she up an had one when she's heaps older an me.

I ain't but bout fifty-six year ole, maybe. An Miz Sarah was ninety."

"Miz Sarah? What're you talking about? Abraham's wife—the one in the Bible?"

"That's the Miz Sarah, an she had one at ninety. I done got all my bellybands an things made about two year ago."

He stood up from the table, went to her, and felt her abdomen. "Dogged if you don't have something growing in there and it ain't no watermelon. But I'll bet a dime it's no baby, feels too much like a fibroid tumor."

"Lawd have mercy, I bet Only's gonna be mad when he finds out I ain't havin no chile. Fo nearly two years I's been makin he sleep on the floor, because I tolt him I was gonna have a chile an I didn't have no need for he in the bed." She stopped laughing and looked serious. "Fo true, I ain't been up to my ole self, but tho't it was laziness."

"Nope, think it's a tumor."

"You can do sumpin wit em?"

"Sure. Cut em out."

"What?"

"An operation; only thing that'll stop that."

"How you do that?"

"Put you to sleep; very similar to the one on Mrs. Thorpe."

"How'll I do about the work here?"

"Get somebody else; you'll not live forever. Man's longer below the ground than above, you've allus preached to me."

"Fo true, fo true. Gawd is kind. The earth is sweet. Death's the peace us all longs fo, an I'll go wit greater joy than the red leaves in the falltime."

"Figure out whom you want to get and I'll operate on you in a room upstairs, so that you can stay right there until you're able to get up. You're too heavy to be dragged around. And I don't want my stitches pullin out. Where's Dessa? Not teaching in the summer, surely?"

"Dessa's home right now, but since she gets that lil state teaty fo teachin, she takes summer courses."

"You decide and I'll examine more thoroughly; then we'll set the day. You'll have to have one of em to wait on you; I don't want that belly of yours popping open once I sew it up."

4

From their watchtowers beyond the golden sun Gawd and Gabriel watched over Catawba, watched its people. Mama Naomi fled Catawba because of Victor's mad cutting. Budda drove the horses unmercifully, lashed them with the whip so that the surrey careened roughly, and Naomi was sloshed as water in a jug in her mad dash to Rahab to hide out with a distant Mure relative until Catawba no longer reeked with ether, until the blood ceased to flow. In spite of Naomi's crying out, Budda drove recklessly at breakneck speed. For Budda was sulky and didn't want to leave Catawba. Miz Naomi was to be tolerated, but Vic and Ole Doc were the two who made his heart beat a little faster.

Victor had ceaselessly infuriated Naomi all her life with his deep mocking laughter, his outlandish indifference, his outrageous conduct, and now this—cutting! On her cook, of all things! Her nerves would stand only so much. Oh well, she had one consolation: Jacob was the apple of her heart. He lived a normal life and was a preacher and walked in the ways of God.

GABRIEL: Well, I's finished puttin down that Miz Big Amazon's operation. She gonna shout Vic's praises over the watershed fo sure. Iffen the peoples don't want to believe she, she'll pull up she dress an show em the scar on she good black belly. And now she floats roun Catawba strong as new.

GAWD: You give that Victor Thornwell plenty credits fo he's good work. He's a simplehearted boy an I wants he to stay so. Iffen he ever gets uppish, I'll chastise em.

GABRIEL: Shorely wish Miz Joanna could have seen em

operate. Done she heart pure good. What disimpatiented ole Satan doin these days? You's been givin em ole boys plenty rope lately an I know most they's tyin up they same ole tricks.

GAWD: Yes. He's trucklin wit em ole elders' heads in Nof Bethel an he'd deny it right tomorrow iffen I cornered he.

GABRIEL: Why's he singlin out the elders?

GAWD: Toadyin wit em because they ain't had a preacher in the last seven years there in Nof Bethel. I don't lack it a-tall the way they treats My servants in Nof Bethel, so I's punishin em good fo the servile trucklin they's been carryin on in that church. But em's My ole Scotch-Irish wit so much red pepper in they tempers they'd fight hornets. An ole Satan's been vexin em.

GABRIEL: Just what's ole Satan been doin?

GAWD: Eggin em elders an that Pulpit Committee to call Jacob Thornwell there to Nof Bethel to preach.

GABRIEL: When did ole Satan go around tryin to get preachers fo preacherless churches? But Jake's a powerful good preacher.

GAWD: One of the best when it comes to preachin, but preachin ain't the question or the point.

GABRIEL: What's the point?

GAWD: Jezebel Inchurch.

GABRIEL: Tho't You lacked em, the way she'd rare back an play that organ. The way she hold that sacred organ seat in Nof Bethel. Remember the Sunday she wanted to go to Babel an got she a substitute fo the organ—but right in the middle of the first hymn she walked right smack back and down the church aisle to the organ an pushed the substitute outta the way an took over? Peoples still talks about that.

GAWD: An mo'an that, since she's got so much money, she don't pay Me no mind an thinks she can buy everythin, even to My Victor Thornwell. Iffen Jake comes there, she'll finish destroyin him one way or another.

GABRIEL: What is You gonna do bout em?

GAWD: I'll think bout em early tomorrow.

Water, water boy, water for my parching tongue. The Green Ponders sing and pray to the great Triune Godhead, way up beyond the shining sun, so that they may reach glory in the sweet by-and-by and shun ole Satan, who with his sycophantic talk would vaunt them into so much sin that it would be easy to take them a toboggan ride to the screaming inferno.

BEELZEBUB: How Green Pond is ragin. I's never in my life seen sich angry waters—sich tempestuous waters.

SATAN: Huh, ain't nothin but preachin, preachin.

BEELZEBUB: Let me push you in an you'll find out.

SATAN: Is you lost you mind? I don't need no preachin or no water. That fire down yonder is good enough fo me to beat the scales offen my tail.

13

It was a clear December day, coat-wrapping cold. The morning ushered in with a smell of snow in the air. Although the sun shone brightly, the old folks could smell snow in the air. They could tell, too, by the shade and tone of the wall of mountains, by the way the wind came over the mountains, by the way the sun last set behind the mountains. Their withered faces were as pages of ancient writing which open to prophesy, then close in a graven mood.

If there was foreboding among the old folks that the skies would sooner or later turn something loose, it was still a bright sunny day in Green Pond, because that's the kind of day God picked out to make into a Preachin Sunday, quite impeccable, set aside from the other six days, which were quite peccable. Sunday: the day the Reverend Jacob Emmanuel Thornwell came south to preach a trial sermon at North Bethel.

Dressed like all get-out, Mama Amazon was bubbling in glory and climbing the steep stairs to the topmost balcony in North

Bethel. Only and Budda were with her and wore their tight-legged, box-waisted pants and felt awe-struck and out of place as a Christian being tossed to some den of carnivorous animals. Yellow Sam and Gee with many of their children were climbing to the topmost balcony to sit with the many other colored people who knew Jake and Vic well nigh as if they were brothers, so close had been their relationship in their growing-up days. June and July were there with their faces shining, their hair greased, pulled straight and gleaming.

Pop and Mama Naomi sat in the honored Thornwell pew upon comforting cushions, but Tommy, who had been dragged unwillingly with them to church every Preachin Sunday since he could remember, was not there. He had grown too big and too rebellious, knowing much more than aged, hoary-headed Ole Doc. Naomi, the old pirate, had eyes already searching for treasures to tote to her secret treasury.

The church filled rapidly as though the people were water being poured into a glass jug through a funnel. The stiff-starched petticoats rattled brazenly, the taffeta swished with a zip. The wreaths and sprays of flowers on the women's hats, the fruits and feathers, leaping as sacrificial fires in God's house, wrought a blinding spiral of color.

Vic took his seat at the organ and calmly looked over the congregation with dreamy eyes. His lazy lips were pursed in thought. He searched the faces casually, then critically, his eyes moving to the first balcony. The seven great columns that supported the seven balconies were heavily embossed with great bunches of grapes, grape leaves, and grape vines, painstaking and tediously carved into the wood by ole Andy in the longest of the bygones, just before he fled to the land of the stardust way beyond the shining blue. Vic searched the seven sides, then up to the topmost balcony where his penetrating gaze picked out Mama Amazon and his heart gladdened at the saintly look upon her old black face.

Mama Amazon saw Vic looking directly at her and pure joy leaped madly within her breast. She shook her head with her disbelief. He had told her that he'd play today, but she'd never believed him. What the crafty elders had done to him to get him to play was pure mystery to her. Sumpin had slipped up on her, maybe she was getting too ole to keep up with the white folks' business. She didn't care, for all she was wanting right now was for that pure music to soak into her soul. Sometime, somewhere she'd find out why he played today. Whatever it was, it was all right for today, because with a Thornwell at the organ, a Thornwell in the pulpit, Thornwells sitting in em fine curved pews, and a raft of Thornwell niggers gumming up the topmost balcony, why the Thornwells were about to take the church over. But, ah Gawd, ole Nof Bethel could stand em, because it was a bold church, filled with sturdy, rock-gutted people.

Then she glanced at Ole Doc's pew and saw that Tommy wasn't there. They'd had a very unpleasant argufying before church and Tommy had walked out of Catawba as rebellious as ole Satan. Mama Amazon feared Tommy would be wild, because as a baby he'd sucked milk from a cow that a black snake had sucked; but she didn't rightly know. Ole Doc had had a great-uncle who had sucked his ma until he was nine years old. Then he'd grown up and run away out West and became nearly as notorious as Jesse James. Maybe there was just a wild streak in the Thornwells and milk didn't matter. She'd done her best and it's no telling what Gawd intended doing with these white folks, if she could rightly say they were white. Purty nigh red. Well, they'd stole the land from a red man. He'd get even with them somehow—Gawd was justice.

Victor saw Jezebel and Robert enter; two deacons led them to their pew. Jezebel was arrayed in a smart fur coat, rich and gleaming, and every lucent hair knew full well that it swathed an Inchurch. Vic noticed her shielded, coy glances, the un-

domesticated burning in her eyes. She was watching every move
he made. Vic thought, *Well, let her call. She's not sick and I
won't go there again. Even if she is, I won't. Or will I? Jezebel,
you're a beauty and a temptress and if the Inchurches favored
me I could—what?*

He continued to play softly, deep and far away. His hands and
feet moved automatically. The congregation was spellbound with
the beauty of the music, its tone enveloped them as burning incense in some forsaken temple.

In this music Vic was with Gawd as He separates the light
from the dark and comes forth in His full blazing glory from an
eddying, amorphous substance of an unplanned world. Gawd
throws out His hands and creates swiftly the waters, the air, the
moon, the stars, the sun. He divides the waters and there are
land and trees, and green grass grows, and Gawd, who is ever-
loving and more than kind, feels pleased with Himself. From the
eddying, swirling, amorphous substance He creates it all. Gawd
flies beyond the newly created and brightly shining sun, His
empurpled robes billowing in the wind, His long white beard
waving. He hurries about, tidying up the scraps of firmament.
The newly created, shivering spirits surround the awesome Gawd
as fresh-hatched wet biddies snuggle up under the feathers of the
hen. Gawd, stroking His magnificent beard—it's no natty beard,
but one more magnificent than the most sainted patriarch possessed in the North Bethel cemetery—points to the earth. And
in this mad moment of playing the organ here in North Bethel,
Victor's soul climbed to heights of enduring beauty and joy and
he snuggled close to Gawd and had no fear. This kept the little
wheel within him ticking in tune and he knew it was good.

The choir filed into the choir loft, followed by an elder and
Jake.

Vic modulated, shifted stops at the same time, and went into
the doxology with tremendous force. Then the adoration hymn,
"Holy, Holy, Holy," was sung and the organ swung the singers

through the hymn with clipping rhythm. The congregation, unaccustomed to such forceful rhythm, dropped wearily to their seats with a limpid thud and dropped the hymn books with a greater thud into the book racks behind the pews. Vic glanced toward Mama Amazon, then to Jezebel.

Jezebel's eyes burned as coals of fire. Her heart smoldered in torment and she was greatly cast down in spirit. Here in God's house, arrayed in rich furs and her fingers weighted down with pure diamonds and the entire congregation awe-struck in her presence, she could hardly control the eating jealousy that gnawed eternally within her.

She looked longingly at her Victor and her agony knew no limit. No matter how much she called, he'd not come to see her, and she had so much pain, oh, so very much pain. Her eyes ransacked Jake as though he were some cast-off garment fit only for a rummage sale. His jowls were plump and well-shaven, he was immaculately dressed, sweet-smelling, even to his breath, and nothing on earth is cleaner than a Presbyterian minister. But she had been too much woman for Jake, she had consumed him too quickly. And Vic had not let her get hold of him; their love lay so near hate that they were always quarreling. She frightened Vic and he kept her at bay.

When she looked, cold and calculating, upon David Kingsley, his wife, and their four sons, her mind filled with bitter memories. *How had old Doctor Thornwell got him into the church? Yet, David Kingsley is not to be trifled with. People think too much of him, if he is Ole Doc's bastard son. He's up-an-comin. The Democrats had sent him to Clover to the House of Representatives at the drop of a hat. It's best,* she thought, *that I truckle to him yet a while because it's rumored that he'll be the governor soon. While I can't forget how hot his mouth burned on mine, there's a possibility, once he's the seated governor, that I can make him row my boat. There're ways, if one contrives.*

One had to overlook Ole Doc, her mind continued, *because he's getting so old. Why, he actually has the Charles Coatworthys coming here to church, and the Cabelus McCobbs of still-house fame. And sitting right down there on the very front row are Mr. and Mrs. Laban Perry and their children; and everyone in Green Pond knows that Mrs. Perry's oldest son belongs to Ole Doc.*

She looked at Louise Tarlton, her sister-in-law, sitting in the pew in front of her, slightly over toward the aisle. She wondered why Louise continued to cast speculative sideway glances at her. She'd been doing it ever since she came into church. Jezebel wrinkled her small nose as though Louise were a bad odor and shrugged her shoulders in contempt as a dog in disgust with his many fleas. *One thing is certain,* Jezebel carefully reminded herself, *Louise Inchurch Tarlton is one of the most blousy hypocrites in this church.*

Jake fed his sermon to the hungry sheep and they cropped it close to the ground. During a drought sheep must nibble closer to exist and seven years without a preacher had been close to deluded digression. Jake wondered as he preached what it'd be like to toady to Jezebel. He led the flock to quiet waters and they drank until their bellies bulged. The length of his sermon had already bulged their bladders, and their kidneys had no place to drizzle.

Louise Tarlton simply could not stand the fury that raged within her any longer. She'd not sit longer in the house of God with such as that perfidiously pharisaical Jezebel. Today Jezebel was wearing a fur coat that cost well over five thousand and here she sat in a cheap, shabby coat that didn't cost a fifth as much as Jezebel's. Robert, her brother, was undoubtedly the biggest sap this side of a sapsucker. Louise took Joe by the arm and they walked immoderately bold from the church during the sermon, immune to the stares of the congregation.

After the service there was a hurricane rushing of the congregation toward the pulpit to speak to Jacob. And among the worming crowd was Miss Lizzie Newcome, who, frail, leaning on a stick, clasped his hand and told him that she was proud of him and that she just knew he had it in him all along.

Vic was trying to slip out a back door when Miss Lizzie Newcome cornered him and made him feel as though he were back in the first grade again. There was about her such brightness and contagious musing that Vic stared at her in disbelief.

"Victor, you've as much devilment in you as ever and you're just as contrary. I watched you the whole time you played. What is it that you do to that organ?"

He stammered awkwardly before her. "Just played. What's wrong?"

"There you go, throwing up your modest fence at the drop of a hat. I simply didn't know that church organs could speak of life, death, the resurrection, the cross, the grave, life in the beginning. Most of the time this one is played it sounds like a circus calliope or a eunuch singing when he's mad at somebody."

Vic laughed boisterously. "Miss Lizzie, you ought to go back to teaching school."

Jezebel and Robert moved smartly down the aisle and no member, by any means, failed to speak to them smilingly, amicably, and with great love, turning their glances of veneration and looks of hate off to dark corners. Jezebel and Robert showered one and all with smiles, light smiles and soon blown away, as things insecure forever do.

2

The seven years of drought were ended and Naomi's rakish soul was replenished, her vacillating heart beating with shining clarity and her corset keeping her body pole-straight, notwithstanding the fact that Tommy had humiliated her and Ole Doc by such indecorous action as not going to church.

This Sunday Naomi sat at the end of the dinner table opposite Pop and gloated fondly over her family. Prattling talk flew around the table amid the clanging of handsome silver against delicate china. For after listening to such divine preaching, Naomi's spirit was as a cyclone; she gainsaid anything to disturb these precious hours the Lord's spirit jarred upon her. To think that she had born a preacher-son to the glory of the Lord constricted her esophagus so tightly that food wouldn't go down, but she kept up her chatter and the Lord knew that her sitting down was comforting and that which she spoke with her tongue was to His glory.

Myra, Jake's second wife, hadn't been to Catawba many times and had met Victor only once. And it had been so long since even Jake had been to Catawba that he was befuddled by the changes. How time did fly; how fast the young grew up. No longer did he hear the squeaking windlass at the well, because no one used it except Pop, who refused to drink the sluicing water from the brazen spigots because it had lost its savor and was fitten only to be puddled in. The electric lights, Pop pointed out to Jake, weren't bad, but sure to breed a generation of speckswearers. The telephone was a jingling gadget, but he hoped the young'uns didn't forget the greatest communication system was between God and man, because that was the line that man was hooked to and there was no escaping it. Jake marveled at Pop's talk.

The entire family was curious to know whether Jake'd accept the pastorate of North Bethel if the congregation called him. Naomi'd hear nothing else and she urged. Pop thought him capable of it, but he'd have to learn the art of truckling and keeping his oil can filled, ever ready to oil the parts that needed it.

Victor was quiet and wondered about Tommy.

Mama Amazon couldn't tempt Jake with enough tasty food to satisfy her overwhelming emotions, although he ate hoggishly and praised her dishes with high-toned words. She trekked to and from the kitchen serving, not allowing her granddaughters that privilege, because in that dining room this day sat a servant of the most high Gawd. Moreover, this righteous reverend had gnawed and suckled at her big fat teaties with his toothless gums and she had given copiously of her milk and he had waxed strong and as a preacher was a power in the sight of Gawd. Fo true, when she went to glory, she had but to point out to ole Gabriel the things she had done upon earth to further the glory of Gawd's name and ole Gabriel had better have every bit of that down in the Books or she fully intended on making him drap his pants right in heaven and laying her hand to his set-down job!

This lovesome Sunday dinner was disquieted by one of the maids fleeing from the front of Catawba to the dining room with a wildly disheveled girl, carrying a baby, close on her heels.

"Pa sait," the uneasy girl blurted, "fer me ter bring this har young'un over har an give hit to you all. Hit's er tater patch that that Tommy come over ter our house an started. Pa sait he wuz gettin ter ole ter be raisin any mo taters."

The family looked questioningly at the girl and then queasily at each other. Pop regarded the mere slip of a girl searchingly with his keen old eyes.

"Where is Tommy?" Ole Doc asked.

"He's run off an he won't marry me," said her scratchy voice, and her eyes were red and swollen. "An I loved em."

"How do you know he ran off?"

"I seed him wit my own eyes swing er freight train yon side er Pecan Lane an he sait he warnt never, never comin back," she moaned.

Big-eyed Mama Amazon eased across the floor and looked at the helpless red mite in the girl's arms and her heart was charged with deep love. "Enty sweet? An a Thornwell, too. Gawd, do have mercy an give me that baby. Looks lack I jest can't stop raisin em Thornwells. Gawd, this coverin a heap of You time. Us had some real fine preachin this mornin an us got a real fine baby this evenin." She took the baby from the girl's arms. The girl grabbed up her dress tail to stanch her tears and fled, sobbing, from the room.

Victor saw the heavenly light in Mama Amazon's eyes. "What are you going to name him, Mama Amazon?"

Her face lighted up radiantly. "Name he fo he's great-grand settin there at the end of the table. An fo short let's call he Tad. Fo first you hears the frogs croakin in the pond an then the next thing you knows, the tadpoles is there."

Vic laughed loudly at her and she scolded severely, "I know you's butted you head agin many instwo-ishions of high learnin, but when it comes to raisin a Thornwell baby, I knows best, because in the days that I raised my shavers, Miz Joanna was livin and she tolt me how, an you's got all em things to learn. You can't live by bread alone, fo iffen you did, the one that had the most bread would naturally do the most of the livin."

3

One day Jezebel turned on Robert, put up her claws as a cornered cat, and snarled, "Robert Inchurch, I want you to see right tomorrow that Doctor Victor Thornwell comes to see me. I certainly have no intentions of having a baby without a doctor just to save you a few pennies. It wasn't my idea to have a baby. That was one of your spawning ideas," she continued, octopuslike, throwing out as much self-defense as she could muster.

"Why must you continue to insist upon that particular doctor?" Robert asked in his suave voice. "He really isn't an obstetrician. He's a bloody surgeon, if one's to believe the tales that float so thickly about this town. And he thinks he is a good one," he continued with his methodical meticulousness. "We could get a first-rate obstetrician from Rahab or you could go to

a hospital there—a hospital, that'd be better all the way around."
An Inchurch had spoken.

"Listen, don't you give me any more of your wily ideas.
You've got me into this trouble and now you're going to get me
out. Is that clear? I don't see why I ever married a stinking Inchurch, for you're so crummy. Why, that old hospital in Rahab
might catch on fire any day. Oh, no, you're not getting me
burned up alive in that old wooden chicken coop." She rained
hot words upon his visible skull.

"Well, we could have an obstetrician come here. A good one.
Get the best. I don't mind the money. It's that Victor Thornwell I don't want around you!" The plans of the Inchurches
were always workable plans and quite flawless.

"That's it. I want the best and I want Doctor Victor Thornwell. He outstrips anything here. When he first returned to the
country here he shocked the living lard out of the folks with
what he did to Mrs. Andy Thorpe. But she lived and she's as
stout as a horse. And she has a big fine husky boy. Look at Mrs.
Helms, and the hundreds of others. He's an artist." There was
too much drawling coo in her voice, sticky hot and peppery
stinging to Robert.

"I don't care what you say. Those have all been surgical
cases; and you know that as well as I do!" An Inchurch spoke
loudly, irked by jealousy as though he had sand under his eyelids and splinters under his toenails. If there were only some
reasonable, some plausible means, some feasible, some suitable
way of getting that Victor Thornwell out of his road—

"Sure, I know," Jezebel spoke softly. "I know that lots would
be dead if it had not been for that Doctor Thornwell. There
are too many patients of some of these other doctors around
here dying for me to trust them. And what did your sisters get
from the famous doctors in Rahab?" Jezebel could scare an Inchurch to death with this suggestion. "Answer me that. And if
you want me to perpetuate the Inchurch generation—though I

hardly think it worth while—you'll get me Doctor Victor Thornwell. What's a little money? Pay him five hundred or a thousand of your moldy dollars if you have to. I don't care. You've got the money. He'll come if you give him enough money."

"But if he won't come from your calling him, I don't see how you expect me to induce him to come. Bait him with money? Maybe that's what he's after. I thought you and the Thornwells had always been good friends. That's funny to me. Money won't buy everything. We had a hard enough time getting him to play that organ in church—and I still can't see why you insist on him."

She laughed. "So an Inchurch has finally run up against someone who can get the better of him? Really, that amazes me no end. It behooves me to behold a skulking Inchurch—such proud possessive people! Poor creature."

"Really, Jezebel, please. I've a little feeling." He arose from the stinging blow slowly, shaking his head to get the Inchurch head gears to function.

"I'm amazed at that," she was pounding while the iron was white hot, "for you've always appeared to me as some sort of a spider. And now you're afraid of poor Doctor Thornwell. Just an innocent, simple-minded boy and an Inchurch is afraid. Shame."

"I'm not afraid of him. I could easily crush him and old Doctor Thornwell too if I wanted. I could crush anything in Green Pond County if I wanted to, and it wouldn't take me long to do it."

She slit her eyes to cunningness, "Ah, I thought so. Then why is it that you're so afraid of getting Doctor Thornwell for my doctor? That should be simple to arrange."

"In the first place I see no need of it. And another thing that has puzzled the daylights out of me is the fact that he is so good-looking and he's bound to have had many women at his feet, yet, why's he never married? And your ceaseless insistence that he be your doctor. Tell me, Jezebel, and tell me the truth, are you in love with Victor Thornwell? Answer me!"

She grew furious. "Why, Robert Inchurch, you, of all people, are jealous. An old ugly humpbacked spider like you—jealous! I knew Victor Thornwell long before I ever knew you. Had I wanted him, I'd have done something about it long, long ago."

"That's puzzling. If you've had chances at him—especially as good-looking as he is, why would you stoop to marry an old humpbacked spider, as you say, like me? I've always had a dubious feeling about that and why you ever married me. Even at night when I'm sleeping with you there in the dark, I can sense it. Jezebel Inchurch, you're lying! *You love that Victor Thornwell!*" An Inchurch had screamed.

"Living with an old humpbacked spider that's as ugly as the devil—in fact, you look very much like the devil, and if you just had horns and a long tail—my, my, what an imp—as if all that's not enough punishment for me! I have to sleep with him, let him paw me with toad-cold hands, feeling me with fingers that creep as snakes. No! All that's not enough. Now he must get jealous. I'll not live with a jealous man."

He grabbed her shoulders and shook her. "Jezebel, shut your mouth. Have you lost every sense of decency, gone completely out of your mind? Cut out this carrying on. You must think of our child that's coming—it might be marked!"

"*Our* child? You're the one that wanted it, not me. And now when I want a decent doctor, one that I can trust, you start accusing me of being in love with him. I won't take that from you. I'll leave you sitting right here flat in this house on your warty behind. Do you get that?"

"Jezebel, you can't do that. Things like that simply aren't done. Do you realize what you're saying?"

"Sure, I realize exactly what I'm saying. And I'll do it, too."

"No you won't, Jezebel Inchurch. I'll have you declared insane and sent to the state asylum. You can't get by with running away. I'll spend every cent I have and hound you to the very ends of the earth before I would let you get away with it. Before I'd let you heap that sort of disgrace upon my head, before I'd be made the laughing stock of this country, I'd—oh, no, old gal, you needn't bother to try that."

"You know, I believe you'd actually do that. Yes, those very things. Well, Robert Inchurch, let me tell you one thing: if you have me declared insane, I'll kill you with my very own hands. You're a whole heap nearer eternity than you think you are."

"Jezebel, let's cut this out; it's getting us nowhere. Let's make some sort of terms."

"My goodness. You started it, not me. I simply asked for a good doctor to attend me and deliver your child and you fly into accusing me unjustly." Jezebel, the good fisherwoman, saw she had hooked him. "If needful, I'll go to Rahab and go through with the same trying things that your adorable sisters Louise and Elvira went through. You'll recall that both of them lost their babies and they had the best medical attention that Rahab could offer. Trained nurses with them night and day. But if that's the way you feel about it, I'll go—it's the Christian duty of women to suffer. It's your child that's coming, remember. It's the last chance to leave a living Inchurch upon the face of Green Pond. Elvira and Louise will never have a child, moreover, now —they're too old; so's Irene, if she ever snares a man. So this is the last chance. But satisfy your own mind. I'll do as you say without more argument. But I do know that Doctor Thornwell is the best doctor."

"That's right about this being the last chance and quite strange that Louise and Elvira both lost their babies in Rahab."

"You do just as you please, Robert. It really doesn't make any difference to me."

"It makes a great deal of difference to me to have a son or no son."

"Whatever you say."

"All right. I'm going to call that Doctor Thornwell down to the bank the first spare moment I get this coming week and see what can be arranged. There's too damn much calmness about him; it's not human. And he seems always to be laughing at you. I'll never forget when he—when they were born. That stirred up more excitement than Green Pond could digest right off. Mrs. Thornwell went crazy and they carried her off somewhere; folks always said there was something the matter with one of the twins' heads. Never did know which one it was, but I'd be willing to bet anything that it was the doctor. Now, the preacher is an all-around good fellow. I like him."

"Reckon the congregation is going to call him?"

"Oh, yes. I think everybody was carried away with him. No doubt they'll call him—especially if I say so. Moreover, we've been without a preacher too long—seven years is too long."

"Well, maybe if you treated the preacher better and didn't fight so much among yourselves, he'd stay longer." Jezebel wrinkled her nose and sat down.

Robert looked at her questioningly.

Jezebel smiled softly and said out loud, "All doctors seem to be in league with the coffinmaker."

Robert squirmed.

4

Gawd's mill grinds slowly but surely. The years turn swiftly, Aprils of warm rain, summers of swallows skimming about Catawba's hallowed eaves. The ivy that the ancient Thornwells had brought from Scotland puts out new white roots and scampers a little farther up Catawba's chimneys each year.

Vic knew in these days that he was traveling over the same routes Granny Joanna had traveled, up and down the same old rivers winding slowly and muddily toward the sea, carrying away the red dirt that the pine trees cried for to protect their bare and bleeding roots. The babbling streams and creeks he forded, often stopping to give his horse a drink. The unfordable creeks frequently had covered bridges and upon these he meditated, examining them as though they were patients.

His billowing spirit was tempered by the hazardous conditions under which he had to operate, with the profound superstitions he encountered. He took careful note and marveled over it. If the signs were in the heel, teeth could be pulled, and if one wet in the road, one's eyes were sure to breed a sty.

At times, especially in the sultriness of hot summer days, he thought of Granny Joanna. He thought of the spittle and the clay and how she had once used hot irons to stanch flowing blood and known the curing power of the great mullein leaves. He thought she would echo Pop in his incessant harping to look into the mind as well as the body.

"You have to be able to diagnose; that's over half the erring in ethical medicine. Take an interest in your patient. Don't worry about money. If you do your work well, you'll be paid."

Granny and Pop went before Victor from Green Pond to Mt. Olivet, were with him at Ebenezer, at Old Hope and New Hope. They lighted fires for him at Old Unity. Purity received him with open arms. Even when he went to Rahab he did not fear, for the Thornwell doctors had been there before him.

There had been two wars fought on this watershed. Men bled and died for what they thought was right. Vic kept that in his mind as he ministered to the sick and to the ailing and did what he thought was right.

The mills grew and expanded and more and more of the folks in Green Pond had a hand in them, in one way or another. They'd long since got mostly away from Ole Doc, though his interest never waned. He kept his sharp interest in them and the welfare of the county and let other folks keep a neat pile of capital in them. Ole Doc liked money as well as anyone and he valued it carefully, but he always preached that it was not everything; what should a brief tenant on earth have to care for?

And Robert Inchurch, who had got in when the way was prepared for him, waxed richer with every turning of the spindles.

The Thornwell Hospital was nearly completed and Vic stopped by. It had been built upon a graceful hill of Catawba's land south of Doubting Hollow, which was south of Green Pond. He and Pop had finally decided to locate it here in memory of Grandma Joanna, because the hill had grown and nurtured a great ancient oak about whose trunk an enormous grape vine had clung well over several hundred years. And because here at ninety years of age Granny had climbed the ancient oak and plucked baskets of grapes to make the strong racy wine for the holy communion in North Bethel Church. In front of the Thornwell Hospital now stood a solid monument, the tree, her great limbs heavily laden with luscious grapes.

5

After a heavy Preachin Sunday, Ole Doc and Naomi sat up late by the fire and talked. The cold barked to get in.

"How's the hospital coming?" Naomi asked, lifting her placid face from the Bible.

"Oh, fine. Six more months'll finish it."

"You certainly waited a time to get it started."

"Wanted to test Victor out. See what he'd do. Give him rope, see if he'd hang himself. But in my estimation he's come around in flying colors. Chip from the old stump."

"You going to give the hospital to Victor?"

"Naturally. It's his hospital I'm having built, not mine, my dear. Even though I might appear as young and dashing to you as Sir Lancelot, I'm not. I'm well in years. I've been on borrowed time a long time. I'll be ninety my next birthday."

"Why, you don't wear glasses yet."

"Doubtful I ever will. See as good now as I did at sixteen. My hearing's all right, too. God has been kind to me, and I'm thankful."

Naomi snorted slightly, an unbecoming sound, but one which she thought became The Doctor. "Well, you're not dead yet."

"Oh, no," Ole Doc said, "but it'll not be as long as it has been. Want all my knots tied and ready to go. Go on somewhere else and pick up a new life and start over, for it's certain that my arrival into this world was carefully and painstakingly prepared for without my knowing anything about it, and it's certain that in the beyond there's preparation being made for me. It was so written out in the stars long ago."

"You don't have to tell me about the stars!"

Ole Doc eased himself out of the chair and eased himself to the window, looking out at the snow falling in the gathering darkness, looking out over the lands that were not now all Catawba's.

"Once ninety," he said, not to Naomi, "the years fly faster than ever. They're slipping by faster than the snow falling from heaven. Time and snow are alike. They have no ending or beginning. They only change."

6

Before Vic went to the bank, he and Pop argued as drunkards do, threw brazen words at each other.

Mama Amazon took back a step, holding her breath, and Naomi cast her face into self-righteousness.

"Quit bucking like a young mule," Ole Doc said. "There'll be lots of things in Green Pond that you aren't going to like to do. If you're planning to stay here—and I take it you are—you're going to have to grin and to bear.

"For when you stick your hand into the lion's mouth, you'll

have to get it out the best way you can. My advice is to get it out with as much skin left on it as possible. To snub the Inchurches would be cutting your own throat. I've known them all my life, even before there was a Green Pond, and they have always ruled. You're foolish, which'll get you nowhere. Make up your mind to that right now, especially where the Inchurches are concerned.

"You go right on down to that bank and see what Robert wants. If there's anything that you can do, you do it. Maybe with your tongue in your cheek, but do it. Especially if you wish to practice medicine here in Green Pond. Get some sham into you. There are lots of things to choke a dog with besides good butter: any rancid grease will do, provided you use tact in getting it down. Don't be so rough—or tetchy, either. Learn to be slow and oily. This is an oily age we're living in. Not that it's any worse than it was thousands of years ago nor any worse than it'll be a thousand years hence. Everyone loves sham and pretense. Truth hurts. Oil soothes."

Vic left Catawba filled with misgivings and out of place. His overdose of honesty worked his Adam's apple chokingly, waves of rebellion still rising in him.

This, indeed, was one of Jezebel Inchurch's most cunning tricks. Jezebel wanted a child no more than a man with a full stomach wanted food. He was filled with such provocation that he could easily shake out whatever grew in her without using scalpel or knife. Then he visioned her affected display of modesty, the coy twisting of her behind, and he seethed with the desire to strip her of all her sexual organs. But that would only make her worse. A resigned sigh escaped him. He reflected upon his destiny and what the stardust held for him. He thought that nowhere in him was there husbandry, and that his life was as the canvas without the paint.

In the distance he heard the whistle of an approaching train and he was suddenly filled with sadness. His breath abated. He stopped, listening. He was seized with a mad desire to hurry to the station, board that train and go—banish forever Green Pond and Catawba from his mind; be swallowed into oblivion.

Leave all that he loved.

Leave all that he loved? Be forever as the haunted or the hunted? Could he not make one compromise, one only, in order to live in this place? For here he must live. It was still as it had been when he was a child: without Catawba there would be chaos.

Vic looked up at the Inchurch bank and laughed, thinking of what Budda said: the Inchurch bank was a skyscraper. In reality it was a modest nine-floored building, hovering on Main Street like a buzzard waiting in some dead tree for a feast; yet the Green Pond *Observer* had praised this new building highly. Jep still liked butter on his bread, Vic thought.

Mr. Inchurch's private secretary greeted Vic with her suave smile. She was a twitting creature who assuaged all churlish sores with her smug efficiency. But today she seemed to have caught the tenor of Mr. Inchurch's rapt uncertainty and now, with the approach of handsome Doctor Thornwell, she made way, bowing a little as though he were some high priest.

Robert was up, bowing nearly from his waist, extending a white, slick hand in good will, smiling, even though his nose-glasses alone made him look oilier than a politician. Vic was offered a seat. He was offered cigars. The atmosphere was of utmost flattery. Robert spoke in his most winning voice.

"Doctor Thornwell, let me once again thank you for playing for church. You've performed brilliantly. Everyone I've met lately has praised you most highly. In fact, we wish you'd consider playing for us all the time. Music is so very important in church. With one brother in the pulpit and one at the organ we could have some mighty good church." *Look at those damned eyes. They are looking right through me,* Robert thought. *I must get him out of my road. I'd never sit in church and listen to him play Sunday after Sunday. I couldn't stand it. Why does Jezebel want him for a doctor? I know why. She loves him. I'm going to make her confess to it. I shall not live with this torturing my mind. He's too good-looking, too tall—all that any woman might desire. I must hatch up some decent way of getting rid of him. I am sure it could be arranged. Yes, Jezebel loves him.*

"Thank you, Mr. Inchurch. That's very nice of you. But I don't think I'll have the time after the hospital is going. I'm planning on a School of Nursing, for one thing—" *Poor old deluded fish, Vic thought, does he not yet know what works in Jezebel's mind? Has he slept with her all these years and not found her out? It's one time an Inchurch has a cyclone by its tail and doesn't know what to do with it.*

"Oh, so you're going to have a School of Nursing? Must be going to be quite a layout. Want to get around some of these days to look it over." *He'll give me no peace night or day. I wonder what he thinks of Jezebel? Is he in love with her? I'm sure she is with him. That's what I've been sleeping with all these years—this haunt. There's no way of telling how he might feel. You can tell nothing from his face; there is no way of probing within him. His face has too much calmness, assurance in it. It is too far away. It is something I can't get hold of.*

"Really, it wouldn't be practical to have a hospital without a nursing school. It'd be almost like having a preacher without a congregation. The mortgage without the mortgagee." Vic laughed too lightly for Robert's comfort. "After all, a hospital is quite a complicated thing." *Why doesn't the old fool hurry up and state what he wants? If he thinks I like to sit here and look at him, he's cockeyed. He sure has the fidgets.*

"Yes, yes. Green Pond really needs a modern, up-to-date hospital. And any time that I can be of assistance, don't hesitate to call on me. You know the Inchurch bank stands ready to back every worthy cause in Green Pond. You've surely heard of the Inchurches golden mortgages?" *That's it! I must get hold of that hospital! There must be some respectable way that I can get hold of it.*

"Thank you, Mr. Inchurch." *Flattery will do no harm here.* "That is most generous of you and I do know what the golden mortgages of the Inchurch bank stand for." *Yes, and what Jezebel stands for.*

"Doctor Thornwell," Robert began by clearing his throat, "Jezebel and I are expecting at our house." *He makes my face turn hot and I am ashamed. I am sure she thought it was he in the bed instead of me.*

"Why, really? I hadn't heard." *What was one more lie in a lifetime? You really weren't up and coming unless you could be adept at slipping them from your tongue as quickly as the batting of an eye.*

"Yes," suavely replied Robert, his voice embedded in oil. *This is the crucial moment. I must use extreme caution in what I'm saying. If he should say no and walk out on me, I'm sunk.* For a brief moment Robert Inchurch's heart was more tortured than a wailing soul in inferno. "Yes,"—it escaped him as the last breath of the dying, as though it took all the wind from his lungs—"yes, we're expecting. But the problem in our case is the doctor—the right doctor. We want absolutely the best doctor. And since you're absolutely the best—and while we thoroughly realize it's somewhat out of your line—we're wondering, would you take the case—for friendship's sake, if nothing else?" *Have I failed? Why is it taking him so long? Is it because he lusts after her and doesn't want to see her with my child? Yes, that's it. Perhaps it is his child she's having. My God, it could be—*

Vic looked, with his soft dreamy eyes, far beyond Robert and made a lazy-lipped reply, "I'd rather save that for social pleasure."

Robert gasped when the full effect of Vic's words struck him in the face. *My God, my God, it is so!*

Vic watched him squirm and he teased, "I assume you'd want

the delivery at home in the Pink House?" *Doctors are never certain of where the noble wish to birth their children.*

The air went out of Robert slowly. "That shall be left up to Jezebel. Whatever she wants." *I don't understand him. Could it be possible he's plotting something? Doctors can kill in such mysterious ways. I can do nothing except pacify him and pay him lots, for he is to be feared now as never before.*

"Well, Mr. Inchurch, if that's all for today, I'd better run along. Life's uncertain and death is sure," Vic said with a mockery that was at himself as well as at Robert.

"Good day, Doctor Thornwell." *I saw the cunning in his face. He's more tricks up his sleeve. If I could only swap places with him. Before long now I shall not be able to get in the bed with Jezebel.*

7

In the cool of twilight after the dying day, Gawd stood stroking His long white beard and looking thoughtfully down at Green Pond and talked to Gabriel, who had finished the most strenuous part of his recording. The snores of the Green Ponders were easily recorded, except the citizenry ate a great many beans and sweet potatoes and there'd be the queer noises that flatus made to contend with.

GAWD: I shorely enjoys My chillun playin down yander in Green Pond. They is noisy, but happy. Lacks lots of contented chillun around My door.

GABRIEL: See You got another chile. You proud of he?

GAWD: Which one you speaks of? They's that many.

GABRIEL: Miz Jezebel's son, Danny Boy.

GAWD: She's been wrasselin long enough to begat purty nigh a dozen or two.

GABRIEL: Didn't You make she outta red Nof Kerlina dirt and right much woman?

GAWD: Fo true. I made ole Eve, too.

GABRIEL: An ole Eve tempted ole Adam to sin wit she.

GAWD: Peoples blames it on account of ho'cum I made Miz Eve outta sich a crooked bone fro ole Adam. I heard em cry out, but they's allus cryin out fo one thing or another.

GABRIEL: They done brung in a contraption called Automobile. I's got to learn how to spell em. Lil ole mens can think up the curiousest things.

GAWD: Better learn to spell em, fo you gonna need to. How you think My ole Vic comin along?

GABRIEL: Recordin plenty-fitten good bout em. He gets vexed now an then at the complicated livers an kidneys an sexual contraptions You's fixed in peoples, but he's mind is filled wit exceptional wisdom an he's fingers wit wonderful proficiency.

GAWD: How's Jacob gettin along in Nof Bethel after two years of sin-slappin?

GABRIEL: Fine, but fixin to run into mo trouble.

GAWD: Trouble?

GABRIEL: You know a up-an-comin preacher is allus wantin to either tear the church up or build another one or do sumpin to impress he's goodness upon the peoples. Well, Jake's Sunday-school-minded, an he wants a new Sunday-school building, an the elders and deacons ain't wantin to oppress the peoples fo the money right now.

Ole Satan hung around the churches in Green Pond, slipping in at night and slipping away before day was clean.

SATAN: Shut you mouth. Wish I could ride in one of these auto-contraptions lil mens is done hatched out.

BEELZEBUB: Wouldn't you look a sight, settin up in there wit you tail draggin on the ground?

SATAN: Guess I could curl my tail up an the peoples would see em, and then the peoples would think I was a high elder.

14

It had grown into a legend, an unverifiable story handed down from mouth to mouth, that first housewarming the North Bethel congregation had for Jacob and Myra Thornwell. It had been lapidated into each heart, stored there, and years later it was talked about with more zest than at the time it happened. It had upset the congregation. There had been divided opinions among the members. There had been tooth-sucking, heel-crunching, and decidedly opinionated thoughts. And it had never died. For the church manse had taken on a lived-in appearance, no longer resembling a lopsided hennery, although the very air about the manse hinted—even reeked—a hircine odor of what hell broth the scroggy hellcats would brew.

"Honestly, Will, she had a naked picture right there on the wall—naked as you when you change clothes on Sat'day night. What sort of sermons will he think up, looking at that naked man and woman?"

"Jepson Grady, you're loony if you mention that Adam and

Eve picture that Myra painted and has hanging in the preacher's study. I know well what the women of this town think."

Helen Thorpe spoke to Andy Thorpe, "I had the time of my life at that reception this afternoon. But Jake has married the wrong woman for this town. She ought to have married Victor. He wouldn't care about the thing that will disturb Jake to pieces. Myra Thornwell isn't going to set good with the congregation. I'll bet anything that picture sooner or later comes down. Myra is a beautiful woman and she shows it in her talk and actions, and that's another thing that they'll find hard to stomach."

"Joe Tarlton, I sure was glad this evening when I called on the preacher and his wife that Jezebel was not sitting there in the way. Quite a relief to go about North Bethel without seeing her. I hope whatever she's trying to have splits her wide open and she never walks again. If that second kid should live, she'll lord it over Elvira and me the rest of our lives. So my prayers are that it doesn't live like Danny Boy and goes on the way of all flesh."

"We've got a preacher's wife at last that I believe can hold her own with Jezebel. And the funniest thing: she has a nude picture of Adam and Eve hanging right there in the preacher's study. Jezebel doesn't know that yet. Lots of the women don't like it; but I hope Myra Thornwell has the gumption to leave it hanging right there, because the instant Jezebel sees it the fur is going to fly, and from the looks of Myra's eyes she can pull her share of the fur. She's entirely too beautiful to be a preacher's wife—Jake always had an eye for sexy women. There's nothing about her that looks religious to me. She's an artist. And she's prettier than Jezebel. And Jezebel's not going to like that. I'm downright anxious for them to get hooked up—feathers, feathers'll fly."

Miss Lizzie Newcome grunted, "Huh, old Eve never had such a muscular man as that to look at. If she had, she would never have gone to the snake."

Myra Thornwell gave Jake a knowing wink when the last of the ladies had gone.

2

When the Thornwell Hospital was opened, young and pretty Sonnie Tizzy, who was thoroughly trained and experienced in nursing, was brought to the hospital by Vic to have charge of it and to help him start a nursing school.

Tizzy was the griping purgative that put a grunt into the hospital's unimpassioned bowels. She was as trim and cocky as a bustling, energetic jenny wren, and all of her that was not rattling starch was pure unadulterated female, clever with her hands and decidedly sure with her eyes.

The Green Ponders, splashing garrulously in their pond, quite naturally speculated in ripples of wonderment what effect the speedy creature would have on young Doctor Thornwell. They patched up a natty romance, planned each amorous detail. But the Green Ponders' exaggerated tree-toad rattles never fazed Tizzy, for regardless of how much her heart might have ached for the handsome doctor, the competent Tizzy never gave them a bellyful-sense of finding out.

Finally the gossipy Green Ponders settled Vic, the hospital, and the nurses as an old rooster in a garrish penful of cheery hens.

From its primeval beginning Tizzy arabesqued within the hospital as an insect about a dazzling light. She lived and breathed it and ran it with her inborn proficiency—a greater efficiency than two dozen men. There was nothing she liked better than a many-roomed hospital to expound her talents.

She had no scissor-clipping tongue nor any shrewd, staccato voice, nor was there any trickery or loathsomeness in her.

From the very first, Vic more or less turned the hospital over to her. While he and Doctor Daniels assisted her in teaching the first three girls, who constituted the first awe-inspiring class of nurses, Tizzy had the chief say-so over them, and this she did most warm-feathered and henly. But she always manipulated things so concernedly that the girls in training were prone to take her in their daily strides as a goatish prophet and a gall-bladder burden, and kept their contumacious dealings and doings as much from her as possible.

With the first several operations in the hospital, Tizzy was all over the operating room trying to do everything from administering the anesthesia to tying the knots. Nothing bothered her personality, she evaluated carefully everything she did. These were clamorous days, and she lent a hefty hand, turning many an ingrained pessimist into a confirmed believer in hospitals. She knew when to be icily sarcastic or toadily fawning with the patients, and they accepted her and yessed her and believed in her as if she were part of the very stardust.

But for a while there were not enough patients for her to charm. Green Pond was leery of a hospital; there was a hospital in Rahab and it had done them for the near hopeless cases that were merely juking the graveyard for a while, and why should they change? All doctors were in league with the gravedigger. Why have a special building to huddle all the patients in? So the doctors could get a whack at more of them more quickly? Vic plowed through dark discouragement and fought against indifference and his own rebellion. He began to be sly about refusing to go out on calls—once he had a few people trusting him the way they had trusted Ole Doc. He invited them to the hospital to see him there. He got them to coming by degrees; and pretty soon they started telling others, and the rooms at Thornwell began to fill. He had not failed after all.

"You see," Ole Doc said, "I never thought it would. But there has to be a slipping from the old to the new, when changes are made, and they have to be made. But folks are ever slow when they see no glamour in the new. Being sick is bad enough under the best of conditions, but to be dragged away from friends and loved ones when you're sick isn't at all inviting. You mustn't expect too much too soon. Man is ever a rebellious creature, son. God had a great deal of trouble getting him to stand up in the beginning—wanted to walk on all fours.

"And another thing: you're going to have trouble with the kinfolks. You mark my words. They are going to ever be in the way during severe illness and near-death cases. They'll be much worse to deal with than the patient. And if you irk them, they'll go to Rahab the next time. A wagging tongue is much worse than a sticky finger.

"Your best days are ahead of you now. For instance, take the case of Jezebel Inchurch: you were her doctor and delivered her fine and splendid and all went well. The next time she has one you can toll her into the hospital, if you're diplomatic enough."

"Pop, what in the world makes you think Jezebel will have another baby?" Vic's eyes were round with wonder and he was beginning to think that something was wrong with Pop's mind.

"Son, don't act so stupid. I've been all the way down the road. I know from actual experience and actual contact and my mind is bright still, even if my pants no longer embarrass me when found gaped open. I hope you can always remain cool and level-headed. I, perhaps, was weaker than you or the temptations were much stronger in my day. But I do know the temptations women are going to throw into your road. And right now Jezebel is using every wile known to a cunning woman—"

"Pop, what do you mean?"

"You know what I mean. I've watched that ever since the first day you started to school. Old heads always see so much because they have both the older and the younger generation to look at with mature eyes."

"So you know?"

"Sure. And she might get you yet. After all, you're only a normal man—quite human. But remember this: she'll have an-

other child—sooner or later. Sooner, I believe. That's one way
she has of you fondling her. And it's all very legal, quite cunning, and very much covered up and quite in keeping with her,
since you've foiled her so many times in her other tricks."

3

The Green Ponders knew to jump out of the path of Doctor
Thornwell's automobile, because at the breakneck speed he
traveled he would as lief splash mud and mule dung on them as
not. And twenty miles an hour was flying like a bat out of hell.
Buggy riders and wagon riders dreaded him as though he were
a great cloud of grasshoppers who devoured everything in sight,
and even said small prayers to God when they started on jour-
neys to be spared the harassing adventure of meeting his automobile. Vic received many sound cursings when he went put-put-
putting past them; but he good-naturedly laughed at them and
threw his hand high into the air in greeting.

But when Mrs. Robert Belcher Inchurch's awesome Cadillac
was unscotched and rolled from a flatcar into the streets of
Green Pond, and she, who was the first woman to drive an automobile in Green Pond, sallied forth and drove it down Main
Street, the Green Ponders were abashed, scratched their seaters,
and talked. Jepson Grady featured her and her automobile in the
Green Pond *Observer*. The Green Ponders read it, talked about
it, and some of them clipped it, sending it to distant relatives, or
folded it neatly, placing it in the Bible to mellow and to yellow
so that it wouldn't have the uncouth glare of fresh writing.

Robert Inchurch purchased an automobile that he might be
driven to the Inchurch bank on Main Street at ten minutes to
nine o'clock in the morning six days a week to ring the golden
mortgages joyously. This left Hump the most befuddled old
Negro in Green Pond. Hump felt that life had passed him by in
one big whiff, with too much toady gusto, because, being brittle

with age, he didn't have the nerve or ability to learn to drive the automobile and to assist Mr. Robert, his lifetime charge, to and from the big bank. So a new upstart, despised by Hump, was hired in his place. The remainder of Hump's days were spent puttering around in the garden, often sleeping in the sun, tending to the horses, and complaining to Gawd about birthin such awesome, noisome contraptions as automobiles—"hoss farts smelt good to what em auto'beals let out."

So the blessed up-and-coming souls in Green Pond began to chortle and to clamor for macadamized roads and asphalt streets, brickbat streets, paved sidewalks. Oh, they cried out in their unadulterated joy, let us adorn ourselves, let us adore this four-wheeled monstrosity, let us try out this four-wheeled academical wonder. We're only two-legged, let us become a four-wheeled generation, let us make something walk for us, let us cruise life away, for it is but a puny day and such a short one.

4

For four long years Jacob had struggled with the North Bethel congregation. Sometimes he felt sad, then again glad as though he had racy wine on his tongue and knew the chatter of the angels. He knew that new unbent straw in a broom always sweeps the cleanest, therefore he had tried to profit by getting in as many first-rate licks for the Lord as possible while he was new and before the congregation started to bend and twist him so out of shape that he really would look as an old runover broom which sat in the corner with its end turned up.

Jake met the Old Boys—Myra's name for the elders—head on and he saw red fury when Pop sided with Robert Inchurch against him, his own son, time and again, times without number. Jake didn't learn fast. Ole Doc kept telling him, and Myra kept saying it was so, that if he wanted to stay where he was he'd have to learn, and finally Jacob Thornwell listened.

"People are too happy to get a little of their evil buried and they certainly don't like for anybody to dig it up and flaunt it in their faces—neither the rich with their big evils nor the poor with their little evils. One can covet two pennies with as much covetousness as one can two million. Now, if you want to blow off at the mouth, get up there in the pulpit and flail the devil out of them. But don't you call any names; because then if you do tramp upon somebody's toes, he'll easily shrug it off and feel sure you're talking about so-and-so over in the next pew, for he's known all along that so-and-so was that way, but he never thought he would live to see the day it would be pointed out so plainly from the pulpit," said Ole Doc, and let the gaze of his keen eyes wander far across the land and into the woods.

Jake listened and learned and his days became filled with visiting and hardly was there time for meditative study. He was coy and clever in his visiting, bragged politely and notably upon any accomplishment that the members might have achieved. He went after new members in an assured manner, backing them into corners, tackling them so cleverly that almost none escaped. For now that Green Pond was growing rapidly, there were many of its citizens not affiliated with any church and Jacob reasoned that they might as well belong to his church as not. He didn't approve of stealing members from other churches as was often the practice; but he wasn't stealing, he was using his high-powered salesmanship for Jesus Christ, and it was keeping him in very good standing with the approving elders.

In four years' time the North Bethel congregation taught Myra and Jacob Thornwell many things. Myra was the brightest pupil. She learned rapidly and never had to have the lesson repeated.

The painting of Adam and Eve came down from the wall in the preacher's study, for, as Jezebel pointed out to Myra, it was an indecent, vulgar picture and certainly nothing to inspire the servant of God to do his best work. Thereafter a print of Jesus praying in the garden amid the flowers and definitely sufficiently clothed was hung in its place to be an inspiration to the congregation as well as the good minister.

Jezebel also didn't approve of Myra's clothes, because they showed too many seductive curves and she cunningly pointed this out to Myra. Jacob seethed with a burning anger that he thought would consume his soul. But thereafter Myra disguised herself in such hand-me-down, dowdy clothes and such comically overdressed, flowery hats, twenty years out of date, that the women of the church thought it their divine right to poke fun at her on any occasion or at any time it pleased their fancy.

But Myra and Jacob fooled them, and that is how they proved they knew their lesson well. Once in the seclusion of their bedroom, they stripped naked; and Jacob, being an extremely virile man, quickened his seed often, and Myra's scent burned his nostrils and he rapturously beheld every curve of her body. And she laughingly said, "Let's bitch."

With Myra he could forget what the years in North Bethel made him think of. He did not wish to think, for when he expounded that question, the answer rose up so big and vicious that he felt the very tombstones sneering at him.

Once in a while, a long while, he felt like running. But where? What was he running away from? And what would he be running to? He took a firm hold on himself—he was quite capable of such things—and quelled the rebellion that rose up so chokingly, and laughed with Myra when she thumbed her nose in the elders' direction and said, "Let's bitch."

And the longer Myra Thornwell lived in Green Pond, the more she felt its strangeness. *I do not understand this town or these people*, she thought, but she did not speak aloud these thoughts to her husband. *Everything is so covered in awed whispers. So churchly. Filled with strange mysteries. I simply cannot make heads nor tails of it. No longer do I paint as I want to, but I do little sketches of their wedding bouquets, their baptis-*

mal caps and dresses, and they brag on my work as though I were from the Renaissance, and I want to retch as my soul shrivels and dries like beans on a string. Jake, Jacob! He'll keep me from drying up before my time!

5

Victor's Gawd so loved the earth that He bent the apple limbs, heavily fruited, toward the ground and the red of the apples glittered and sparkled in September's sun. Catawba was yet fruitful and peaceful. Gawd weighted the pear limbs with weights of gold. The big oak in front of the hospital snuggled in brotherly love to the bosom of the earth. In Ole Doc's footsteps, Vic was clever with knife and wax and string, and inserted many buds and matched many grafts onto scroggy saplings, and wisely removed offending limbs and knots, and he threw wood ashes about the trunk of the great oak, seeing that its butt sat in ashes, and praised Gawd eternally.

The hospital loomed up imposingly upon the south hill and stood with outstretched arms to receive the ailing and afflicted flesh. Vic's knives and scalpels were whetted, lying waiting with their gleaming edges.

On a visit one day to the old homestead, John Mathis told Victor that he didn't mind the thought of going to hell. He knew he was going right straight to that hell Cora had shouted so fiercely about and that was all right with him. Because if Cora Mathis was in heaven, he wasn't wanting to go and be in her company.

"No, sirree, I'd take hell any day. Why, I've had that much sweet peace and rest since she died, more than I knowed was upon the face of the earth."

Vic chuckled and wondered what made John think Cora had gone to heaven.

"Why," said John reasonably, "according to the way she carried on: readin her Bible, praying, living might nigh in the church, playing that infernal organ, and chattering like a goose in the preacher's face. For two hours the preacher raved and ranted over her dead body setting there in North Bethel Church. Why, he punched her ticket so many times that she can't miss, can't help but be right in the middle of heaven, tart-tongued as ever. Heaven ain't gonna change that tongue. And she's probably running things up there like she did down here. Iffen she is, why I say straightway: give her more power, for that'd be the only thing she'd ever be satisfied with. I just ain't wanting to go there and have her powering over me. Let me go in peace onto the other place. They say it's easy to get to where I'm going, so I'll probably get there without too much trouble."

"John," said Vic, extending him some money, "I brought you this to help you out. Late getting here with it; best I could do under the circumstances."

"I don't need that. Why, I've got every penny of all that other money you gave me. I'm an old soldier an get a pension— though I ain't one to be favoring no government teaty; but I might as well take mine as the rest. It's all in there under a brick on the hearth in a glass jar. So when I'm gone, and as things look now it won't be many more years, you get that money. I'd rather you'd have it as anyone else. I never see a living soul but you. I most probably'll die right here by myself and iffen the buzzards ain't et me up, you bury me and take that money, because I'll have no more need for it."

"Where do you want to be buried?"

"Anywheres except beside Cora. I don't want mine and Cora's worms to get to fighting and I know they would. I'd just as soon be buried right down there beside the creek."

"I'll try to do that for you," Vic said.

6

In this day and time Green Pond grew and waxed strong. Bricks were hauled into Green Pond to build more and larger mills, better industry. Railroad sidings switched off here and there right into the bushes. There was excavating. The ring of hammers on nails. The ripping of saws through planks. The Green Ponders built cotton mills to the south of town with sure-fired zest, and to the north they trekked, squatting in the red mud erecting the singing spindles, westward toward Rahab they built them, and out east toward Old Bethel they went with bricks and mortar. The company houses were hurriedly hammered together about each mill, and no longer was there a cotton field in sight.

Uncle Prince Blue cried out loud and thought that was bad, for he thought they ought to reach right out of one of the big shiny windows and pick a handful of cotton and yank it inside and spin it right quick; but lo, they fashioned offices up and down Main Street and traded and bargained in cotton and brought it up from Egypt.

Robert Inchurch, with his years of crafty experience aptly at his mind's door, saw to it that his interests were furthered whenever possible. He allowed no newcomers to start anything without the approval of his eye and the stickiness of his finger. While Green Pond now supported two other small banks, the Inchurch bank was old and tested and so were the Inchurch interests in the mills. Occasionally a minor firm would get its toes into the ground and hold on tenaciously, but Robert and those he selected with great craftiness saw to it that it didn't happen too often. Although as the town pushed farther and farther out, and Jepson Grady cried louder and louder in the Green Pond *Observer*, it was getting harder and harder for Robert and his minions to maintain an absolute rule.

Robert brought in many experienced technicians and they

applied their knowledge and their skill, for they were schooled men and had learned to figure the machinery upon paper and not as the old from instinct and intuition. Indeed, throughout the red land there was prosperity from the humming of the spindles.

Charles Coatworthy had pulled completely away from under Robert's clutches—and quite artfully, since they belonged to the same great church—though the process was as painful as the escape of a hooked fish from the line. He had slyly moved beyond the limits of Green Pond and there constructed three mills in a row, blending the four-room company houses artistically into Coatworthy Village. Charles held his torch high in North Bethel and praised the Lord with all his might, because his mills spun and spun and his yarn was always in top-notch demand. He taught a Sunday-school class, and under Jake's supervision they began a small outpost Sunday school in Coatworthy Village, which later swelled into a church, and Charles conferred upon it the name of Coatworthy Memorial.

7

The roosters in Green Pond pulled the scowl of darkness from the eastern gate with their metallic crowing and the sun escaped into the heavens to plow all day long through the deep blue. It looked impossible that a man's soul could leave the red land and fly straight to heaven beyond the disk of the shiny sun. Needful things for the body were so subject to the reaching-out hand of every ordinary person that the heavenward flight was put off as long as possible, so Jezebel reasoned, stamping her trim feet and tossing her coils of copper and gold hair.

"Cut out your stalling, Missy," Jezebel shot at her maid. "You're going to tell me who is the father of the child you're carrying. You're one of those stinking Thornwell niggers and just as stubborn. I know all about you—Ole Doc Thornwell is your grandfather. I have my own ideas of who it is." Jezebel's voice was shrill-commanding. "Tell me."

"Miz Jezebel, I don't rightly know," Missy meekly replied.

"Missy, you're lying. Who have you been lying with?" Jezebel squinted her eyes, gritted her clenched teeth, and the muscles of her lips were taut. "Tell me. I'm going to have it out of you before you leave this room." *She's been with Robert somewhere here in this house,* Jezebel thought in hot anger. *I wonder how long it's been going on? She's too haughty to have anything to do with her own color. No, she has to have the big cheese or none at all. Robert ought to have his tail end kicked and I've a good mind to do it.* "Missy, quit standing there staring at the floor like a ninny. Tell me who it was. I've every right to know. If you don't tell me, I'm going to shake you until your fine teeth rattle right out of your mouth." She stamped the floor, the coils of flaming hair vibrating on her head.

"Miz Jezebel, I done tolt you one time I ain't rightly certain." Her eyes came up dartily and back to the floor. *Iffen I can once get out of this house,* Missy thought desperately, *they ain't nothin goin to bring me back. I tolt Mr. Robert she allowed to find out, but he say he don't care and he's wantin som lovin and he needs me fo I warms him up mo hotter than Miz Jezebel an he keeps slippin back fo mo an mo.*

"You ought to be ashamed of yourself, Missy. Getting with child and not being able to stay here and tend to Danny Boy and Elizabeth."

"I don't care," Missy spoke with bitter assurance in her voice.

"Why, you stinking bitch," cried Jezebel, reaching crowning glory in being able to call another woman a bitch. "You have more brass than a dozen brass monkeys. Sure. Just go away and leave me with those children, and as much as they think of you."

"I can't help that," she replied. *She ought to tend her own chillun. No wonder they thinks mo of me than they do her. I've got her chillun and I've about wore out her man. There's not much mo roun here fo me to get my hands into.* There was green foxiness in Missy's face and Jezebel was stunningly puzzled.

"Undoubtedly you're the most ungrateful whelp I've ever laid my eyes on. You—a cheap, two-timing Thornwell nigger. I take you here into my house—this flabbergasts me." *I know it's Robert; she's too smug. But what can I do about it? She'll go off and tell it. What if it should get into the church? I must do something about it. But what? I've never known but one situation that I couldn't scheme out of. If it's true, I'll never admit it, and then it'll not be true.* Jezebel bit her nails, looked over her fingers in studied thought at Missy. "Tell me, have you not secretly been lying with Robert?"

"No, ma'am, Miz Jezebel, I crosses my heart an body." *It'd only vex her mo to know the many pleasures I took wit her man. Even she flay me till I dies, I'll not tell her now. That'd be gettin even wit her mo better an tellin her.*

"You're lying. Robert Inchurch is the father of your child. Come on and tell me that it's true. You're too stinking proud to lie with your own color. You would pick the most influential man in town to lie with you. How'd you do it, you little yellow hussy?" *No, you'd better not tell me. Let me always keep guessing.* "Now, you get out of here, Missy Thornwell, and don't you ever come back, you dirty yellow slut." *And I thought I was getting even with the Thornwells to have one of their offspring as my servant and I get a little hussy who crawls into the bed of my husband and sleeps and sleeps and sleeps. Oh, my God, the Thornwells and the Inchurches are all crossed up.*

Missy hurried from the Pink House as though she were virtually being driven with the wind because behind her there rose all that heaven forbade. Missy carried herself as straight as an Egyptian, toted her knot south across the railroad tracks, Main Street, and straight on to Yellow Sam's in Doubting Hollow.

8

After a long sunny afternoon nap upon the roof of the Pink House, Jezebel stood in her dressing room and began to grapple with her fiery beauty. After all, Victor had taken excellent care of her during her last confinement, but it was no more than she had paid for. But really, he had worked wonders with her: her breasts were as snug as a budding girl's, her hips so seductively curved that men turned to stare, and her belly was as flat as a palm leaf and her legs as trim as a deer's.

Now she was ready to go yonder to God's house and dicker with the ungracious preacher, Jacob Thornwell, who screamed at the top of his voice about the narrow, winding path to heaven and how hard it was to find. For during the last years, by having two children and enjoying the professional touch of Doctor Victor Thornwell, her work in the church had gone greatly begging. But now with her belly flattened, her kidneys in round, firm condition, she fully intended to make it up. She didn't like the organist nor the way he played, nor what he played. She now planned to connive until she got his seater off the organ bench. She'd not wait on Robert to do it—she liked to do some work herself.

Jacob opened the door, but upon seeing her, his face lit up with an honest-poor-servant smile and he graciously invited her into the office. She swished in past him. *God might rule heaven, perhaps in some remote time the earth,* Jacob thought; *right now, it is Jezebel's rule.*

"Have a seat, Mrs. Inchurch," Jacob said, "and make yourself at home." *That bitch'll do that whether I ask her to or not. Why do I call her Mrs. Inchurch? What upon earth does she want? If she pulls my tail feathers, I shall yell. She has something in that —what did Vic say it was?—mollescent brain. She should have softening of the spine and hardening of the arteries: that would be more in keeping with her lustful nature. She is so covetous. I shall preach upon that soon and I shall preach right to her— my words pelting off as water on a turtle's back.* Jake smiled masterly enough to remove a whole mountain, but it didn't budge Jezebel. "How are the children—little Danny Boy and sweet little Elizabeth?"

"Thank you, they were fine when I left home. I believe Danny Boy will be a wonderful preacher just like you," and her laughter was filled with the jellied malice of mankind. *So this little warty preacher sits here and he'd chastise me for my sins if I had any. I remember when I used to pinch his little behind and now he sits upon it with malice toward none and I shall get my way.*

"That'd be nice," Jake smiled suavely, "but let us hope a much better one than I am." *What in the world does she want?*

She smiled off-handedly before she pursed her lips and said, "What did you think of the music Sunday?"

He listened to her talking on and on about the choice of music and no soul in the organist's playing and sundry things and he did not really hear them because it did not matter if he heard them. The result was the same; the result would always be the same. She talked on and on and he put in comments at the right moment. He slumped in his chair and his countenance was soured. He was filled with loathing. She had unmercifully seduced his body in the bloom of youth and now she wished to capture his soul and cage it as though it were a bird.

Jezebel was saying, "That man's playing in church is an abomination in the sight of God!"

After she had gone, anger shook him as a chill. "My dear, what would you suggest that we do about the music?" She had won. And Jake pounded his desk with his fist as some carnivorous animal attacking prey.

9

Now as the ever unfilled clouds of greed were strangling Europe in war and America looked every minute to be sucked into it, Green Pond grew so rapidly that its very roots were heard at night plunging, delving into the earth, anchoring themselves, coming into life abundantly. The few remaining pine trees which the cotton fields had spared cried at night before their day of execution. The price of land sprang upward as a toadstool will overnight.

All the eastern red lands of Catawba, that which lay between Catawba and Green Pond, were sold in lots at what Ole Doc thought was a fabulous price. Here the exclusive homes of the rich, the high-salaried, skilled craftsmen, went up rapidly, vying over the largeness of the houses and the spaciousness of the lawns.

Mama Amazon called upon Gawd to have mercy. "Green Pond is just lack a pig rootin in the garden an he ain't got a bit mo sense of when to quit than no nothin. Only, you might as well go on back in the thickets on the creek somewheres an rid you up a few lil patches to work, because wit that Sunset Boulevard and New Haven developments taking in all we's fields, there ain't no other place."

Only meditatively shook his head, "Fo true, I hates to see so many of the fields an the ole tenant houses go, but I guess em niggers'll have to move to Doubtin Hollow. Yellow Sam's sellin lots, too. Shorely ain't gonna look lack the same place no mo. I'm shore glad I had all the strawberry patches an the fruit trees Vic budded behint Catawba. I reckon we'll just live on lack we's been doin. Got plenty to eat an ain't nobody wantin to sell us right now."

So they would sit and talk about the strange times that were upon the red land, and being old and remembering it all very well, they spent joyful hours recounting the places they knew the first wild strawberries to be, which ditch bank had the sweetest dewberries, where the first blackberries bloomed and they'd be sure to be ahead of blackberry winter, or where a certain big snake always gave them the hot-belly and escaped their hoes, and of the plum bushes, which were the sweeter, the red or the yellow.

But it was all in the keeping of Gawd's time, maybe. For the ones that had been middle-aged and old when they were shavers were long ago gone beyond the river; or they hoped they'd gone beyond the river. One could never tell about people.

When the Thornwell Hospital was first started, Mama Amazon had come to teach some of the younger Negroes of Green Pond the proper way to prepare food, because she'd served in a great doctor's house all the workable years of her life, and proper food and she were akin. The Negroes were almost convinced that she also owned the hospital, to hear her talk, and they laughed. "She's ole-timey, way back yonder in the slavery time, and don't allow no foolin in she mind."

No longer did Budda till Catawba's warm red acres, because Vic had long ago brought him to the hospital and put a white coat on him, and he trucked patients to the operating room, lifted them to the operating table, strapped them down, later rolled them back to their rooms.

He had pleaded with Vic to let him fix himself a bed and chair by the big boilers that heated the hospital and Vic granted it and there Budda lived, never going to Catawba except for a visit. He spent the long winter nights, when he was free of his other hospital duties, quarreling at the big boilers, shoveling coal into them, and enjoying life by himself. Occasionally he spent some time in the kitchen with the cooks after supper and kept them in stitches of merriment mocking the patients. And Budda's years were long and he spent them all at the hospital until people so associated him with the hospital that the two were inseparable in the Green Ponders' minds.

From the rifle range in the faraway distance Vic could hear the booming of the cannons against the mountainsides and he thought of the eight boys in the hospital who were so viciously torn up that he had had to call into play resources that he didn't know he possessed to make a stab at saving their lives. Man was created to stand unmerciful chopping up and to live under adverse conditions, but how this new method of automobiles smashing people up would be he didn't know and could only surmise. Medical science must learn swiftly to cope with whatever new ways man maimed himself.

These had been his first cases—and eight of them at once—smashed and torn by an automobile. He had found it much different to anything he had ever encountered. Some of them had as many as two broken places in the same leg bone or arm bone. The lacerations had been deep and those that had cut important blood vessels the most tedious to work with. People were living too fast. With the war raging in Europe, they seemed to throw reckoning to the wind and live for all they could get today.

"Tizzy, how about you teaching my classes in anatomy and surgery this evening?"

"What are you going to do?"

"Get ready for the next automobile wreck. I imagine we're going to have to learn to sew them up rather rough and fast. Or what's your opinion, Tizzy?"

"About that I don't know, but that old man in 515—have you decided what to do?"

"Let the family decide that. You must always consider the family, Tizzy. It's cancer. It'll have to be exploratory, and whatever I do to him very much experimental. I'll not bother today, the family'll hunt me up soon enough."

"Dying is so depressing."

"Why, Tizzy, bless your heart, you're getting poetic. Poetry and a hospital don't mix. Do you have anything better to look forward to than death? Your years, like mine, are none too far from the toboggan slide. I think we should concentrate more on getting them into and out of the world as painlessly as possible."

"You have the most animal-like attitude toward life, Doctor Thornwell."

"That so, Tizzy? Thanks. Why should I coddle myself into the belief that death is for you and not for me or souse my soul into some tomfoolery when my very infallible instinct as an animal tells me that it is not so? Dying is as natural as the gay-colored leaves falling from the the trees this fall. The leaves shed no tears, but splash themselves with color and go gaily. Death shouldn't be an abomination to anyone."

If they were actually sick, all men were brothers and all women sisters: Victor meditated upon that a great many hours of his life. Why, if their anatomies were so nearly identical, was there somewhere such a vast gulf between them?

In the great Pink House, doing his morning toilet, Robert looked up and saw it: the Thornwell Hospital. On yonder hill, growing so firmly, embedding itself into the people's mind and hearts. It was added to, new devices brought in, new clinics and young doctors added to its staff. And he saw it, saw the great oak in front of it with the grape vine entwined securely about its gnarled trunk and growing there. His people, the Inchurches, had fought to get that vine, but old Joanna Thornwell had driven them away. That tree, a symbol of integrity and perseverance in medicine. There seemed to be no way of stopping it. Upon the slightest pretext Jezebel'd rush to it, with the flabbiest of excuses she'd had his children's tonsils out, adenoids removed, their appendixes removed—where would she stop? To him it was distasteful and made him bilious. But how to take it away from those Thornwells?

10

Vic found Uncle Prince Blue dead in his fireplace. There was only a small fist-size burn on one side of his face; the fire must have gone out before he fell from the log on which he had often slept sitting up.

Telling Pop about it, Vic fell into a melancholy mood, watching the embers on November's hearth and listening to the crickets recount to him again of the going of Uncle Prince Blue. "I'm glad I found him, for I'd have hated for wild dogs to eat him."

Pop said slowly, almost sadly, "You know, son, ole Blue was one of the most magnificent men ever was—and don't you let anyone who ever laughed at his dozen pairs of pants tell you different. Must have been at least a hundred and nine."

Vic mused, "I guess he was rowed across the river all right. He used to talk so much about it and made it so plain, I'd sometimes feel like I was standing right there on the bank and the next one to get into the boat. He always had such a look of peace on his face. I never saw that peace ruffled but once, and that was the time Cora Mathis slapped him in North Bethel. It was the first thing that popped into my mind when I found him there in the ashes of his fireplace."

Ole Doc sighed the gentle hardly-whispering sigh of the very old. "He's better off gone. I doubt whether he would have made it there alone through another winter. There's something in the rising and falling of the sap in the trees or in the weather that has its effect on an old person or a lingering person like that. I've noticed it all my life. Our first killing frost was late this year and the minute it came, Uncle Blue went. There're slick-tongued fellows who'll say that was a coincidence, because that kind of fellow has an answer, without rhyme or reason, for everything that exists between heaven and hell. But I don't know."

The Thornwells sat long at the fire and thought of the years that Prince Blue had known and the years that had come upon the watershed. Wars fought upon it and wars fought away from it, to which the best of its young men had gone. Finally, after years, they'd heard through the government that Tommy had been killed in the war in Europe. Vic thought of Tad here in Catawba and of Tommy, whom he had seen too little of.

Pop grinned at Vic's worries. "Oh, well, Tommy was at that stage. They get about that age and they'd fight a circle saw. Nearly every generation or two has to have a war. Although God only knows why. Still, it's a good way of thinning out the population—and the more you thin out a thing the better it grows. Contagious diseases have the same effect. It's a method of keeping things balanced. Nature uses violent means to balance things and to keep law and order. When doctors feel kinda smug over licking some persistent disease, nature allus sends another for them to baffle. But it's a good thing, for it adds zest to a man and gives him something to live for. What would life be if it were not human and imperfect?

"When Tommy ran away and left that child, we couldn't see it then, but we can see a little farther down the road now. Tad may be the only means of carrying on the Thornwell name—so often I've seen life hang by a mere thread, but it makes it zestful."

Victor went to the piano and played a plaintive song, the song of Yellow Sam, so tenderly that it was like a great requiem. A requiem for a dead Thornwell boy and a requiem for Uncle Prince Blue, the son of an African king.

11

BEELZEBUB: That's awful heap likker you's got there, Satan. I tho't the churches had done discommandmented all likker here in Green Pond.

SATAN: Fo true, but you can order off fo a gallon, which I's done, beins I's a very-much law-abidin citizen.

BEELZEBUB: You ain't gonna disrupt the peace of the land, not the way you lacks pleasures. How's Miz Jezebel? Ain't heardt you make no talk of she lately. Still got religion, I know most?

SATAN: That's my gorgeous wench. I keeps a fleet of imps busy feedin her new ideas. She's on the throne of grace in Nof Bethel now and still got the give-mes.

BEELZEBUB: What you think of automobiles?

SATAN: Habit-formin. But I wish they'd get mo speed into em. Have too many flat tires.

BEELZEBUB: Clever men'll add the speed.

SATAN: Hope so. This war ain't helpin us much. Not wit the preachers givin the soldiers testaments to put over they heart.

BEELZEBUB: Yah, churches is havin days of prayer, days of fastin, an days of not eatin no flour bread. Looks lack eatin corn bread'd make em mad?

SATAN: They'd be goin back on they raisin. Us got to get sumpin rigged up agin that parcel of Baptists and Methodists that's floodin this town. I'll bet a scale offen my tail, there's been fifteen new churches built in Green Pond in the last year. I'm gonna have to depetize a right much larger squad of imps.

BEELZEBUB: You know Jake's got a new Presbyterian church started? That Charles Coatworthy is the instigator of em. Now Jake's tryin to get ole Miz Big Amazon and Yaller Sam to start a Presbyterian church on Third Street in Doubtin Hollow. I know most they'll never get that little bit of water to stick on em kinky heads.

SATAN: Shet you mouth. Can't you think up nothin but down-in-the-lip stuff?

November's chill slipped through heaven and Gawd prepared much snow for earth.

GABRIEL: Lil mens is havin right much war on earth.

GAWD: Yah. Wiped out Tommy Thornwell. He's better off here wit Great-granny Joanna. She'll straighten em out.

GABRIEL: What is You lookin at so?

GAWD: Down yander in that Thornwell Hospital, I's watchin Vic patch up them fellers that was tore up in that big Cadillac early this mornin in that fog. Vic's callin into play resources he didn't know I give him, tryin to save em up.

GABRIEL: Was they all that bad tored up?

GAWD: Yah. Wanted to see what Vic'd do wit em. He's gonna pull em through alive. But look, Vic missed catchin up that muscle in that feller's neck. He'll never be able to lift he's arm, but he'll live. That doctor's plenty baffled.

15

Ole Doc followed Victor to the hospital religiously, with tottering, uncertain-feeling steps, his crablike hands holding securely to the automobile door. Riding upon asphalt streets was a never-ceasing marvel to Pop, but not the intense, variegated drama found on horses and in buggies and sulkies in his day; nor were the gas fumes the earthiness of horse flesh that he had known.

Mama Amazon and young Tad Thornwell waved them out of Catawba's back yard; Tad liked the hospital as much as they did, but Victor was very stern about Tad's regularity in school.

Going down North Philadelphia Street, Ole Doc recalled Nora Kingsley, who was now long dead. Now David lived in that house and was an astounding wonder with law, holding the Green Ponders in the palm of his hand as though they were but a few Mexican jumping beans. Pop wondered what technique David used with the Inchurches; it must be some sly trick up his sleeve, for they never failed to side with him. Pop was joyous that

David had inherited many Thornwell traits and was shrewd enough to deal with the Inchurches. And his old mind thought in marveling intensity of God quickening man's seed that the egg might be fertilized. There were those that claimed it had no right to be. But God created man ever fruitful, and He sprouted those seeds that He wanted to grow, and He thinned and He harvested according to His gracious notions.

Along the way this showery April morning, pink-faced buds lifted the lids of their sepulchers and girdled their waists in green as actors make-up before their entrance upon the stage. And Vic drove along, muselike quiet, lethargic and absorbed in thought. He misled all who might observe him, for his celestial thoughts were too realistic for the average imagination.

In the elevator going up to the operating rooms with Vic and Pop were the operating-room nurses who had just come from breakfast.

Pop noticed their winsome, rubylike smiles and fresh, soft faces, the reeking cleanliness and paper-crispness of their uniforms, and also their preference for standing closer to Vic than to him. His elephant-wrinkled eyes filled with the laughter of youth in spring and about his mouth was the hushedness of moonlit lovers.

"Victor," Pop said in a tease-filled voice, "you've no excuse now for not marrying."

The nurses giggled and Vic looked at Pop abashed. "Why Pop, I brought you over here to court so that I could learn your art. You've got such a way with women." The nurses laughed.

In the scrub room, Vic found Budda sitting lazily upon a stretcher, ready to go after the first patient. "Budda, see can't you bring me an appendix," Vic said, looking the schedule over. "I want something easy to start with, though it'd be my luck to run into something bad with just a simple appendix. Miss Ware, help Pop get scrubbed up. He's quite determined to assist me today and he don't like to wash any too well," Vic chuckled.

"Moreover, he sees absolutely no need of washing and then putting on gloves—pure tomfoolery." He brushed his fingernails briskly. "Miss Appley, I want to try some of that new catgut. If that old salesman has filled me with a bag of hot air, I'm going to tell him about it."

The operations moved along swiftly all morning. Vic's hands seemed to move caressingly slow, deliberately fondling as though they were clock hands ticking the hours of a man's life away. His rhythm and tempo were a swing song; here behind each life was the skeptic's joy. The room was permeated with the stench of ether; the quietness bored holes into the occupants' eardrums.

Upon the operating table Budda and a nurse lifted a man whose bald head, sallow complexion, blunt, sawed-off nose, and dehydrated skin made his face resemble a skeleton's and who was well past the prime of life. His face was quickly covered, the ether started. The laparotomy sheet was placed and exposed the grim, rigid belly. The assistant nurse slapped a scalpel into Vic's extended hand. He took the scalpel, felt it snuggling there as though it had come home to roost, and then it flew downward toward the abdomen with a terrorizing certainty. The abdomen was opened smoothly, horizontally; the nurse mopped and caught up squirters; then Vic cut twice vertically, catching up the vessels, tying. He urged the nurses to wipe up the blood faster.

Aged Pop stood beside the operating table, the flame of healing burning in him as brilliantly as it had fourscore years ago. There was in his weathered face a boyish glee, yet all about him hung the peace of Noah's dove. He was the old doctor unjealously living in the young doctor. He had had his day. He praised God on high for permitting him this view.

That's my son, Pop thought. I never knew what love was until he was born. Of the many children I have fathered, none of them was as this son across this table. He's wholly mine. I shall not die, but live on in him. Ma sure would be proud if she could

*see this. I've a hankering that she is not far away; just close
by, looking on. His cutting is a work unparalleled. He was born
with that in his digits. Now I can put two and two together and
it does make sense. Things that I didn't understand about him
when he was little are made so plain to me now. How I wish
that I might go back over it all; live with him again; but it
takes a lifetime to learn and then you're ready to die. If someone could write a book for the young to go by, but it can't be
done. If it were done, they'd not read that which is written,
because the young are ever filled with forward-looking thoughts,
and see the old as clumsy failures.*

The lower abdomen was laid wide open, the flaps of flesh
pulled over backward, weighted down with clamps, and Vic with
his sensitive left hand felt cautiously the hot bowels. The assisting nurse caught his eyes, then their eyes dropped spiritlessly into
the wide-sprawling incision, and Vic's look was I-told-you-so.

"Sew him up?" asked the nurse.

"No——give me a moist strip." And he made straightway to
wall off the descending colon. There was now in his fingers the
utmost delicate touch. It was as though he were throwing sticky
butter to and fro in his hands and it was only his manipulations
that kept it from sticking to his fingers. The hot guts he moved
through his fingers gently, separating, freeing until every gut was
from the patient's body. Then his fingers were here and there
and there and here, considering where to take out and how much
to remove.

*I wonder does Pop know, Vic pondered, and what's he think-
ing? He warned me of these forked roads in my youth. I can't
be too hasty here. This man wants to wake up and to live a few
more years. When he went to sleep there was trust in his eyes.
Had he not trusted me in the first place, he would not be here.
If I had two more years to live, and knew it, what would I do?
Is it possible that I can give him four? If I could, just for a few
moments, get closer to God. But in these moments of uncertainty*

*when I reach out gropingly for Him, He seems to evade me;
then He comes back, enticing me to put trust into my callow
wings; but there should not be trust in my own wings, for without His aid I should not fly at all. Oh, the crisscross design He
so artfully tucked into man's guts! Is that not justification for
my hesitation? As complicated as the stars of the heavens, and
who would be fool enough to say that he knew all about the
stars? No. Pop doesn't understand, I'm certain. He never dealt
with things as I'm having to do. Sometimes he tacked the guts,
which had been spilled into the dirt in a knife fight, back into
the abdomen, if the guts were not actually mutilated themselves;
but here I must decide what and how much gut I can take from
a man.*

"Pulse, Miss Ravel? Keep that ether steady; it'll be some
time yet."

"Fine. He must be as strong as a bull."

"Pop, I want you to go down to Ward 210 someday and look
at my pet. He's a scavenger if I've ever seen one. Looks worse
than this old fellow here. In the last five years I've taken out
his gall bladder, removed one lung, half of his stomach, his
prostate gland, his appendix, one kidney—each time is more like
an autopsy than an operation. Trouble is, I never get any
money, but old Avis seems to enjoy my operations. I wonder just
how far I can go with him. Bet his brain would be interesting."
And Vic grew silent. *And what could I possibly find out about
the man there? There is no art to measure the inner man.*

"Um," Pop grunted, more fascinated with the movements of
Vic's hands, that worked automatically, methodically as he talked.
Each time a nurse offered Pop a stool, suggesting that he was
fatiguing, Pop scoffed and stood unmoved upon his own two feet.
As Pop watched Vic, his thoughts washed into North Bethel
cemetery and to the weather-black stone that marked Mary's
grave. He was young and just home from medical school. Somehow he always meant to marry Mary. They'd meet on a moon-

lit night when the trees were clothed in green, when the honey-suckle climbed helter-skelter, giving off its deliciously sweetened breath, when the night was alive with the songs of mocking-birds, when frogs chorused by the river. There by the winding river they met engulfed in the river's scent and mist; there their hearts beat as one, for God had made it so between a man and a maid. He made the night seductively beautiful, their hands clasped, their lips met, and God had made the night most mad-dening. When Joseph was born, Mary was as silent as the tomb; she loved her doctor and she shielded him. Women, she said, were much stronger than men—it was as God so planned. Later she had gone about with him over the watershed helping with deliveries and they had worked as one. Folks had talked because talk was dirt cheap, but that was as far as they did get. And now somewhere there was Joseph, the president of a university, and Ole Doc's eyes came back to the hands of this son who handled the bowels of this man as though they were hot molasses candy.

"Give me a continuous suture, nurse," Vic ordered. "Let's get the old fellow patched together; he's been out a long time." *Boy, you can't do a thing with Pop! He's stood through this all morning as easily as I have. He's never mentioned that this was can-cerous. I know he saw it; you can't fool his old eyes so easily. He has been the quietest this morning I have ever known. I wonder what criticism he would make of my work?*

2

Way before dawn, Mama Amazon made her way down the back stairs of Catawba, letting her hand slide the well-worn handrail that ole Andy had carved in the long bygone, and to the kitchen to get the fire started, because it was chilly before daylight these April mornings. She had to get Only's breakfast and get him to the back fields of Catawba by daylight, for if he were to live and feel good, he had to get out and get the good morning air. Nothing but white folks and sick people stayed in bed until daylight—and they didn't amount to nothing.

Only and Dish came through the kitchen, blinking sleepy-eyed, rubbing their eyes with their fists, and hurried out to the back porch to wash their faces. Only stepped into the yard to scan the heavens, to note the condition of the stars, and to study the descending, waning moon. Being a farmer and knowing that all he had was controlled from that which was above, he went through this ritual every morning upon rising.

"Bigma," said Dish, breaking a piece of bread to sop molasses with, though not before she had asked Gawd about it, because one simply didn't break bread in Bigma's kitchen without first talking it over with Gawd, "what's I goin to do today?"

"Before the folks gets up, I wants you to clean that lower parlor where the big piannas is. An you polish em piannas plenty-fitten, fo I wouldn't have nothin to happen to em fo the world. Then you do the main room an front stairs, then get their bedrooms in the south wing and that south-wing living room. By that time, it'll be dinnertime and this evenin you can pick strawberries iffen Only needs you and make yourself some money. Will you need em, Only?"

Only laughed with a mouthful of bread, "I'll need em iffen Ole Doc don't picks as many today as he did yesterday. That ole feller picked over two hundred quarts yesterday. About as many as I could. Had to be paid, too. Him ownin all Gawd's creation, an out there pickin strawberries as hard as the field hands. He's proud of that money as a boy. He didn't have a pocket to put em. You know he sewed up every pocket in he's clothes years ago, said he was gettin too ole to be puttin things in he's pockets; so he carried that money right on here to the house. It's lyin up there on the fireboard. The way he was wantin to be paid off an the way he carried it right straight on here to the house, you'd tho't he was about to starve." Only snickered.

"He's that much lack he's ma," Mama Amazon laughed. "Why, she birthed chillun until she was so ole she could hardly move. Take me along an she'd set on a chair an tell me what to do, an if she was lucky enough to get a dollar an didn't have to trade em out in gooses, chickens, feathers, dried fruit—why, she'd get right into that buggy holdin that dollar in her hand an ride right back here to Catawba wit em. That's been years ago. I declare, us ought not be up here talkin about the dead befo daylight."

Dish sopped her molasses, snickered at her grand's sayings. So often did her grandchildren dig into Catawba's buried past that Mama Amazon was uncertain at times of which age she lived in.

Vic scrambled into the kitchen, excited and upset, his hair uncombed, his night clothes thrown about him togalike.

Mama Amazon jumped from her chair, her eyes gleaming, mouth agape, and hands thrown upon her hips.

"What in the name of Gawd's wrong wit you, boy?"

"It's Pop."

"Pop, what?"

"Pop's sick. It's his heart. I've not examined him very much, but I know that's what it is. I want to get someone out here that knows a little more about it than I do. You go call Doctor Frye. Tell him it's urgent and that I wish he'd come before I go to the hospital. I've three operations scheduled for this morning."

"That's gonna make that doctor mad—this hour."

"He can get glad."

"Gonna get well, enty?"

"No."

"You mean to stand there an tell me Ole Doc gonna die? An jest this mornin us was talkin about how many strawberries he'd picked yesterday."

"Afraid it's so. Regardless of who we are or where we are, it's coming to us all. We wear out. He's stout and he may hold out for several months, then he may go with the very next attack he has. Once this morning I thought he wouldn't pull through this attack, but he did."

"Ole Doc's done been that bad off, an you ain't come down here an tolt me about em?"

"You'll have plenty of days wrestling with him yet. He's never been sick a day in his life and he's going to be a problem to wait on. I could never get him into that hospital—unless chained. Take Pop some breakfast—a little coffee, maybe. Got any likker? Take him a good shot of likker."

"You's fixin fo Miz Naomi to throw a fit now."

"One more fit won't hurt nothing, she's been throwin them all her life. She's drunk on the church, and what's the difference in drunkness?"

Mama Amazon rolled her eyes and shook her heavy weight toward the front of Catawba.

After Doctor Frye left and after Vic had gone to the hospital, Mama Amazon trudged through Catawba, singing in a low, woebegone voice, singing about hating to see that evening sun go down. She heard Dish in the lower parlor cleaning, but she dragged on to the kitchen. She saw Tad off to school and her eyes filled with tears. She moved over to the table, dropped down in a chair, buried her head in her arms, and cried.

"Oh Gawd, what is You gonna do wit Catawba?"

3

Dawning, and then the rising red sun over the red land. Doves mourned. Whether these were Noah's doves or whether they were common doves with the ability to mourn sadly Betty Mae Hill didn't know, because she was hurrying so fast to the mill that the lonely doves only tore her heart with sadness. She wished that she might sit all day long on some sunny red bank and not have to lift a finger to tie one blessed knot on a speeder frame. For once she was shut up within the mill, she could only look out the window. Her heart would grieve all day long for April, sprawled out beyond the windows. Her mind would rip and snort with the tender memories of her girlhood in Aprils of the bygones.

Betty Mae Hill was old beyond time.

Betty Mae recalled when Minnie taught her spinning; taught her how to tie knots—like a damn spider she had tied knots. She remembered Granny Swaps: how she used to poke fun at Charles Coatworthy and give him a good solid cussing every now and again because he toadied to the Inchurches. She remembered that she was only Betty Mae and she was filled with living. She was endowed with a blessed suppleness and was as limber as an honestly worn dishrag. She was not careful of her clothes, for she no longer wished to impress anyone. She no longer cared what men thought of her. Decorum could caress where she could not.

At the speeder frames, she greeted the boy she was teaching. "God, you're lookin bright and pert this mornin. I wish I was your age agin." She hurried down the side of the frames, tying the knots with the dexterity of a surgeon's hands.

"Betty Mae, reckon I'll ever learn to tie as fast as you?" the boy asked.

"Hell's fire, you'd better iffen you wanta make anythin." Betty Mae spat out with her snuff, the words flying to the boy, the stuff to the spittoon. "Of course, you're a boy, an you can allus go back up here in the mountains an get you a gal an bring her down here to work in the mill. When she finds out she can make thirty-five dollars a week, she'll work her blessed ass off for you."

"Aw hell, Betty Mae, I'm gonna learn to tie em knots. Give me time."

"You'd better learn this right off so's you can get into some of this easy money that's floatin round like dust."

"Where's all that money at?"

"Hit's everywheres. Big wages peoples makes in these damn mills. Why, I can walk outta this damn cotton mill an go to another one an go to work tonight iffen I wanta. I am jest that damn free. Hit's mighty right and my right. An I was born wit em! An that's jest about what's gonna happen iffen that damn night hand don't go to leavin his work runnin better. Has the things in a doggone stinkin mess every mornin. He'd stayed in Georgia or the mountains or wherever he mighta come from, for all the better he works. They've scoured the damn red hills lookin for hands to run these mills since that war started, an that's the reason they got so many no-account'uns."

"Then you're a good'un?"

"Uppity squirt! Iffen I was you—hell's fire, yes, I'm a good'un. I learnt back on em damn frames what was pulled wit steam an jerked an jumped like somebody sewin stitches up a tomcat's ass. Ole Granny Swaps learnt me on spinnin. That's in the days when we got a dollar. It shore is a pity Granny Swaps couldn't of lived a few more years to draw one of these pay envelopes what has five-dollar bills in em. Po' thin, she's been dead now for years an the damn cotton mills keeps on spreadin an sprawlin all over God's creation. Tell me they's buildin three more out on Kinfolks Road on the road to Old Hope. I don't know where in the name of God they's gonna find hands to run em."

She muttered, fled up and down the length of frame with a spurning look on her face. Her hands darted in and out of the flying spools and the crawling strings. At the end of the frame she wiped sweat and complained of a headache. She fumbled in her cotton-sprinkled, grease-smeared apron pocket for a small purse.

"Here, you run over to the shack yander an get me a dope an

powder. Get one for yourself iffen you wants. Gettin so I have to take several powders a day an dope wit em. I wonder what's in em damn powders."

When the boy returned with the two opened dopes, he gave Betty Mae the powder, which she dusted on her stuck-out tongue, holding the lip of her chin tight against her teeth to keep the snuff and powder from getting mixed, and then they stood at the end of the frame drinking their dopes. The boy offered her the change, but she told him to keep it.

"No need for me to hoard up money—can't take that into the beyond; it's got to be sumpin else. It comes easy, I say let it go easy. It ain't the hard money we uster earn. Why, Granny Swaps tolt me of the time when they didn't even pay in money but in pasteboard that could only be spent at the commissary where there was more flies than beans, more worms than raisins, an every damn bag of taters was deaconed. Hell's fire, I got plenty of foldin money an can go right down on Main Street an go into one of em spick-an-span groceriments an buy up somethin fitten to eat iffen I wanta. Usually I don't have time, so I jest give my order to that feller that runs a store here on the hill an lets him send em out. Hell, he charges me three damn prices an weighs his thumb to boot."

Their dope bottles were drained. The powder was taking its effect on Betty Mae. She felt effusively sentimental and put her arms around the boy, running her fingers through his curly hair and pulling him against her belly. For somewhere in her effete body was a last spark of woman that the powder had touched off. She felt his worm firming and pressing against her leg.

"Honey, come home with me tonight."

4

Summer came with a deathly stillness. The nights were filled with a mysterious-looking blue and never black dark. The earth bestirred all her children to gorge themselves amid the fruiting time so winter would befit them snugly.

Ole Doc lamented bitterly to be taken downstairs to the lower parlor where he might have the pleasure of Victor's piano playing. So the lower parlor was turned into a semibedroom. And while Pop's disease didn't keep him in bed but a small part of the time, Vic thought he ought to rest lying down as much as possible. Both the day and the night nurses spent their time in Catawba, ensconced in Catawba, and quite enamored with Ole Doc.

"Here's something I want to tell you about, son, while my mind is clear," Ole Doc said to Vic when they were alone. "You've noticed, I assume, that there're days my mind's not so bright—I'm addled. But it's this—say nothing about this until I'm laid in the mausoleum. The hospital's all paid for and the deed is recorded at the courthouse in your name. No one can ever take it from you legally. I had to use a good bit of the money received from the sale of the front acres of Catawba to finish paying for it. Catawba here and the rest of her acres have also been deeded over to you, and I want you to look out for the colored people here on Catawba to the best of your ability. And take care of your mother. I have left her nothing. You've surely, by now, discovered that she is a kleptomaniac?"

"Yes."

"So far it's not been so bad; but there have been evidences of it from the day you were born. I've covered it up, for her sake, as much as possible. There's so little scientific and medical knowledge yet of her kind of case. One can only speculate; but she'll bear watching. You do that. That's the reason I'm leaving her nothing. I've left you considerable more than Jake and I've told him all about it, too, for I want you to be responsible for her. You can never tell about that mind of hers."

"Do you suppose that, by any chance, Jezebel would know about this?"

"I'm quite certain she doesn't, and if she did, she'd not know what it was. Jezebel has a mollescent brain: she's not a thinker —her type never is. She's too driven by a primitive instinct— a female conniver. She's like a cat at night in the dark when no one is looking that smells a fresh piece of meat in an iron box; and driven by desire, she'll wear all the claws off her feet, wear her teeth down to the gums trying to get to it. Moreover, Jezebel is interested in things that she wants for herself. That's been my way of seeing her ever since I delivered her into the world. She came into the world that way and she'll go out that way. They all go out as they come in. Ever notice?"

"Considerable."

"About your mother—whatever you do, don't say anything to her about her condition, because if she knows about it, and I believe she does, she'll not mention it. These spells when my mind goes and I'm irrational—I know as well as anything when they're coming. That twilight, slipping from rational to irrational, from one condition to another, I can sense or feel things that I'll do or say, but I have no control over them. Whether your mother is like that or not I've no way of knowing. But whatever you do, be tolerant and unbiased with her. She may get worse as she gets older. She's not broken down with age yet and she's taken good care of herself."

"Does Jake know about this?"

"No, and don't tell him. It might only hinder his work. It certainly wouldn't do any good. If he stays on at North Bethel he'll have enough to worry his head without dragging in too many unpleasant affairs."

"It's a wonder he hadn't noted it."

"He doesn't have a doctor's eyes. How many operations do you have for tomorrow?"

"Six."

"Anything interesting? Anybody I know?"

"Just routine. Don't think there's one you know. Most of em

from the mill villages—Betty Mae Hill has a stone-filled kidney. Most of them pay good, now that the mills are running full time. That's where most of my cases come from. The doozers down-town, lots of em, go to Rahab in these moneyed times. They'll come back when times get tough wanting bargain-counter in-cisions, and dogged if I don't have about half a mind to let them have them, but right now I suppose they think they're getting superincisions in Rahab."

"Son, you're just on the threshold of a most important ad-venture. The next fifty years will see a tremendous movement in the field of medicine."

All during Ole Doc's lengthy illness, Vic didn't tarry at the hospital more than was absolutely necessary, but lingered at Cat-awba with Pop. Often he played for him, often they talked, and sometimes they sat on the veranda silently communing.

5

Robert, with his natural proclivity to grab, didn't need too much prodding from Jezebel to gobble up most of the Inchurch mill stock from Louise and Elvira, leaving them only the fringes of interest. But when it came to the Thornwell Hospital, he was on one side and she was on the other. He watched Jezebel taking her Sunday-school class of teen-age girls to the Thornwell Hospi-tal to make bandages for the local chapter of the American Red Cross, and he was rent with fury. And he looked up at the ancient oak whose body had been scarred many times by fierce lightning, who pulled the gnarled grape vine to its bosom, and he saw it growing there in the yard of the Thornwell Hospital and he knew full well it had furnished the grapes for years to make the racy wine for the holy communion in North Bethel. And he was filled with a fright akin to none he had ever known.

At the hospital, the Sunday-school class, with their leader, Mrs. Robert B. Inchurch, seemed to have come at the wrong time.

There was a great blowout of confused talking between the superintendent of the hospital and Mrs. Inchurch, of which they couldn't make heads or tails.

"But, Miss Tizzy," emphatically stated Jezebel, tossing her head belligerently, "I simply don't want you showing us how to make the bandages. Moreover, Doctor Thornwell promised me definitely that he'd show me how this morning. He promised me yesterday over the telephone." *That old sneaking heifer has him hidden somewhere from me,* Jezebel thought. *I called Catawba and the nurse told me he'd left early for the hospital. I know this cunning hussy; she wants him all to herself. She looks just like someone who has eaten something forbidden. She lords it over him, but I'll taunt her until she tells me where he is.*

Miss Tizzy looked her disgust and it filled her voice. "I thought I had explained to you that Doctor Thornwell is operating this morning and can't see you. Isn't that sufficient reason that he can't show you how to make the bandages this morning? He told me to instruct you." *If I could only tell this classy rake what I think of her,* Tizzy thought. *If she thinks for one moment that she's fooling me with her covert nature, she can mock someone else with it. She'd like to have the man I have here under my thumb. Foolish fish.* Tizzy spoke as stiffly as her uniform was starched, and her manner was crisp as her dress.

"Why can't you go tell him that I'm waiting?" *I wonder what she'll bring up now to keep me from seeing him? It's people like Tizzy who cause so much trouble in the world. She always has harsh words and bitter criticism of all the folk she comes in contact with. She's always finding fault. She's hurting this hospital with her domineering. Why does Vic have an old dried-up cow like her trying to run things?* Jezebel tapped her heel on the floor, which was her most excellent way of scoffing.

"Do you realize, Mrs. Inchurch," Tizzy asked, moderately scornful, "that in an operation a life is usually at stake and you simply can't stop it just any moment that you might choose?

How'd you like for some doctor to leave you lying on the operating table for several hours with a gaping incision?" *This's the most exasperating ass I've ever known. What will she think of next? She's not going to get to see him today. I bet it'd take her two weeks to fold a simple piece of gauze under his directions. She can see him next week or the week after that. He said he didn't want to see her today and she's not going to get to. I'll see to that.* "He had four minors and two majors scheduled for today. Perhaps it'll be the middle of the afternoon before he finishes." *Surely she'll not wait that long. He should be through in another hour.*

"Oh, that soon? We'll just wait, then." Mrs. Inchurch could be cunning when she wanted to see the Doctor. "Although, you know, when you have a husband and children, you can't be out at all hours," she taunted Tizzy. *The old fool wants him for a husband herself! I've heard how he carries on with her; I know.* "You won't mind, will you, dear? Where'd you want us to wait?" Her voice was light. *I'll fix that old bitch!*

Tizzy swallowed a mouthful of sighs mixed with acid and said, "Oh, anywhere except in the waiting rooms. They're for sick people." *You're sick in many ways, old girl, but I don't think Doctor Thornwell will help you today. So hang around, you won't bother me.* Tizzy hurried down the hallway, walking briskly, entered her offices, and shut the door.

From there she called to the head operating-room nurse, leaving word for Doctor Thornwell to fade out—and nothing else needed be said. After the operations Vic went down the fire escape and disappeared from the back of the hospital. Jezebel stayed, sharply waiting, until well after dark before she could admit she was foiled. Her Sunday-school girls were modestly exhausted, delicately mortified.

Jezebel clicked her heels together; trickery by Tizzy! Someone should hear about this, mainly Miss Tizzy. She hurried about desperately to find Tizzy, but when she found her, the buttered nursing smile was so filled with quavering sorrow that Jezebel was baffled and could only stand and listen to her.

"I sent him word that you were waiting. He's left the hospital long, long ago. You know," Tizzy's voice was airily light and very politely scornful, "he's the doctor around here and what he says usually goes. I'm only a nurse. I'm so sorry that you've missed him, Mrs. Inchurch." Her voice dropped. "You'll have to try again sometime—soon."

6

"Doctor Thornwell, Doctor Thornwell," Nurse Perry called urgently, knocking on the door of an upstairs bedroom in Catawba, "come quickly."

Unclothed, Vic snatched the door open. "What is it?" he asked, running his hands through his hair.

"Your father," she uttered in a greatly distressed tone, "has disappeared. His clothes are lying on the floor, torn to shreds. I can't find him anywhere. I was in the kitchen getting a midnight snack and when I returned, all I found were his clothes."

Vic picked up Pop's clothes that had been ripped into rags. "You'd better be thankful you weren't around when he had that spell. These clothes are comparatively new and stout and look what he did to them. Wherever he is, he doesn't have a rag on."

"How'll you ever find him?"

Vic walked across the room. "He went out this way, because this screen door doesn't come all the way shut unless you push it to and he failed to do that."

For a long time Vic stood in Catawba's yard baffled, wondering in which direction he should strike out to find Pop. He felt sure that Pop wouldn't go toward town. Then he thought of the Thornwell homestead, but it was doubtful whether he'd had time to get that far. Vic went through the back yard. The katydids sang gratingly, scarring his musical memory. He walked with the beauty of the leafy shadows. He followed the tapering earth as it slanted off toward the bottom land along the boiling river. Through the swamps he heard the bullfrogs booming and the small frogs peeping, the weird lonely call of snipes, mockingbirds singing, catbirds quarreling for daylight.

Coming upon a round grassy knoll, sparsely wooded, with the scent of green corn blowing upon him, he stopped and looked far down in the bottoms where the view was unbroken. He saw Pop startlingly naked walking serenely along, his hands folded behind him upon his rump. Vic watched him a long time.

Pop walked there in the light of the young moon, wrapped in the river's mist, forming a celestial picture.

The heavy scent of the earth, the sugary odor of blooming flowers filled his nostrils, and Vic was helpless as to what he should do, so overcome was he with the awe-inspiring scene that sprawled before him, a scene that spoke unerringly of life after death. He had never seen Pop with such strange restfulness and crowning peace. Vic walked toward Pop.

"Pop, Pop, what're you doing way down here?"

"Are you a stranger in these parts? Do you not know that I live here? Do you not know that I was born here out of this mist nearly a hundred years ago, and that it's not long until I go back into this mist? I've reached the place in life where I am sublimely happy. Death, so far as the body goes, is man's crowning achievement. This peace that I have now, shortly before I go, is such luxurious peace that I wish that every man might taste of it and know the joy of being born."

"Pop, are you sure this isn't one of your spells?"

"I had a spell before I left Catawba."

"Why did you tear your clothes so violently?"

"It's the flesh and the spirit struggling—the spirit to squeeze itself from the body. You've not struggled long enough yet to understand. You're a mere blundering doctor. That's all gone from my life. If the crown is the flesh and the crib the spirit, won't the spirit come forth victorious? Because it is so written. So far there's no art to separate the spirit from the man. We live here in the bodies of animals. God so created it in the beginning. It's so fitted that the strong man shall put the weak man's neck to the wheel and make him turn the wheel for him, for the rich man to steal from the poor man—these are the animals."

"Let's go home, Pop. You had Miss Perry distraught with worry."

"Yes, Miss Perry is a lovely young lady, as pretty as any I ever courted in my day. Why don't you court her, son? Or are you still secretly in love with Jezebel?"

"Jezebel? Of all the dread creatures!"

"We had another word for it when I grew up."

"If she keeps on running over to the hospital like she's been doing, I'll have to hire an extra nurse for a bodyguard."

"Is she that desperate? She'll get you yet. She's Cora right off the block."

"I don't see how in the devil you walk barefooted on this rocky ground."

"What're a few briers and stones in a lifetime? One can't always walk the primrose path. There's surely more to life than fine shoes, for why do we talk here? It's mystery, not an archive. Man's a pretty smart old booger and getting smarter. I won't be hanging around to see what he'll do in the next century, but in my century he was born and he died. I'm not filled with stoicism or apathy, but if Jesus rode an ass and Jezebel an automobile, basically, what's the difference? Man has always sought his Utopia, his Fountain of Youth—his God—but what would he do with this body if he found them? You know what? I'd like to see John Mathis to talk over the war. I remember a night like this that I turned a couple of Yankee prisoners loose instead of killing them. Always glad I did it, but it'd been too bad if I had got caught up with."

7

It was a hot summer evening and the gnats were about Gawd's ears and the stars were mean about winking at night and acted like sacred secrets.

GABRIEL: You gonna call Ole Doc home soon?

GAWD: Won't be long off until I sends an angel south.

GABRIEL: He's purty nigh a hundred; I got a whole bookful jest about he's doin's on earth.

GAWD   Won't have much mo to put in em. I know most Miz Joanna'll be glad; but Miz Big Amazon'll be sad. But fo jest a lil while. For her sadness is My sadness and her gladness is My gladness. An we haves the chile-lack beliefs.

Always padding about Green Pond, sniffing the dung heaps and getting chicken manure between their toes, Satan and Beelzebub kept up a fancy-free gossipry.

BEELZEBUB: I thinks us ought to sally forth to Babel fo the summer lack all the oldest families do. This place stenches. Miz Jezebel's rushin up to rejoice she kidneys an liver. Lack to find out what goes on there.

SATAN: I don't lack you sleazy excuses; better stay here an work on these churches. When's the las time you been in Nof Bethel?

BEELZEBUB: You know you sent me there to see Mr. Jake not too powerful long ago—a moonsoon, maybe.

SATAN: Never did report.

BEELZEBUB: He's frustrated; prattles a great deal to he's self about he's he-goats an he's she-goats. He's spirit's often cast down. Sudiebelle Wilson—you know she live up Nof now—blowed in here not long ago an shook him up good. An when's the las time you listened to Jepson Grady recite about Green Pond?

SATAN: Hump! I'm scared of him. He chants too much poetry. An he's one of Ole Doc's chillun—him an Ossie, too.

BEELZEBUB: Uh-um. I found out Miz Jezebel's been trickin em sister-in-laws of hern into knittin a heap of socks fo the soldier boys an then she steals em an shows em to the reverends as her own work. Fur flies in em in-laws.

SATAN: You know Missy's done had a lil ole red-headed baby?

BEELZEBUB: You don't mean it?

SATAN: Yes, sir; head's redder an this dirt.

16

Missy was once again on hand within the Pink House, caring for the two beaming and impossible Inchurch prodigies, Danny Boy and little Elizabeth. And Jezebel was extremely glad to have her, because there was no longer any jealousy in her over Robert. Between the two of them, Robert had had his last fling and now lay drying on the pantry shelf like an old prune. If he were boiled up plump and round again as prunes will do, he would squirt right down again, Jezebel thought gladly. Certainly there was nothing about him to consider and she felt sure Missy felt the same way, so Jezebel met Missy on friendly terms, as women will do when the man has been eliminated.

But Missy would not come back to the Pink House to work unless she were permitted to bring the shining Goldie, cute-tongued and alert already. At first Jezebel said no emphatically; but when the Inchurch monstrosities were irreverently driving her into nasty, hair-pulling fits, Jezebel sent for Missy and conceded to her wishes. For, as Jezebel reasoned, the boy Goldie was getting large enough to learn to do light tasks about the yard and kitchen and she was never one to hold grudges. Moreover, it'd be a blessing to get the pesky children off her hands.

So Missy came back, leading the shining Goldie, and they most comfortably parked themselves in the Pink House, right where they felt that they belonged. The minute Missy cut her eyes at Danny Boy and Elizabeth they knew delight, for Missy's lap was exceedingly soft to their bodies, her singing very soothing to their ears, and they called her Mama far oftener than they did Jezebel. Little Elizabeth thought Goldie's hair was far prettier than any of her dolls' hair, and she patted it and ran her fingers through it, to Jezebel's chagrin.

Hump, the old Inchurch coachman, wizened with age, his bright red tongue hanging out on his woolly chin as a lizard sunning itself in a straw pile, quarreled and fussed unmercifully at Goldie, who was helping him to polish Miz Jezebel's newest limousine in preparation for the trip to Babel, the land of pure delight.

Jezebel was stunningly and smartly dressed this hot morning and her little seraphs more radiant than evening stars. Since Missy was Jezebel's size, she sailed forth in Jezebel's cast-off clothes, and the chauffeur was as handsomely outfitted as a general. They were in the limousine, ready to take off, feeling as inspirational as the breath of a summer morning and overgiddy with the prospect of pouring out their souls to the Lord up in Babel.

Hump and Goldie waved them good-by and the dazzling limousine moved lugubriously into the street and nosed toward Rahab, hence on to palmy Babel. They moved smartly along on their course and soon squalid, overheated Green Pond was behind them.

Missy was satisfied. She had not thought ever to be back in the Pink House, much less back on her own terms and riding in kingly splendor toward the much-talked-of Babel, where Miz

Jezebel would cool her soul. This was the life, and nice, too. Goldie was as smart as a brier. He could cunningly look out for himself there in the Pink House. He could already use one of Miz Jezebel's commodes with subtle grace and had a horror of going to the bushes. He already knew how to lord it over the Negro servants and they stood in awe of his flaming red hair and sky-blue eyes. She smiled faintly, letting her ever-refined airs settle about her as she mused that a strident voice got nobody no nothin.

All morning Miz Jezebel's limousine nosed upward to Babel, continually passing in the ungracious road oddly shimmying vehicles that moved snakily snail-paced toward lovesome Green Pond, where the humming spindles called night and day for workmen.

All the red land of the watershed had been stripped smooth of its laborers for the mills of Green Pond, and still the cry went out as a dreary voice in the night for more hands. All the glittering, scintillating hillsides that surround Green Pond had been raked bare of human flesh and more urgently did the hollow voice bellow, as a cow for the bull; forever and forever the call flew across the red terrain.

The hands came. They threw the old bedstead, the old bedtick, the old stove, and a couple of straight chairs upon a wagon —later a truck—and into a company house they moved, grabbed up the hot string ends so rapidly that the spools never knew the hands had been changed.

When the call had reached far away through the hills and into the mountains, the people had heard the cry and had trekked down the hills in search of the promised land. And as they came they built houses of worship; the coruscated Baptist came and the itinerant Methodist, and they built themselves, on every red hill that surrounded Green Pond, tabernacles and praise-houses to worship the Lord and testify to His goodness and His mercy and His love.

2

News flew swiftly around Green Pond that Cabelus McCobb, of stillhouse fame, was dead at his ritzy residence on North Philadelphia Street. He'd given up his earthly holdings of mill and bank stock, bonds and securities, and fled—everyone was uncertain to where.

The red land baked cracking dry in late sultry summer.

"Doctor Thornwell," said Miss Shelley, hastening across the lower parlor to the French doors that led directly upon the green terrace, "what're you doing out there? If I turn my back, you're up rambling around. Come on and eat a bite of breakfast. It's mighty good this morning."

"I'm taking a little pee," Ole Doc replied, standing out in the grass barefooted and with only his drawers on.

Shelley stood in the doorway, laughed at him, "You're going to kill that grass with that urine. You should have used your jug. Looks like you'd be afraid someone'd see you standing out there wetting so bravely."

"I've passed beyond all that tomfoolery, Shelley. I'm doing nothing wrong. I'm simply taking a little pee, like I like to do. I don't think God intended I wet always in a jug. If He had, He'd put a jug onto me somewhere. Fear? I'm too close to God to know what fear is. Only those without God know what fear is. Shelley, take off some of these days from your busy nursing and loll about and let God get close to you—you're missing something, something very special, I'm afraid."

"I might be, at that, but you come on and eat a bite of breakfast," she urged, opening the screen door for him, assisting him by the arm into the room. "That's certainly a lovely bowl of flowers. Who sent it? It must have arrived last night after I was off duty."

Pop seated himself before replying. "Oh, that infernal Jezebel brought it out here last night. One of her methods of contriving.

She's an ingenious old plotter. She wants everybody to see her contrite heart and praise it, but behind all that she's a schemer. She came in buzzing like a stupid bee, when in reality she's more like a wasp; for she can twist that behind around and about and sting you before you can say hiss-cat. I've known her all my life—in fact, I delivered her and she's been scrouging and pushing every since."

Ole Doc fell to thinking and looked at his breakfast tray. "Shelley, you ever thought about man's hands: how he's reaching out, groping, feeling upward—like plants? All reaching up for something higher. He starts it in the cradle and keeps it up all his life."

John Mathis came often to see Ole Doc, and they talked of their way of life, for Ole Doc considered John to be his most understanding friend. They talked with tongues of wisdom, saw with eyes of understanding, heard with ears that were attuned to catch the undercurrent of the melody of life. They were capable of looking beneath the sunsets, beyond resplendent moonrises. They were overwhelmed with the beauty of memory and their thoughts were far too deep for tears. Knowing his overgenerous life was coming soon to its close, knowing that the slipping-away time would soon be upon him, Ole Doc prized John most highly, for now in their old ages they were welded with having lived and with the nearness of their time of departure.

Here the sturdy Scotch-Irish had come and lived. Now all that day and time was gone, because so many strange people lived in Green Pond that he hardly knew anyone any more. After all one's old friends, loved ones, and acquaintances were gone, there was nothing much left for an ole feller to do but go on with them; but in their time, they had had their day.

Mama Amazon stood in a far-off corner and observed Ole Doc and she was, indeed, extremely low in her mind, because no man reckoned with Gawd and got by with it. He'd reach out sooner or later and call one to account. Here before her was the oldest of the old Thornwells. She'd thought once Gawd intended to swat them all down like so many flies, but now she was uncertain, for there was Tad, a full-grown boy, looking just like Ole Doc. Ole Doc would leave him a message, a heritage, a way of life. Mama Amazon looked down at her black hands and then to the ceiling of Catawba. This was her home. She knew nothing else. Yet how had she got mixed up in it? The dirt was red, the people very near red, and she was black—ah, Gawd must have an eye for the colorful, the way He splashes it around.

3

Jacob and Myra dropped past every evening after Vic had repeatedly warned Jake that Pop couldn't make it much longer. Now that the North Bethel congregation had presented them a handsome automobile, which Jezebel had been instrumental in bringing about so that the preacher might appreciate her contrite heart the better, they spent the greater share of the afternoon calling upon the members of their congregation.

Myra kept herself in odd clothes and hats. It was a far better show than Jake was capable of in the pulpit. Since Pop's illness, the Thornwell pew in North Bethel was thinned, and only Naomi, Tad, and Myra held forth.

Naomi descended Catawba's stairs as regally as any queen every afternoon at the hour Jacob usually arrived and seated herself in the lower parlor with Ole Doc and the nurse, waiting.

"Hello, Pop," said Jake, coming across the room to him, and Pop arose, though tottering, and stanchly shook hands. It had always been his custom to do so; not to shake hands before sitting down was a leaky, untrustworthy manner. "Feeling better? Looking mighty good," Jake continued.

Ole Doc sat down willfully and looked up at Jake with decided scorn. "At ninety-eight I feel spiritually wonderful, but I'm sure you weren't inquiring about my spirit; and physically at ninety-eight I'm worn to a frazzle—just plain flat frazzle-assed, which you could see if you'd open your pesky eyes. Son, I hate to see a man trying to follow the Lord and his eyes so changeable that he looks right crosseyed and may fall into the next ditch he comes to."

"What passages of Scripture do you want me to read to you?"

"You're doing the reading. I'm listening, though I'd like some of my favorite passages."

After the reading, Jake started to pray.

"Jake Thornwell, when did you get so lazy that you have to squat around like a pesky toad to pray? You stand up there in the presence of the Lord to pray."

"What's the idea of that, Pop?"

"I've never seen a sincere, God-fearing man to hunker over in a chair like that and pray. Especially a preacher."

"Pop, times have changed."

"God hasn't. Or has He? Does each generation have some different God? In all probability it is likely, for they change everything else, so why would they not change their God? And they say, 'Look at us and our God, the old ones and the old God didn't know how it was done.' Yet they are born and they die and time moves on."

4

Deep within Mama Amazon's heart there stirred a desperate prayer and she was rent to her soul with a grief that could not be uttered. There was no mist in her eyes, no catch in her voice. Work, talk, crying, laughing, playing, singing, and anything else that a human being did from the beginning to the end stood away back on her waiting list. All roads turned sooner or later and this was the road that had the big turn in it. Never in her years here in Catawba had she remembered an evening like this: when the sun came into the lower parlor as it was now in such dazzling radiance, nor when the crickets there on the hearth did the most plaintive crying she had ever heard, nor when the songs of the frogs came up so sweetly from the river and the low bottom lands, knowing that they would be buried in the mud for the long winter's sleep. Nor when such a dying breeze quivered the tree leaves. And yet in that same little breeze whispering around Catawba there was a song. She was uncertain of the melody, but it was a song of remembrance. It was the kind of music that bored deeply into her. The great clock here was ticking the hours of a man's life away in Catawba.

"You want a bite of supper?" Mama Amazon asked, breaking the golden stillness.

Ole Doc looked at her a long time, his eyes far away and into some strange land, then he turned his head slightly, gazing toward the sinking sun. "No, Mama Amazon, I won't be needful of your good cooking; I do well to sit here and to breathe. I've patched up lots of folks lots of times, but there's finally an end."

"Yes, sir. A few mo risin's an settin's of the sun an that ole road turns."

"No, it never turns; it forks.—Where's Naomi?"

"She's upstairs readin she Scriptures, I suppose."

"When Vic comes home from the hospital, tell him to come in here. I want him to play for me. He's neglecting the piano too much for the hospital. He takes it too seriously. He can't keep up at the rate he's going. He won't save them all—I never did. I have abated many fevers, lessened the family's anxiety, alleviated many pains, reduced inflammation in joints, and relieved much suffering of the body, but there was always a quota which I could do nothing with. While times have changed and medicine now stands upon a new dawn, there'll be other things to pester the doctors. They'll butt their heads against the wall many times and wail with their troubles, but their troubles will blow away like dust. God never intended us to know everything or there'd be no interest in living—nothing to struggle for. Without a struggle life ain't worth a hoot."

Miss Shelley got up, came to Ole Doc, and started taking his pulse.

"Shelley, you needn't do that. I know you're obeying the Doctor's orders. But there's nothing you can do. When an old thing is worn and falling to pieces, why try against all odds to hold it together?"

"Oh," Shelley laughed, "I've got to keep in practice. It's time for your medicine."

"I'll not take it; Shelley, I'll not take your concoction another single time!"

"If you don't take it for me, you'll have to take it for Perry," she said, glancing at her watch. "It'll soon be time for her to come on. I believe you like Perry the best."

"Don't know as I do. I don't want no stinking medicine. Tie up my shoes, Shelley. I've been sitting here all day with them untied."

"You ought to take off your shoes and lie down and rest."

"I'm not going to lie down any more. You tie up my shoes. I look like a frustrated person sitting here with my shoes untied. I never could stand frustration."

"Have your way."

"Mama Amazon, tell Tad I want to tell him good-by as he goes off to school."

"He wouldn't miss doin that fo the world. But I declares he oughtn't be goin off to school wit you so bad off, though he's done sent he's trunk to the station."

"Bad off—I'm dying. No need for him to hang around looking at my old dead body. It'll be spent and gone. If I've done nothing to live on in his heart after I'm gone then I should die forever. His life is just beginning and ahead of him and I'm expecting big things of him. He's a Thornwell—and I'll be watching."

Tad came to bid Ole Doc good-by and Ole Doc stood and stretched forth his palsied, creeping hand and Mama Amazon forever swore that when he clasped Tad's hand there was a flare of light brighter than any lightning she'd ever seen.

Tad was on his way to catch the night flyer to school and Mama Amazon followed him to the front of Catawba. "You great-grand'll be gone when you gets back an you won't be seein he no mo on this ole earth. But I could tell the way he was lookin at you that him an Gawd's placin big doin's upon you shoulders."

Heavyhearted, Mama Amazon stole from the room, leaving Ole Doc, who loved the red land of the watershed zealously, sitting before the fireplace in Catawba, sitting there the calmest she had ever known, waiting for that never-failing train to come through and to pick him up.

The farther she got from him the fuller her eyes got with tears. It was a good thing she had Dish here to help her, for times like these tried her old soul so she didn't know what to do. If Vic could only, only get back from the hospital in time to play just a little bit for him, because he was going now so soon and that little bit of music was all he was asking for. All he was hoping to take with him.

"Dish, you'd better light a fire in yander. Gets mighty chilly after the sun draps these nights. He's settin in yander dyin wit he's shoes on—so help me Gawd—an the only thing he's wantin is a lil bit of music."

"Bigma, dead peoples pure scares the daylights outta me—sucks the breath right outta my body—"

"Gawd, Dish, he ain't dead yet."

"The way you was tippin around an—"

"You'd better get that fire started!"

But Victor was late leaving the operating room for Catawba and across the operating table was Tizzy who knew why, and who knew no one knew what went on behind her mask.

The gloved surgeon's hands pulled the rotten, ulcerated stomach from the man's incision so swiftly that the nurses and assistants looked on in awe, their movements paralyzed. The bright operating-room lights intensified the humid, pin-dropping quiet.

But Tizzy only looked over her mask at Vic, glad her smile was hidden by the mask. She had had a hell of a time with Doctor Thornwell on this case—it usually was the patient.

This man, leaning on his wife and cramped double with pain, had hobbled into the hospital in the afternoon. Vic diagnosed his trouble as ruptured ulcer and advised operating immediately; but the wife wouldn't consent until she had scoured the countryside for his many relatives to get their consent also. Vic blew up: time was running short, the man had waited too long now. The wife was still arbitrary and had her way. Vic washed his hands emphatically and walked out.

But Tizzy had rounded up the kinfolks, got their consent, and by early night had prepared the man for the operation and got him upon the table and anesthetized. Then there was the long roundup of Vic, cooling him off, scrubbing him up, and getting the scalpel into his hands.

Long after dark Vic entered the lower parlor to find Pop sitting before the fire, laughing softly to himself and semidozing. Vic pulled an ottoman up beside him and dropped upon it, remaining quiet. Looking about the room he noted Perry sitting under a floor lamp by a table writing. He got up and went over to her.

"If you want to take off tonight, you may," Vic told her. "You haven't been off a single night this week. Should I have to go back to the hospital, I'll call you."

"I'm not sleepy," Perry replied, "but I could go upstairs and lie down to read."

Vic played many variations of Yellow Sam's melody and the effect upon Pop was effusive serenity. Cooling calmness soaked into the room as water into a sponge. Vic got up from the piano, went over to Pop, and dropped down upon the ottoman.

"How's that, ole man, did that set good with you?"

"That," Pop replied, "was absolutely the best yet. I'm sure if you play like that when I'm gone, I'll hear you and be greatly rejoiced. For those sounds you've made tonight don't merely scar heaven's face, but live forever—that sound wave keeps traveling out and out, there's no end to it. Yes, play that often for me when I'm gone—deep and melodic as the black people'd do it. We'll always remember that as Yellow Sam's melody, for that's to whom it belongs. The white folks can't steal that—they steal everything else. But so it's been through the ages, stealing from one another."

Vic reached over and took Pop's senile hands in his. "Do you really think that song will live forever, keep on traveling?"

"Yes, and I can't explain it. I didn't create the world, so you'll have to ask the Fellow who did. Of course, there're plenty of quippy fellows who know the answer to everything. They could answer you right off without scarcely giving it a thought. I have spent lots of my life thinking upon that subject and have come to some definite conclusions, but not all the way."

"Have you talked this over with Jake?"

"What good would that do? What does Jake know? I doubt seriously that Jake's capable of one solitary solid thought. When he was young here and growing up he spent the greatest share of his time chasing gals, and since he has been in school and preaching he's been delving into books, and none of that is conducive to thinking. You stand a better chance at thinking than he does. You're where life's more juggling and paltrier. You've seen it in the raw. People with their hair let down as I've seen them. Son, I've always thought you had a keenly developed sixth sense which permitted you to see under things, to catch the meaning of things from the twitching of a face muscle. You know, if I had my life to go over and knowing what I know now and in this day and age to begin living, I'd study the human brain.

"God did His masterwork in the human brain and eventually doctors'll go right in there and work with great safety. It's merely a matter of time and they'll surely relieve much suffering.

"God did His work all right, but somewhere along the way man has made a hell of a mess out of it. I shall go out trusting that it's like they say it is, for that would be much better than not trusting. I should hate to go out not trusting and then find out that there was a hereafter, so I shall go out trusting.

"It's like being born. I certainly didn't know I was to be placed here on the red land of the watershed between the two rivers, but I was—for some reason. I can't say why. And here I'm going out and I don't know where I'm going or why, but I know I'm going somewhere. I can feel it. There're some things you simply can't say, for you don't know how. While man's as glib-tongued as the glibbest of creatures and he's juggling and he's scratching notes and he's making speeches—he has a heap of questions to rake up yet. Some of them I doubt he ever finds the answers to."

They fell into silence. Both of them studied the flickering fire, listened to the pesky insects, to the clock ticking the hours of a man's life away. Then out of the silence Pop asked Vic to play again for him.

Vic put everything he knew how to into the music. He kept it soft, but it breathed and lived and oozed from every nook and crack of Catawba. All the loneliness of a lifetime came from the piano. It covered the red land. He reached a soft passage; he had to lean over to catch the sound; and then he heard Pop scuffling. Vic turned in time to see him standing up, his arms stretched, reaching.

"Help me up!"

Ole Doc slipped away so easy, standing up with his shoes on. Mama Amazon wanted to know, "Was he steady on he's feets?"

Vic could make no sense out of the whole distorted inter-
mezzo. He could only see the short movements that connected
the big ones into one song. If he could get off and look at the
whole, it might make some sense. Yet did it matter whether it
made sense?

After the great sorrowing throng had gone, Vic locked the
mausoleum, turned, looked across the cemetery, and then down
at the key lying in the palm of his hand. Vic thought that Pop
was sumpin like right out of the Bible—he'd begat so many chillun from Gawd.

The warm noonday sun filtered through the finny-fingered
leaves of the mimosas. Butterflies arabesqued among the tombstones and immutably possessed the earth in tranquillity. Vic's
memory drooped and he apostrophized Pop until he became
quite clairvoyant. Man's life was as a book: its scribbled pages
his twistings and his turnings, his fidgetings and his squirmings.
Yet the big and the little alike faded into oblivion.

Pop was now within the stardust, beyond the disk of the shining sun.

5

In Green Pond autumn was ferociously cruel and prowlingly raw
with death, a deathly atmosphere of foreboding and lurking
evil: this influenza epidemic. The privileged plague went into
whatever noisome hovel or handsome house of the rich it wished
and right early cheated the people of their lives, hemorrhaged
them to death often, omitting any pomp or ritual, and coerced
them out into the unknown beyond.

Doctor Victor Thornwell, skinny, disheveled, overworked, and
hollow-eyed from lack of sleep, skulked in Tizzy's office and swaddled his spirit with a cup of steaming coffee.

"Who was that on the phone, Tizzy?"

"Your buddy," she laughed loosely. Then her words flowed.

"What do people expect? This hospital'll hold only so many patients. If those mopey undertakers'd get those bodies out of that third-floor hallway, we could put a few cots in there; but now that there's so much meat for them, they seem to have full stomachs. So—the Inchurches will have to die at home."

"Inchurches die at home? What is it, Tizzy?"

"That was Robert Inchurch trying to get his mother into this hospital. His sister Irene died a few minutes ago."

"So Irene is dead?"

"Why Victor, was she one of your cutie-pies?"

"Cutie-pie hell, Tizzy," he snapped.

"Have you tapped those pleural cavities?" Tizzy asked, pulling back the scrim over the window and gazing into the fog-cowled street.

"Did ten. Strange there's pneumonia mixed with this flu. One boy made a hell of a racket. When they arrive at a stage they need to be drained, they never die."

"Why don't you hide out of here and rest—nobody'd find you in the graveyard," said Tizzy.

"I've got that exploratory to do on Alf Logan. He has me stumped; I can't pull a diagnosis out of the air like a magician."

"It can wait another day! Go on," snapped Tizzy. "I'll keep this old plague-ship sailing. Later, you can look at Alf Logan's entrails—and I bet they smell."

So Victor thought of John Mathis. John was all that was left, except Mama Amazon, of what was really Pop. Naomi didn't seem to count. He would go see John and they would talk: a suitable surcease from what he was going through here.

No peaceful smoke came from the chimney of the old homestead on this raw, chilly day. Vic pounded upon the door sharply, but there was no reply. He heard the pig grunting gratingly loud in the pen; it sounded as if it hadn't been fed. Vic went into the house through a shuttered window.

He found John dead, his head hanging over the edge of the

bed, the floor beside him covered with blood that had come from his nose and mouth as he had bled to death from a hemorrhage. Influenza.

Vic stood in the center of the cold, clammy room, suppressing the raging grief that rose in him and then he felt surfeited with life. He revived himself with a sigh and moved toward the bed. The room was filled with preternatural gloom. He'd have to work rapidly—John lay rigid and unbending.

Vic got dry wood from the wood box and taking a piece of fat pine kindling he made shavings of it with his knife, deftly and quickly so that it would ignite rapidly. He reached upon the fireboard, found a match, struck it to the pine shavings, and built up the fire as carefully as though he were performing a most exacting operation. With the fire going, he hurried out to feed the squealing pig, the hungry chickens, and to milk the cow.

He returned to the warm room. It was out of the question to get a busy undertaker out of Green Pond to bury John, so he'd have to do it himself.

Vic stirred about to make the coffin and finally betook himself into a closet on the second floor and there he beheld the thick tongue-and-grooved boards, lovely satiny, over eighteen inches wide, which had been cut from the heart of a huge pine tree in great Grandfather Andy's time. Surely ole Andy wouldn't mind him prying loose four handsome, satiny boards for a coffin. He must hurry because the dreary November days were short.

He located John's tools, then returned to the closet, pried and prized and hammered, and the old house groaned every time a wooden peg was splintered as if it were a living person being mutilated; but Vic worked as though he were beset with quippy jeers. He felt that ole Andy was directing him and that his Grandmother Joanna and Pop clapped their hands in approval.

He dragged the planks into the room where the fire was, and there he hammered and sawed, talking to John as though he lived.

When the coffin was finished, Vic turned John over to see what he could do with him. He ought to have on better clothes to go into Gabriel's presence, but Vic saw no way of getting the clothes on the stiff form unless he broke some bones, and he didn't want John whimpering and limping in Gabriel's presence, complaining of cracked-up bones. He had, at least, got through life with his bones intact, with the exception of this missing thumb that Cora had accused him of shooting off himself to get out of fighting. He ripped the fresh clothes in the back, laid them over John, and pinned them together in the back after the fashion of a shroud. So John could face Gabriel, at least.

He used the quilt and pillow from the bed to cushion the bottom of the coffin, and Grandma Joanna approved, and when John was laid into the coffin Vic hammered the lid on with nails, then wondered how he'd get him out into the yard and into the grave.

Vic jumped up out of the yawning grave and hurried to the pigpen. He took two short pine poles that would go lengthwise through the door of the house. He carried them into the room, prized the coffin upon them, and slowly began to roll it out into the yard. Once the coffin was over the open grave, he let it down to the bottom of the grave with cunningly contrived and manipulated grape vines.

He stood the shovel in the corner of the house and looked at the fresh grave. So John, too, was gone into the beyond.

6

"Why, Victor, what brings you to North Bethel's manse?" asked Myra, opening the door. "This is, indeed, a pleasure. I never get to see enough of you."

Jake laid his paper down. "I think you doctors are falling down on your jobs, the way everybody is dying these days."

Vic was filled with derision, but it was transitory and he dropped into the chair that Myra indicated. "I suppose you've cured all the diseases here in North Bethel Church?"

Myra's eyes crinkled with laughter. "You really don't know how Jake cuddles and coddles his diseases here," she said. "Why, one of them actually buys his underwear; I've secretly hoped she'd try it on him."

"Is it all that bad?" Vic asked.

"You ought to live around this manse a while," said Myra. "Why, I'll have to get my very soul back from Jezebel to have one to take to Gabriel."

"Aw, Myra," said Jake, "it's not that bad."

"Jake Thornwell, don't you sit there taking up for Jezebel In-church—as many times as she's had you sniffling. You're no man: you're a toad! What on earth does that woman do to you men?"

"Does she do something to men?" Vic asked in a beguiling manner, hiding his smile with his hand.

"Not all men," said Jake, and Vic read his thoughts of the long bygone.

"You know, Vic," Myra began thoughtfully, "I've always noticed something peculiar about you and Jezebel: the tone of voice she uses when she speaks of Doctor Thornwell. I don't know what word to use to describe it. I sense it, I can feel it, I know what it implies and suggests, but there's no word for it." Then she looked questioningly at Vic, "What in the world do you hold over that classy hussy's head?"

"Myra, you're on church property," Jake rebuked.

"Jake Thornwell, shut your mouth. There's nobody here except Vic and he knows I have to blow off steam once in a while or I'd pop wide open. I wish this influenza would get that bitch."

"Myra, Myra—"

"Vic, I wish you'd open your brother's skull and see what is wrong with his warty brain. The sly way Jezebel Inchurch has persecuted, tortured, and bemeaned me since I've lived here is inhuman. Why, folks treat their animals better than she treats me."

They talked for a time about the epidemic, but soon Vic had to go. There was always the hospital. Influenza still called its dreaded tune, bringing people in burning hot with an ungovernable fever and sending them out in a short time, clammy and cool, rigid in death. From floor to floor Vic made his rounds through the hospital halls; he moved among the irrational, who cried incoherently. The cots were side by side in the hallways and there was barely room for him to wedge through. He wondered what Pop would say, could he see this hospital so overcrowded. Yet Pop had predicted, when the ninnies had scoffed and jeered at him for building such a big hospital, that the day would come when they would see that it was far too small for Green Pond.

Vic stopped and closed his eyes tightly and thought of Pop's spirit hovering so nearby. Hovering here over this great building that stretched out its arms to comfort and to help.

Now Vic was Old Doctor Thornwell—the old doctor whom people trusted, whom the people came to, beseeching and begging for help and health.

Outside it was November's raw chill and cold and cloud; inside the Thornwell Hospital steamed with warm death. The woman had her hands to her face as she was walked down the ground-floor hallway, held by a nurse and a relative.

"Did she say anything more?" the relative asked with timely concern.

"No," the woman said with quivering lips, "she just died. She's dead—dead." And her sorrow grew loud in the heated, crowded hallway and her tears gushed through her fingers and spilled away and her thick voice went on, "She's dead—she'll never, never talk again."

And Vic's fists clenched, for his hands could do little more to stay this dark angel from his multitudinous visits.

7

In Heaven Gawd was ferociously violent and unmindful of His earthly chillun's cries. In His wrath He kept Earth disagreeably chilly, and a disease-breeding fog draped it night and day.

GABRIEL: What You means by rushin things up? They's dyin that fast now I can't put em down.

GAWD: I think you better empurple you pen, fo that flu plague's off on a rampage an I don't know when I'll let em up.

GABRIEL: John Mathis is gone. Vic found he's body and dug he's grave an buried him out to the ole Thornwell homestead.

GAWD: Yes. And I also see that contrivin hocus-pocus Jezebel's fled Green Pond, scared to death she'll die wit the flue. Wearin a big piece of asafetida tied openly about she neck. Wouldn't want em ladies in Green Pond to ketch her doin that. Also, I see Vic's overworked. The Thornwell Hospital's overcrowded. He's walkin out often in Nof Bethel cemetery. He considerable perplexed.

The Low-Region boys loved death, enjoyed the flu plague, glad to see so many cheated of their lives, their spirits coerced to the beyond before they had a chance to put up any bargain-grabbing petitions, each spirit accorded an abode suitable to it.

SATAN: Us shorely is gettin we's share outta this mad flu plague Gawd's done turnt loose on lil mens.

BEELZEBUB: Yah, an lil mens thinks Gawd done turnt agin em. I hears em cryin out an prayin at night in Green Pond.

SATAN: Most of em don't have time fo that; it kills em too quick; don't have time to get fo'giveness. But it shorely helps us out lots.

BEELZEBUB: That's the nature of lil mens: hangin round, waitin around fo bargain-counter repentin's.

Book three

Book three

17

Green Pond would send David Kingsley to the capitol for its governor. Jezebel was in the midst of the affray, hauling the women voters to the polls, making certain that their votes were rightly cast. It seemed a forever drawn-out process of getting David Kingsley historically seated in the capitol, where he connived for Green Pond, getting black tar roads strung across the country, which the people cried at contemptuously, saying they'd stick up in the oozy tar and perish in the sun-hot, immaturely snatched from the face of the red land.

It was rumored that the Inchurches would choose someone to be successfully groomed as an elder to succeed Robert—for sooner or later, of course, all good elders go to their rewards in the stardust and successors are needed. Jezebel wanted one properly trained her way. Give a man a taste of Inchurch fortune and Inchurch power, she thought, and he would lend himself willingly for training—scratching the Inchurches' backs as he learned.

Except Vic.

And year after year Jezebel pulled the strings and her puppets acted.

"Really, don't you think the flowers were lovely this morning? I believe the church was the prettiest I've ever seen. Jezebel fixed it, of course. It was simply lovely." *If that Jezebel Inchurch don't quit wringing every weed she has in that Pink House yard and bringing it here and ramming it topsy-turvily into the gosh-awful-looking containers, my hay-fever is going to get so bad I'll simply have to quit going to church.*

"Oh, yes, Mrs. Robert B. Inchurch is pouring at my reception. Really I don't know what I'd do without her." *Mother did that. I hadn't even invited the old devil.*

"Yes, I think the choir robes are such pretty colors. Yes, Jezebel was the chairman of the committee that selected them." *As many years as I've had in that line of work and she gets just what she wanted.*

"Didn't you think the new choir director did superb this Easter morning? I thought it was lovely." *That's more of Jezebel's work. Where on earth did she pick up that grotesque creature? He couldn't hem up a tune in a barrel of molasses. I believe she has all the elders bewitched.*

Little good it did for anyone to accuse Jezebel, for she was far, far beyond any wrong doings. Jezebel lied bewitchingly, with her honeyed smiles looped from ear to ear. All that she did was singularly right and virginal and that which others did was abated with the fat of ole Satan.

Nothing could be done with one so divine as she.

Jacob Emmanuel Thornwell knew it well—and therefore made no effort. Myra Thornwell continued to let off steam to Victor behind closed doors and to let the ladies of the congregation go on laughing at her and praising the pictures they let her draw. She relished bitching as much as ever, but she relished not so much her husband.

2

The mad, roaring years rolled forward across the red land as human and earthy things will do and Doctor Victor Thornwell went into many bowels and beheld Gawd manifested there, and sometimes he alleviated the trouble, sometimes he removed the trouble with his scalpel and his deft fingers. He placed his hand into many upper abdomens, slowly withdrawing ulcerated stomachs. So his days, standing solidly by the operating table; he played with many coral-like stones from gall bladders and kidneys; his days and often his nights were filled with a steady stream of operations. He tacked in here and pulled out over there. He lightened burdens. He relieved suffering.

The red land grew rich with machinery and industry. The natives learned to live by the turning of the wheel and vaunted themselves over their successes. The pecks in the mills thumbed their behinds at the straw bosses, walked out and readily walked right into another mill, so plentiful was the work and so adept at twisting the string ends were they.

Green Pond cried night and day as a colicky baby for more and more power, and the power companies damned the rivers high and higher and flooded many fertile acres of the lowland.

Only cried out to Vic and pointed it out to him, "So you's sellin all the big bottoms fo the backwaters?"

"Nothing else much left for me to do," Vic stated. "They're offering too much money. Besides, I'd only be temporarily standing in their road. I'm like the rest: a mere cog in the wheel. Now don't ask me what kind of wheel nor where it's going, where it's running to, for I don't know. Today life is but a cogwheel. I hate to see the scenes of my childhood go."

Only murmured, "They might as well kivver it with water, fo iffen they turns many mo crazy peoples loose like that county agent up there in the courthouse, they ain't gonna be none of the country left nohow. That ole county agent come out here and staked off em terraces fo me and bless Gawd the first big rain come, every one of em busted. I could make a mo better terrace than that an I ain't never butted my head agin no big agri-culture schools. Looks like they'd teach the common fools that water tends to naturally run downhill, but not this agent wit he's frisky, big talk: tries to make em do some other how. Nobody can sin agin nature too much an get by wit em. Not a one of em terraces they made had enough fall in em and I told em so at the time, but they let me know right quick I was just a nigger."

"Only, you have to overlook some folks: a small amount of learning goes to their heads like too much rain to cabbage heads in the spring."

"Every bit of that big south bottom is goin?"

"Yes, I'm thinking about the big woods behind the old homestead, too."

"I know Old Doc'll turn over in he's grave the minute a ax goes into em big trees; many years as he guarded em," Only said sorrowfully.

"I realize that, but conditions have changed greatly since Pop left us and he never cringed nor whimpered when he sold the front acres of Catawba. You know, it's funny: so often I phrase a question to ask Pop, only to realize I can't."

"I feels the same way in my head."

"Seems as if we had lived in a fable or were the characters of a parable."

For a long time they stood silent and gazed over the south bottom lands of Catawba, then Only spoke, "Iffen when all that backwater gets here, there ought to be some powerful big catfishes in em. I imagine a body could drap a hook in most anywheres an pull out a big un. Uncle Prince Blue sure loved to talk about em big waters—allus said the big waters made a slave of him. He could never get the troubled big waters fro he's mind."

"I suppose the water'll be backed to those willows down yonder. Tell you, Only: make us a flat-bottom boat and we'll keep it tied up there. When we want to go over to the old homestead, we can ride."

"Won't that be sumpin? Can't believe water'll spread all that great distance—that'll be lack an ocean or mo."

Beyond Green Pond proper, south of the Thornwell Hospital, lay Doubting Hollow, where Yellow Sam had set himself up in many righteous businesses, where he ruled wisely as a king, where the sluggards and the slothful came often with flattering lips and darkly sticking fingers and he corrected them and showed them a better way of life. It was here that Jepson Grady often came to discuss with Yellow Sam the things that should be done for Doubting Hollow and then Jep hammered it home in the Green Pond *Observer*. Here was the colored Third Street Presbyterian Church that Yellow Sam and Mama Amazon had founded under the evangelistic guidance of Jake. Its congregation were the first-class Negroes of eminence, high-spirited, keenly perceptive, and leaders in the social development of Doubting Hollow. And here Dessa was a leader in the schools. But the streets were unpaved, narrow, tortuously winding, often squalid with litter.

Mama Amazon never missed a Sunday without going to the Third Street Presbyterian Church in Doubting Hollow. Yellow Sam, whom she had raised to do right, was a vastly high elder there. June and July and their families belonged. Mama Amazon had many grandchildren who came there to Sunday school to learn about the sweet little Jesus Boy, whom everybody said was white, but that made no matter, for someday the black cherubs would be as white as the whitest white. They were all equal in death. When there were many to be baptized, Mama Amazon was right up at the front helping the preacher, wiping the water off the little black cherubs' crinkly hair lest too much water give them a cold. The visiting Baptist Negroes scoffed at her, saying that little old tat of water wasn't enough to feel, much less to save a soul from ole Satan. But Mama Amazon shook her head at them in simple disbelief and told them that they had no ideas of the powers of strong Presbyterian water.

Vic threatened to sell Catawba because it was so big and bundlesome, burdensome to keep up, and so outdated it looked odd sitting on Main Street. He could build a ritzy house in Forest View or South Hills.

But Mama Amazon grew so angry she jumped with all her weight upon the rail fence behind Catawba and sermonized powerfully to Vic. She wanted to know was he out of his mind? Had he taken sumpin at the hospital to effect his brain?

"I wouldn't be caught dead in one of em po-white-folks' trashy houses. Ain't got but ten an twelve rooms, the ceilin's low lack a chicken coop—a body'd pant in there lack a parrot in a cage fo a drink of water! Trashy! Why, they front stairs ain't half fine as Catawba's back stairs what I travels up an down every day of my life. I don't see what you's coming to, Victor Thornwell! You's had the mo better raisin. I never raised no trash: neither black nor white. No, I don't see what's happenin to you or the times. The tender succulent roastin' ears Catawba's ground has produced, the hams that smokehouse has harbored, the golden peaches from the trees! And my Gawd, today everybody's eatin outta tin cans and paper pokes an ain't a thing got a bit mo taste an chips from the woodpile!"

She comforted Vic and he was filled with compassion. "No, Mama Amazon, I'll never sell Catawba as long as you live to love it and I can make enough money to keep it going." Then he scoffed, "But any day now I'm expecting someone to rush to the hospital wanting me to scalpel them a new anus because the old one is no longer in the style."

Mama Amazon's mouth dropped open and she stared at him, "That's my caul-headed chile!"

Naomi went in and out of the stores of Green Pond, filching and pilfering, ramming whatever she was cunning enough to lay hands to into the folds of her outmoded skirts and waists and toting it to Catawba. Her turned-up pug nose and fat protruding cheeks behind her smart veil always created the expectation that she had lilies of the valley bestrewn about upon her hat.— Man's life runs from worm to worm, the wriggling, the wriggling —she tittered often and folks gazed silent and dumfounded at her, their mouths falling open like dredging machines. They thought she was like an old Daniel who had too much backbone for the lions.

The illegal stills cropped up, squatted in thickets along the creeks, sweated out their white juice, and the bootleggers became more sought after than the preachers in Green Pond. The automobile tires clicked along the cemented highways, carrying the male and the female to the bushes for sugar stealing.

Then one day Green Pond's Main Street was extended far beyond Catawba and the younger generation rode carefree and gaily upon it and beheld Catawba as they passed and were amazed at the well shed, the well box, the well bucket sitting right on the side of Main Street as Pop had left it years ago. Catawba became the greatest pointed-out place in Green Pond. People even made up many strange stories of Catawba and rocked their children to sleep with them.

The legend of Tommy Thornwell began to take root in the red land, chiefly planted there by Jezebel, who favored its cultivation at her Country Club parties.

"I vividly remember the Sunday Tommy Thornwell stuffed a pillow under his coat and waddled into North Bethel Church to the very front seat and sat down while his old daddy was preaching."

It changed often, this tale: he'd ruined many girls—he'd been shot at and run out of the country—he'd been caught naked in bed with a married woman and her husband was still after him —he'd run way out West somewhere and married an Indian.

But in the Thornwell Hospital babies popped into the world

night and day. The switchboard operator pushed her plugs wildly and answered many questions.

"Grandma ain't er-lookin nat'al wit'out her specks," said the woman to the switchboard operator in the hospital lobby. Grandma's spirit had fled, so the woman went on to say, beyond the blue of the stardust on a Preachin Sunday night and now she was ready to ransack this hospital for Grandma's glasses. "She wuz a good woo-man an we ain't er-wantin her buried unfitten. Not our Grandma. An we're aimin to hold up puttin her in the groun until we find em specks." Her tongue spoke, her eyes brimmed with water, and she shook up the switchboard operator, who pushed her plugs wildly, "You've misplaced Grandma's specks. Find em, find em. Stealing from the dead."

There are no means to discern the inner man, what goes on in there; and it is best that one man cannot look into the heart of another, for there one might see things that are best left unseen, Vic muttered, scrubbing up.

3

The shadows of evening were lengthening across the faces of Elvira Dodge, whose husband had suddenly died years ago, whose body was huge and round as a farrowing sow with the fat of old age, and Louise Tarlton, who clung to her husband as a drowning being to a raft, and whose body was as old and skinny as a fence rail. Ever since Jezebel Mathis had been in their family they had fomented an intoxicating hatred toward her, the devil's beauty, who smelled and dressed like a gaudy harlot, who gnawed as certainly at their decorum as an ugly barbarous worm in wood.

So now without misgivings, they said to themselves, ruefully and blightingly, as they sat down to coffee in Louise's living room, that it was time to retaliate and to let the devil's beauty bewail her gluttonous lot. They filched tidbits from the coffee table, held their cups correctly and in the prevailing style, and poured out hot words about Jezebel as water gushing over a dam.

"I've taken my last smurky slap from that intolerable Jezebel," said Elvira, gazing at Louise in scorn and showing no fear, "and you're going with me and we're going to drag her before the preacher if we have to tie her and drag her." She crossed her legs smartly and pulled down the hem of her dress.

"But really, Elvira," Louise said in a wizened fuddle, "I haven't said a thing to Joe." She ended punily in dismay, although she loathed Jezebel with a high-toned hatred which fertilized her soul until it writhed unbecomingly in torment.

"Louise Tarlton," Elvira scorned in a mannish voice, "you're old enough to no longer care what men say about you. The only thing that has kept me from going to the preacher or the Session with Jezebel years ago was Mother. She thought it'd be an outlandish disgrace. Now that she's gone and I no longer wear mourning for her and I'm old and don't even care what people say, Miss Jezebel is going to get her toes roasted. The Thornwells have always been good people, and why that Jake Thornwell, who is trying to follow the Lord, lets that Jezebel Inchurch browbeat and cow him first one way and then another is beyond me. When Jake first came here, I thought, even had very high hopes, that he'd rule the church wisely and get Jezebel and her mischief down to where it'd not be so squalid and noisome; but since he has come, she seems to have gone from bad to worse. And now I fully intend to take a hand."

"Oh, Elvira, this'll be dreadful. What if it were to ever get out among the members of the congregation what we'd done? Oh, it'd be the most unbecoming and singular thing to do. People would hand that down to their children for ages and ages to come and it'd never be forgotten. You know how things like that live on and on in a church." She whimpered in a whisper, regarding her sister searchingly, and reflected upon the situation.

"Leave it to me," Elvira coaxed, "I'm not afraid of it getting out. Jake Thornwell will never tell it and you'd never squeeze it out of Jezebel Inchurch with a cider mill. I'm not taking another thing from her. I'm calling Jake and making an appointment for this evening in the church office. We're going right today. Jezebel might think she's God's chosen one, but I'll show her."

"Elvira, will you use your chauffeur? He might talk. You know how Negroes are."

"No, I'll do the driving myself, use one of the smaller cars. That'll eliminate that possibility of it getting out. I'm anxious as you to keep it covered up, but I'm just as anxious to call her out into the open and let her squirm like the worm she is."

"How will you get her into your car? Reckon we'll have to stoop to pushing her? Oh, this is terrible."

"No, when she finds out we're going to visit the preacher, she'll break her fool neck getting into the car. Have you ever known her not to be overly anxious to go to the church, and especially to see the preacher?"

"Are you going to call her first?" asked Louise, trying to allay her plowing fear.

"You know I'm not going to call her. She might start telephoning around, trying to get wind of things."

"Are you sure she'll be at home?"

"Yes, I've checked that. Robert is out of town and there's nothing in particular doing anywhere. So if we get there about two thirty, just when she gets up from her afternoon nap, we'll be able to catch her. I'm going home now," Elvira continued, getting up, putting on her wrap, "and call Jake. And provided everything clicks as I feel sure it will, I won't call you; but if I call you, you'll know without me saying so that the jig is off for today."

4

Jezebel bounced out of the Pink House and into Elvira's new, expensive car. "My, my, Elvira, another new car? You must change with the moon. I'm still driving last year's model. My, it takes money to buy things like this," said Jezebel in her most charming, poverty-stricken voice, leaning her red head against the rich upholstery, feeling the fabric of the seat with her hand, then putting wonder into her jig-dancing, yellow eyes. She looked at Louise, who sat in the back seat with her and who felt as if she were in a cage with a panther, who cringed notably and was beginning to sorely blame Elvira for this reckless adventure.

"What's happened at church that I don't know about?" Jezebel asked banteringly, directing her question to Elvira, who was putting the car into motion, nosing the heavy vehicle into the street and toward North Bethel Church.

Louise looked at the dreaded panther and longed for firearms. Jezebel sniffled her nose, twitched her shoulders, waiting for the answer.

"Oh," Elvira began lightly as down in a breeze, "we want to keep abreast of all the local gossip. The telephone's entirely too slow and uninteresting."

"I'm sure glad you came by for me for I certainly don't like for my mind to wool-gather sitting at home and I love to be at the scene when the facts are smoked out," Jezebel laughed off-handedly.

"In this restless, drawn-out affair, you'll be right there when the facts are smoked out, although you might feel sorta rumpled-looking when the infuriated affair is threshed out," ironically replied Elvira, nosing the car through traffic slowly, and keeping her spirits in a holiday mood.

"Really? Has something like that come up in the church? I thought things were going fine." She questioned brushingly.

Then to Louise, "Didn't you think the music was divine Sunday?"

"Brilliant," Louise said, unadorned and flat.

Their smiles were as toothsome and glittering as a tooth-paste advertisement as they rode churchward. When they had alighted from the car, gone into the church office, and seated themselves about in odd chairs, Jake held a small prayer, then listened cautiously for the woes and complaints which he somehow felt in his bones were coming.

Elvira had made certain that she was seated between Jezebel and the door so that there could be no sly slipping out, and now, fussing with her clothes, she took to the floor, speaking outright plain. "Mr. Thornwell, Louise and I have a very disagreeable affair to call your attention to. It's quite distasteful, but we know of no other way to settle it. It is this: ever since I've been president of the Auxiliary here at the church and the two years I was president of the Presbyterial, Jezebel has made it her job to slyly poke fun at everything I've tried to accomplish or to do to further the Lord's work, and it, to me, has been very demoralizing and from her view point, quite unchristian, so I want you, as an honest preacher, to put a stop to it." *Of all the ungodly things,* Elvira thought in desperate anger, *Jezebel is no more affected than had I given her a spoonful of cream. Does she mean to sit there and try to lie out of this? Yes, she'd like to try something like that. She hasn't connived and contrived all her life for nothing. She's well-grounded in that art. She knows how it's done. After she's torn my nerves to pieces for all these years, criticizing, making bemeaning remarks, her mockery, then she sits here right under the preacher's nose so snugly, thinking she's going to get out of it. Oh, no, she'll pay and pay dearly.* Elvira's face was deathly white, her lips had thinned to a mere thread, her eyes burned with a hot consuming light.

"Why, Mrs. Dodge," Jake began slowly, toying with the ink on his desk, his eyes avoiding hers, "I had no idea there was any such thing going on in this church." He was lying diplomatically and officially converting his conscience into a gaming device, for right now he thought that anything became a dignitary. Then he moaned within, *Oh, Lord, don't let Myra find out about this, for I'll surely become much lower than a toad. Much, much lower. What can I do with these witch women? They have me any way that I might turn. Jezebel will never humble herself if she has done this and I'm quite sure she is guilty. I know that old gal well. I was raised up with her. She usually got whatever she went after from man to mouse, and now I'm only a mouse, but once I was a stouthearted boy. Yes—Myra said you are but a mouse.*

"Yes," responded Elvira, feeling more buoyant, wedging her cause, "but I didn't expect you to know anything about it. That is the reason I'm here telling you about it." *What has happened to that man? He used to be one of the most straightforward and uplooking boys going and here today he sits not even looking me in the face honestly. What has charmed him so on that desk? I've noticed that twice he's cut coy, sideways glances at Jezebel. Does she have him ground down under her heel that much? I'm not leaving this place until it's out in the open.* "It's quite true," she continued, "everything I've told you about the affair, and I'm simply sick and tired of it. If you don't want to believe me, ask Jezebel. She's sitting right there and I'm certain too splendid a Christian to stoop to lying out of it."

Jake cleared his throat, coughed, and his face flushed, "Yes, Mrs. Dodge, I see her." *Why must I be twisted and tortured with this smelly affair? There's so much selfishness in them that it's doubtful whether any good could be found. What'd Pop do in a situation like this? I'm sure the minute I ask Jezebel, she'll lie out of it as quippy as a crow. It was born in her—it's her nature. Shall I give up the last shred of integrity in me? Shall I crawl in the dust as a toad and let Jezebel squash out the little life that's left in me?* "Mrs. Inchurch, surely you're not guilty of this accusation?" *There, I've opened the way for her to lie out of it—I've made it very easy. Now she'll take the cue, the sailing will be smooth. We'll get by this way. To dig down to the bottom and get the truth would tear the whole church asunder—there'd be no place for me to preach, I'd have no money coming in. Yes, this is far the grander way. Let everything fall back into its old haunts, its old ruts, and become the same old stronghold, then they can fare forth daily with their sunny goodness. I'm no longer even a toad, a warty toad—I've sunk beyond—beyond redemption. I'm stamped inside with the marks of hell. Though I skulk, the hellhounds shall find me. And I can no longer go fighting upon Armageddon for the Lord God Jehovah.*

Then Jezebel answered cunningly, her eyes mischievous, knowing that there was no method that either her foolish sisters-in-law or this silly preacher could use to probe the meaning from her inner heart. "Really, I'm dreadfully shocked. To think that my own dear sisters-in-law would deliberately haul me into church and accuse me so very unjustly is most humiliating and quite embarrassing." She sat completely surrendered, the glowing halo of divine righteousness sparkling about her. "If I have said anything that has been slightly amiss, it was only for the good of the church and our dear Lord." She wriggled her nose as a rat sniffing a noisome cheese. *So help me God, when Robert Inchurch hears what his stinking sisters have done to me, he'd better do something notoriously rash to them or they'll soon be running this church in their outlandish ways. Of all the wormwood and gall, bringing me here and accusing me—oh, the wizened bitches. All right, old sisters-in-law, I'll get even with you somewhere along the way—and I'll go to your funerals and stand over your coffins and stick my finger into my eyes so that I can squeeze out one little drop of water for you. So they don't like the way this church is being run?*

The dove of peace descended upon Jacob and he was capable

of lifting his head and there was a slight sheepish smile. "You see, Mrs. Dodge, there's been a misunderstanding all the way around," and he flipped his hands washing-like and aimlessly together. "Just one of those little mishaps that we run across on our struggling way to heaven. So forget it, for you've all done wonderful work for the Lord." *That was a close call. You've gotta watch these old women, for they're not half as dead as they look. And Jezebel, the varmint, you can always depend upon her to lie out of any bad situation she gets herself into. Oh, God, don't let Myra find out about this, for if she does, I'll hear about it until my hair has turned as white as a November morning's frost.*

"Well," came slowly and unconvincingly from Elvira, "perhaps I was wrong or a bit hasty." *I'm quite sure I'm right. I wouldn't have been so tortured all these years. No, I can't be wrong. She's lied. And he's taken up for her. Which is the worst? So we no longer have a decent preacher. There sitting before me is the shell of what used to be a man, and what has Jezebel done to him? Little did I think I was heading for this. I shall remember from now on that Jezebel is very unlikely to lose at anything she sets her stubborn head to. So she has won again. And what is her gain?*

Louise stayed in far-reaching silence, being a woman of infinite patience, but her thoughts plundered and towered within her. *I told Elvira how it'd be. It'll take a sharper person than her to lick Jezebel at her sly tricks. I hope that when I die and if I must go to hell, I hope I beat Jezebel there so that I can throw the first big shovelful of red-hot coals upon that head of hers. Has the devil endowed Jezebel with eternal youth? She looks as sleazy-slick as somebody twenty-five years old.*

The trio tripped blithely from confession. Elvira hauled Jezebel back to the Pink House and their good-bys were a lovesome sight.

5

Green Pond was built as the circles form when a pebble is dropped into a pond: the circled waves nearest the center the highest and gradually fading out to smaller ones. Green Pond was the hub and its many roads its spokes of existence. In slippery moonlight the greater rings of Green Pond were wrapped in foretelling mysteries.

The apex of each little red hill that circled downtown Green Pond was the little shiny Baptist Church, its little steeple clasped to its bosom in prayer and looking right straight up to God in heaven.

The Reverend Jacob Thornwell before his upper-crust congregation, many wrapped in the skins of animals and the feathers of fowls, had once upon a time denounced the encroachment of these hagborn prophets, but he might as well have kept his mouth shut, for when the sowing has been completed, no man can censure the crop. Now Jake's sermons grew more melodramatic and he moaned in the pulpit and dabbled at his eyes and his sophisticated congregation had no admiration for his goodness.

Nature, the erudite teacher, is crudely unmindful of the lives of her pupils, so Victor thought, and remembered that in his youth he had tried to outrun the dark shadows cast by the cumulus clouds, but he never did. Something always got in his way.

Standing beside the anesthetized young girl on the operating table, Vic looked to the whispering purple mountains that loomed up friendly and inviting beyond the hospital in the azure-mystic haze. He was greatly cast down in his soul and his mind spewed as the frost will do the earth. The operating room was exploited to stillness by his waiting and the operating-room assistants stood as though afflicted with a form of petrifaction.

Vic turned slowly and looked at the girl's abdomen exposed in the opening of the laparotomy sheet. He touched it with his gloved index finger, shook his head, brought his gaze upward, and stared sadly at the assistants, thereafter dropping his vision into the opening of the sheet. The assistants saw his jaws clench and his muscles work furiously and they knew he was fighting a murderous hatred within himself. They saw wave after wave of perceptible murmurs rise to his lips and die without being born into audible speech.

No, girl, no. Why'd you do it? You've not many more hours left of this life. There's not much that I can do with you. Who's to blame? In your desperation you've gone to an abortionist. How you must have suffered. In this mad roaring age too many girls, just like you, are climbing into automobiles and riding the highways and spending the night in erotic play. Yet, that's what God so created you for. He made you first boy and girl, male and female. He made you in the beginning. Where'd the twist start? Is it from civilization? Then what's civilization gained for man, more than a pond filled with troubles? Is there not enough trouble in the pond already?

In the apparently dry state there were not only two chickens in every pot but enough white moonshine likker to cook them. Night after night Vic returned to the hospital to sew up the slit throats of the bootleggers. The bell ropes stayed smoking hot, ringing loudly for Jesus. The preachers of the red land of the watershed grew more excited and flailed the devil out of ole Satan and belabored genuinely, and a new church rose upon the bosom of the red earth, its little steeple denouncing the evils of the Jazz Age. The flappers, painted as gaudily as Egyptian harlots, stole their sugar in the bushes and scratched chiggers for a fortnight.

The Country Club during the Christmas season threw thundering parties of trivialities and hunted up an unashamed, responsible bootlegger. They drank and ran unsteady hands into each other's clothes, feeling, feeling.

The Green Ponders careened in prosperity and bragged of

their cunning bootleggers. This was the land for the people, the uncorrupted people, and they drank themselves into dizzy heights and went to bed, waking up the next morning with a dreadful hangover.

6

Gawd hoped Gabriel didn't mess up the genetics of the Thornwells, because their genitals had been going plenty strong, but He had to watch Gabriel for he was getting that absent-minded and He had a heap of things to keep looking about on Earth, especially Green Pond. That race of doctoring Thornwells was enough to keep a body guessing.

GAWD: Young Tad Thornwell is gettin on mighty fine in the dissectin rooms in medical school. Lackin em, too—chip offen the old block. He'll be needed back in Green Pond to help in that Thornwell Hospital, fo it's growin, an lil mens is feared of Me an worser scart of dyin.

GABRIEL: Yah, Vic's puttin on right-much age. How long is us been recordin about em Thornwells?

GAWD: Years. An they's been an interestin set to deal wit.

GABRIEL: Ole ones was stanch believers.

GAWD: Young'uns, too. But changed a lil. Changes is good.

GABRIEL: Don't look lack You changes much. You's been hittin that ole oak tree in the hospital yard wit bolts of lightnin way over two hundred years might nigh now an ain't killed em yet. Goin to?

GAWD: Might up an do that some mornin in the by-an-by. They no longer makes the racy wine fro he's grapes fo the holy communion. Serves weak grape juice that's lost its savor an fittin only to be puddled in.

Satan roosted in Green Pond now, rooked the Green Ponders each chance he got, and rollicked them straight to Hell.

SATAN: Where you been at, Mr. Beelzebub?

BEELZEBUB: You know blamed well you tolt me to take a oil can an oil the preachers' bedsprings! I'll swigger you can think up some of the awfulest things.

SATAN: Knows what I's doin; you be quiet, you hear me?

18

The Green Ponders woke up one morning from a drunken sleep
to find their subjective worlds in dubious condition. They cried
right straight up to Jesus and bewailed their lots unmercifully,
pointing out to Him their self-righteousness, questioning His reason for taking away their folding money, wanting to know why
there was no work upon the face of the red land. The sun rose
each day and sailed through the gallant heavens. Gorgeous was
the moonrise—A Carolina moon, heralded in song and story—
but who cared for that sort of stuff when one's guts growled to
pure beat the band for something to gnaw upon? The stars—
the galaxy of stars—the milky way, all of the milky way—
sprinkled the high-ceiled blue by night boldly and without end
—beyond and beyond, forever and forever, no end to eternity
—and cast plenty-fitten stardust earthward; but little men were
too egotistical to see it. The grasses of the fields came up brazen
green. The trees budded and bloomed and copulated boldly,
with the help of bees, and fruited. The cows bawled and itched

for the bull. Turkey hens ran to the gobbler, squatted, screamed when the gobbler tore up their backs with his sharp toenails, and sneaked away to lay their eggs. The people heard the dear earth goddess and her daughters, Nymph and Mermaid, groaning with the goodness of the earth, and every man, urged by a primitive emotion, longed to make a garden.

Yet it was hard times throughout all the red land of the watershed from Babel to Baal, from Rahab to Unity, from Goshen down Kinfolks Road out to Old Hope. Typhoon Ai bemeaned his Tabernacle congregation, accusing them of stealing from the Lord Jesus, because the collection baskets held only small pieces of silver, and folding money was as rare as raindrops in a drought.

Jake cringed and skulked, fearing he would starve to death, because, even though he had thousands of dollars tucked safely in the never-failing Inchurch bank, the mighty deacon who had served North Bethel capably as treasurer for twenty-five years had been unable to pay Jake's salary now for five months. This catastrophe caused the Green Ponders to drub their spiritual catacombs, casuistically seeking an answer that they never found.

When the Green Ponders were stricken with catalepsy, when fear and frustration bored deeply into every human being, when the banks closed one by one and the people faced each horror bravely, their eyes cast wild, furtive looks, their tongues fidgetly moving, declaring they would have to go to hell to see a banker with his gold because so many of the bankers were slitting their throats and the hellhounds were right there to lick up the blood.

The Inchurch bank came through unmolested, for once again the Inchurches had been connected congruently with good Federal money. Although there had been nights Robert had taken his whipping tongue in hand and made each cringing bank employee dig and scratch laboriously on through the night until bleak dawn. Then they had met, with a mystery-story air, the southbound express and there, under the direction of the pistol-wearing railway mail clerks, unloaded canvas bags of money and carried them in single file, under the watchful eyes of the Green Pond policemen, to the Inchurch bank, while the moneyless and hungry stood gawking in the street.

The depression was more of a moral than a financial dip. Robert forever held the financial umbrella if the sun shone, but in pouring depression he withdrew it and was sheer distrust. Being an indefatigable worker and seeing the fields ripe for the harvest, Robert Inchurch, who was an excellent harvester if someone else worked the crop, gobbled up block after block of Main Street property as it went upon the chopping block. He snapped up priceless bits of real estate simply by being there when they were sold. He dickered for whole chains of cotton mills and got them for a song. He picked up almost everything he wanted in Green Pond with the exception of Catawba and the Thornwell Hospital, and here he sheepishly drew the line for two reasons: he was immortally frightened of Doctor Victor Thornwell, and Doctor Thornwell, having far more of the shrewdness of Ole Doc in him than most people suspected, made certain that the Thornwell Hospital didn't go upon the block. Howbeit, Robert had secretly and constructively plotted, even to reconditeness during his sleepless nights in bed beside Jezebel, a safe means of destroying Victor Thornwell. But Robert stayed very much out on a limb when he considered the destroyed Doctor Thornwell. For even though he destroyed Doctor Thornwell, he was afraid the man would still live on, because there was something about him that he couldn't quite put his finger to. Was it the grape vine of security entwined about the mammoth oak there in the hospital yard—that vine that brought that wine up from the good American earth? Did that protect Doctor Thornwell from his grasping fingers? Something—it was something that drove fear into Robert Inchurch's fearless heart as nothing else could do as he lay there beside Jezebel.

2

Where Sandy Peeler's people were or where he originally came from, Vic didn't know. Sandy had been brought into the hospital from the village of Pecan Lane—a place where the scum and ruffian belabored in the Inchurch mills when their spindles turned, but at this time it was rare that the mills operated. Here by day and by night the tired, emaciated males took pleasure with the wearied bodies of the females. Children of the squalid, dusty streets made grim mischief with dogs and cats: tying tin cans to cats' tails, hanging dogs by the neck with ropes. They laughed tinnily, tinkling and rattling their hours away boisterously. Their frisks and capers were as tadpoles in a scurvily stagnated pond. They scrutinized the scudding scrupulous, thumbing their noses at them. Every day was a big to-do. They smoked the butts dropped into the gullies, occasionally in desperation they chawed a thrown-away tobacco quid, and always they begged for nickels for dopes. Nights they prowled uptown Green Pond, filching, swearing, courting, going to the shows.

Little Sandy's belly was swollen with the microbes that fought over him and Vic went all out to save him. He cut and drained and watched and prayed and it took a long time. The youngster had fight and the hardness of Pecan Lane, and his body, or soul —Vic often wondered which, in a case like this—fought at Vic's side and they won. And the surgeons and the doctors and the nurses were filled with courage from living with Sandy Peeler through the dark-crawling shadows.

When it came time for him to leave the hospital, Tizzy and Vic were greatly cast down in their hearts and Tizzy spoke to Vic, "It kills my soul to see that boy go back to what he came from, especially after we've put out what we have to save him. He'd have been better off dead as to go back out there and be kicked from pillar to pillar. Since we've cleaned him up and fed him sufficiently, he's a cute-looking kid. And so ingratiating."

"Yes, Tizzy," said Vic, detesting the quiver in his voice, "I've thought about that. And I'm going to try to do something about it. I'm going to take him to Catawba."

"An old bachelor like you? My God!"

"Well, why not? You forget: there's Mama Amazon—I wouldn't swap her for ten thousand of your upper-crust mamas. She's earthy and wise, and she teaches you sumpin that makes you independent—that makes you adventuresome and not afraid. You become the primitive man that lived perhaps a million and a half years ago—a hairy little man, a cold little man, who shivered in winter in a cave—who, when he saw the great sun returning declared a holiday—for he knew there'd be food and warmth."

Tizzy's mouth dropped open. It was all right. Sandy went to Catawba, and if Sandy had had any folks, they wouldn't have cared.

3

Across the flaming hilly red land, Jezebel and Robert owned, according to the Green Pond County courthouse records, a multitude of run-down farms, which had been fleeced, with first one and then another underhanded method, from the unsuspecting "pimps"—as Jezebel was wont to call them. A pimp, Jezebel knew, could never understand one of Robert's tricky mortgages —it was doubtful that she could herself. And Jezebel looked after these farms and called them God's Acres, because she used the loose money they eked out to do good unto the church—at least, it was delightful preacher bait. And these farms had produced much forty-cent cotton during the World War years.

But then one day, almost before day was clean, the boll weevils scurried upon the red land, forged into the communal cotton land. God had endowed each little turtle-backed bug with a steely bill. Being bugs of cruelty, smart and with persevering instinct, they began, upon arrival, to puncture holes in the juicy cotton squares and to back their butts over the holes and to lay eggs into the holes. In the cotton squares the eggs hatched out into vicious grubs, which swelled up the squares, turned them yellow, and knocked them from the stalks.

There was no cotton. Jezebel grew alarmed.

She and Goldie drove furiously through the red land; Jezebel exhorted her tenants to poison the boll weevils, jacked them up so high they felt dislocated.

"De Lawd put de boll weevils here, Miz Jezebel. I couldn't rightly pizin de Lawd's lil creature. No'am, Miz Jezebel, I can't be goin agin de Lawd."

"You stinking niggers make me sick." And she shuffled her plump rump in the soft seat of her automobile and patted the thick carpet with her feet. "You either poison that cotton or look for another house. Get out of mine."

"I'll jis have to move, Miz Jezebel, fo I can't be pizin no boll weevils. An dis ole place, I'd hardly call it a house. I think hit look lack a ole Southern mansion."

Jezebel ordered Goldie to drive on and the tenant muttered, "Boll weevils's here Lawd, boll weevils's everywhere, an that Miz Jezebel an em ole boll weevils is jest alack."

The general run of Green Ponders suffered and the roads running east and west, north and south were filled with weary hitch-hikers going from one mill town to another searching for a place where the spindles turned, but there was darkness over the face of the watershed and nowhere did the spindles turn. The power and energy were still in the lines but the wheels and the levers stood idle for the lack of someone with gumption enough to throw the switch. A great murmuring arose among the people.

Often after a lengthy day of grueling operating, Vic came to Tizzy and they'd talk far into the morning. He cautioned her repeatedly never to turn a single soul from the hospital because one couldn't pay.

"People can't help it that they need operations and medical attention in times like these. If we can simply get enough to keep the hospital running, I can easily get along without my fee," Vic pointed out to Tizzy. "I can't let Pop down now."

"Don't worry, they're walking right out without paying."

"I think we'll get by, though it might be a tight squeeze. I don't want to reduce the Nursing School—since we're on such good footing with the state board. How's Kenny getting along?"

"Fine," said Tizzy. "Believe she'll make a good nurse. Her leg never seems to bother her; never tell she has an artificial leg. But bound for you when you set your stubborn head to something. I've never understood why you took so much interest in her."

"Good. I'd like for her to specialize in operating-room work, for I'd like her there by me. Perhaps by the time we get the two new wings built and the new operating rooms ready, she'll be through training."

"One minute you're talking poverty-stricken and the next you're expanding beyond all imagination. You've not enough patients right now to fill one floor of this hospital."

"Tizzy, you still jump to conclusions too quickly; that's not good in good medicine. You've seen the day this hospital could have used four times this many rooms and in all probability we'll see days like that again. I've the money saved to build those two wings and I think it'll be a good idea to get started while labor's available. People need work and that'll help. I believe Pop'd approve. And there's Tad coming along."

"Yes," Tizzy laughed, "to take over when your old shoes are too runover for you to stand up in."

"For some uncanny reason," Vic said, "I've always thought Pop bestowed a great medical gift upon Tad before he died. And the next time Tad comes back over here to the hospital, you observe him. See don't you think he's lots like Pop. I see nothing of Jake or Tommy in him. All I see is Pop. There's something about Tad's hands that makes me think I'm looking at Pop's hands—it's amazing. And he's gal-crazy too."

Tizzy said slowly, "You know, Vic, you Thornwells are the queerest people."

"Don't see where I'm queerer than you. Queer, you've never married."

"My dear boy, neither have you. Moreover, after you've spent as many years as I have pushing smelly old men about in a hospital, you'd have no desire whatever to go to bed with one."

4

Jezebel spent her afternoons with her bridge club at the Country Club, nibbling sweety fat pastries while her long red fingernails flipped the idle cards, but it was chiefly a gossipry, for life would be weary without it.

Doctor Victor Thornwell, the famous surgeon, was hauled upon the card table for dissecting quite often. Their ears were cocked for this disembosoming. This uncouth boy he'd picked up from Pecan Lane—*well!* Liz suggested that it could easily be his for she'd heard said often that he'd had intercourse with more women than any other man in Green Pond. But if he'd stooped to pick a Pecan Lane woman—Ethel made as if to up-chuck.

Hearing this, Jezebel's heart stopped beating and she grew absent-minded with the cards; for winning at cards seemed now so little for this she'd just heard was more than she could bear. How it recalled the candy pullin in Catawba when she was a girl. Her co-player noted it and delighted in aggravating her. The prattling talk flew about the card table and rang in Jezebel's ears as a million gnats on a hot summer evening, rang in her ears and grated on her nerves worse than Ma's tongue.

"They say he's a brilliant boy. Very musical. Doctor Thornwell has spared no expense in getting good teachers for him. He's won several important honors in both organ and piano."

Oh, God! Jezebel thought, *he could have got that talent from Vic. This is real. This is not something held over from some other world.*

Robert, a busy, busy man, wondered where Jezebel might be; but he stayed late at night at the bank, thinking and figuring: the Thornwell Hospital at times occupied his brain but he could never arrive at any safe way of controlling it.

But the great Thornwell Hospital loomed up high into the sky, high above the great oak. All night long its elevators rose and fell, like the pulse beating in a man. The nurse gave orders and pushed the stretcher. Toward the delivery room she pushed, shouting, "Doctor, it's her fourth child; her water broke while she stood downstairs waiting to get on the elevator." And down the hall she went to the delivery room. And another tiny red pebble was dropped into the pond.

5

The little earthy men in Green Pond cried out in their fiscal misery. They swore the bootlegs of flour given them in the relief lines were filled with white worms and the small sacks of tobacco were disdainful in their sight, because they had to roll their own cigarettes. They looked up to the gallant sky and wished the grasshoppers would come up out of the river and devour the land. The sun was as red as blood, the earth about them redder.

Jepson Grady walked often by the pond and concentrated upon the plight of his beloved land. His hands were folded and lay loosely upon his rump as he sauntered about. And his kind eyes were crow-footed and chunked and knocked brimful of wisdom. He urged the merchants to advertise their wares and to not stand meltingly in their doorways; and that little parks be made by the idle men. He exhorted the people to plant mimosas, crepemyrtles, Judas trees, dogwoods.

The Garden Club, of which Jezebel was naturally the instigator, came all out for beautification and Jezebel's mopping-up action was absolutely ungeared and her periscope was on high seeing that plenty of lubricant was smeared over her egoism in the Green Pond *Observer*.

When Green Pond was in its darkest hour, when the people were dull and without a spark of hope, Jepson Grady came forth with plans for the Joyful Cotton Boll Parade and presented it to the Merchants' Association and the merchants shook their heads scoffingly, disagreed violently. But the more Jep pointed out to them the advantages of placing their industry before the world, the more their resistance was broken down. And Jezebel, being the guardian of Green Pond as well as of the North Bethel Church, fell into step with the proposition.

The day of the Joyful Cotton Boll Parade, God turned the sun loose a few minutes early by the clock, letting it ride high into the infinite blue and burn hell-hot down upon Green Pond. But God didn't fool the country people, for they stirred way before day was clean, doing their turns, making everything in readiness to drive in their jalopies into Green Pond to spend the day, munching crackers, cheese, and peanuts, to behold the jubilee, which Jepson Grady had jogged them into doing with his writing in the Green Pond *Observer*.

Main Street was bestrewn with cotton and as nervous as an adulteress among the elders in church. Sweet Green Pond, as fair and unbeholding as any of her thousands of sister towns across the face of the country, groaned with creative birth pains as the Joyful Cotton Boll Parade moved down her Main Street. The floats came and they were works of art. The most creative minds in Green Pond had belabored on them for days. They were awe-inspiring; they were breath-taking; the comments on them were amazing and profound. But all of this ballyhoo was mere trivia compared to the uproar Cyrus Hill and Betty Mae and their float brought to the crowd that so aptly found itself represented upon Green Pond's Main Street the day of the Joyful Cotton Boll Parade.

Cyrus Hill, whose stubby beard was as a molting rooster's feathers and nearly as long, sat listlessly upon a Hoover cartload of indescribable furniture—warped iron bedsteads, the enamel chipping from them; old cane-bottomed chairs, with the canes sticking out threateningly to anyone's behind; an antique iron stove, rusty in the places it was not black and greasy; dirty, filthy, much-mended bedding; a bureau with a mirror larger than the Hoover cart; a coop of scrawny hens, cackling wildly; an old washpot and several dented tin tubs tied under it, hanging dishonorably; a safe, with tin doors, filled with disharmonizing pans and dishes.

Betty Mae Hill sat higher upon the household goods than old Cyrus and she looked like a bowl of elegant dish gravy. She looked to the right and the left, taking the cheering crowd in honestly. There was now no cringing, for she rode with great dignity—and time had passed her by. Cyrus, with his slouchy hat pulled down to his ears, drove the old mule sternly and fussingly.

The throng of people descried this float of Cyrus and Betty Mae Hill and roared with laughter. Jepson Grady hadn't exaggerated one bit. This was befitting for these days and times which were upon the face of the red land upon the watershed between the two red rivers.

Then the congregation of North Bethel became unduly alarmed when Robert Belcher Inchurch began to hand out crisp one-dollar bills to his Sunday-school class of boys. They scratched themselves and knew something dreadful from heaven would strike the red land with a tremendous jolt. His good deed spread through Green Pond and nebulized, it flew in the wind to the utmost corners of the country. The old folks chawed and spat, saying that it was very peculiar, but they had known the Inchurch generation since buck was a calf and right off they couldn't recall an Inchurch ever being touched in the head this way; but times did change and it was possible that a people would change regardless of what they thought about it. God moved as He saw fitten and disregarded many of man's give-mes.

6

Mama Amazon and Vic went to Ole Doc's tomb on Christmas morning in a blinding snowstorm. Mama Amazon wanted to walk all the weary distance and this delighted Vic. She carried with her the monkeybush, the magnolia boughs, and bits of exotic berries that were found about Catawba. Mama Amazon trudged along, her heavy weight tiring upon her feet and the ferocity of the snow a drawback.

"Gawd only knows," Mama Amazon lamented, "I ain't wantin this Christmas day to dawn wit'out some plenty-fitten boughs at he's grave—snow or no snow. Much as he believed in things lack this."

"Do you believe all that strong in things like that?" Vic asked, and humored her along the way.

"Believe?" And her face rippled with surprise. "Believe mo'an I believes in myself. But you's got to be lack a chile; Christmas is fo the chile an only the chile fo the hereafter. An boy," and she grew profoundly concerned, "you believes the same, fo you was raised that way. There's nothin to this life but a parcel of troubles—an sometimes they weights you down powerful much."

"Aw—you know I didn't mean it that way."

"Don't care what way you was a-meanin em," and she trudged along. "Ole Doc was a heavy case in he's time and there'll never be another lack em."

7

Missy was terror-stricken the night Robert came to her bed and tore every garment from her body. She fled naked, screaming wildly, from the servants' quarters and up the stairs to Miz Jezebel's bedroom with Robert coming helter-skelter behind her, grabbing for her, apelike, with every lunge he took. Missy's screams grew so piercingly loud by the time she reached Miz Jezebel's bedroom that Miz Jezebel was out of the bed and had the door opened when Missy dashed past her and into what she thought was the holy of holies. Jezebel, being groggy from being aroused from sleep so suddenly, didn't have the presence of mind to slam the door shut and Robert was into the room.

"Missy," Jezebel yelled shrilly, "what on earth are you doing up here naked as a jay bird? And quit your screaming. You'll wake up the whole town."

"Oh, Miz Jezebel," squalled Missy, her voice rising to a wail as she jumped into the middle of Jezebel's bed with Robert clamoring into it behind her, "Mr. Robert, I think, is done losed he's mind or sumpin. He tore all my clothes offen me. Call him off, Miz Jezebel; can't you see he's right after me?"

"Robert Inchurch," Jezebel stormed, "what in the world are you doing?" But Robert didn't hear her and proceeded gorilla-like after Missy.

Jezebel hurried across the room, grabbed Robert by his shoulder, pulling him from the bed, and he turned on her with the raging fury of a trapped beast. They struggled noisily across the room.

"Turn me loose, Robert Inchurch," Jezebel shrieked, trying to stamp her foot scoffingly, trying to put authority into her voice, and trying to quell the sickening waves of fear that rose up within her. "You stinking, dirty vermin! You disgusting worm! *Let me go!*"

But his hold was tightened upon her. The situation had no

verities in it. It was crazy from one end to the other, verging upon the supercomical, and very unbecoming and singular to the gentle people of the Pink House. During the terrific struggle Jezebel's night clothes were ripped from her, even to the metal curlers in her hair. Once she succeeded in snatching herself free of Robert, she cried for Missy to come with her and to bring covering from the bed and they fled into the street. Robert followed them to the front door of the Pink House and there he stood, shouting wild threats at them and laughing lugubriously.

Jezebel and Missy stood in the middle of deserted Third Street with bedclothes topsy-turvily twisted about them and looked with horror upon Robert.

"What in the world are we going to do, Missy?" asked Jezebel, who had always been quite capable of frightening the town councilmen to sniveling servility and jerking out great handfuls of dear pastors' tail feathers, but who now stood cringing servilely and very much unable to make up her mind.

Missy predicted dire physical annihilation. "I don't no'am. He's a wild one!" She giggled, drawing the quilt close about herself, knowing she was in the open and could outrun most anything.

"You're mighty little help," snapped Jezebel. "Quit your silly giggling. Let's do something. I'm not standing out here in the street all night without any clothes on." She patted her bare foot on the pavement, giving Robert a deadly look. "Robert Inchurch," she commanded sternly, "what's wrong with you? You go on back into that house and go to bed. You look like a ninny standing there. An Inchurch ninny!"

Robert laughed hideously, more nerve-shattering than a ghoul at a feast. He flayed his arms erratically wild, churned about on the veranda as a wild boar, and hurled savage gibberish at his wife. "I'm an Inchurch," he boasted. "I've run you two sniveling whores into the street. I'll not have you fouling up the house of an Inchurch. This is my house. I'm an Inchurch."

"Robert Inchurch," Jezebel cuts crisply, deadly, "shut your dirty mouth. So help me God, I believe you're crazy as a bedbug. People'll hear you and then what'll they think of an Inchurch?" she clipped, razor-sharp.

"People," his wild laughter rose higher, "people? What do I care about people? I'm an Inchurch. And you," he said, pointing threateningly, "are a tricky whore, a dirty sordid whore. You've tricked me, you've fouled up the house of an Inchurch. Yes, I'm up to your tricks. You're more crooked than a Scotch corkscrew—"

"Missy," said Jezebel, tapping her bare foot, "go to the police station and get the law. There's nothing else to do. I'm not letting him get his hands hold of me again."

"Miz Jezebel, I ain't got on no clothes."

"I don't care. Go on like you are."

"But, Miz Jezebel, what'll the policemen say wit me walkin in there wit jest a quilt wrapped around me? That's awful."

"Missy Thornwell, I don't care what the stinking policemen think of you. I want some protection. You get right on down there and bring them back with you. Hurry. I'll try to keep him entertained right here on the porch so he won't come into the yard. He acts like he is charmed with something on the porch. He must be charmed with being an Inchurch. Hurry!"

"What must I tell em?"

"Good Godamighty, tell em! Get on down there. Don't stand there asking me a million questions. Run!" Jezebel gave Missy a shove, letting her quilt fall to the street, and then she furtively caught it up, rewrapping it about herself. The only thing that bothered her was that Naomi Thornwell would find out about this and gloat.

8

The news of Robert Inchurch's insanity flew about over Green Pond and was on the tongue of everyone. The easy-flowing voices sucked upon it as bees their blossoms, the ill-natured and slothful spoke insolently of it. The congregation of North Bethel stood abashed, chagrin smeared over their faces, and their whispering was profound. And Robert lay in a private bed in a private room of the Thornwell Hospital.

Art Lily, whom Robert Inchurch had been grooming for years, and Ahab Hennessee, whom Jezebel had picked up, were grounded and stooged into the Inchurch tradition until they were quite capable of moving the Inchurch fortune onward, especially under the shrewd, foxy guidance of Jezebel, who made them sit down with her and go over the books each week. She paid them lavishly with money and smiles. She often did niceties for them, but she knew that too much temptation placed before them might cause them to form the very bad habit of taking out portions of money which looked pleasing to their eyes, so she used her high-pressure, backslapping womanship to be sure to keep them looking forward to the straight and narrow roadway.

And Jezebel had a continual reason for coming to the hospital. Her visits there were not all rounds of joy, for though Vic did not always dodge her, he was often with Tizzy or Kenny or one of his other nurses and Jezebel cringed when she saw him place his arms about a nurse's shoulders and walk down the hallway intimately with her on his rounds. Then Jezebel suffered the darkest human misery that a woman could suffer and still live. She called down the wrath of God upon those other women. She called them all sorts of loose names. She dug their graves one by one.

And she felt fright, sometimes. She knew that they were older, much older now—but she could push that thought from her, for were there not still sweet years ahead? Where Victor was concerned there was no time and she was as a girl of seventeen. *Oh, Ma, Ma, why did you so cruelly and abruptly interfere with the stardust that time?*

Each time she came to the hospital to see Robert she felt the fright and each time she pushed it from her. She would not be beaten; Vic couldn't hold out forever. She'd get him someday. He'd have no excuse when Robert was gone. So she counted the days of Robert's lingering illness one by one—slowly. How time dragged.

9

Doctor Thornwell and his boy, Sandy Peeler, were in the lower parlor at the two grand pianos and it was the much-looked-for hour for them, caressingly and rapturously rare. Being a surgeon kept Vic from playing with Sandy as often as he would like. Vic had the old piano, which had been Mama Naomi's in her heyday, and Sandy, who had shown a remarkable instinctive love for music since the day he was brought to Catawba, was at Vic's newer one.

Victor subdued his playing and kept his ears keenly cocked, catching every note of Sandy's rich musical tones. As he listened to Sandy's playing he felt overabundantly rewarded for the trivia he'd put forth to snatch Sandy from the sordid destruction he was heading for. His heart swelled at the thought of Sandy, the thought that he'd done something for a fellow man who loved him with a childishness which was almost unbelievable. Shorely, as Mama Amazon said to him, his cup ought to be lipment full.

Whether Sandy's first concert in Green Pond was an unmistakable success or whether it was unmistakably the beginning of his downfall, Vic only guessed. Jezebel Inchurch descended from her throne. She gazed at Victor and praised Sandy, and the following week Sandy was asked to take the position of organist at the mighty console of the North Bethel Church.

Vic shook his head and recoiled his spirit from this danger. But Jezebel would not take no for an answer, and Sandy, towering young with worlds to conquer, begged that he might be allowed to try. The affair was threshed out and Sandy Peeler went to the pipe organ at twelve years of age when his legs were barely long enough to reach the foot-manual. Vic knew he was enmeshed in one of Jezebel's haunting traps and he lived in utter dread of what would happen.

But the years turned by without getting too rumpled-looking and Sandy grew and waxed in love and admiration in the eyes of the North Bethel congregation.

Mama Amazon was overjoyed to see Tad coming home a full-fledged surgeon, ready to roll up his sleeves and to go to work in the Thornwell Hospital. He had studied with as much vim as Vic had ever shown, although he'd hurried to Catawba and to the Thornwell Hospital each holiday that had rolled around to get encouragement from Dad, as he called Vic, who had ironed out his large group of worries and sent him back to school with a frenzied desire to surmount the complicated surgery. He had spent his summers in the Thornwell Hospital dogging Vic's steps and taking everything very seriously—too seriously, some of the nurses thought.

But the height of his joy had come upon the rare occasions when Vic was doing an exploratory and permitted Tad, with gloved hand, to go down into the patient, feeling around, getting the lay of things, to learn to feel which organs were normal and which were abnormal.

But Tad still had lots to learn for there was complaining at the office in the hospital. "Five dollars for that?" the young man asked, extending the forefinger of his right hand. "Why, he put in only one clamp in my finger and charged me five dollars."

"Ought to see what he done for me for nine dollars," another said, comparing repair work.

"Tad, boy," said Vic, after he'd overheard this and cornered Tad, "I've sutured all night for just the smell of blood."

"I'm not rotting here without being paid!" Tad exclaimed. "Of all the work I've done in smelly dissecting rooms, then learning to cut upon a living, breathing carcass!"

Vic hid his chuckle. Here was Pop all over! Life was a circle. Tad was a believer in clamps; he still loved suturing, just to see how fine he could make his stitches. For a moment he thought he was Tad and looking up he thought he saw Pop, saw him smiling.

10

The sun banked in the humid hot summer evening as though once again Joshua had commanded it to stand still. It threw its redness streakingly across the face of the red land that was quiet and filled with luxurious green growing things. The insects buzzed in the humidity, sweat poured from the folks in Green Pond, and they complained of the unbearable heat. The earth groaned deeply and contentedly with its birth pains. The bell ropes rang out at sunset for Jesus, growing smoking hot in their ringing, and all the land was filled with prayer and all the earth's creatures looked toward the banked red sun disk and clapped their hands in supplication.

Ole Satan went to and fro to see whose pie tasted the best.

"And two hundred years ago," Vic thought, "there were no hospitals. Two hundred years from now—" He dared not think. He wouldn't be here to worry about it; what difference did it make.

One generation was about as good as another. There was no difference in them. Each one of them thought it was his day and he had lived accordingly. So would they in the generations to come. What was old-fashioned and what was new? What was barbarous and what was unbarbarous? Was man more than a boll weevil or a bean beetle? What was he to forget in this day of living? Was there anything to forget? Anything to remember?

Tizzy came to him and they talked far into the night about a man's life, about the beginning and the ending, the coming in and the going out. And he did something to Tizzy's soul that she couldn't understand. After one of her talks with him life looked different, and she loved him for what he was and nothing more.

11

Satan was so overjoyed with the news that Beelzebub brought him to the hovel where he was drinking a can of beer that he jumped up and poured the beer atop of his horny head.

BEELZEBUB: Great day in the mornin, ole fool, is you tryin to up an baptize youself lack em Baptist I seen comin up outta Jenks's millpond?

SATAN: You astonish me: em Baptist was baptizin wit liquids: this's beer I'm drinkin. I got the presence of good mind, boy. An I'm shorely glad you's brought me this good tidin's of the troubles of Jezebel's daughter. She just like she ma.

BEELZEBUB: That's some parcel of sin an no tidin's.

Gawd looked down from on high with great sorrow in His voice, His tongue in mourning, His uttering pure sadness.

GABRIEL: What is it, Gawd? Why so greatly cast down in spirit this mornin?

GAWD: It's that music, pure beauty, comin up fro Nof Bethel this mornin. Never knowed when I created Sandy Peeler in Pecan Lane that I was puttin sich beauty into he's soul. He's sendin it all in pure sweetness to My throne, such music as draws nothin but pure sadness fro Me.

GABRIEL: You should temper he, Gawd.

GAWD: Don't want em tempered. Wants em jest lack he is, fo he ain't gonna be on Earth that long. I never made he fo the Earth. I made he fo song. To play at My throne. Jezebel'll get he outta that church when she plans don't work out right and that'll kill Sandy in the long run.

19

May is the sentimental month, the month of Elizabeth In-church's socially prominent wedding in North Bethel Church. But Elizabeth stayed in the semigloom that she was born in. She felt her life ebbing toward its end—there'd be no cruise to Europe this summer, no house party at Babel—nothing, nothing but this wedding.

Elizabeth, gowned and veiled, standing at the door of the church, her bouquet trembling lightly, waited for the organist's cue. And no tears would come to her hard-rimmed eyes behind the veil—there was only the mad stirring of pregnancy within her overbold belly—the fruit of many promiscuous sexual unions with he-boy Buckgin.

She had had everything in life but love.

She had had a magnificent education at the chawin-an-dippin school, she and Buckgin, who had learned to carry the ball across the field, cheered to manly exhaltation. They had learned, these scholars, about the ball game—oh, just any ball game. And

Buckgin wanted to play all night long and he had punctured Elizabeth one night of rough game, punctured her with his hungry horn.

Any minute now the organist would give the cue, Elizabeth and Buckgin would meet at the altar. To please Mother! Mother hated Buckgin because he, a Baptist, a raping Baptist, had punctured her darling daughter. Oh, Mother had raved. This, too, must be covered by the church.

Elizabeth still stood waiting, waiting in full wedding splendor, waiting at the church door for the organist's cue for her to go down the aisle to meet Buckgin. She trembled and she shook, but no one could see behind this frothy veil.

Elizabeth and Buckgin were bound together by two rings.

And Jezebel looked on.

2

Budda fumbled conscientiously with his many keys in the dimly lighted hallway of the west wing of the Thornwell Hospital and he succeeded in finding the right key, opening the door of the most expensive room in the hospital for Lovebird and Lovebird, who stood, puffing and panting, with their little wagon. In the room lay the crumpled-up form of the eminent banker who was dead. Lovebird and Lovebird bewailed Robert's grotesque condition, but assured Budda that they would make a presentable repose of his shaggy remains.

Budda felt doubtful of the times; whether to be sad under the oppressive shade of death or whether to rejoice with Gawd over the burden Robert had been delivered from. However, Lovebird and Lovebird were unconcerned with Budda's disturbed emotions, but made ready, in kindly haste, their departure with the weird body, and Budda followed them to the elevator. He went down in the elevator with them and Mr. Robert, whom Budda eyed in masterly disbelief.

Budda came to himself watching the vanishing tail lights of the hearse going out the paved, circular driveway. He listened to the wind high in the tall pines soughing. There dipped into his bosom an unearthly loneliness that he could not recollect as ever babbling there before. He jarred his head with the palms of his hands and suddenly he had the longing to go to Catawba and to Mama Amazon. The other orderlies could hold this hospital down for a while.

He split out down through Doubting Hollow, heading westward toward Catawba. Night life was coming upon the streets in the hollow as he passed through. Girls rolled their behinds freely; radios blared, sending moonlit, seductive songs through the air; young boys danced boisterously and scooped up and down the streets behind the hip-waving girls; small children played marbles and hopscotch in the squeezed-up yards. The whole place was wrapped in bright April night and there drifted in from the rivers the dwindling, puny songs of what few frogs were left.

Budda challenged his wandering feet for hanging behind and to pick themselves up, for he had a long journey into a far country to make, seeking something he had lost and could only find at Catawba.

Once in Catawba's yard Budda stopped dead-still, letting all his life parade about him, for now he was old and understood much that had once been hidden from his eyes.

He entered the upper back parlor gingerly, stopping before Ole Doc's portrait that hung silently above the small marble-topped table upon which the only light in the room burned. And as Budda looked up to Ole Doc he knew that he was no longer needful of any earthly thing. The great man had fulfilled his order in his allotted time, for he had been a happy, rock-gutted man and lined the land with his good works. Budda keenly watched the eyes of Ole Doc there on the wall as they followed him about over the room. As he started to leave, he turned for another look, and the soft brown eyes were still following him and Budda was charged with desire of all that was good.

He turned again to the three little sturdy steps in the corner that led to the door that opened to the back stairs where Mama Amazon and Only lived. As he stepped up the three little steps, he let his hand slide softly over the little handrail and he tried to vision the ancient Andrew Thornwell who had wrought this rail from a pine tree. And now there was Doctor Tad—that was important, for he was a mighty fine doctor, everybody was saying.

"Gawd, Budda," exclaimed Mama Amazon, lurching up from her chair, patting herself on the forehead, looking wide-eyed, continuing to speak with outrage somewhat trembly on her lips. "Scare the livin daylights outta a body an be done wit em. Enty lose you mind creepin in here that way? Just lack a hant. You had mo better raisin an at. What's wrong wit you?"

"My goodness, Mama, the way you's cuttin up, you'd think I'd come fro the grave, instead of jest over to the hospital. I allus comes in this way and never undergoes a great deal of preliminaries about enterin. I declare, youse's got fire. Don't you know it's spring on the outside or is you just done hardened you hearts agin the rich livin of the great outdoors?" Budda asked, coming standing before the fire as though it were the dead of winter and his blood were very thin. The firelight glistened upon his white hospital coat, which he wore every chance he got when he left the hospital because it marked him when he sailed forth, and he had an overdose of Mama Amazon in him when it came to be selected for the who's who—even of Green Pond. And Green Pond definitely had a who's who, though it might be questionable and somewhat hazy.

"Son," said Only, biting off a large chaw of tobacco, as much as the inside of his cheek would endure, "get you a chair an pull up to the fire."

"Yes, set down, Budda; a lil fire feels good to ole folks these chilly nights o spring. Where's Vic and Tad? Gawd only knows, they never comes home very often no mo."

"They's busy," said Budda, taking a chair beside Sandy, then looking at Sandy's book, asking, "What's you readin, Sandy?"

"*Macbeth*. Next year we'll read *Hamlet*. I can't wait," Sandy replied, easing his chair over in order to make room for Budda. "Is Dad still operating?"

"I don't know iffen he be still operatin or not; he done twelve today."

"You don't say," Mama Amazon butted in, and then, "He's goin to outdo heself some of these days in the times to come, shore as Gawd made him. Enty right many patients in the hospital?" she asked.

"I bet so," Budda vowed, buttoning up his stiff white coat to call to them its dignity and what it stood for. Then he began to speak in an enriched, far-off voice, filled with mysteries, "I don't guess us'll be seein Missy much mo over to the hospital, though Gawd only knows she an Miz Jezebel shore plied it in the time that Mr. Robert was a-livin."

Mama Amazon bobbed her busy head and she regarded Budda in questioning awe. "*Was* livin? What do you mean, Budda?" Sandy quit studying *Macbeth* and searched Mama Amazon's face.

Budda regarded his white coat and spoke as one of the eminent, "Why, he's dead."

"Jesus do have mercy, why didn't you tell us? Do you think us is mind readers? When did he die? You acts so vast aloft and distinguished-lack."

"Oh," he began, as though it were obnoxious trivia, yet secretly marveling that he was keeping them in suspense, "he been dead a good while, but they had to do the autoppin, so Lovebird an Lovebird couldn't get he until a few hours ago and I had to stay there an wait."

"Was Miz Jezebel an Missy there wit he when he up an die?" Mama Amazon asked.

"No, enty nobody there. I fount he when I went to take he's supper. Vic say he been dead fo several hours. Vic couldn't make up he's mind iffen he died in he's bed or the floor—us fount he on the floor."

"Ah, Lawd," Mama Amazon said, " a vast rich man have departed this here earth. An in he's time the touch of he's fingers to the pen have oppressed many, many, bowin em low wit they necks ever near to the choppin block, the ax swung threatenin'ly always above em. In he's time, he own half of Green Pond County, as though it was hisn in the beginnin. He ain't takin em wit him. I never will fo'get that time I took that tore-in-two five-dollar bill to the bank an ask he was it any mo good; an he says, holdin up the two pieces, 'Ah, Auntie, I think maybe I can give you about two dollars on it.' I didn't know no better neither!" She doubled over with horseplay laughter, bobbing her bushy gray head so vigorously that Dish had to stop combing for a bit.

"Yes, sir," said Only, spitting into the shifty fire, "he was one mo case in he's time. He tried he's best to get a whole block o houses away from Yellow Sam in Doubtin Hollow, but Yellow Sam was too sharp fo he and I think good ole Jepson Grady wised Sammy up somehow. That Jepson Grady is a good man, powerful lack Ole Doc."

"I declare," said Budda, after they had finished speaking their minds, "youse ought not be talkin so much about he. I kinda got so I lacked the ole feller there in the hospital. I allus had to tend him. But I never knowed nothin much about him until he come to the hospital. He shore believed in em nose-glasses. When he'd get on one of he's big spells of talkin about the rats gettin into he's money an he's property an carryin everythin off, he'd blink at me lack a big owl an tell me to never trust silver or gold fo rats lusted after that mo'an anythin on earth. An when I'd tell Miz Jezebel that the rats was carryin off Mr. Robert's silver an gold, why she'd hush-hush me up wit her hand an tell

me that she already had that an fo me not to worry my head
about it. He raved about many thin's that I didn't know no
nothin bout durin he's illness. I believes the ole feller was
lonely—you know, never did nobody come to see em. Wonder
why?"

"Budda, didn't nobody know he was up there in the first
place, so how could they be goin to see him? Miz Jezebel kept
that kivvered up good. I'll bet a dime when it comes out in the
paper, it won't say nothin about him dyin in no local hospital.
Budda, you been around that woman all this time an ain't
ketched on?"

"Ketched on? What you means, Mama?"

"The only reason Miz Jezebel has kept Mr. Robert in that
hospital is so that she could be aroun Vic as much as possible—
he's still her loadstone," she laughed. Dish stopped combing,
listening, and Sandy Peeler became all eyes, wondering what
shadowy illusions were crouched about Dad, the only person to
whom he had ever felt very close in his life.

Sandy was wise in the ways of life, for the turbulent current
which had tossed him from monotony to a life that was most
pleasing had sharpened him. He was old beyond his frail years
and he grasped the profound truth of old age, the time in a
man's life when the last drops are so sweet, so much sweeter
than when the cup is lipment full, when events take on a marked
and measured meaning.

So this night, an eventful and concerned night for the Green
Ponders, Sandy tried to keep along with the Macbeths, but a
lonely, weird hunchback kept getting in his way and blurring
the typed pages and his brain swayed as though it were dimmed
autumn. So he stopped reading and thought of his music.

"Lawd, Sandy," said Mama Amazon, slapping her hands
into the bless-pat manner, "you'll have to play fo the funeral
whenever they haves it. I'm shore gonna hear that. I'm goin
real early an climb into the balcony. I knows that's gonna be

some fine, vast funeral. It naturally takes em kind to get an In-church into the ground—I wonder do the worms appreciate it any mo better? He was too busy grabbin fo money to build he-self a scropugus, so he'll have to be contented wit the white worms an tree roots. Course now, they might put em in one of em fine termite-proof boxes they uses fo the vast rich, but it won't do no good. All he's life here on the red land he have had the boll weevils in he's hair, so some worms won't hurt nothin now."

"Dad said it was microbes he had in his brain, and not boll weevils," said Sandy.

"Hit was a sumpin up there, fo true," said Budda.

The soothing night wore away into its middle. Mama Amazon talked in her fancy voice, peppered with mockery and remem-brance.

Sandy, a bit of uncertain imagination, the substance that tears are made of, listened to her as Vic had listened in his childhood, and his imagination was as a hummingbird's tongue that can get the drops of honeyed sweetness from the almost unobtaina-ble crevices in delicate flowers. And Mama Amazon was filled with simple human affection and honesty about herself and everybody else—that, Sandy knew, could be counted on, counted on to endure—to pass all things, beyond the stardust, beyond the galaxy of stars.

Muggins, the Boston bull, sat at his feet and often indicated, with smooching whines and little know-all motions, that it was bedtime; but then Sandy would pacify him by scratching his tail bone with his toe and Muggins would be contented to sit, all-eared and all-eyed, and listen the longer. Sandy was uncertain of this sweet-jawed death that Mama Amazon spoke of. He feared it. He didn't like to be about the hospital too much where Dad and Tad stayed the greatest share of their time, for there were too many people rolled out the back way and they were always covered up on the little wagon. And even when Dad came home and Sandy sniffed him, he always smelled of the hospital and cold, clammy death.

3

Ossie Grady laughed at Jep, "Good, I'm glad it isn't an Inchurch wedding. Don't strain yourself, old boy."

The Green Pond *Observer* came out with an immense picture of Green Pond's beloved banker, who, it said, had rendered incalculable significance to the betterment of Green Pond. It listed his pallbearers and the honorary pallbearers, whose names filled a whole column of the paper and whose bodies, once seated at the funeral, would fill over half of North Bethel's pews. The news elaborately recorded his good deeds so that his name lived on forever and was not scorned into oblivion. It was written into the stardust. It was written forever and all times. The two-column editorial extolled his virtues beyond any shadows, beyond any sticky question. It was read, with great tooth sucking, by the he-goats and the she-goats of Green Pond, compassionately, and their commendations were as the white sands in the bottom of the sagacious red river. They whispered it about the entire watershed on their thick, fat tongues.

But only Jepson Grady knew what Victor thought of his adventure into the Inchurch's thinking contraption. With his little trephine Vic had bored a hole into the Inchurch skull to see that avaricious brain. And he sawed and hammered and made quite a few buttons and took quite a squint at the apparatus, with Doctor Tad doing much more than assisting. But Robert Inchurch's forlorn brain had not a great deal of information to leave posterity.

4

The lights in the Thornwell Hospital were on from its bottom to its top. It stood out in the gathering darkness singularly restful. Doctor Thornwell and Nurse Kenny Kimball watched Budda truck the patient out of the operating room, a little girl whose liver had been badly torn by indirect violence, and the tear Vic had sutured with mattress sutures, using a round, non-cutting liver needle.

Nurse Kenny sighed, "Patients are rushed in here and we rush into the patients. Reckon she'll make it, Vic? That was a bad tear."

"How'd you know?" Vic asked solemnly. "Doctor Springs didn't seem to think so and he was right into the incision with me, tying and clamping off."

Kenny shrugged her shoulders, "I'd hate for Doctor Springs to get hold of me—there's never much wrong with anyone, to hear him tell it. It was your face. I've not worked with you all these years for nothing. I can tell from the wrinkles on your face just what's down in the gaping incision, be it obstructed intestines or a hardheaded pancreas. And your grunts, Vic, are works of art when your fingers touch a hardening liver."

Vic headed for the washroom, skinning out of his gloves. "Kenny, I won't be back tonight to whip together another torn liver. Anything bad comes up, call Tad—though it was a joyous battle with this liver and sometimes, Kenny, I wonder what in the devil I'm battling against and for. That little girl would have been much better off dead. What is there to sucking air in and out a few more years; what is this living that everyone talks about? But everybody loves it."

"Get on out of here. What are you trying to do, throw up a fence?" asked Kenny. And he was gone and Kenny stood watching him go.

Her face blocked itself with filed records, including a deep symphonic rest that had been the chronology of her life since she donned a nurse's uniform. When she had first loved him, she had been jealous, and then it had grown into something warm, and now there was never any feeling of it being annihi-

lated. He was the one being in her life that stood far above re-
proach.

And Victor left her and he wandered through the night,
scared and affrighted. He stopped walking and looked sadly
across a moonlit place that used to be a cotton field and his soul
reeked with a singular loneliness. The April wind blew strongly
about his tired face and he listened tentatively to it, sopping up
its tats of melancholy. His mind quaked with thoughts of the
long bygone.

And he wandered on through Green Pond's mystery-shrouded
outer rings until dawn, and the birds gave out song and the red
sun rose. What had been a cotton field was now Cornbread
Corner, as the unsmiling sign rightly avowed, and Vic turned
into Cornbread Corner and wandered about freely through its
narrow, rowdy streets.

Way in the morning he heard North Bethel's big bell tolling,
summoning what remained of Robert Inchurch, and Vic's fear,
which had not abated through the night, increased. Deep within
him there was a fearful tremor, for he knew now sooner or later
Jezebel would catch him when he was standing this still and
then he would have to face her and have it out once more. He
had kept clear of her all these years, in spite of her babies and
her Red Cross bandages and her husband; in spite of Sandy and
the church organ; in spite of the way she looked at him and
invited him and what she had managed to do, once or twice, to
his blood. They were both of them getting old now; but she had
never stopped rubbing her hands up and down her hips; and she
would never think she was old; and she would never let him be.

The wind, the strong fragrant wind of April, blew over the
purple, lofty mountains and into his face and his mind turned
to Gawd and he nuzzled close to Him. And there arose in him
a joy. Small children playing in April's after-the-rain mud
looked at him questioningly; and he looked at them with a
tenderness. And his heart was touched with contriteness. And

his thoughts returned to Jezebel now that the curtains of their lives were drawing closer together, closer together today than they used to be. When the curtains came together, there would be darkness—unless there was stardust.

5

Jezebel had lain lathered in her grief in her bedroom and be-meaned and belittled her would-be friends and the floral offerings as they were brought to her one by one. But when Sandy Peeler dropped by, dashing and so tall and long-jointed that he looked to be put together with hinges, Jezebel turned on her array of smiles. She discussed the funeral music for Robert with him in eagerness, in a lily-lilting voice. Even with sky-blue eyes and sandy hair, inclined to be curly, there was something imperatively marked upon Sandy that gave him an uncanny resemblance to Victor, so Jezebel lay in her bed and soaked Sandy into her system, feeding the light within her as the lantern wick feeds the kerosene to the flame. Cautiously eying Sandy, she wondered could it be true—there had been so much talk over her bridge table!

Missy had got Jezebel up, washed her, gowned her, and taken her to the funeral.

Of the seven preachers who filled North Bethel's pulpit, Jake had the center chair, with the immane tall back and handsome carvings, and he was flanked on both sides by three ministers and they looked steadfastly over the multitude.

For the Inchurch funeral, Jake now came forward and stood at the great gold Bible, reading in his most lugubrious funeral voice. His mind was as turbulent as troubled red waters, now that he had reached the greatest prayer-state of his life upon the red land, when the very life in him had been squeezed out, as all the juice is squeezed from the grapes to make the wine and there is nothing left but the mashed-up, soggy pulp which has no beginning nor any ending. Jake read: "Let not your hearts be troubled—"

The Inchurch funeral was an unmistakably big to-do.

6

Sometime that summer and somewhere around Green Pond's chastely pasture, the Ministerial Association had let the bars down and the sinful likker dealers had once again slipped into Green Pond in a twentieth-century vehicle and opened their legalized likker stores upon the main drag and displayed their sin-bottles more glittery than the serpent's eyes. The angry churches were demonstrative and indubitably conclusive—hell was popping. The intensely hot and ardent preachers' sermons burned fierier than the likker. North Bethel attacked the likker more violently than it had ever attacked the Northern Presbyterian Church. Jezebel, who was the monstrance of North Bethel, swore vengeance upon this likker.

That summer the earth was silvery at night from the light of the moon, by day it was golden by the light of the sun, the mockingbirds sang of eternity, dishonest crows built flat-sticked nests atop the tallest pines, possums wagged their young in their pockets with the youngs' tails hanging out in the open, and Mama Amazon and Victor often went fishing on the backwaters with Only rowing them over the placid red waters, its pinkish spume settling about the fishing corks.

"Sandy don't know what he's missing," said Vic, threading a worm on the hook. "Don't see why he has to practice so much on that church organ."

Mama Amazon gave one of her big hoots of disdain, "Ain't so certain it's allus church organ."

"What do you mean?"

"Sandy's powerful gal-crazy this summer."

"That's natural; they get that age, you know."

In an operating room on the seventh floor of the Thornwell Hospital, Vic belabored over an intestinal obstruction. All night he had been harassed with imperative emergencies. At midnight there had been a young man with acute appendicitis with perforation over which Vic had sadly shaken his head. Nevertheless it was often amazing how Gawd had fashioned the insides of a man so that he could rot away, even to bringing about the dreaded complications of fecal fistula, and still see the day when he could take up from his bed and walk. Then there had been two cases of perforated gastric ulcers, both with a beginning peritonitis, within several hours of each other.

"So this is Betty Mae Hill," said Doctor Thornwell, philosophically and reminiscently, to the nurses who were caring for the intestines with pads and hot saline as he brought them out from the peritoneal cavity. "Well, she's getting to be a ripe old age and a bad set of guts here in my hands. We'll probably get her through this and she can stagger back into the Inchurch mills to grab up hot string ends. Ought to be getting good at it by now, started when she was six. She's had the tired patience of a tick who might lie in waiting for as much as eighteen years for his first bite to eat. That's predestined in the stardust, Kenny." Their eyes met over their masks. "So I cut out a length of rotting gut, cut to where the blood is bright and greedy to go on living, and then I put the guts back together. Kenny, shall it be end-to-end or side-to-side or end-to-side anastomosis? I must leave no loose string ends hanging around: she never did in the Inchurch mills."

"You're getting too tired," Kenny said, dry-mouthed. "Better let up. And when are you going to see Mrs. Inchurch? She's chortled for you all summer."

7

Doctor Victor Thornwell trudged through the blinding snow-storm which the dark hours of early morning were rushing upon the face of the red land as leaves trembling in moonlit windy trees. He was swallowed into the hungry jaws of the tempestu-ous storm and he was, indeed, very glad that he was walking. He sapped a certain strength out here in the open, battling with his Gawd. He threw his long legs rapidly in front of him as if his life depended on it. Here feelings and emotions welled into him that he could not describe. Life here was wrapped in a mys-tery that excited curiosity in him, filling his mind with sweet torment.

There was nobody stirring; the town was solitude and loneli-ness; the street lights cast flimsy shadows; the wind whipped over the tops of the buildings and blew gusts of snow up and down the deserted streets. At times it was in a spontaneous, whirlwind dance of youth and then it blew softly and grievously quiet against the dark edges of the buildings and was in whispers of the aged.

Arriving at the hospital, Victor entered the front door and he glanced at the switchboard operator, noting that she was push-ing her plugs into the board, talking steadily into the mouth-piece; he went up the steps to the first floor and went down the hall to his office. And there he found Jezebel waiting.

"Jezebel, what on earth are you doing here at this ungodly hour of the morning?" She stood leaning against the edge of his office door, wrapped in a fur coat.

"What are you doing here yourself?" she asked saucily.

"I'm a doctor. We have to get out in all sorts of weather and nature is never too kind to us old fellers." He was serious, his mind filled with myriad, topsy-turvy questions. "We have to take what is sent on us, renounce the weather, and go on. It's rough out this morning and that's why I can't get it through my head why you are here."

Girlish mischief played about her mouth. "Perhaps I have a pain. Perhaps I couldn't sleep. You surely know how it is when you can't sleep? Perhaps I got stranded here in the snowstorm. Oh, there could be many stupid reasons why I'm here. One of the main ones, quite naturally, was to see you. I felt sure I'd picked a magical hour when you couldn't escape me so easily as you've been doing and at this hour I didn't think that band of your nurses would start getting between you and me. I still remember that you have a fondness for getting up way before daylight and tramping around. You never will grow up, will you?"

"What's the big idea in getting me grown up so fast? I've plenty of time for that yet. The hours before dawn have always fascinated me. I usually can live closer to Gawd that way. When daylight comes and the busy day begins and the people push and shove in the trade of the day, there's not the tormenting beauty to be found that was so abundantly flung about just a few hours earlier. I've always lived for those bits of sheer beauty that come my way—and I don't like to miss out on them. See?"

"You never go to church and surely you have no knowledge of God. Yet you're always bandying about with your being so close to Him. I simply don't believe it. Here you are, sixty-some years old, and have never joined the church. I wonder what old Doctor Thornwell would say about that—he being an elder and all—and what does Jake say?"

"Jay-bell, you amaze me no end—you amaze me more than the stars of heaven and all eternity—and no man understands that amazement. So you came here to the hospital to give me a lecture on joining your church before daylight on a snowy morning? Indeed, this is most strange. Quite bewildering."

"Victor Thornwell, I see nothing so strange about it. You could always make the biggest mystery out of almost nothing.

You won't come to see me, so why shouldn't I come to see you?"

"Why in the world would you want to see me?" He looked up and down the hallway. "Let's move back into the office and sit down." He closed the door. "You surely could find many more things upon the face of the red land to amuse yourself with besides me. Surely now with the Inchurch fortune resting snugly and securely in your lap there's nothing else that you want."

"You bewilder me and you club me as nothing else can do." He helped her and she slipped her fur coat off her shoulders and leaned her head back on the seat of the chrome-framed, leather-cushioned seat. "I have not been prudent in coming here, and I know you will do nothing but mock me and pelt me with your tongue. I came here this morning to throw all my cards upon the table to you and to see what you'd say about it. Why is it that we cannot pick up from here and go on together? You certainly have in times cared a little something for me, and for me you have always been the only thing going. I used to ask myself would I always be so foolish over you—even when you were old—and I find that it's much worse today than when we were younger. Vic, for God's sake, let's do something about it! Robert's out of the road now. We don't have as many years left as we did. I've existed through the years with this one hope burning in my heart! It's winter now and very cold, but this warmth here, within, with you, Victor—let us have love!"

"Yet when Robert tried his best to take the hospital away from me—to beat me out of it—you knew what he was doing, I dare say. For all I know you might have aided and abetted him. I have forgiven your Robert his impetuousness and his many pilfering mischiefs, for what good does it do to hold within my heart grudges against the carcass of such as he?"

"Oh, Vic, don't be that way. He was an evildoer and an oppressor all his life. Had I tried to stop him from trying to take the hospital and Catawba, he would have been right down on me. You have no idea how jealous he was of you. He knew deep within him that I never loved him, and that the only person I ever loved was you."

"No, Jay-bell. You have what you want in your church and the Inchurch fortune and I have what I want here in the hospital. It would never do for our lives to cross more than they have. I go my way doing what good I can. There might have been a time—but we have run into a dilemma, and as Pop so often used to point out to me, the forked roads. I have no life of my own. You have been the center of your life."

"Vic. Vic." Her eyes became moist. "You'll have me crying the first thing you know. Do you remember when I cried that night in Catawba a long time ago? I haven't cried since lo those years ago in the long, long bygone. You're the only person that can make me cry, but no wonder. You have been the only person I've ever loved—and now it looks as though I'm losing you for good. The years that I have planned and dreamed of this. Vic, tell me it isn't true."

"Yes, it must be true. It is for the best. We do not see alike now. Perhaps had we started off together younger we might have been all right; but now, no."

Jezebel's eyes brimmed with tears. "Tell me, my lord, what is right about me? I'm tortured through the day. I suffer sleepless nights. What I would give for one good night of sound sleep! I jump at the least noise, startled at my own lurching shadow. Nothing seems secure. My nerves stay screwed to the screaming point. What will I do? Where shall I find peace? I can't go on this way."

"I'm sorry for you, Jay-bell." He glanced at the clock on the wall. "I have five operations scheduled for this morning. It'll soon be time for me to get on up there and get scrubbed up. You know, Jay-bell, each operation brings me a more lasting joy than the previous one. It does something to me that any individual love can't equal. Perhaps it is love itself—for man and his weakness."

"Oh, God, Vic." She took his hand into her lap, patted it, her tears dropping silently. "Vic, don't drive me out. It shall break my heart into a million little pieces and each one of them shall rise up and cry out to you day and night."

"You see the clock hands are turning—there might be someone besides you who wants to go on living. I'm sorry."

8

Jezebel left the hospital in the swirling snow and hoisted herself into her waiting automobile, whose engine Goldie had kept idling to keep himself from freezing to death. Goldie cut corner-eyed glances at her when he helped her into the automobile, for he knew where Miz Jezebel had been and for what purpose, and he hated to have to do the laborious driving through the snow to the Pink House before he could fetch this strange news to the other servants.

In the back seat Jezebel crossed her shapely legs and tossed her swinging foot in spurious sophistication and shrugged her thin and delicately curved shoulders under the warm furs in mock disdain. At sixty-nine years of age, she was nobody's slouch. Her appearance was as deceiving as herself.

Nobody knows the actual grief and pain I carry in my heart now, she thought. *I can never put it into words; you can't make words for losing the one thing you love most in the world.*

For the time being she was down, but she would never give up hope. All the rowdy years of her life yawned before her and she went through them cautiously, looking, picking them apart piece by piece to see where she had tripped up. If there were only some way that she could go back and start all over again; if there had been some way she could have dodged the wagon whip in Ma's hand. She had fought getting old as though she had been fighting the battle of Armageddon and what had it wrought her? *That man!* That two-legged man yonder in the Thornwell Hospital.

Tears welled into her eyes and she bit her lips and shook her head. He'd be laughing way up his sleeve at her, if he only knew in what condition he had her now.

Well, she had begged for him for the last time! He would never get another chance to refuse her. She'd never give him that satisfaction again! Or would she?

By a supreme effort of will, she kept the unbidden tears from falling and she gathered the cloak of her bitter humiliation about her, the cloak of her hurt, this last hurt that she would ever let Victor Thornwell give her. And then she cast around in her mind for something with which to pierce him, to hurt him to the inner heart, to make him feel the raging pain and the grief and the sickness that she felt as she rode to her great Pink House.

Passing through the main part of Green Pond she continued to cast around in her mind to fetch something to get even with Vic and pay him back for all the years that had led to this very morning. What would it be? She'd make Victor pay and pay dearly.

Ma had interfered too many years ago with the wagon whip, whipped the stardust too furiously. Bitter hate and plotting remorse filled her chock-full. Love and hate lay so near together in the scale of human emotions that it was easy to modulate from one key to the other. She'd take what was left. If she couldn't play in the major scale, she'd play in the minor. And her brain fermented with weird plans.

9

The years twisted and turned and in these green days Jacob had grown to be an old bald-headed man, whimperingly stingy and poverty-stricken. He walked as a mechanical mannequin, and the very life had been squeezed from him. His days were tedious; he went about making his pastoral calls; he went through the hospital sketchily once a week, saying many flighty prayers and hurrying onward as though he were about offal. His wit was most effectively displayed before the gentle ladies' clubs and the men's clubs of Greater Green Pond. Often he drank too many of their drinks and felt as a breeze among the leaves of the trees and wondered the next day if they had noticed it and laughed about him afterward.

The church was no longer as it used to be. The assistant pastors preached often and Jake sat in the Thornwell pew, a deserted lonely old man, and his mind was filled with much dissatisfaction.

The church's interior had been reworked. The great glittering chandelier was gone to make room for indirect lighting. The sacred seven columns, with climbing vines and tendrils, the leaves and grapes, were chopped out; the young robe-flapping assistant preachers preferred the open chancel. There were long-robed altar boys running about the church lighting a multitude of candles. There were altar vases filled with flowers, and higher in the center a huge brass cross. The hostesses, the secretaries, the directors ran hither and thither over the church night and day. And the organist was forever at the job.

10

Mama Amazon trudged about in the kitchen of Catawba long before day was yet clean. She punched the fire, watching the sparks fly up the chimney with her wrinkled, world-weary eyes. It was hardly cold enough for fire, but a cheery fire warmed old folks' hearts and this morning she was most needful of having her disturbed heart warmed. She listened to the chirping crickets out in the yard and shook her head sadly and hummed to the good Master, reminding Him that it wouldn't be long until she came home.

Only had been gone from her for a long time now, even many of her children she had buried. Her days upon the red land of the watershed with the Scottish Presbyterians had been happy ones, each one fulfilling its portion of the predestined stardust. But now she was getting tired and going home filled her ever wakeful hours and even in her sleep she was never certain of whether she was going home or just for a cat nap, for she felt sure that death would be that lovely a sleep.

Mama Amazon wanted this breakfast to be long remembered by Vic and Sandy. She had the table set like it was for one of Catawba's old to-do's and she knew she was fooling no one except herself. She was simply living in a shy, childish, make-believe world, but she wanted them dining in style once more and that to her would be soothing as medicine to the sick, it would take the sting and torment from her old heart.

With breakfast ready, she would go get Vic up, if he hadn't been called out on an errand of mercy in the dead of the night; but he was there breathing in restful sleep. He had always slept so sound and peaceful as if he never had a care in the world. She believed to her soul that he could fall sound asleep right after one of his most harassing operations. She guessed it was because his goings-on inside were at peace.

"Sandy, what're you going to play in church today?" Vic asked.

Sandy's head emerged from looking into his plate, his eyes flickered as a fading song, and he dropped his face, gazing unconcernedly into his plate, shutting out all reality. Then he murmured thickly in an unchanging voice, an uneventful voice, "Nothing."

"Nothing? Why?"

"Dad, have you been so well hidden behind that operating

mask that you didn't know I was fired a long time ago?" and Sandy's face dropped into his plate.

"No, son—I had no idea. Is there sumpin I can—"

"No, Dad, there's nothing you can do," Sandy's voice drifted as unreal and remote as moonlight upon the red river, filled with haunting shadows and lengthening illusions. "You'll have to excuse me, Dad, I'm all washed up with a headache." He rose from the table and walked measuredly from the room, his body seeming to flow along.

Mama Amazon caught the puzzled look upon Vic's countenance and took it to her heart, then she swooped it upward with the speed of a hawk ascending with prey, for all her erstwhile philosophy gave her a calm burning of skilled rightness in the wilderness of doubt and she confirmed Vic's dishonest misgivings. "There's sumpin bad wrong wit that boy. He's been as bereft as people under a wagon load of grief fo the longest time. He's palm-waving an singsong joy is been blowed away fro he and he wanders as a scapegoat in the scrub oaks."

Victor's voice was filled with concern, he wiped his mouth with the linen napkin, stared thoughtfully at the myriad flimsy shadows the candles cast. "How long has this been going on? Sandy's spent entirely too much time downtown. He's never had the hankering for rambling in the woods and along the river and the play places about Grandpa Andrew's old house that I used to have. Of course, I've no right to expect that, I guess."

"No," she answered flatly. "Sandy's weak, an when sumpin goes wrong on he's insides, he takes the easiest road out. He just naturally ain't rock-gutted. I think—I don't think neither, I knows: Sandy is drinkin lack a catfish in the bend of the river. An he'll keep on until he's just lack a hog an got to get down an wallow in em."

"My Gawd, drinking?" Vic exclaimed.

"Yes, sumpin has happened to that boy somewhere. You

watch em shifty eyes, em flutterin fingers. That ain't the Sandy that uster be. An he never cracks a book no mo. An I did hope he'd finish that last year o college, fo in high school he uster come to we's room an study he's fool head offen he's shoulders. I bet iffen it wasn't fo you, they'd done had him throwed out of that school too."

"What caused this, Mama Amazon?"

"I haves my own suspicions about that," she said, chunking up the fire as though she were destined to chunk fires and make them mind her and sing happily for her. There was a poverty-like silence in the room, a wishinglike atmosphere in the air, yet it foreshadowed a headfirst collision, a brewing of bearing-down storms which perhaps would reach maniacal action.

"What is it?"

Her old eyes flickered up to him, then dropped into the smartly burning blaze. "You know how Miz Jezebel is?"

"Jezebel? Why, Jezebel was the very one who wanted Sandy to play that church organ years ago." But a sickly fear took root in him.

"I didn't say she didn't want Sandy to play the organ—at one time," Mama Amazon said. "But times and peoples changes. Tell me, Vic, enty turned she down?"

She saw his head fall into his raised hands; she hated to see her caul-headed chile suffer like this. There was nothing she could do but go on like she had been doing. She had lost weight until she was thin. She had smothery spells once in a while, but she would not give up. She had been too long in the house of these Thornwells not to understand them, too long at Catawba not to be as tough and rock-gutted as any of them, and she wanted always to ape Ole Doc and be steady on she feets when she went. She had Dish to do the heaviest part of the housework, but when it came to waiting on the doctors, Mama Amazon did that. She let Vic be and she cleared away the dirty dishes of the half-eaten breakfast.

11

BEELZEBUB: When was it this here good likker come back to this here country? Lack olen times, enty?

SATAN: Oh, it's been quite a few years—the year Elizabeth Inchurch Buckgin died.

BEELZEBUB: Well, she died shortly after she was married.

SATAN: Yah, she was pregnantly married in holy wedlock in Nof Bethel—so it ain't no need fo you to be countin on you fingers. You ain't no ole woman nohow. At that time Miz Jezebel was glad to get she married off pregnantly—even to Buckgin the Baptist.

BEELZEBUB: That makes all the Inchurches dead and gone but Danny Boy an Miz Jezebel. Believes Gawd's gonna wipe em all fro the earth.

SATAN: Yah, strange times in the land. Chillun is upsettin they parents every day. It's blamed on the big war, but I's enjoyin this new war.

BEELZEBUB: Competition's good in this land.

SATAN: So's this new wine an beer they's sellin here in town. What'll the churches do about em? Us had a hard time gettin em back. Hope they don't discommandment this likker too soon.

BEELZEBUB: Why?

SATAN: Me an Miz Jezebel's done spawned a good plan an he's startin to work powerful good, too.

But Heaven was wounded by the transgressions on Earth, bruised and made sore with iniquities, and the angels hid their tears.

GAWD: Don't no mo hear the sweet music comin up fro Nof Bethel. I feels so downright sad.

GABRIEL: You oughtn't let em happen.

GAWD: Oh, well, he fo the best; my angels I want home. I never created he fo down yonder long. Not my Sandy Peeler.

GABRIEL: Yes, Sandy's very frail. Won't take that rotgut long to destroy he's body.

GAWD: That's what I'm aimin; I just misses My music fo today.

20

Sandy was a long-gone fellow. There was nothing anyone could do. Vic's heart broke every time he brought Sandy back from some scummy hovel to Catawba and saw him slip away into his likker-born dreams again. His heart broke whenever he went after Sandy and whenever he didn't go because he was too busy to make the long, fine-tooth-comb search that finding Sandy required.

The old folks of Green Pond knew about it, nodded their sage heads, saying wisely that blood would out, and they were opinionated and compared the past with the present and sputtered a great deal about what ought to be. The winds of heaven spurned the arty formation of the great cumulus clouds that boiled and spumed in the blue up yonder and spurred them to a squally trot.

On one of those sad, periodic searches, Vic scrouged into an impossible parking place on Main Street, slithered out of the car.

His long strides outstripped many popeyed onlookers who behaved childishly and stared at him after he had wisped far past them. Green Pond was taking on its singularly incurable night life, that was diffused and agitated with untoward goings-on—without pause it hiccuped, miffed, and fretted, and over it all was a gauzy glow of integrity filtered to familiarity with the glowing lights. He heard the church bells ringing out their acclaims for Jesus. The whole street was as brilliant and gaudy as a circus poster. Rutting boys and girls clotted together in fledgling amatory and the night wove a spell with their wispy ways more than the deep-graven gusts of spring.

Radios shrilled and trilled and blared forth their wares, he noticed with a delightful grin on his face. There was preaching among the preacher boys on the corner, he heard the hymns anticked straight up to God. He searched and siphoned the haunts where Sandy's incurable thirst for whisky now led him: the taxi yards where the gossamer raglike taxi drivers hung about waiting for the trumpeting calls of the whores to be driven out into the nostalgic countryside with their men—the cheap cafes that smelled acridly of wine and beer and spittle and spume and sweating bodies—the railroad stations where the cheap and tawdry tarts reeked of indecencies—behind North Bethel where there was an alley that was brambly clustered with honeysuckle vines where the novelty boys and girls went often to do their erotic playing—but in all these there was a not-thereness. Sandy, for this night, seemed to be a long-gone fellow—as before, and before, and before.

Vic drove, circling Green Pond's Saturn-like rings, streaking through the hot-dog-strung settlements. He hoped that somewhere along the way he would find him: that little frail Sandy Peeler that used to be. That wisp of fragile humanity who was suspended here between the finite and the infinite, who was gentler than the wee lamb that followed the good shepherd and whose life was as the nectar in the great white magnolia blooms. Yet Vic knew that such fragility was not long for this earth. That substance, between a tear and a dream, was salt that no longer had any savor in this mad day and time, and it was so easy for the unsavant and too physical to tramp such matters down. Life was scabbed in cruelty and grew more unsavory each day, its waters tossed and splashed over the shoals of time. As he searched for Sandy he tapped out prayer after prayer upon the steering wheel of the car as though he were counting out a rosary. His mind clotted with thoughts, never in frustration or exasperation, but methodically heavy-flavored with suspended intuition. Vic's own integrity kept him balanced.

Skinning to the outer edge of Pecan Lane, just beyond the rows and rows of four-room, square houses that constituted the bulk of Pecan Lane and to the edge where the sturdy-rooted pecans flung their leafy arms skyward, drenched chokingly in glittering moonlight, Vic stopped beside the rusty fence, leaning and warped like an old man, trying to hold its dignity against the onrushing madness of a new and encroaching people, whimpering disgustedly by the side of the road like an armless beggar.

When Vic beheld the fence his heart was so rent with grief, his mind so corroded with memories that he clenched his teeth to restrain the tears. All his life spewed up before him like a geyser. A gauzy feeling filtered to his fingertips and he reached out into the air as though to feel the past in it. As he walked aimlessly he listened intensely to catch the sounds out of the air that had been produced here fifty, seventy-five, a hundred years ago. They were there, if there were only some way of catching them. His lips worked, his eyes were misty, "No, Gawd, no. Let me a little closer, closer—tight and don't let me loose, don't let me go; let this body of mine go. Dying is so easy. Let me not mock the very earth from whence I came. Man, against time, can't always keep the wrinkles from increasing in his face or his hair from turning white. When the leaves of the trees have spent

434

their course, when the time comes for them to go, they slap
paint upon themselves and go gaily, and a poet's breath of
frosty air doesn't necessarily have to blow upon them to get
them into the mood. It's sumpin deep within the subjective
lives of the trees which bids them put on their gay grave robes.
But for man, that tempered creature, there is no such fanfare,
because, even though he be wrinkled and bent, he is too busy
laying up his worries for tomorrow, which might and which
might never come."

Here nearly all the Inchurches were buried. The place was
vine-grown and weedy. Here Jezebel would be lain when she
was through with her earthly mischief. A ferny smell arose from
the earth. The dilapidated, ancient Inchurch house was gradually falling down. It had caved in in the middle, sweeping downward from its massive stack chimneys. The porch had caved in.
Somewhere out there in that moonlit thicket stood old man Inchurch's crumbling sarcophagus with the solid flat stone for a lid.
Vic knew that by now many popeyed rodents had burrowed
through the crumbling lime and bricks and made their homes
within it.

As he stood there meditating upon the years of his life and
all the things that the energetic stardust predicted, he heard
voices coming from within the thicket and he listened, trying to
localize the source of the voices.

GIRL: Listen, ain't that a car out there in the street?

BOY: I ain't heard nothing but you wetting. Hurry up and
come on. I'll be out of the notion toreckly.

GIRL: I guess you can wait a minute and give me time to
wet.

BOY: You wetting on top of that thing? Ain't that a grave?

GIRL: Don't care. Ain't hurting me none. I like to get high
in the air to wet. Don't see why girls have to squat anyway.

BOY: You oughtn't to be wetting on a body's grave. That's

where the ole feller's put that built all these mills in Green Pond. He's of high honor and ought to be respected.

GIRL: I don't care.

BOY: Hurry up. I'm already about out of the notion to.

That could be Sandy out there, Vic knew, but what was he to do? Here was Pop's forked road. Vic stood and debated.

2

Winter piled up her snow high against the foundation of the great Thornwell Hospital where it imposed in the south hills of Green Pond. The great oak on the front lawn that supported the ancient grape vine was gowned in flimsy gauze as though she were a great lewd lady on the loose. The earth was silent under the weight of the snow.

From a cozily warm chartroom on the seventh floor in the south wing, Tizzy and Kenny drank steaming coffee and looked across the treetops and the rooftops at the lazy, peaceful smoking chimneys; upward the gray-black clouds continued to push themselves southward uncompromisingly, assuredly doped with more snow. Between Miss Tizzy and young Nurse Kenny Kimball there was now not even a shabby degree of jealousy over Doctor Victor Thornwell, but almost unthinkable unvouched understanding.

Tizzy had grown up with the hospital, she had helped to set up the first furniture, put curtains and shades to the windows. She had worked as a field hand. She had been young then, the muscles in her belly capable of a push. Her education had never gone to her head as water sometimes does to cabbage heads and she was quite capable of downright sweaty work, and now that her hair was frostlike she kept it rinsed blue and still ran the Thornwell Hospital efficiently. She often pondered, filching into her memory, recalling the number of girls she had painstakingly taught in the Nursing School and she always made sure that all her student nurses were adequately coached to sail past the state board at examination time. To what degree she loved Doctor Thornwell the nosy Green Ponders had yet not found out. There was never anything they could actually put their fingers to, but —well, but. And in her lengthy years here in the hospital she had worked with Victor through darkness and light, through good times and bad times. She had seen him fail, she had seen him surmount medical obstacles beyond the pale of known medical science, to hurdle cases that no other doctor would touch, such incurable love and curiosity did he have for humanity. His charity operations were uncountable. She had seen him perform almost a miracle with this girl, Kenny, a ward of the hospital.

Kenny could argue and discuss with Vic in a joyous fervor and there would only be that kindly gleam in his eyes and the soft reprimand that sent her scurrying forward through the days and nights. He had given her the best education obtainable; he had given her special coaching for the state board examination so that she flipped past the examining board incisively and her postgraduate work in various hospitals was merely a sauntering song, and once back here in the Thornwell Hospital and head of the operating room she and Vic ironed out, as noisily as crows in a public debate in the top of a tall pine, the complicated kinks that were forever snarling up affairs in the operating rooms.

Kenny set her cup down. "Vic worked on that old woman from one o'clock to six this morning. She'd keep fading out, we'd have to wait until they got her doped up before we could go on. Right now I'd give anything for a couple of hours' sleep. Don't see how Vic stands it, as old as he's getting."

"He's slowing up, too," said Tizzy.

"Takes too many pains with his patients. Why, he spent five hours with that old hag. We struggled to save her life. Next week she'll be home, fighting like a sow cat and her drunk husband'll slit her throat again just to see if he can."

Vic entered quietly. He dropped into a chair beside Kenny and pulled her into his lap. "Tizzy, how about a cup of coffee? Nobody on earth can brew it like you." Then he caught Kenny's doll-like face between his gentle hands.

Kenny laughed, "You'd better be petting Doctor Vernon."

"Why that, Kenny?" Vic asked.

"Did you know he did a cholecystotomy yesterday and it should have been a cholecystomy?" Kenny asked.

"I didn't," said Vic. "That's very unfair to the patient to take the stones out of the gall bladder and sew the gall bladder up. It'll probably fill with stones again—and the same thing over. There're too many rackets like that in medicine. Doctor Vernon is hardly skilled enough to ligate the cystic duct and cystic artery when the gall bladder is removed. Things like that make it bad on doctors and hospitals, but I hate like the mischief not to give him a chance."

"Better do something with him," said Kenny. "You weren't so easy on me. Remember that first kidney operation—the most difficult position to arrange—I set up for you? Boy howdy, you didn't let me off. Now with these breakable tables, setting up for some of those difficult operations is a cinch. Why, you can break the table right under the gall bladder, throw that region upward, bring the organ right out from under the ribs where the most clumsy infant could operate."

"Now, Kenny," Vic remonstrated, "let's not be too hard on old scrawny doctors. Give em a chance."

Kenny thumbed her nose at him and left.

"While you're going, Kenny, you might as well have the operator page Doctor Philips and tell him that I wish to see him."

Tranquillity filled Vic, rested upon his slightly stooped shoulders, and all his years on the red land were with him and he thought of his life as a surgeon and the revolution in surgery. Now he used the Trendelenburg position, the dorsal position, the Sims position, the lithotomy position to go into men and women and there to observe the intricate design Gawd had so fashioned and there to behold the ugly marring by disease. Man was most wonderfully made. Vic could easily remove a badly diseased duodenum and by reconstruction, close off the old outlet of the stomach and with his scalpel make a new opening to which he could attach the intestine, and the man's digestive tract would go on doing a respectable job. He could patch up for a little while many leaks and holes in a man, but after all, no matter how much reanastomosis was done, a man finally played out. He did not slip, he did not err, he sutured his vessels firmly, and he praised Gawd on high for granting this gift to his fingers. When he went, he wanted to go straight forward as Pop had gone. He had tried to be objectively and subjectively honest with himself and it had put him into lots of trouble.

There came a knock on the door.

"Come in," Vic said.

"Did you sleep well last night, Doctor Philips?" Vic asked of the doctor who had entered.

Doctor Philips looked puzzled. "Oh, fine, thank you. But surely that wasn't what you called me up here for?"

"Indeed, I like to know the welfare of the surgeons who operate here in the Thornwell Hospital. You surely know by this time that I make it one of my foremost interests? Did you have a nice time at the ball game day before yesterday? I suppose you know who won?"

"Great game. Never enjoyed myself better."

"It pays to enjoy yourself as much as possible in this world. You ought to go in for baseball. I imagine you'd be better at that than surgery."

"What's up? I don't catch it."

"That isn't amazing. The little girl who was brought in here with a tricky appendix, and whom you were supposed to operate on and didn't, but trekked off to the ball game, is going to die. Now listen, Doctor Philips, we're all human and we all make mistakes, but one more slip-up like that out of you and I'm going to see that you go out of this hospital—in fact, that you never go back into another. Thank you and good day."

Vic turned and looked out the window and gazed across Green Pond. Tears stole to his eyes and he bit them away. He grew elegiac and dropped into a great mist of melancholy. Were all men equal?

He heard the voice of his doctor friend from the Far East, speaking to the Medical Society of Green Pond: "I was born on foreign soil of a minority group; I've known, as a child, what it is to have them yelling 'Foreign devil, foreign devil!' And have them push around me, feeling my head, my arms, my body. Yet, today, in an overcrowded public vehicle, they'll push over, scrouge up, making room for me to have a seat. Yet here in Green Pond I can't get up and offer my seat to one of a different color, for it is forbidden by law."

Day in and day out the people of Green Pond toted their array of pains into the Thornwell Hospital. Doctor Thornwell remained as contagious to women as the seven-year itch and his communicable laughter, shaking his belly, resounded through the halls of the hospital. The nurses drank him as though he were a racy wine; his homely traits fetched them on the run and time and again they flung themselves in his way, hoping to be chosen to push the dressing trays along the hallways as he made his rounds. Or they clambered into his car in stunning numbers when he asked them for a ride and they went ecstatically happy in large numbers and came back to crow over the ones who had had to remain on duty.

The Thornwell Hospital was now overrun with doctors, surgeons, specialists. The callboard stayed lit like a neon sign night and day.

Not long ago there had been a woman surgeon, and when Doctor Tad had seen her dark silent eyes above her mask at the operating table, his eyes had got a gleam and glint in them that Vic had never seen there before. Could this be love?

Vic had drawled, "Well, Granny Joanna was a good'un in her day and she never pulled her pharisaical robe tightly about her in stand-offishness, but went right to the seat of the trouble of the patient—and the trouble was usually in the seat."

Babies popped into the world night and day. The elevators clattered and clanged up and down all night long, for no man could stop his entrance into the world. The doctors and nurses hurried and then they waited and there'd be string of curses and sometimes screams.

A great noise hung in the air, there were unmerciful groans renting the air, and the puny wail of an infant, another little stone in the pond, another little circle of waves started.

None of the other doctors ever knew how much Doctor Vic charged for his handiwork; nor did anyone know when he laid a doctor in the aisle for stupidity.

Vic knew that he could button a man's bowels together and increase his trivial years so that he could withstand the pressure of his brother's foot upon his neck, but what was predestined in the stardust he didn't know.

"Dad, what a seam you sew," said Doctor Tad to Vic, as they ripped off masks and gowns, heading for the washroom. "Nothing in the whole Army to equal you. Funny you don't like clamps."

"Make too many sore bellies."

"What do you think of this new experiment they are doing in replanting kidneys?"

"At least whoever performs those experiments will learn the

knack and whack of good suturing and fine detail work. I know it's good that doctors keep busy."

3

In her old age, Naomi, with internal cancer greatly metastasized, slowly ascended, at nine thirty Sunday morning, the magnificent stone steps into North Bethel Church as queenly royal as the most gracious opera singer. No longer in Green Pond was there such a thing as a Preachin Sunday, for there was preaching all the time. The church doors were never closed and the bells stayed alive for Jesus, booming and clanging, giving rise to a varied and awe-inspiring variety of noises.

Smiling, Naomi began her climb, but not before she had shared her spirit with sheer delight at outright pilfering from the parking meters along the street. She carried a little gold key about her neck that was in the shape of a cross, but it was a parking-meter key that she had once filched from one of the policemen and she had found this little magical weapon a joy when she came to hand-to-hand combat with the stubborn parking meters. For by opening a number of the meters and purloining their contents, her pennies and nickels had a tremendous financial pressure upon the collection plate. When the devout deacon who waited upon her when the offering was received saw her flurry of pennies and nickels tilt the plate sideways, his eyebrows were wholly lifted in searching surprise and he had the feeling that he was dealing with an elegant old pirate; but openly he never dared question it, for he was a chivalrous deacon who was supposed to promote harmony and prosperity and he calculated that although the extravagant display of pennies and nickels never helped the church much and were definitely burdensome to count, she was, undeniably, presenting her offering to the Lord in good faith.

She placed her trim little dainty toes upon the first hallowed step and started up the heavenly steep with heroic exertion. She was such an enthusiast, blindly devoted and doggedly intolerant, that folks were never certain she was all there.

Now all alone in the world, as she put it, Naomi never missed a blessed service at the church. The members acquiesced her as a harmless old toad and let it go at that. She and Myra always sat together in the honored Thornwell pew and the Sundays that the assistant pastors preached Jake sat with them and Naomi's innocence and guile were as untroubled waters, her benign spirit presided nakedly and unashamedly.

This morning as she went up the steps her tread was decidedly secure and her little waist was hardly larger than a lighthearted ant's. She had stuffed an outlandish amount of packing into her bosom, making it stand out rather improperly, still, she hoped, with prestige. Her skirt and petticoats rattled eloquently and icily enough to make her feel gushing. Everyone who saw her thought she was dressed for some shocking event in another world.

Nearly to the top of the great stone steps, the merciless old plotter and pilferer stopped, sighed, and turned around looking with casual disapproval over the sprawling town.

She had been The Doctor's wife. She would let anyone know at any time, any day, about The Doctor and the vivacious days when she was fifteen, when she had outsmarted Sherman and his fire, when she had cheated so many women and become the mistress of Catawba. Ha! A brick house that the old rascal couldn't burn so easily as he had Father's house.

Those loud and resplendent days were gone into the bygone; but still life was serious and not, as some would have it in this modern age, a preposterous adventure. In the becalmed Sunday morning, Naomi stood there on the stone steps and floated around most deliciously, then turned and moved apologetically, her thoughts aligned along the pilfering way; and she bickered a little raucously to herself.

Uncle Simon saw her coming and he was a trifle shocked; his old watch could never be trusted for the correct time to ring the big bell for Sunday school, but that Miz Nee-oom-mee was knowledgeable and never missed hitting that front door right on time.

Naomi stopped in the great arched doorway and listened reassuringly to the big bell tolling out the Sunday-morning invitation, summoning the corruptible to come.

With a slinking yet concerted effort, Naomi slyly turned her head across her shoulder and looked down the dizzy length of steps she had climbed, and she fluttered her waxed eyelids in amazement.

Standing there in the doorway of the church she looked pathetic and lonely and far away. Yet arrayed about her was the outmoded dignity of a church and only a becoming sentiment that aptly and precisely fitted the occasion. Its blood, the racy wine, was gone, and now in its place was a thin, watery grape juice.

4

It was gentle spring in sweet Green Pond. The gardens of the upper crust were wealthy with the multicolored blossoms and cool luxuriant greens, and the patches of the lower crust were filled with tomatoes, beans, and corn. Without segregation the great golden sun worked upon the upper and lower crusts' greens and there was no division of the shades of green.

As the idea of the hypodermic needle, perhaps, came from the fangs of a rattlesnake, so trepanning came from the ancient Egyptian skull-borers. Vic assisted Doctor Tad, who was schooled in trepanning and who, with his little trephine, opened the skull of a man. He did it with exuberant energy, his hands, in keenest dexterity, moved classically and scientifically and, indeed, he was a marveling wonder to the assistants and nurses who worked with him.

Across the chair from him, Vic thought: *Are these Pop's hands —hands that I see before me, probing and delving with inborn instinct? Come, who is it that answers these questions? I have not the answer. Yet these hands are before me still. Oh, wanted, wanted someone to tell me, tell me the answer.*

Jepson Grady, the great old erudite man of Green Pond, walked haltingly, observing shrewdly, to the office of the Green Pond *Observer*. He stopped, chattering with David Kingsley, the kindly old judge, discussing the events of the day, and they moved slowly to their eminent posts.

Jep remarked to Vic, the only one besides his sister Ossie to whom he made such remarks any more, that Jezebel had a look of waiting about her, waiting to be a Gold-Star Mother. "If she doesn't get a telegram soon," Jep said, "I think she's going to send Danny Boy a poisoned box of goobers. She's finally pushed him up to a major, you know. Though it's my opinion that in this Second World War he does nothing more than tear off bits of toilet paper and hand them to the general—naturally, a matter of routine."

Boys and girls dragged themselves to school, and the teachers, looking at these discrepancies, sadly shook their heads in bewilderment and were greatly cast down in spirit and knew their bookish learning was nugatory; yet, being expositors of knowledge, they knew they must cram some synthetic whims into the wool-gathering minds of the rowdy and opinionated lot of the Mom-dollies.

Vic was still stubborn and rebellious and Tad watched across the table as he was doing the appendectomy. Tad noted Vic's slowness, ragged cutting, clumsy and awkward fingers, his muscles stiffening. He'd seen Vic do a simple McBurney in five minutes and today it was going to take him six and a half minutes. It'd make him fighting mad to tell him so.

Tad was the proud father of two sons. Tad and the lady surgeon had found a greater communion than mere medicine.

The North Bethel Church scorned the racy wine Granny Joanna had once fermented for the holy communion, and females publicly displayed as much sinful skin in church as they wanted to and clicked their high-heeled shoes upon the hallowed stone steps and walked out of church forever, because no longer could the solemn Session church them.

5

Each time Vic raked Sandy from his drunken, sordid existence, took him to the hospital, and straightened him out, he slipped away as soon as he was capable of making his wobbly legs brusquely obey him. He dove Vic to incredible despair; the evil he engendered became more and more irredeemable with medical aid. Vic knew that alone now Sandy stood in the mercy of heaven or the curse of hell. Jezebel with her cunning should be dealt with swiftly, but she wouldn't be; she'd go scot-free, and continue on a refined, never-to-be-questioned scale.

In Pecan Lane, where night life was shaking off the scornful day—Pecan Lane always scorned the light—and taking on the nuzzling warmth of darkness, Vic stopped in the red, washboard street, climbed from the car. He stepped upon a rickety porch and knocked upon the door. Waiting for someone to answer, he looked with considerable admiration at the huge geraniums growing in tubs and buckets with touch-me-not gusto.

"Well, well, iffen it hain't Ole Doc Thornwell," lightly exclaimed Betty Mae Hill, twisting her hands around in her long dirty apron in a feeble attempt at drying them. "Won't you come in, Doc? What brings you way out this way?"

"I won't have time, Betty Mae. I'm out scouting around for

Sandy. You haven't seen him, have you? I haven't seen him in quite a time, now. He has reached a stage where I can do nothing with him," Vic said, regarding her medically, surveying the surroundings with alacrity, yet with the studied thoroughness of a hunting hound.

"Yes," she began, "I see him every two or three days." Her voice was deathly flat. Her tall, paper-thin body was akin to all that which surrounded her and still in harmony with nothing in particular, for she was of a different stratum than this which huddled up about her, she was as a tat of golden butter left, after the churning, on the buttermilk. She stood with her arms akimbo, and her little knot of a belly had a string tied squeezingly tight above it.

Yes, she told him, Sandy had wandered right back to the place he started from and she had seen him many times and wondered about him. He was running with the young sprouts that knew everything. There was no chopping them down, for, albeit you chopped them down, say tonight, they'd sprout full-grown by tomorrow's rising golden sun. She didn't understand this younger generation. In her time, everyone—including the young'uns—worked, she remembered most piercingly; but today everybody had banker hours. No longer was there a night and folks went to bed and slept decently under the watchful eye of God in heaven, resting their toil-worn bodies for another day of wrestling with their work; but now they slept on the job, keeping one eye cocked for the boss man and the other reposing, dreaming of the seductive night, when once again they might take pleasure. They trusted not themselves nor anybody else. They took pleasures all night long with one another. They sneaked into each other's bedrooms, they hooked themselves together standing up behind the machinery, they clambered into automobiles taking their pleasure at seventy miles an hour. They rubbed each other's thighs in the picture shows where great actors beat each other over the head with fluffy chiffon pies and a real good story where the fat man rolled down the steps a hundred times and got hit with two dozen juicy pies. They rammed their hands into each other's clothes and the more the fat man rolled down the stairs the stickier their hands got. Still and all, she pointed out, in this day and age they were not yet satisfied with that; women took pleasure with women and men with men—she'd heard tell of that as a girl among the educated upper crust, but now it was among them all—the women were like cows in a pasture without a bull.

"It's gettin about time you found Sandy," she ended thinly, her voice catching in her throat.

He told her that he had tried, but failed; and that he could only guess at the cause, for he would never dare speak it out openly in Green Pond—because things like that simply weren't believable. Because, too, since now he was old and much wiser, he knew there were lots of things much better left unsaid. It was obvious to everyone. If he did tell these things, none would ever believe them and then he would stand with his lips as dumb as a scapegoat and his tongue parching dry in his mouth. He wanted above all to retain his well of joy, for it never to run dry. If profited a man nothing to lose it.

"Iffen I see Sandy again, which I'm most sure of, do you want me to call you at the hospital? Iffen you was to hurry, right then, you might catch him before he got too far away."

"Yes, I'd appreciate that, Betty Mae; and thank you many times."

"No need to thank me, not you," she added with something extra special in the tone of her voice. "Not as much as you done for me in that hospital."

Victor drove forward through the all-loving night and heard the whippoorwill call out sagaciously for a drought; the symphony of night insects kept their instruments at a heated staccato. The earth was filled with fruitification and profoundest bliss existed in the labyrinth of dark mansions above, but here among men was the squirming of maggots.

He drove past Connie Hennessee's All-Night Praise-House, thinking that he might find Sandy there, for his gang frequented her place, if they never went in; albeit he had heard that she came often into the noisome street and drove great mobs of them to her altar where she wrestled with them until dawn to get them saved up good and on the side of the Lord fighting the battle of Armageddon. Her meetinghouse stayed open all night and many drooled and wept in maudlin emotion.

Past midnight he drove slowly past many of the large tents where the cheap commercial preachers rejoiced their livers nightly, but he knew that by this time most of the old scamps had pulled down their festive flaps and gone piously to their hovels to sleep off the hazardous frenzy they had gone through in extracting rattling and folding money from the throngs whose hearts were in a great darkness.

He even went so far as to go to the Prayer House where heavy Honey Daddy preached while his black cherubims fanned the buzzing flies and pricking insects from around his swarthy neck. Honey Daddy called the wrath of Black Jesus down upon their rusty hides and many were struck dumb with the spirit and lay writhing in the sawdust. Multitudes of them fell prostrate at Honey Daddy's feet and he extended them a very gingerly blessing under his great and many-ringed fingers. The worshipers marched the Holy March about the aisles of the Prayer House, passing before Honey Daddy's great gleaming eye, and as they passed, his vision knocked the ones who were consumed with fiery devils to the dust and their piercing screams rent Green Pond's night air, even the chilly dampness that issued up from the rivers. He told them straightway that Jesus loved them, but that he, Honey Daddy, loved them much more than Jesus the Jew. The worshipers turned their pockets wrongside out and the immense tin tubs were heaped with money when the offering was taken. There were two roustabouts who did nothing but carry the heavy tubs of money to Honey Daddy's armored vans, for where money was concerned, Honey Daddy trusted neither Jesus nor God.

There'd been times Honey Daddy had been slapped into jail by the white folks, but they could do nothing with him. They would like to hang him but they could find no lawful reason—and he paraded whenever he pleased about Green Pond in his great Cadillac. The law blocked the legal flow of traffic and Honey Daddy had the street for himself, his trumpeters, and his angels. He would not be driven to dark Golgotha, he would not be impaled upon the white folks' tempers. This is Honey Daddy, the son of I Will Arise. Neither would they be casting lots for his purple bloomer under his great white robe.

Doctor Victor Thornwell moved forward through the lonely night, searching out the hiding place of Sandy Peeler. He searched many of the roadhouses and the camps and the dives, but nowhere was Sandy to be found. It seemed that he had vanished from the face of the red land.

At dawn Vic gave up the search as an exceeding evil and hurried on to the hospital to administer to his own tired and worn spirit. He knew full well Sandy's life hung under the certain shadow of death, that his light was as a fizzling candle in a storm and all too soon it would be snuffed out.

In the hospital he proceeded to the dining room which was yet unoccupied. He blundered on into the kitchen and fixed himself a tray. Returning to the dining room, he hid in a corner where he might see everything and not be observed himself. He ate slowly; his soul was buried in deep grief.

Somewhere within him came the knowing feeling that he would never see Sandy again. Even after he had almost physically battled the elders of North Bethel to get them to at least stintingly grant him some practice time at the organ, it had done no good, although he had been assured through the grape

vine of both the church and Sandy's gang that Sandy did practice some. But it also seemed that he never let his whisky alone.

Tizzy was the first one to enter the dining room. Tizzy was
getting old, he observed. After all, he thought, eventually every
well ran dry. Although she was still capable and efficient. He
wouldn't swap her for a million in their younger years. She was
immaculately crisp this morning. Her hair freshly blued. Her
sharp eyes surveyed the dining room in one take-in-all glance
and her eyes caught him on their first round.

"So you're hiding this morning, Doctor Thornwell," she
laughed, coming to him with her hospital walk. "Are you going
to help Doctor Tad do that brain operation this morning, that
tumor? That man surely has some choked disk, so Doctor Lester
has discovered," and she continued to give him a great deal of
information on it, which amounted to almost a strange jargon.

"Tizzy," he regarded her with astounded weariness and his
voice was as an engine with missing spark plugs, "I'll help; it
might be very interesting to delve into a human brain this
morning. After all I have beheld last night of what the human
brain is capable of creating, it might not be so bad this morning
to once again look inside the human skull and behold what
Gawd has fashioned there, for no man can understand it
either from its beginning or its end."

He sounds like Ole Doc, Tizzy thought, and ate her breakfast
in an opposite corner.

6

Uncle Simon grunted in horrible disdain when he discovered it
and fled to the church manse to tell Reverend Jake as fast as
his old boatlike feet would carry him. His old woolly face was
splattered with chagrin and shame: somebody had stolen the
great gold Bible from North Bethel Church, the sacred gold
Bible was gone. The young assistant ministers had put it to

disuse and stored it, preferring something modern and quite up-to-date.

Jake was unalarmed. The stealing of a Bible was a minor incident in his life and he dismissed Uncle Simon's worries right early and sent the old man tottering back to the church, shaking his head and wondering what the times were coming to.

But Jake knew better. He simply didn't want to open up any more old church sores—they never healed as it was. He knew that Bible's history full well, from mouthy history and from the actual written church records which recorded all sorts of sins and lay moldy and dusty in the church's archives and quite ready for publication, but no telling when ole Gabriel would get to it—he was that slow. And Jake certainly wasn't caring for an earthly airing of it. While the church would never let Nathan Corn Saddleberry become a member, it had accepted his handiwork, the hand-bound, gold-backed Bible, and used it for worship throughout the years; but all this had been brought about when he was a boy, by his mother, before he grew up and got to be big and sinful.

The old folks handed down the mouthy history: Uncle Prince Blue was Nathan Corn Saddleberry's daddy, they said, but Saddleberry's mama had told the Session, when churched for having an off-colored illegitimate child, that a big black bull had frightened her and marked the child. That was true, the old folks said, for what was Uncle Prince Blue if not a big black bull? It was always chawed over that way and the old folks knew. And everybody knew that Sudiebelle Wilson was Saddleberry's daughter and by the skin of her blessed feet she had escaped Green Pond and turned out better than expected. Some folks said she was a famous hat designer and the mother of Johnsie Murray, a very light yaller, whom anybody could see singing and shimmying and dancing with white men on the sinful screen and whose voice came over the airwaves. She was a knockout, folks said. Johnsie Murray, granddaughter of Uncle

Prince Blue, son of an African king, shimmied and danced openly with white men.

Nobody else would want that old Bible, Jake thought. It had been Sudiebelle who had slipped back here and taken it. Jake didn't much blame her. She had some feelings. He simply didn't want it talked about, aired out. The biggest sin of the church was its own evil-wagging tongue.

7

GAWD: Put that horn down, man. Is you tryin to frighten lil mens?

GABRIEL: Aw, I's seein could I outblow em automobiles' horns on earth. They's dudin it aroun. But they drownt me out. Can't hear my own ears no mo. You got some powerful noisy chillun.

GAWD: That's bad. Too much blowin. Fo'gets Me lack I was a has-been or a never-come-no-mo. There are em that thinks it's blasphemy to look upon Me as a flesh-an-blood Gawd. Thinks I should be a spirit an nothin mo. Then there's others that thinks I am an absurdity an a fake.

GABRIEL: Yah, the way em churches is hypocritin around.

GAWD: I's afraid Danny Boy gonna meet he end in the Battle of the Bulge. Then won't be none of em left but Miz Jezebel. Let she squirm some mo.

GABRIEL: There's Goldie; don' You fo'get lil ole Goldie, now.

GAWD: I ain't so dismindful. That Goldie, he don't go by no Inchurch name. He go by the name of Thornwell. Who's Miz Jezebel deaconin an jimmyin now?

GABRIEL: Mostly the ration board, that's what I mostly puts down. Ho'cum she that way?

GAWD: Hard-to-obtain things is always fascinated womens. You shorely remembers about ole Eve, her cravin offen that tree? An now since Miz Nee-oom-me is done come home to us you can understand mo better.

GABRIEL: Yes, an I'm a-watchin my pocket.

In this day Satan had no trouble pronging up plenty of sin. The vegetable marts closed with the sinking of the red sun and the preachers raised the flaps of their tents with the appearance of the seductive night, dealing in all-healing wonder-working with the soul.

SATAN: Shootin de peoples in de rump wit salvation.

BEELZEBUB: I'd ruther have one of em big-gutted doctors jug me in de rump wit he's needle—be lack lil mens and keep on an on livin.

SATAN: I wish you would quit wit you disgruntlement.

BEELZEBUB: Us gonna have to pump water into the Baptist church yet.

SATAN: What's that you say?

21

Any profound, unusual mass movement is started by a master thinker—or plotter. Jezebel, with her churchly whip caught firmly in her jeweled hand, had cut across the ministers of the Green Pond Ministerial Association, whacking and chopping most unmercifully upon their seaters until she pushed them into a mad frenzy to do away with Green Pond's unchristian liquor stores. The preachers flayed and flogged their congregations from their pulpits as though they were beasts in a training arena; the clicking and clattering of their tongues, the staccato-pounding of their fists upon the Holy Bible deeply moved the notable members and they either signed the petition, asking for a referendum, or the preachers sent them, delicately mortified, straight to hell—a burning hell. Jezebel drove doggedly onward against her foes in this, her most famous war, and her smile was as the golden sun spinning through the blue upyonder, for she didn't have Jesus' leniency toward the drinkers and the whores of Green Pond. She thought they were ruining the town for her.

And once again the nigh-spirited dispensers of coddling spirits were driven from Green Pond into a lonely world.

2

As the big weights in the grandfather clocks in Catawba run down stopping the clocks, so does the life in a man run down.

Early Sunday morning, Sandy hopped into Main Street as if he were a sparrow hunting a large cake of dung to attack. The first faint light of the east was breaking uncleanly in his face, a nervous, emaciated face with big birdlike eyes, beaked nose, gaunt, pallid cheeks, and chin bones wasting away.

But Green Pond was dry—suddenly and all-to-itself—and Sandy Peeler on Main Street this Sunday morning, looking in the windows at his old tempter, could get none of it, nor any other day of the week besides. There in the window of the first tawdry cafe was an array of beers. Fire danced within him. It was a ritual fire dance every Sunday morning at 5:00 A.M.—and it had been for the weeks since he had joined the club. But the temptation at this hour was so much easier to resist. The doors were padlocked securely—and never again would they be opened since the heated election of yesterday had settled that once and forever. How sad, he thought. Still, everybody that was self-respecting in Green Pond was at home abed at this ridiculous hour. The thick glass kept his threadlike fingers from the bottles, the fire he so craved as the diabetic his water. How many did it take to brighten up a hangover? He couldn't remember.

Passing a wine shop further on, Sandy stopped for a little squint—wine—red wine—and just a bit of white wine. With his long fingers he traced the outline of a bottle upon the glass, patting it—Baby, baby, b-a-b-y. Saliva rose in his mouth. He swallowed, gulped. Boy. Did he have that old feeling? Weak-kneed, jelly-legged, trembling. But never again. The doors were locked.

Main Street's light was now much stronger. He could soon be within the church if he picked up his weary feet. Once there, he was safe for the moment, at least. The elders of the North Bethel Church had said that Sandy Peeler might practice upon the great organ for one hour, one hour in heaven out of a week of mad hours of gnawing fear. He had to face every day now, he thought; the alcoholic doors would never be opened again.

He was passing the ABC stores, the greatest temptation. Sandy still loved them, even though they were locked forever against him. For weeks now, he had not been able to trust himself down this street late in the evening—especially Saturdays. Saliva rose, flooding his mouth. Those lovely Saturdays. Sunsets —blazing red—kinda like Mama Amazon's ole Satan, he thought wistfully. The doors would be wide open. So many fellers milling about. Fellowship, laughter, tinkling, cheap glass—"Hi ya, pal. Have this one on me"—Sandy's stomach turned over.

He stopped. Everything was serene. The buses weren't running yet. What an hour. His eager eyes missed not a single store that held his true love. Then he reminded himself that he must move faster, get away from here, lest he take his very fist and smash the glass. He thought of Vic and knew that by this hour he was hurrying toward the hospital—always working, doing something for somebody. Why couldn't he have been like that? He moved faster, swallowing, gulping.

He was going up the magnificent steps of the North Bethel Church—long, straight, high—why, it was as if he were walking right straight up into heaven.

He entered the nave. This was definitely heaven. Here in the cloistered gloom of the church he was safe from the harassing temptation. To bed at night with the chickens, as folks said out on the farms of the watershed, which was the red land forever stanch and unyielding; pull the covers over his head so that he'd not hear gaiety, tinkling glass.

He crossed before the chancel rail—right where the Reverend

Jacob Thornwell usually had stood preaching in his morning coat and striped trousers and bright red boutonniere, and there Sandy knelt in the gray morning gloom, asking God for mercy.

Sandy knew somehow he was pure bad, clear to his middle. Things were wrong with his goings-on inside of him. They cut up too big a to-do. He thought of all his drinking, the Nances and the Daisies he played with, the whores he caroused with. He reeked of sin. He hadn't wanted it, but somehow he had got started, he didn't know how. Daddy Vic had been so good to him, why was he bringing all this?

Dad had never approved. Dad had tried to help him—but why?

Then he thought of the old dame, Jezebel.

He asked God to look out for her, for she was in as bad a shape in her middle as he was—maybe worse. Nobody would ever know what she had killed inside of him; he trusted blindly that God did know, was looking down, seeing it all. Was this, too, somewhere predestined in the stardust? Sandy didn't understand the stardust.

At the mammoth organ, which held the Inchurch name in embossed bronze, he was as gleeful as the little towheaded boy to whom Vic had taught organ. He pressed the switch, heard the motor whir, flipped on stops, and his left hand moved. Creeping upon the swell manual, the long threadlike fingers of his right hand picked up the melody of "When at Night I Go to Sleep" from *Hansel and Gretel* on the great manual. His left heel on low D, his right foot sought the crescendo pedal—this was his orchestra, his world.

Surrounded by story angels in the lofty windows, he played as an artist. Rest washed the haggard lines of his pallid face; the pinkish-violet light coming through the saintly stained windows on his yellowish dirty hair turned him into a cherub.

The Reverend Jacob Thornwell jumped straight up in bed so violently that his toupee tumbled under his single bed. He scrambled so noisily for his robe in the dim dawn that Myra awoke, yawning, snuggling the covers about herself.

"What is it at this unearthly hour?" she asked sleepily, getting up on her elbow, feeling the metal curlers on her head with her free hand.

"Music," Jake snapped, trying to get into the red and yellow robe. "After all I've been through tonight. Now it's music. Organ music. Don't you hear that organ? Music at this ungodly hour of the morning!"

"Don't be so upset about it," Myra said. "A body would think that the world was on fire and this was Doomsday, the way you're cutting up and everything—you sure can make a heap of fuss," she continued to jabber from her single bed opposite the open window where the damp morning air and organ music poured in.

Slamming the door, fuming down the stairs as though he were a lit stick of dynamite, his now very bald head quite red from the anger that had flooded it, he moved along as fast as his fat old body and formless heavy monk's-cloth robe of brilliant red and yellow permitted him to do.

"That idiot! That Sandy Peeler. Vic ought to have to put up with this. I'm going to put a stop to it," he muttered, grinding his teeth, grimacing his face. "Music! Organ music at five o'clock. It's a good thing he got his practice in while I was in Europe, for he'll not wake me another morning with this infernal playing."

The manse's door was left ajar and Jake's bare, fat, pink feet trudged onto the dewy grass. He charged across the lawn to the church like a bull in a cool green pasture. He snatched open the back door of the church. All night long Jake had had the bellyache from eating too much of dowager Jezebel's heavy dinner in the Pink House, the occasion being the celebrating of his return from Europe. And when he did get to bed, the trains ran and blew all night long, cars honked, blew—the scum of Green Pond never slept, it seemed. Now when things were quiet and he could sleep in the early morning, there was this infernal organ music. He glared devilishly.

Much against the elders' wishes, Jake, eight weeks ago, before he had sailed for Europe to the first postwar World Council of Churches, had had the Alcoholics Anonymous group come in a body to an evening service. The crowd upon this particular night had been electric. The elders were so impressed that when Doctor Victor Thornwell asked them to grant Sandy Peeler some practice time at the organ, they granted him one free hour per week—to Jake's bitter, belated chagrin.

Jake climbed the back stairs to the sanctuary laboriously, puffing with each tiring step he took, and he resembled ole Satan very much in his flaming robe, his red bald head poised above it most notably. Puff and up he went.

In the dimness across the church, in the eerie light which so resembled the deep monkish gloom of some faraway monastery, Sandy Peeler saw something he had never seen before in his short life, even when he had the shakes. Rats and snakes he was acquainted with, but this thing yonder—that was ole Satan. The slick bald head—Sandy could see right where the horns sprouted out of it. The flaming robe, moving stealthily, deadly up and down the aisle. Sandy knew that behind that figure was the long tail that Mama Amazon had so aptly and vividly described. He could not see it, but he knew it was dragging up and down the aisle behind that thing. Sandy thought that this was as dying. No pain. It was as if he were dead drunk. He played from his subconscious unearthly music, playing for protection from God. Surely beneath God's wings there would be protection; God would care for him. The story angels observed from the windows and Sandy's spirit was, for this moment, as big as space itself. Themes unknown came from his fingertips.

The organ was in such full force that the church vibrated.

The pale light in Sandy's hair caused Jake to slow his pace—was this not the town drunk playing? No organist of this town had ever caused such music to come from that organ or any other organ in Green Pond. It was sheer, startling beauty. Something crumpled up in Jake. That face over there at the organ, partly buried in shadow with the pinkish-violet light slanting over one side of it that seemed to form a halo, could it actually be possible that this was something that belonged to another world? Was this an absurdity of his mind? Some false creation? Heresy? Was that a heretic at the organ? A blasphemy against the church? Was that an angel at the organ? He had thought all along it was the town's drunkard. He became stilled with thought and placed his hand absent-mindedly and quite by accident to his head and drew it away in stained horror. He had forgotten his toupee. He suddenly felt naked. Naked in church! This must be a dream, an aftermath of the dowager's dinner. Damn all precocious dowagers' dinners. Damn the twentieth-century church; nobody believed in what he saw. Was this the strangeness that had followed his twin brother Victor all his life? He felt as if the great day had come and all eighteen hundred of his neurotic members had arrived, coming especially to hear him preach. He began tipping backward. This was most offensive to good taste. This was like the earthy passages of the Bible which he could never read. He stepped backward much more cautiously, trying to make his bulky form invisible, for now the only thing upon earth that mattered to him was to get safely to his boudoir and get his toupee. What if people should see him?

Sandy rocked the organ far more than his allotted time and Gawd was there making the world into flesh as he played. And Sandy was made to know his weakness of the flesh and his spirit gnawed and tore within his body and came through his fingertips in great music that would never die. He knew the vast and troubled people of Green Pond could not find the surfeited peace which he was finding here. He nuzzled so closely to Gawd that he had no idea of where he was and in him there was no void, empty crying. Time would soon run out here.

Here at the organ, all that Vic had taught him of life flooded through him. His short years upon the red land crept through his mind one by one. He played to Mama Amazon, who he knew was sitting in the topmost balcony clapping her hands. There were his happy years at Catawba. There were the nights when Mama Amazon had made him get down upon his knees and begin, "Our Father—"

He didn't realize it was time for Sunday school to begin until he saw Mrs. Robert Inchurch hurrying through the church to her Sunday-school room where she taught. She wrinkled up her nose scoffingly at him when she passed the organ and he quickly shut off the organ and hurried into the back alley without anyone else seeing him.

He wandered through the cemetery in his ragged filthy clothes until he came to the back side of it; here he climbed over the rock wall and through the honeysuckle. He dropped down into the street, cutting, as the crow flies, between rickety buildings and weed-grown back yards and down several filthy alleys and made his way to the railroad tracks and sat down on a cross tie.

After seeing Jezebel in the church, he would give anything for a good stiff drink. It was useless battling with her. She had licked him long ago. Where he was going to get that drink he had no idea. If it were only yesterday with all the old joints open, it would have been easy for him to have bummed one of the fellers out of a drink. Or could he have run into one of the good-looking Nances from Rahab, who some week ends worked Green Pond, he could have had a good stiff drink, sure enough. But, he thought dejectedly, with everything under lock and key from yesterday's elections, there was not much of a chance. He looked up at the sun, shutting one eye, gauging its height into the heavens. It was early yet. All the fellers were sleeping. They would be out in the by-and-by.

The hot sun grew unbearable on Sandy and he crawled up the railroad bank and under a low-growing bush which afforded shade. Here his tired, emaciated body fell into an exhaustive sleep in which his whisky-burnt nerves and flimsy muscles danced and jiggled as puppets on a string.

When the day was well spent he was aroused by laughing voices on the railroad track and he scrambled to his knees and crawled on all fours to the edge of the cut, looking down to where he saw some of the fellers.

"Hi," he called to them, "Where you going?"

"Come down, ole organ grinder, we gonna have a party."

"Got sumpin to drink?"

"You bet, ole organ grinder. Them ole church shitpokes ain't stopping us."

"Say, organ grinder, your pants are unbuttoned."

"Who cares?" Sandy asked. "What can't get up, can't get out."

Sandy fell in with them and they cut across town. They talked of their gals, and openly and boldly discussed their copulations of the night before, and their times were numerous and they described everything quite plainly. They dredged up tidbits of frivolous talk and sounded off loudly. They yelled and whistled at the high-class rutting boys and girls who rode by in cars. Sometimes they called them sharp, pointed names. They giggled over the upper crust who ran Green Pond and let that disintegrated body know what they thought, although it spilled its gingerness upon the summer air and was not recorded from oblivion.

That night they assembled themselves in that air of man-about-town into an old, dilapidated building in the shadow of a church in one of the outermost rings of Green Pond, and drank a most deadly concoction of paint thinner, shaving lotion, and rubbing alcohol, and their manner was of most charming grace and extravagant politeness, which proved, after several hours of gulp-ingly swallowing the scalding stuff in rapid jerks, to be fatal. Their din of screaming dying, worked to a deafening uproar, almost drowned out the flimsy ringing of the church bells, so great was their agony. One of them died nicely and quickly within the building, but the rest fled into the streets as rats will do when they have taken certain poisons. Four of them died dili-gently in various streets not too far from the building where they had held the party. Five of them staggered, blind and crazy, screaming at the top of their lungs until picked up by an ambu-lance and carried, siren-screaming, to the Thornwell Hospital. Sandy Peeler was one of the remaining five.

3

Doctor Victor Thornwell lifted his head slowly, looked again wistfully toward the striking figure of Catawba looming up as solidly as a mountain boulder away across Green Pond in the treetops. His tear-filmed eyes beheld unrealities. His soul reeked, lonely and gall-like, with an insufferable grief, and he was de-pressed into the nethermost regions and he was beset with the feeling that he was inadequately capable of coping with this form of disaster. Without doubt, this was the most evil concoc-tion yet to ferment in Jezebel's pudding-stirring brain. She had as surely murdered Sandy Peeler as though she had plunged a knife up to the hilt into his weak and timid heart.

Jezebel had the heart of an old mud turtle, whose head would snap on viciously even after it was severed from its body. But why had she done this to him? Why had she done it?

Sandy had not been meant for this earth. He was too fragile. He had always been a wisp of make-believe. The little sprite of a spirit that was almost but never quite there. Something that no mortal could get hold of and hold, and he had gone hesitantly and avoidingly, a wisp of trivia.

4

Jezebel had always looked upon Vic and the nurses in the hospital as a cocky rooster with a penful of hens and she bet he didn't let them suffer.

But then Goldie had come home from the war in one solid piece and much better-looking. He was suave and polite and knew all the ropes. His voice had a gentle purr in it. Danny Boy had not come home, but his great sacrifice made her a Gold-Star Mother. Now she had a most elegant and handsome chauffeur who drove her to the services at North Bethel when Danny's earthly remains were at last returned and placed beside the other departed Inchurches.

When she heard of the untimely and horribly grotesque death of Sandy Peeler in the newspaper, her comment was brief. "Just another soul in hell," she said, and sent an immense sheaf of roses.

Missy, at fifty-five years of age, was refined and oily. Her hair was not gray for she kept it dyed and it was always curled and in place. She was matronly and mature, but with a stunning figure that still made the men of Green Pond gasp. Her voice was low, soft, cultured, and she knew how to get her way. What she said in the Pink House was meticulously observed and with punctiliousness. Miz Jezebel signed the checks still; but Missy usually told her what for and for how much. Missy gave Miz Jezebel right much leash because no dog should be confined too much; a little airing now and again did her good.

5

The cheap movie houses were filled nightly to overflowing with rutting boys and girls. The little roosters danced and spurred about the little pullets. They laughed in the homesick moonlight and, without any ritual, ran their flimsy hands into each other's clothes in erotic play as Jezebel had done Victor in the long bygone. It was chancy doings, but worth it. Ole Doc had said years ago that they pushed into the world like beans popping up the hard, crusty ground, urged to get here and with a greater urge to begin to praise the great hereafter with their sexual organs. Was life more than a scribbled page in a book, a thin paper page that blew about in the wind and was soon blown away as things fallible are?

The many handsome cars, their tires singing, raced on the cemented roads that led in all directions in lucidly dramatic importance and lounged most lousily and loggily across the face of the red land.

And Victor Thornwell was still a loadstone to Jezebel, though there was no way that she could think of to keep in touch with him any more and she would not have him know it for the world.

The Reverend Jacob Thornwell preached in his morning coat and striped trousers and bright red boutonniere. The churchly fathers longed to strip from the Bible the act of Jesus making wine and the church now served watered grape juice and Miz Joanna's racy wine was an outcast. The assistant pastors, robe-flapping, overruled Jake and there were two morning services for each Sunday, two choirs, two choir directors, two rival organists. There was the nine o'clock service and the eleven o'clock service. And, as in all things, Jake finally became reconciled.

Jepson Grady pushed the Negro High School's valedictorian and salutatorian atop of The Green Pond *Observer's* front page and crowded the running congressman and his family off to the corner at the bottom, and in a two-column editorial he edified the brilliant achievements of the Negro school. Miss Odessa Few's handsomely engraved invitations to the Chitterling Strut which she was giving in the House of the Sons and Daughters of I Will Arise was on the society page and it was listed in the social calendar from day to day quite calmly.

What Yellow Sam had accomplished in Doubting Hollow

would benefit the race of mankind yet to come—for he had not stood for the disused and the undoing. But his staccato voice whipped things into concerning shape as he had shipped the teams of horses there at Catawba, and that which was corruptible he had striven to correct. He went about it good-naturedly, discreetly, and methodically. The citizens of Doubting Hollow often hooted at him, but when it came for a stanch go-between between them and the white folks, it was always Yellow Sam's lot to do so and he went between smart and well-knowing.

In the time of youth, in the long bygone, Victor had known himself and them to be young and straight and brave as the morning; now they were all of them stooped and in the evening of life, the late shady evening—that time when man looks with disbelief, caution, and even precaution.

6

In an operating room on the seventh floor of the Thornwell Hospital the doctors and nurses wrestled with an old man's life that hung by too thin a thread.

Doctor Victor Thornwell used the scalpel, but Doctor Tad Thornwell felt and felt deeply in his bones that Vic was getting too old for such a testing operation.

The skin incision was made and sheets clamped to the subcutaneous tissues to maintain sterility of the peritoneal cavity. Vic deepened the incision slowly through the fascia and muscles. Eagle-eyed Tad watched, for he had seen Vic do this same thing much faster. Vic went on to open the peritoneum and he was slow, he fumbled and he fumbled and he grunted and he grunted. Tad thought he would never get the stomach and the jejunum delivered into the red gashing wound. Then Vic seemed to play dreamily as he stripped the jejunum free of its smelly fecal content, like he was a little boy playing with a water-filled balloon.

Tad felt bad, he felt bad all over; he hated to see this, this slowing up, this falling away, this hesitating Vic was doing. But Vic was determined, he needed no help, he had never had any. When the head operating-room nurse slapped the intestinal clamp with rubber-covered blades into his hands, he perked up and applied it to the jejunum; then he applied another to the stomach. Then he seemed to slow again, to dream, to lapse into his youth, the assistants listening to his mumblings, mumbling names of people they weren't acquainted with.

He seemed to deliberate, to hesitate when he brought the stomach and jejunum into proximity; he used the linen thread as though he were going to lasso something.

He sweated profusely and Tad noticed and wondered what caused it; it was too excessive and the nurse continually mopped it up.

The assistants and Tad padded off the field with hot gauze pads, protected the sheets with additional towels.

Tad saw Vic across the table, bent and stooped with age, fatigued and fumbling, holding on bravely. *He is too old, slowing up too much for this sort of operation; such an operation requires such dexterity of finger and mind, no deviation, delicateness of touch. He is going to have to give up whether he wants to or not. I have been urging it, but he won't listen. And folks still trust him; but I am afraid this old fellow has trusted too far—though he wouldn't live many more months at the most. He is going to have to give up whether he wants to or not. I hate to see him go, but it will be bad fo the hospital for him to keep on bumbling.*

"Doctor Thornwell, he's fading out. There's no pulse," said the anesthetist, stopping the ether, searching further for the pulse.

"Give him some digitalis, he'll make it," said Vic, stepping back, shaking the sweat from his face. Kenny rushed to him, mopping his brow. He was in a spot, she knew, she had never known him to sweat like this.

Vic felt that he was a child again in Catawba's back yard, there near the old rail fence, just below the smokehouse, helping Pop to castrate the pigs. How proud he had felt the first shining steel his fingers had clasped, as though it meant life itself. How he had cut and haggled, torn and smeared about in the bright red blood until it had turned a dull black, black as the blood was doing here within this rotten carcass.

He laid his gloved hand on the patient, felt the muscles jerking, slowly twitching, halting as if he were a machine running down. The last bit of air escaped from the body.

Vic turned his stooped back to the operating table. Tears welled into his eyes and trickled down his sweaty face. He dropped his head, his shoulders slumping in defeat like a whipped dog, a lonely, disappointed-with-life dog who had never had a master. The nurses crowded about him, untying his gown, slipping off his mask, peeling off the thin rubber gloves from his hands.

Tad helped him get his clothes on after he had washed up.

And Victor Thornwell wandered that day, lonely and dejected, until late in the evening, when his weary steps turned him toward Catawba. At Catawba everything would be all right; like a small boy nearing home he quickened his steps, but at Catawba he got the greatest blow of his life.

7

No one knew the moment of Mama Amazon's death except Gawd and Catawba. Vic knew that Gawd had been richly rewarded and that the big old rambling house had quaked loudly to its inmost soul as she went.

He found her sitting in her big rocking chair before a small dozing fire there in the big old kitchen which she had loved more than anything on earth unless it was him. Her hands were upturned, folded loosely, and in one of them perched a much-used dishrag. It looked as though she had been working about in the kitchen as usual and had come over to the chair to sit down and die as though she wanted to rest a few minutes. She had gone steady on her feet and that was what she had always wanted to do; she had longed to ape Ole Doc.

When Vic could dry his shameless tears, he hurried as a very small boy to the undertaker, thinking it would be indelicate and very impolite to call on the telephone and he had come back with the undertaker and saw them pick her up gently and take her forever away from her beloved Catawba.

He tried to be eloquent in approval, but his spirit dwindled into clattering, clamorous thoroughfares and there he saw life zipping by with a big hello and toady gusto. He felt imperceptive and dazed. There in the back yard of Catawba he looked up toward the starlit ceiling and he questioned himself as to who he was and from whence he had come. He felt rimmed in and time unsufficed and nowhere tonight were there homely sounds to warm the goings-on in his heart. Catawba's big to-do was over. He left Catawba, walking slowly and feeling benignly broody, creeping in the magical hours before dawn, cantering the un-questionable in his mind, drinking strangling gulps of all that was so stanchly illuminated within him.

He looked painstakingly slow and inquisitive among the many elegant coffins the undertaker had to offer before he selected. He took the utmost care in selecting a dress—a big pink one with many ruffles and much, much lace like she had worn when he was little—and all the time he did it, it seemed that her big hoots of laughter continued with him and he felt when he had finally decided upon one that she approved with a smile.

He and Jake nearly came to powerful blows over putting her in the family mausoleum. They argued in the church office as though it were a Session meeting. Jake in his dried-up voice protested in anguish.

"What'll my members say? You dragging her here into North

Bethel cemetery and putting her into the family mausoleum. Have you gone batty?"

Vic broached him with the certain gait of a sure-footed cat. "I don't give a rap what your sniveling members have to say. Their mouths are no prayer books. There are whole sections of that cemetery out yonder that the slaves were buried in."

"Oh, but that was a long, long time ago. They were slaves, besides. That's quite different to this day and time."

"Oh, the old family horse! Jake Thornwell, you've bowed down and truckled here so long in this church until you can no longer call your soul your own. What're you so afraid of? Your servile, darty looks are those of a condemned man. You grieve me greatly to see you so low." Vic boomed luxuriously loud, "You undoubtedly are the most afraid creature anywhere in Green Pond."

"But you don't know my members—I must live on with them."

"Your goatly members? Who is afraid of them?"

"Get out of here, Victor Thornwell. I don't care where you bury her. I'm washing my hands of the whole affair." Jake was abashed and electrically charged with such a flux of chagrin that he slumped in his chair and a look, wholly venomous and vengeful, streaked from his weak and watery blue eyes.

"Yes, but I want you to conduct her funeral. You know as well as you are living she'd want you to do that above all else. As much as she thought of you as her preacher-boy." Vic looked despondent, thought of the oncoming ordeal.

"Oh, I'll do her funeral. I'll turn on my most eloquent harpings and really I don't mind her being put into the mausoleum, but you know how people'll talk—you know how deliberately sluggish and reluctant they are to forgive ever and there's no need to embitter any more of them than possible. Every precaution I can take is, I've found out, the pill that grips the fever I suffer with." He was woebegone.

"I don't give a damn. I'm not worried about what your royal consorts will have to say about me putting Mama Amazon into the mausoleum. She's the only mama I've ever had and a stomp-down good'un at that, so I want her entombed right where I'll be put someday. Right across the aisle from me. Someday she's going to wake up and I want her to put her hand on me and tell me that it's morning and time to get up as she used to do when I was a child."

Now as Vic left the locked mausoleum, the great basket of red roses nodding peacefully at its door, and wandered aimlessly through the cemetery, his mind was rusted with many thoughts that naturally rust a man's life toward its end.

What more could be expected of religion if not to bring peace? Mama Amazon had trusted lavishly in her destiny; her head must lie low as anyone's and she would take up as much space in death as though she had been a ruling queen. Oh, she had trusted most stanchly in the stardust. She had shown Vic how his feet could always walk on the crest of the rainbows and be disdainful and leery of the tricky pots of gold at their bases. And never again would the Lawd be calling upon her to furnish niggers fo the world—she had done what many hadn't, she had furnished plenty.

She had paused often to talk to and praise the Master, and Vic was certain that she and Gawd were stanch cronies, two good'uns that could whip ole Satan any day they took a notion; they just let him have his way fo a lil while, fo a lil while and toreckly they would do sumpin about em!

Vic walked on through the enclosed cemetery; he saw the transfixed tombstones flinging BORN IN IRELAND—BORN IN SCOTLAND. Rushing boldly and madly all about this plot, so restfully and tranquilly concealed, was a scrouging and scrambling town so filled with torment that it tormented itself and was spreading from here-to-yonder and all over Gawd's creation. But it had been predestined in the stardust of what a man's life should be long before his time here on the watershed. There was nothing, nothing he wished to inveigle.

8

Gawd stroked His majestic beard and looked down upon the hallowed ground that is the red land of Carolina. He saw the folks walking and He heard the folks talking and He talked to His angels there in the sky.

GAWD: They's near Me an I hears em, but seems lack to Me they's still got awful heap of give-mes. Almost mo'an I can disstomach. They was never contented wit My racy wine fro the vine that climbed up the ole oak tree there in front of the Thornwell Hospital. Ever wantin new an glitterin things.

GABRIEL: Gawd, You oughtta bind an chain ole Satan.

GAWD: I created everythin good an nothin bad, because it wasn't in My nature to make badness; they gets sick and twisted somewhere in their middles down there along the way.

GABRIEL: No, no. You never did create no badness. Only goodness.

Ole Satan no longer hung about the Pink House.

SATAN: I's that disgusted with that Miz Jezebel, I could puke right here in this street in Green Pond.

BEELZEBUB: Always thought she was you gal.

SATAN: Huh, done got too ole. Can't get a thing to foment in she ole puddin head no mo. Just a ole lonely woman hangin on borrowed time. No good to me no mo.

22

All during his years of retirement from the practice of surgery, Victor still had it in him, the greatest love of his life. There was no other opiate, no other food, no other vocation. He frequented the hospital to offset his loneliness, he wandered the halls, an old stooped man, but with a rapid gait, and he stuck his head into many of the doors and talked with the patients. He bored the hospital staff; he bored the interns and externs, the nurses and the supervisors, the orderlies and the maids with his ceaseless and incessant prattle of the past. He wore them out with the old stories he told and everyone ran from him when he was seen coming. Often he would stop at the chart desks and boldly invade the charts because things there interested him.

As an old man in the hospital, he wandered its haunting over-crowded hallway where he saw fresh-birthed mothers, lying head to foot, strung down the great lengthy hallway, groggy, their lips thick with mumblish-voiced talk, dark shadows under their eyes.

He peeped between each screen he passed by and he saw them and he marveled that no man controlled his entrance into the world and each entrance was welcomed, happy-armed, and all the philosophy that Mama Amazon had dosed him with flooded and swelled upward within him. And he saw this multitude of red pebbles filling the pond, starting the waves, sending out and out like a great tide.

The switchboard operator worked madly with her plugs; she shouted into the loudspeaker—oxygen wanted in south wing, oxygen wanted in south wing; Doctor Effigram, you're needed in Emergency, report quickly.

And the orderlies and the cooks and the maids, easygoing, ran rampant in the hospital; they washed the whites, they fed them, they dusted and scrubbed behind them, they trucked them to the operating room, they put them on the bed pans and took them off, and they held the vomit cups.

The call board stayed lit with the doctors' names, with the names of the healers. And these doctors, pathologists, and technicians beheld Victor as Ole Doc, a has-been, for he didn't know how it was done in this day. He was old-fashioned and away behind the times.

Tizzy still held her supremacy and was obeyed, for today she had many supervisors under her who did the greatest share of her work.

Then one day there came an urgent call through the switchboard for Doctor Victor Thornwell and Tizzy answered it, finding it to be Jezebel. She hunted about for Vic for two days and finally located him.

No longer did Vic wield the scalpel in any of the operating rooms upon the seventh floor of the Thornwell Hospital, but out in the back there were many grassed plots between the cemented parking places and the cemented driveways and here, during the years of his retirement, he had wielded the knife as ferociously and as delicately as Pop or Granny Joanna had ever wielded it in their heyday. Cutting and slitting, budding and grafting. From the entire circle of the blessed-turning earth he had had shipped to him strange paradise apples, stunted peach stumps, singular plum scions, weird bits of quince, and every conceivable oily nut, and he had worked the top of the one to the root of the other, and through grafting and budding he had stunted them into a pure shining art. He nurtured them and he fed them and he put a million bees buzzing among the blossoms to give them a good copulating, for he didn't want them suffering as Jezebel had suffered throughout her life and he laughed and he muttered and he talked to himself.

And the vines and the scions yielded singularly and copiously and the little trees' little limbs drooled and drooped to the ground, laden, heavily fruited with succulent fruits, more succulent than Jezebel's flouncy hips had ever been upon the organ bench to the sacred high elders who looked up askingly.

Victor held out the fruits of the vines and the fruits of the scions to the student nurses, externs, and interns who walked these walks numerous times daily, that they might take nourishment; and these offerings were sought eagerly and devoured in gratitude. He did these things, for he never knew any other way.

But his big restless spirit was disquieted.

Tizzy finally found him in the cool of that September morn. "Doctor Thornwell, aren't you ever going to answer your very special telephone call?"

"Nah! Let the ole buzzard keep on calling. Let her call until she's burned all the lines down. She's hooked to nothing special!"

"You're being naughty, Victor."

"Don't see as I am. There're other doctors who might like to take a look at the devil's beauty's carcass. I've looked upon it too often and know all its parts by heart."

"She calls so insistently. What'll I tell her?"

"Go tell her I'm an old rooster up here in a penful of hens."

2

The next day was Sunday, and during the middle of the afternoon Vic was called upon to perform an operation upon a middle-aged woman who had been rushed in by ambulance in a dying condition. No other doctor was available. He didn't want to, but he had to.

The abdomen was laid open, weighted down with hemostats —a yawning cavity from which blood-tinged, watery fluid spouted up, pouring over the sides of the patient, completely blacking out the interior. Doctor Thornwell urged the assistants to mop faster, to sop up the putrid fluids. A mass of rotten matter was in full view, its odor saturating the operating room. The noises of clearing throats sounded, then the operating room grew tomblike silent.

Sweat poured from Vic and the place was filled with super-tension—taut nerves, drawn as snapping tight as violin strings, the nerves as easily cut as a horsehair from the violin bow. The sweetish, sickening odor of ether mingled with the fetid odors of the incision saturated the atmosphere.

Vic's brow rained sweat and Nurse Kenny mopped it.

"Doctor Thornwell, she's fading out. There's no pulse at the wrist, can scarcely feel it at the temporals," said the anesthetist, stopping the ether, holding her ear to the patient's nose listening, birdlike, for her breathing. "But little breath."

"Give her caffeine," said Vic, stepping back, shaking the sweat from his face. Kenny rushed to him, mopping his brow.

"Give me some drains," he commanded, continuing to shake sweat. "There's nothing else to do but fasten in several drains and put in a few through-and-through sutures and call it lights out."

"She's going, Doctor."

3

Doctor Thornwell dropped into the chair of his desk as if he
would never rise, slumping as a sailboat in dire need of wind,
wind that perhaps would never blow again. Flopping his seemingly disjointed elbows upon the desk, dropping his chin into
his upturned palms, he gazed out a seventh-story window of the
Thornwell Hospital at the blazing, sinking September sun whose
rays jeweled his wet, dreamy brown eyes. He looked toward the
west and he saw huge domineering Catawba loom up among
the treetops in the faraway hills like a Scottish castle in medieval
ages, like a giant prehistoric bird with its wings spread. It was
empty. It was deserted. It belonged to a bygone. Once it had
been a big to-do and its rambunctious goings-on had been accepted here on the red land of the watershed between the two
red rivers. And his thoughts corroded his mind with all of that
which was written in the stardust about a man before he was
born and of that which he did through his life as he tarried
here upon the face of the red land and of that which he would
do after death, and his life began far away beyond the disk of
the shining sun—as Mama Amazon had pictured it to him as a
child.

Nurse Kenny Kimball cautiously opened the door and came
across the room to him, putting her hands upon his shoulders.

"Vic, don't let it get you so. There was absolutely nothing on
earth you could do to save that woman. She was dead when she
came in. You did absolutely everything that could be expected
of a surgeon."

Motionless, he gazed out the window, saying an inaudible
prayer, his eyes rigidly staring, his lips barely moving. *Oh, Gawd,*
he thought, *what would Pop say? Is the road forked? Is it in
the stardust? That which is to be or that which is not to be? But
so do the things of life dog a fellow's footsteps. His days are few*

*and quite useless. For what earthly reason would beast or man
tread upon the face of the earth?*

Kenny shook him gently, "Vic, Vic. Come on. That undertaker will soon be here; you've got to sign this death certificate."

"Always there's one more death certificate to sign," he murmured. "What good's a death certificate? For some fool to read
with a sticky finger? I'm licked. I'm licked. I'm through."

"Don't be ridiculous," Kenny flipped. "People have to die
sometime. Here's as good a place as any. We make em easy.
Why, that woman went out as peaceful as blowing out a candle.
You should have seen how distorted she was with pain when she
was dragged in here. Those old bodysnatchers will be here in a
few minutes, if they're not already hanging around, and they'll
floss that disfigured old sister up as she was never flossed up before in her life. They'll stick her in an expensive-looking box—
oh, it's most elegant."

"Gotta die, gotta die. That's why people are born, Kenny," he
spoke huskily. "Gotta die. Yes, man comes into the world pushin
and shovin as beans against hard cakey ground and he's pushed
and shoved back into the ground after the big to-do is over.
What's it all about? I'm defeated. Do you know what that word
means, Kenny?"

"Oh, sure." She pushed the certificate across the desk to him,
handed him the pen. "I went to school a couple of days, you
know."

"You should have gone three days," he said ironically, taking
the pen, "and maybe you would have learned sumpin, Kenny.
Learned you don't know anything." He was busy with the certificate. He stopped, staring at Kenny's legs. Perfect. Pride swelled
into him, arraying itself about him. "Come here, Kenny," he
said, reaching across the desk, catching her hand and pulling her
about.

He caught her doll-like face between his gentle hands. "Kenny, look me straight in the face. I want to ask you a question and I don't want any lies."

"Why, Doctor Thornwell, what in the world has come over you? You have the most stormy soul," she said. "But tell me, what's this profound question you'd ask? You know I'd never keep secrets from you. I've been here in this hospital all my life—you know all there's to know."

"Are you happy?" His eyes leveled the question at her.

"Is that the profound question?" She laughed. He nodded. "Why? Have I seemed sad and lugubrious to you—even mournful with melancholy? I hope not. I never wanted to appear that way. I enjoy my work here. For me, it's the life—never a dull moment, always something new coming up. We really have fun going after em—"

"Yes, Kenny. You're giving me a very good description of what I can see, but what I'm really interested in is that lil ticking, those goings-on inside of you—that's what each fellow has to live with and not this gibberish we encounter in this workday world. I thought maybe you ought to get married. This day and age is breeding too many disjointed bachelor girls who sooner or later will wreck havoc with our way of life. It's unnatural. I thought perhaps your leg stood in your way."

"No. It never bothers me. I've always been too interested in working here in the hospital to give the boys much of my time and thought. But it might be that I would be better off with a man of my own. Especially since you suggest it. You usually don't fling around much stupid advice."

"Kenny, I've a horrible story to tell you. I think you'll understand it and appreciate it and forgive me."

"Forgive you for what?" she asked in disbelief. "As good as you've been to me. All you've done for me? You certainly weren't under any obligations. And without you and this hospital, I'd never have had a home."

"Oh, that's all outward. I had a bad thought about you once."

"Bad thoughts don't hurt anyone."

"Only the thinker."

"Well, that could be—seeing it from your viewpoint. But what's this thought?"

"The night you were born, I delivered you because other doctors don't like charity cases if they can wriggle out. That made me mad. Then, when you started making your entrance into the world, coming foot first, that was bad, but when I saw that you were a long-legged girl I flew into a rage. You ask Tizzy sometime, she's always shared me with you. I was seized with a hideous frenzy—a madly insane desire to take my two hands and kill you before you ever breathed. I saw no hope for you. I was rebellious against nature, eternity, Gawd. That's what I wanted to tell you, Kenny."

She caught his face in her hands, pulled his head to herself, and kissed him. "You wonderful man. Now you're forgiven. Is that the reason you've done so much for me?"

"Perhaps," he rose to go.

"Where you going? To see Jezebel?"

"Jezebel? Does that ole gal still have the nerve to call me? She's not getting me."

"She has called about every three hours, night and day—for a week now. You'd better go on. You know how she's stuck on you—she might be ill and need medical attention—hardly anything else at her age."

"No, I know that ole gal plenty well."

"If she dies, you'll be sorry."

"Reckon?"

4

Vic came out the front door of the Thornwell Hospital whose threshold was worn hollow in the center where the countless

thousands and thousands of ailing and aching, lonely and frightened, hysterical and imaginary people entered with their gripes,
their groans, their grouches. From all the red land of the watershed here between the two rivers patients poured into the hospital
as water down a stream—from Babel to Baal, from Ebeneezer
down Kinfolks Road to Old Hope they came. Through wind,
sunshine, stormy weather they dragged their weary selves, bent in
agony with ruptured gastric ulcers, burst gangrenous appendixes,
locked rottening bowels, stone-filled gall bladders and kidneys.

He was leaving it all behind. Behind him stood the massive,
modern Thornwell Hospital; and it had cost aplenty—his life.
He had once been lord and master of it. He used to give the
orders and they were obeyed; when he spoke, there was moving.
He had been a giant in his time, yet now he was old and
whipped, he could not even whisper one word to shut up the
pain within him—nor would tears.

This was left for the oncoming generation, a new set of people
whose gibberish was important for their day.

Once on the sidewalk, he stopped and gazed up through the
tall pines at the hospital, piercing the heights, a beacon light.
There was his whole life, wrapped up like a Christmas present in
scented pine. The shade-sprinkled green grass, the tall whispering
pines whose roots plunged deep into the red earth, the climbing
wisteria and honeysuckle, the masses of aged azaleas with their
riot of color in early spring, followed by the watermelon-red crepe
myrtles in the heat of summer, the delicate pink, heavily-scented
mimosa blooms with the hummingbirds and hummingbird
moths after each flower. He stood listening. The wind always
sighed here in the pines, always soughing. Lullaby. Rocking with
the wind as Mama Amazon had rocked him in the wooden cradle
long ago.

He walked across the lawn to the ancient oak about whose
trunk an enormous grape vine had clung well over several hundred years, to the oak that Granny Joanna had climbed at ninety

to pluck the grapes for the holy communion in North Bethel. He minutely and meticulously examined her body, looking at the many places the lightning had struck her through the years, looking at the places her great limbs had rotted and fallen away and she had healed herself. He looked up among her leafy limbs at the bumper crop of luscious grapes hanging there for the harvest. But no longer was there a brave Joanna to climb her and pluck the fruit for the racy wine; besides, the church no longer needed it. The church had given the wine no warning that they would ever part; but then, the wine knew nothing of the dangers in the secret charms of today's church, so the wine had been found guilty; but Vic forgave her, and loved her, for he could see Gawd in her roots and her limbs.

Cars scraped the curb, coming to abrupt halts. People crawled out, banged doors, talked subdued, whispered on the hospital ground.

Vic stood, head dropped, listening, waiting for those rare moments when there were no squeaking brakes, banging doors, dragging feet, smelly whispers. A golden moment, for just a fleeting second when he could hear his beloved pines soughing. The soughing made life come to easy terms on the inside. He threw his long legs out in front of his body and swung down the maple-shaded street.

He left Pine Ridge, turned down Trumbull, and headed across town, walking, swinging his cranelike legs, keeping time as an orchestra conductor would tap out a score with a baton, swinging both arms in movement contrary to the movement of his legs.

He had been caught; he'd had to do sumpin he didn't relish and it upset him. He must get away, be completely alone. To be alone on such a noisy street—he'd go to Pop. Pop would understand. Pop would listen—there was no one else that would listen, he bored everyone else, bored them no end. And Pop could see that little something within that was making such a big to-do right now and lacked a long ways of running smoothly.

He approached the railway station, whose bright red-tiled roof looked like a picture from a Chinese story book. On the end of the roof was a sign proclaiming to all who cared to look that this was GREEN POND.

In the distance he heard the whistle of a Diesel engine. 39 was coming north—a big four-unit Diesel engine. He slowed his steps, his arms became calm at his sides. He listened intensely, hearing the train whistle drowsing in the hollow, velvet-fogged tone. It did not excite as many dreams as the old steam whistle had when he had been in his far-back youth. Yet within him today it—this Diesel, even—created a surge of loneliness. Way off he could hear the rails clicking.

Victor milled among the mumbling people, squirmed alongside the railroad tracks, his long legs snipping as keen-bladed shears, and arrayed about him was an outstanding homelikeness which made people stop, turn, and stare at him. "Dogged iffen that feller don't make me think of somebody I've seen somewhere, but right off I can't recall who." The people shook their heads and stared.

He crossed over to Main Street—a quiet, Sunday Main Street, yet so ritzy were its shops that it looked to be, in miniature, a bit snatched from the most swank of the big metropolises. He remembered the time when it was unpaved, noisome, filled with flies and animal dung, but now it stretched, shining and gleaming far beyond Catawba. Where it was racing to and what it would do or what was written in the stars about it Vic didn't know. It was like a dream he could not quite remember. There were the bank buildings—the Inchurch bank was still the tallest. The large department stores, the exclusive hat shops with their feathers and ribbons and bits of veiling. High atop one of the bank buildings was one of the radio stations.

So, plopping along to North Bethel Church, he began to retrospect, trying to recapture how it must have been in the beginning.

5

At the gray, lonely dawn the hurricane rains were eddying sharply, slapping Doctor Victor Thornwell's tired old face with the ferocity of a superangry woman. The newspaper boys called her Hurricane Hazel. The first noticeable dash awoke him instantly, and he lurched up so springingly that he had to throw his hands against the mausoleum to support himself. He jolted the sleep from his head and looked at the tempestuous storm sweeping hissingly against the ancient stones that held their puny flares—BORN IN IRELAND—BORN IN SCOTLAND—BORN IN IRELAND—defying above the bosom of the red earth there in North Bethel's tree-shrouded cemetery.

How very long and tiring this night had been. The storm doubled up with intense fierceness. But Vic's soul was rent with joy. He threw his hands high above his head in supplication and there was a great crying and gnawing in his subjective self to be loosened and set free, to be unfettered. This storm was the maestro. All else was disquieted, afraid, and filled with misgivings. Wrapped here in the little vine-shielded cemetery behind North Bethel Church, he was buried alive almost in the center of frightened little Green Pond, which he had seen grow from a mere bubble to something that spread and crawled, capered and romped, dickered and jimmied, lied and cheated itself all over creation. Yet here it would always remain a church and cemetery, because great Grandpa Andrew had so willed it. He had trekked all the way from Scotland bearing the flaming torch of Presbyterianism to the red land of the watershed.

Vic moved around to the front of the mausoleum, put his nose to the small glass high upon the door, and peered in as a small boy looking at some desirous object in a store window. Within the two top drawers were Mama Naomi and Pop, then the next two drawers were Mama Amazon and Sandy Peeler, and his, he looked sharply, trying to discern it in the gloom, would be right over there opposite to Mama Amazon's, "fo someday she's gonna reach right across that aisle an say, 'Come, hon-chile, it's time fo to get up, the Lawd's done arrived.'"

The lengthy years upon him didn't keep Vic from walking at a brisk, swinging gait that was astonishing. Momentarily the gustily sweeping hurricane bewildered him and he considered in which direction he would go. However, it meant little, for the glow from the little fire within him gave its eternal warmth and he would have peace by day and by night. This anxiety which had so often come forth in him most chokingly was quelled. He had left his car keys with Tizzy, so driving was out of the question, but he could walk. It had been many years since he strode forth in such a rebellious storm, but this morning he felt like flying.

Scurrying around the corner of the church, he thought of the forsaken organ, but it had been so long since he had played that he doubted whether his hands and feet would work coherently. Sometime he would like to try it out, but not this morning.

Passing the Pink House on Third Street in the storm, he felt sure any observer from within would take him for a lonely tramp. He wondered what Jezebel was doing. He thought certainly she would still be enjoying her sleep in her massive four-poster bed, especially at this ungodly hour. She might as well be enjoying it, for like him, she didn't have so many more years here on the red land of the watershed to enjoy, her time was running low, her weight coming close to the bottom of the clock, and before long she, too, must go. It wouldn't be long until she went to her winter home in St. Petersburg. He wondered why she had been calling him so much lately.

The further he went the faster he walked and the more his mind dug into the past, worming out little doo-dad happenings and events with a clarity that he sometimes questioned himself. He knew he bored the middle-aged and the younger generation with his ceaseless drabble of his early life, but what was an old fellow to do? Go off somewhere and talk to himself? Still, he had had a bellyful of living, so why bellyache?

He wanted to go through Catawba once more before the hammers and the pinching bars of the wrecking crew began to flay and prize and pull it down, hammering it down into oblivion and henceforth from the sight of all mankind. He wondered what Pop would say to him for selling Catawba; but Mama Amazon was gone and there was no woman left to love and to cherish Catawba, without which Catwba would eventually crumble, dying a meaningfully slow and tedious death. He had thought it better that she go at once. Something powerful, like a big ship, like a time, like a civilization.

Victor entered Catawba, which showed no signs of life any more in its great high-ceilinged, yawning rooms. It had been stripped and gutted of its life's blood, bled of its old handsome, priceless furnishings. His footsteps echoed in the hollow rooms. He ascended and descended the many stairs. He peered out the windows. He opened and shut the exquisite old doors. Shudder after shudder choked him. He counted here in sweet remembrance those hallowed days of his youth. Each corner held its lonely heartthrob. In this storm, he doubted whether the workmen would begin wrecking Catawba today. They would not start until the weather faired. Catawba had a few more hours. Madly burning tears came blindingly to his old eyes.

He had never known anything else. He thought of Mama Amazon's noble and notable life here, of the love and devotion she had lavished upon Catawba. She had cared for it more than anyone else. She had had an overdose of the mother instinct. He could feel the warmth of her soft black hands upon his body when she fondled and cuddled him as a child; when she instilled into him a love and devotion that he had never known elsewhere. Always her memory dogged and haunted him and there was no separating her from the flesh. How wise she had been. How she had understood life. How she had used to tease him about Jezebel. How she always wondered what his children would look like.

He went out the back door of Catawba. All the barns and the outbuildings were gone long ago, only the well shed with the old well bucket still sitting for a reminder of another day. Where the rail fence used to be, where the cows and geese and turkeys used to trod, where the paled-in garden used to be—the upping block where Pop got on his horse and the ladies into the carriages and surreys, the orchards, the vineyard, the cider mill, the ash hopper, and all those things that had been with his childhood and in Mama Amazon's time were gone. Now in their place were many red and white filling stations and business establishments and only Catawba remained to hold up steadfastly her belief in another day. Now soon she must go. The powerful mechanical dinosaurs would come belching forth their odorous oil and gas fumes, rare upon the famous trees, and with great grating growling, gnashing and grinding their gears, push them down, destroying them, marking them into oblivion. Tomorrow and tomorrow would come creeping and sliding across the face of the red land and laugh at what had been. He had seen them born, he had seen them die in countless numbers; yet each one lived glibly in one's day, for it was a great day and not to be reckoned with or questioned.

He stepped into Main Street and hurried on through the swishing gale as fast as he could go. He had circle after circle of Green Pond to yet go through before he reached open country, and then it would not be very open. Surely no good would come of scrouging this many people together.

He passed a settlement and this place he remembered as the place where Uncle Prince Blue's old dilapidated house had stood in its time. All his youth flooded through the network of his mind and he sadly picked out portions at random, but it had all happened so long ago that it seemed unreal.

Miles out he turned off the superhighway which Robert Inchurch had dickered for in his time, stealing it, getting it brought through Green Pond, increasing the fiscal value of his material things. He remembered in the many elections that he had frightened the voters to his way of voting by telling them what the "niggers will do," and so Robert Inchurch had swung whole campaigns to his way. He remembered the times that Robert and Jepson Grady had cut each other through the Green Pond *Observer's* pages. Now all that Inchurch generation was gone save Jezebel; he wondered where that abusive fortune would go with her passing. He wondered whether she had ever thought of it.

Heading toward the backwater and toward Grandpa Andrew's old house, he passed through a new raw and naked settlement, where houses were going up rapidly, where there was no pavement, nor any lights or running water. This he knew was called The Willows—though where the willows were he did not know.

He had to bail water out of a boat before he could ride. Once out upon the rain-swept red waters, which hissed up fiercely, he pointed the boat northwesterly and to the alcove of Grandpa's house.

The giant pine trees bent and swayed on the hills above the house. Right then he was glad that he had never sold that timber. It was filled with too much rest. Gradually all the trees of the red land had been cut away and this was one of the very few remaining big woods and as long as he lived it would remain so. Other than a small share in the hospital, this was all he owned now. Here it was like a quiet sanctuary, a place of tranquil rest, hidden from the eyes of men. Here were none of the annoying contraptions men had created in civilization, here nobody could find him.

He saw Dish's Ford coupé sitting in the yard under the huge English walnut tree. She had used the wood road to come in here, which she invariably did. Since he had sold Catawba, he had remodeled this old homestead, fixing it up as old-fashioned as he could. He used only kerosene lamps for light, Dish cooked before the open fireplace, and if she kept on improving she would soon be able to make fire mind her as well as Mama Amazon had ever done. He had cool spring water to drink, and he gobbled it more thankfully and greedily than a primitive man. It was the simple life. Here were no blaring radios, no hurly-burly, no rank-erous blowing automobile horns, no clanging church bells, no pushing and shoving in the day's trade—only rest, sweet rest, here was what a man longed for as he turned toward the great end, toward the time he would lie down with his fathers, with the bearded patriarch—he cared not to lie in the canon of saints.

He saw John Mathis' tombstone there in the yard. In the far-off he heard a train, but through it all there was nothing but quiet for his soul to drink.

As he tied the boat up at the edge of the bank, he saw Dish standing poker-straight, her arms akimbo, her tufts of hair plaited neatly, in the doorway; he saw the bright cozy light the fire from the fireplace threw about her.

"Ho'cum you didn't come yesterday?" she called to him as he approached the house. "I had supper all ready an waitin an you never come."

"Oh, I got fooled into a nasty operation, waylaid, and never got here."

"Well, come on in here to the fire an change you wet clothes. You looks lack some vagrant tramp. I declare to Gawd, iffen folks could see you now, they'd run fro you," she laughed gleefully.

"That," he began stoutly, "is exactly what I want em to do."

"What you want fo you breakfast? I just knows you's hongry. I bet you ain't et in Gawd only knows when," Dish said solemnly. "You might as well throw that suit o clothes in the fire. Ain't no cleaners ever get em straightened out," she laughed. "I don't see where in the name of Gawd you been to get yourself in sich a beraggled shape."

"Oh, I had a good dinner yesterday at the hospital. With Mama Amazon's grandsons and granddaughters there cooking, the food is bound to be good."

"Did you know Yellow Sam's grandson, Ernie, won the state championship in speakin down to the University?" Dish asked.

"Hadn't heard about it."

"Ho'cum you don't never read the papers? Ernie's picture was in the paper and everythin; the picture was most big as the one of Mama Amazon when she died."

"By the way, I think I saw Dessa get off the train late yesterday. Wonder where she'd been?"

"Oh, comin fro she summer home. Gettin ready fo school; Lawd, she's gonna hold down the presidency of Emancipation Proclamation Academy until ole Gabriel blows he's horn. Ernie was one of she pupils—she teached he up right."

"Dessa's gettin old. How time flies. It seems only yesterday we were kids there on Catawba's red rolling acres. We were happy and now all that's gone. Only the partial fragments I have assembled here do I have to remind me of that long bygone. We had a good time, too. But today a five-year-old spends more money in a half day than we had in a whole year. Material things don't bring happiness. After breakfast I'm going upstairs and pile into bed. Today'll be a good day to sleep, the rain pounding on the roof and the hissing wind in the trees."

Rolled into a feather bed which was well over a hundred years old, whose feathers had been pulled from the squawking goose by his great-grandma Hannah, he listened to the storm tear violently against the old house and he fell into deep untroubled sleep.

6

Budda said, shaking the rain water out of his white hair, "Dish, don't you be foolin me. I know Vic's out here. I been runnin all night long in the rain lack a wet dog tryin to find em. All hell's done busted loose in that hospital yander in town and we's got to have him there to straighten things out. I wonder where in the name of Gawd he's been keepin he'sself? How long's he been out here?"

'Oh, not long; he's upstairs sleepin."

"Where in Gawd's name has he been? I wasn't bout to go in that graveyard lookin fo him last night in that big storm; and I'll bet that's where he was."

"Why in the world would he want to spend the night in there? —But he's a case, a heavy ole case."

"Gawd only knows. But I hear Miz Tizzy and Miz Kenny both say he left out right after that woman died on the table. Say it was a wonder he'd ever tried to operate on she. But I tell em, they don't know Vic. Me, I was born an raised up wit em—an he's got mo guts an determination right now than all these pine trees put together up here on this hill, iffen he is bent an ole."

"Iffen the woman's done dead, what's you runnin round in the rain lack a beraggled possum tryin to find em fo?" she laughed bountifully.

"It's Miz Jezebel now. She's bad off," he sucked his teeth.

"*What?*" Dish arrayed herself in alarm as a clock will do at times.

"Yes, she was brought into the hospital yesterday evening about two hours after Vic left. Doctor Tad say she's in bad shape. The doctors all looked her over, but then they stood back offen she just lack she was a cornered polecat."

"Fo true, she must have real sharp pains."

"Doctor Tad say she appendix done busted on her an she's

swelled up might nigh lack she gonna have a baby. He say onless
sumpin is done quickly, she won't last long."

"An you's been out huntin Vic all night?"

"I is. I come down here to the boat landin last night about ten
an I see all the boats is there an I knowed he'd left he's car at
the hospital an I knowed he wouldn't walk all the way round the
mountains to get in here—that'd be twenty miles. An I hunted
all over town all night long except in that graveyard an I ain't
found him. An he's got to be to the hospital, fo Miz Jezebel ain't
lettin none of em other doctors tetch she. Hurry up now, Dish,
and wake him up, fo I got to get back to the hospital."

Dish climbed the stairs. "I'll have he down here in a jiffy.
You bank that fire fo me, because I don't want it to go out
while I'm gone to drive youse to the hospital. An I got to get
back here in time to milk the cow fo it gets dark; get dark early
today with this storm goin on. Better check the water in my
radiator. I don't want nothin to happen to my Ford."

The trio left the old homestead, climbing the steep wood road
in the swirling storm. The pine trees had no time for soughing,
they were lashed so furiously by the hurricane. Dish drove. Vic
and Budda were crowded into the seat with her; and once after
reaching civilization, they still had a long ways to go before
reaching the hospital.

7

Vic stood in the street looking up at the great hospital already
lighted in the early grayness of the storm. He scanned the windows and the many floors and wondered which room Jezebel
was in. He listened to the maddening ferocity of the wind as it
lashed the pines, beat and rattled on the huge magnolias, rho-
dodendrons, azaleas that had been mere cuttings he had rooted
in a shaded sand bed behind the hospital. Many of the pieces
here John Mathis had helped him to root. He looked them over,

letting the tender thought of each one's creation ooze about in his mind. Across the rain-swept lawn, under the great oak that held the grape vine, Vic stared, because, for a fleeting second, he thought he saw John, then Sandy, Mama Amazon, and Pop looking up at its great branches—he saw the peace and rest upon their faces as in a dream.

He brought his hands out in front of him. These used to be surgeon's hands, skilled hands, trained hands, the hands of a healer. Hands that had never belonged to him, they had always been empty hands, empty because they belonged to others. Hands that had spent a lifetime probing and filled with a wonderful curiosity. They'd been uncanny sleuths and gone into the countless thousands and thousands, and there with their tender touch, soothed and righted untold wrongs.

He moved forward and through the great front door. He saw the afternoon switchboard operator working madly with her plugs and he heard the amplifier calling Doctor Johnson. The smell of the hospital, that delicious smell, rushed over him and surged about him. He saw Tizzy stick her head out of her office.

"What room's she in?" he called to Tizzy.

"Room 618, and don't forget she's still a queen."

Vic paced out of the elevator on the sixth floor. He heard the hollow-voiced amplifier calling Doctor Bell to surgery. He saw Doctor Tad swishing down the hall in his quickened hospital tread. Vic thought of Tad's new baby son and wondered was that what caused his quickened gait.

"Dad," said Tad, omitting any unnecessary fringes, "your old gal's here and she's waiting for you. She says you're the only doctor going, the only doctor that she wants tending to her."

"How is she?" Vic asked, and Tad discerned a concerned tone in his voice. Or was it because Vic was talking to him? It was that special tone that Tad had heard all his life.

"Not suffering too much now," Tad began, casually flippant. "We've done all for her that she would let us do, though she's swelled nice and plump. And she's strong as a bull. Her heart's unimpaired. She might pull through, but she's waited a time."

Vic looked at the floor, thinking slowly. "When did she come in?"

"Brought in late yesterday. I was in surgery, and she was brought in while I was up there. When I first saw her she was chortling for you with great gusto."

Victor moved toward Jezebel's room, but stopped and said to Tad, "Better see about an operating room and get set up. Guess I'll have to go into the ole gal—she's a she-cat, after all. Might be interesting in there. I've often wondered."

"My God, Dad! Do it by yourself?"

"Oh, you and Kenny can help."

When Doctor Victor Thornwell entered Mrs. Robert B. Inchurch's room he had the feeling of entering the cage of a very ferocious black panther, because her yellow, feral eyes were glazing with such fierceness that the leopard spots blurred and ran together as some mishap on the movie screen. But he strode most bullheadedly and severely doctorlike up to her bed and thumped her swollen abdomen as though it were a watermelon. The emotions shifted so speedily over his face that there was no telling where one stopped and the other started. He cleared his throat, walked around the bed, and looked out the window among the boughs of the trees that clapped their hands in the storm joyously. Her head turned slowly on her pillow and she looked at his back. He turned after ages and came to the side of her bed.

"Ole gal, you're getting mighty old to let things like this happen to you," he said in a far-off voice, a voice that oozed briefly and sweetly.

"Why don't you do something about it, then? Why don't you stay here in the hospital where you belong and tend to your patients? You always were famous for trekking about and hiding in the countryside. Where have you been? It has taken them over twenty-four hours to find you," she began in her browbeating way, and her eyes danced.

"That had nothing to do with it. Your trouble began about a week ago, I assume—that was when you needed a doctor. Haven't you got sense enough to know when you are sick? Surely seems that you are getting old enough to know that."

"Victor Thornwell, I like that. I turned myself purple in the face calling you all last week, and you wouldn't come. What am I to do when you won't come?"

"You could have called some other doctor. I'm not the only doctor in Green Pond today. There are some hundred and fifty. In fact, there is one doctor for every five preacher-boys that are running loose up and down the streets."

"You're the only doctor I want fooling with me. You've been my doctor all my life. I don't want any other. I've money to pay. What is your price?"

"You'd rather die as go to another doctor?"

"Yes, any day."

"Well, Jezebel, that is exactly what's going to happen to you," he cut at her bluntly, and for the first time in his life he saw a slight flinching in her, but it was gone so soon that only the quickest of eyes would have noted it.

She shot at him with her old fury. "Victor Thornwell, you impudent, despicable brat. Don't you stand there and tell me I'm going to die. After I've belittled myself for a week calling you and you wouldn't come to see me—after I've stooped so low as to literally let the undertakers drag me here into your old stinking hospital—you've got the gall and wormwood to stand there and tell me I'm going to die. I've a good mind throwing something at your stinking, impudent head."

"If you don't like this hospital, why didn't you let them drag you into another one—Green Pond, you know, now has several others, including a hoss-hospital. I feel sure some of them would have admitted an old war hoss like you."

"I like that. You would like to see me in a hoss-hospital. Well, right now I wish I were a good horse—I'd kick your behind for a month of Preachin Sundays."

He moved over to the window, and stood gazing at her with profound admiration. She was a spunky gal. His mind was corroded with thoughts of their youth in the long, long ago. She had always been lively and too pretty and she excited him and made him mad.

She dared not even look at him, but fumbled with the bed sheet. Her whole life was overrun with unfathomed depression; she could never recall an hour when she had sunk into such depth of melancholy as this. She did not see Victor as an old, slightly stooped doctor. No, she saw him as he was in his youth, as he was in Catawba, as he was when he had come home a full-fledged surgeon, the first one the watershed of the red land had ever known. Those were the days. They had hope. Today they had nothing. It was empty and void. He could have been hers. But Ma with the wagon whip had got into the road. Now Vic said she was going to die. She didn't want to die. She didn't feel like dying. Some other day, some other time. He was joking. He could save her. She had groveled at his feet all her life. He had always been good to her. He didn't know what it was to be mean. He would save her—those hands of his would, they were filled with an eternal love. He surely wouldn't let her down, let her go, turn her loose, no, never loose.

"What's the matter?" she asked shyly. "There you go hiding—you've always done that."

"And why not?"

"Perhaps it is as well: I don't mind dying. I mind only leaving you, being separated from you."

"You've never had me."

"It wasn't my fault."

There was a long pause before Victor asked, "Are you ready for

them to prepare you for the operation? I was thinking about it
—there are several new discoveries I might try—"

"My lord," she began, and there was a definite quaver in her
voice, "any hour that you are ready you may take the most grue-
some, the most ominous-looking knives you have and begin slitting upon me anywhere you wish and if I die, I shall die happy,
for nothing in this whole wide world so sets my skin afire as
the touch of your hand. What is it about you that has bewitched me all the days of my life? The few jeweled times in
your youth that you came from your throne and put your hands
upon me and your arms about me are the most treasured things
I possess. And I shall take that into eternity with me, that and
that alone.

"I would have had you, you mark my word, but Ma got in the
way with the wagon whip; and after that you were never so bold
as I, for had you been, I would have still had you."

"Jezebel, the nurse is coming to prepare you for the operation.
Say your prayers, Jezebel, if you have any to say." He marched
with his long strides, more of the lurching of a bullfrog than
the walking of a man, out of her room and down the hall to find
Doctor Tad still waiting. He put his arm about Tad's shoulders,
"Come on, let's go to the dining room and see can we have
supper and coffee before we scrub up."

They sat in a corner of the dining room, out of view of many
of the diners, and ate and looked out the window at the storm.

"Dad, she'll never make it, especially at her age; she's eighty."

"She's a tough ole gal though. While women are considered
the weaker sex, they're far stronger than men. It's proved in the
birth rate: a girl will make it where a boy will die. It's the way
Gawd created it. Frankly, I don't think she has the chance of a
worm before a hungry bird, but I always did say she was like
an earthworm: pull her in two, both pieces'd crawl off in opposite directions."

"There's another thing I want to know, Dad: what was between you and her? Why'd you never marry her?"

"You flabbergast me—must sit up nights thinking em up."

"Great-grandpa, Ole Doc, would never let flouncy hips like that out of his sight. Talking about your seed roosters."

"It's about time we go to the operating room. Imagine the ole gal is ready and waiting. You know she killed Sandy? Now would be a good time for me to get even with her."

"My God! What do you mean, killed Sandy?"

"It'd been easier on her and me and Sandy for her to have shot him as to do what she did. But let's forget and forgive. Now she's waiting for me to save her."

"You still going to operate?"

"Am I not the doctor she has been chortling for?"

"But I had thought once anesthetized, you'd let me take over."

The abdomen of the devil's beauty was laid wide open and her breathing was stertorous and contented and trusting. From her opened cavity blood-tinged, watery fluid spouted up.

He'll never do it, Doctor Tad thought. *He can't clean out that abdomen after he has opened it. I've never seen such haggling and cutting, worse than a pup chewing upon a tough meat skin. The raggiest cutting. And slow. Somehow I've got to get that scalpel out of his hands without hurting his feelings too much. Why did he ever want to attempt this? She'll never live to die naturally; he'll kill her right here on the table.*

The desire to heal still flamed hot as the sweat that poured from Vic and he couldn't keep his thoughts where they should be. They wanted to ramble, chase off into the long bygone. He'd say she was tough. A tough ole gal, Jezebel Mathis. The attendants heard him mutter Jezebel Mathis and they looked at one another askingly. He thought he was alone with her and their faith was renewed, revived, and relived as in Catawba a frosty night years ago. But here he could make no promise, no promise to her. Their love had never got quite together, but it had always been like it was here: the one haggling on the other.

8

But three days after her operation, the spunky Jezebel overshadowed her lather of misery, her veil of narcotics, by running up her arbor of glittering jewels. She was put into Fowler's position. And Missy came with her nugatory contraptions to pretty up the spunky creature. Jezebel slapped red upon her face as though it were an old granary, her fingernails were tapered and painted. Her large jewel casket was opened in her presence and she selected the costliest pieces with cunning wisdom and artful proficiency. She upbraided Missy sharply for any bit of clumsiness. She thought her eyes a trifle too puffy and she shrugged her shoulders in disgust and averted her eyes from the mirror in misery.

Her diamond necklace was so long that it went about her withered neck with confidence five times and then dangled celestially over her shriveled and lifeless breast with ecstasy. Only on rare to-dos of social prominence had the Green Ponders ever seen that necklace. She had rings, studded with countless diamonds, for all her fingers, and many of her fingers were honored by the steady presence of as many as four rings. Her bracelets ran the gauntlet of human endurance and the imagination of a hundred jewelers and were set with every conceivable stone known to social Green Pond; they arrayed her flabby arms from wrist to elbow. She had jeweled pins of magical length and combs set with an amazing amount of precious stones for her hair, and since Missy couldn't use the cover-all dyes to advantage in bed, Jezebel used many combs for her hair to cover the places the dye had washed out. Her earrings, great long pendants of shining gold, flopped about as the bell ropes in the churches. Jezebel smiled triumphantly when she touched them and recalled the time when as a girl she had slipped to the old witchlike colored woman's house and let the old woman burn a hole through her ear lobes with the smoking hot needle so that she might wear earrings.

Her room was the most expensive in the hospital and her flowers arrived in such massive arrangements and in such numbers that the nurses in the hospital silently cursed all clumsy florists and made remarks of stinging nicety about them.

Jezebel fought for her life with the guts of a swarthy she-bear. To the men and women healers of the hospital her fighting courage was a much talked-of marvel and they tirelessly trod into her room and thumped upon her ever-swelling abdomen, shook their heads, and walked out in dismay. She called ceaselessly for the penicillin, because she had read somewhere that it was a cure-all savior and she violently shook the stand that held the saline and glucose solutions which were constantly fed into her veins by the Murphy drip.

During the days that she lay dying, her life in a shallow pool, Doctor Victor Thornwell took to the road. The hospital with Jezebel within it remained the hub of his living but he swung about it, trying to view it from many directions, hoping perhaps one view would change the inevitable conclusion being played out there.

Out at Tad's handsome home in South Hills, which Vic had bought, Vic played with the fifth generation of Thornwells he had known, and wished that Mama Amazon could be here to see them. Still he felt she was looking on. He told the three little boys vivid, unbelievable tales of his youth in the long bygone. He brought them many presents, and the boys didn't see why he couldn't stay with them always. But he continued to rove like a rogue that he was.

In the Blossom Shoppe, late one afternoon, he bought the largest and most expensive yellow chrysanthemums that Reola had in stock and she laughed at him, accused him of having a gal

somewhere, and through it all Reola dickered and jimmied with
him, trying to find out when Jezebel would die.

He carried the chrysanthemums to the hospital and with the
nurses and the doctors standing as so many gawky effigies, he
marched stanchly, and as straight as his stooped shoulders permitted, to Jezebel's room. Much talk flew about over the hospital
and it was discussed upon every tongue.

When Jezebel saw the chrysanthemums her thoughts rushed to
a bright October in the long, long bygone when the you-and-me-
that-used-to-be had stood by the paled-in garden of old Mrs.
Ives and looked at the huge chrysanthemums nodding in the
chilly autumnal breeze that came from over the bright purple
mountains. They had been young then, and now Jezebel knew
what he had meant, and her soul was flooded with remorse. She
turned her face from him and looked out the window. He placed
the flowers by her bed and stole from the room.

She heard his soft-padded hospital tread as he left the room.
She lay dying, and for a long time she gazed out the window at
the limbs of the trees, the limbs of the ancient oak filled with
the luscious grapes to make the racy wine, and Jezebel recalled
how racy the wine was in the old cup that was passed among the
communicants in her girlhood. Ma'd given her no warning that
she'd ever part from that racy wine. And she needed it now:
that from the tree out there, it was youth and Victor.

Finally she turned back and vigorously shook the stand that
fed the life-giving fluids into her body. Then she lay for a long
time staring at the flowers. Tears filled her eyes. She reached over,
yanked the big fluffy petals from the stems of the chrysanthemums, and threw them as high into the air as possible, and continued to do so until she had destroyed each gorgeous bloom,
until her bed and the floor were covered deeply with the petals
of gold. She lay for hours watching the petals decolorize, grow
darkly, curl and shrivel in sweet death as they had never done
in life.

Mr. and Mrs. Henry Leg sent her an extravagantly large basket of red roses and Jezebel had them sent at once to the cooks in the kitchen without even looking at them, but stared off into the corner of the room with the disgusted look of a dog scratching his fleas. "My, my, how that Leg & Leg Department Store has grown." Henry's head, severed from his body, leered at her from the foot of her bed and she pulled the sheet over her head and looked at her swollen belly, which she thought was a vast mountain.

Gentlemanlike, old Judge David Kingsley came to her in urgency with a great batch of papers for her to sign. When he questioned her about some changes being made in her will, she told him to get the hell out of there and that she would write one out to suit herself.

"There's Goldie, poor Goldie to consider. He can have half the Inchurch fortune. What is gold to me? It might as well go to him as anyone. He may breed a new race of people that will not suffer as I have suffered. The other half can be used as a memorial to the eminent Doctor Victor Erich Thornwell—he needs a stone raised to him. I'll write out what I please and you'd better see that it's carried out."

"My heart is strong," she told the nurses. "The doctors say there is nothing wrong with my heart—it is strong, it is strong." She told them over and over, day after day, night after night as she lay rotting and dying.

Jacob, a clumsy dotard, his manners in great nicety, his voice that of a cracked bell, his life standing out jaggy and open as the chestnut bur when the chestnuts have fallen out of it, came to read the Scriptures to her and to pray. He read of the cool green pastures and he remembered how hot her lips had been in their youth. He read of the prepared tables and he remembered how eagerly her belly had pressed against his. He read of the shadow of death and he remembered how tight her arms had been about his neck. He prayed and he was once again a little boy down on his knees beside the big four-poster bed in Catawba and Mama Amazon was making him repeat after her, "Our Father—"

Early that morning Vic laid his warm hand upon her damply cold forehead, already sweating in sweet death, and silently left her room. He knew that her great bodily energy was about burned out, that it was but a matter of hours before she would go that day. She had fought for nine days and nights and there was but little energy left in her body to be burned up.

A short time later he came out of the boiler rooms with a two-edged ax swung over his shoulder and marched, to the bewilderment of the hospital staff who saw him, down the corridor and out the front door to the ancient oak that had nurtured the grapes for the racy wine for the holy communion for years.

The hospital and its attendants were subject to sudden outbursts, drastic changes, emergencies, to man's sudden entrance into the world, his quackish qualms while he lived, his unwarned departure, but Ole Doc Victor Thornwell out there on the lawn cutting down the ancient oak changed things a bit. Operations were halted or stopped completely while scrubbed-up surgeons actually peeped out the windows. The colored maids and orderlies and cooks rolled their eyes and knew death was riding a white horse.

But Victor had dropped his coat upon the lawn, thrown his old hat off, and taken the great gold cuff links of Ole Doc's from his cuffs and with the double-edged ax was making chips fly punily from the base of the ancient oak. With several uncertain whacks he had managed to sever the grape vine at the base of the tree, and the stump of the vine looked like the neck of a man who had been fresh guillotined and the blood now gushing out. And the vine cried, its sticky glisteny tears dripping back into the red sobbing land.

Victor mopped sweat slowly and looked at the tough old tree and chopped upon it doggedly. The ancient aboriginal oak cried against its executioner, its rich-smelling chips ingloriously spilling about its trunk. High in the heavens a jet-propelled plane went by at a speed faster than sound. A lonely buzzard circled the lofty blue.

By midmorning the pile of chips about the tree's trunk made a small carpet, but Vic was still chopping and the grapevine bleeding profusely.

As he chopped, he muttered and he mumbled, "Her skin was too tough, I couldn't do anything with it. I couldn't save her. Why would I want to save her? I'm cutting clean here, no one can say these chips are ragged. The church never gave this old tree any warning that it would leave her when it no longer needed the racy wine. And so what's the need of this foolish old oak standing up here holding an unwanted harvest?" He stopped chopping, mopped his sweaty brow, and looked up to her room. "I made her no secret promise, we never exchanged any tokens in the church. . . . Somehow our love never quite got together."

Up in her room, Jezebel no longer viciously shook the stand that fed the life-giving fluids into her rotting body. Her eyes were walled and staring; she was the quietest she had ever been since her rambunctiously wenchy life began.

Jezebel's nurse heard her mutter and mumble and hurried out to the lawn where Victor haggled upon the ancient oak. "I expect you'd better come. She's finally given up and is going fast."

Victor looked at the shattered oak that he'd been unable to fell and slowly dropped the ax, then moved into the hospital and up to the sixth floor. He opened the door of her room quietly and entered softly.

"Victor." She knew that it was he without looking, because all her life she had known when he was about her whether she looked or not.

"Yes." He answered her very softly.

"Hold my hand."

"Yes." He picked up the shockingly jeweled hand.

"Darling?"

"Yes."

"Maybe, just maybe with you holding my hand it'll be easier."

"Easier?"

"To get across—I can't get across."

This was most strange; yet true. Like something Vic had heard in the long bygone—oh, long, long ago, from someone else he loved very dearly. "Why, Jezebel?"

"The boards are so rotten under me—so very rotten."

"They are?"

"Yes, they keep breaking through—my feet can't find firm ground—I keep slipping—beyond the stardust, perhaps, there's space—space for my feet to find firm ground—where they won't keep breaking through. Vic, oh, Vic, the boards are so rotten, so very rotten under me!"

As he covered her face with the sheet, through the open window came the splintering crash of the ancient oak as it came to the ground, seeking the bosom of the earth, seeking the home from where it came in the beginning.

9

And Gawd caused a great storm to appear out of nowhere and Gawd shook Green Pond fiercely. He sent great bolts of lightning earthward, striking North Bethel's imposing steeple, sending bricks and mortar and debris piling into the street. He cracked the great bell and it and its rope came tumbling down. He uprooted oaks, tossing them about. His angry breath roared through the town, ripping off roofs and caving in plate glass. As suddenly as it had begun it ended, and He placed a beautiful rainbow in the east.

GAWD: I never created any badness. Only goodness. It's certain that the chillun all comes into the ole world alack and they all goes out alack. I make em that way in the beginnin. Sumpin gets in em between they comin's an they goin's that makes sich strange critters out of em.

And Catawba is gone into the crumbling dust, its roots torn from the red sobbing land of Carolina. And the tall pines sough for Heaven's glory and their roots plunge further into the red dirt. Catawba is gone and Ole Doc is gone and Mama Amazon is gone and Vic sits waiting in time, waiting for an answer to the question, that question that itches so unbearably.

GABRIEL: You gonna let our ole Vic know anythin mo better than he knows, Gawd? You fixin to give em the answers?

GAWD: I ain't rightly sure yet. I ain't sure about any mens. Maybe I let em have the answers fro time to time; maybe only in the sweet by-an-by; maybe toreckly. It depends.

GABRIEL: It depends on what?

GAWD: It depends on em peoples.